Also by William H. Gass

FICTION

Omensetter's Luck
In the Heart of the Heart of the Country
Willie Masters' Lonesome Wife
The Tunnel

NONFICTION

Finding a Form
Fiction and the Figures of Life
On Being Blue
The World Within the Word
The Habitations of the Word

Cartesian Sonata

Cartesian Sonata

AND OTHER NOVELLAS

William H. Gass

BASIC
BOOKS
A Member of the Perseus Books Group

Cartesian Sonata and Other Novellas was originally published in hardcover by Alfred A. Knopf Publishers in 1998. The Basic Books edition is published by arrangement with Alfred A. Knopf.

Published by Basic Books,
A Member of the Perseus Books Group

Library of Congress Cataloging-in-Publication Data

Gass, William H.
    Cartesian sonata—Bed and breakfast—Emma enters a sentence of Elizabeth Bishop's—The master of secret revenges.
    1. Didactic fiction, American. 2. Good and evil—Fiction. I. Title
813'.54—dc21   97-49462
ISBN 0-465-02620-6   CIP

Manufactured in the United States of America

00 01 02 03 / 10 9 8 7 6 5 4 3 2 1

THESE NOVELLAS ARE FOR MARY

CONTENTS

Acknowledgments   ix

CARTESIAN SONATA
   The Writing on the Wall   3
   The Clairvoyant   25
   I Wish You Wouldn't   43

BED AND BREAKFAST   66

EMMA ENTERS A SENTENCE
   OF ELIZABETH BISHOP'S   144

THE MASTER OF SECRET REVENGES   192

ACKNOWLEDGMENTS

Earlier versions of *Cartesian Sonata* were published in pieces: "The Clairvoyant" (called here "The Writing on the Wall"), in *Location* 1, no. 2 (summer 1964); "The Sugar Crock" (called here "The Clairvoyant"), in *Art and Literature* no. 9 (1966); and "I Wish You Wouldn't," in *Partisan Review* 42, no. 3 (1975), as well as in *The Pushcart Prize* (1976-77). "Emma Enters a Sentence of Elizabeth Bishop's" (then in the form of a short sketch) appeared in *The Iowa Review* 24, no. 2 (1994), and subsequently in *Hard Choices: An Iowa Review Reader* (Iowa University Press, 1996). The final version came out in *Conjunctions* (1998), and in its final form, with photographic illustrations by Michael Eastman, in *Conjunctions* 30.

Cartesian Sonata

CARTESIAN SONATA

The Writing on the Wall

This is the story of Ella Bend Hess, of how she became clairvoyant and what she was able to see.

There was nothing in her childhood to suggest it. Her gift was the gift of the gods, not a natural product of her past, I am sure of that. It was a true gift: free and undeserved, as beauty is supposed to be, or the descent of the dove: inexplicable and merciless.

Marvelous is what I mean. Miraculous. Mysterious? Surely not a word so weak. Yet it has to begin with an *m*.

You see how little pride I have, to let you watch me fumble. I could have sent that wretched word away and written what I wanted, you'd have been no wiser; but I haven't got that kind of courage anymore, the courage of the liar. My will, somewhere along the way, has grown most deathly tired; now I have the scruples of a worn-out thief—fierce, painful scruples—and I wish I could recover everything I've stolen from my stories over the years; maybe then my angry blood would quiet. Of course, they do catch up, these phrases that I've condemned, poor awkward creatures, and occupy my dreams. They remind me of a row of prisoners, rapping on their bars. They shout their names and shout their names. I laugh with all my nerves. Well . . . prison is my only metaphor.

Is it right or honest? After all—Ella Bend—where is she? Isn't she as much in all those scraps I threw away as in the scraps I saved? Threw away, mind you, when they held her name. Where else did she have her life? I'd given her a long nose, I remember—no good reason why. Now her nose is middling. I made her sing a bawdy song—a poor idea. And I cut the nursery scene entirely, the whole scene, you understand, where she comes in, more than half asleep, the baby bawling, frightened, pawing at the darkness, helpless as a beetle on its back. When Ella touches him she shares his skin and feels him stiffen. Just then she understands the dreadful quality of his confusion. Her mouth falls open. She strikes the air.

I've never had the experience myself. How would it be to bump things like a spider? Anyway, there were too many principles against the passage.

I didn't give her a long nose exactly. She *had* a long nose. Now it's gone. I decided she looked too much like a witch, and since she really was a witch, it wouldn't do to have her look precisely like one. If I weren't honest you'd never know; you'd think her nose was middling. So it is. My god, don't blame poor authors. Think how shameful it would be to say: Ella Bend had a long nose, which I shortened to a middling one because a middling one made her look less like a witch, although a witch is what she was. You won't find many who've got the guts. They make a cheap product—skimp on the goods. If you want my advice—don't buy.

Passage is the right word. *Passage.* Every sentence is a passage. So I changed her life; changed it; not in advance but afterward, after it was over. That's real magic for you, not the merely manual kind. What is this art but the art of appearance? I make bright falsehoods to blind the eye.

Maybe it was *merciless* I meant. Beauty is often a curse, and I suppose clairvoyance could be. Now: what do I mean? You realize that time has passed—another thing the cheapskates hide. Time. Whole weeks. A lot happens. My mother dies. I am caught by a famous disease. Or nothing happens. My mother does not die. I am not caught by a famous disease. Do I still intend whatever it was I did? Ella Bend is lucky to be alive. I have a terrible pain in my head. Of course she's dead. But not yet. She doesn't die in the story. At the moment all she has is an altered nose and nervous eyes. Think if that were all you were.

Cassandra's curse wasn't clairvoyancy. It was not being believed. Suppose it had been Cassandra who saw but who also disbelieved. That would have been more interesting.

I wonder if you understand about that *m*. The other day I idly scribbled twelve of them in the margin of a canceled page: mmmmmmmmmmmmm. They doubtless affected my mind. I was writing away, "the descent of the dove" and all that, when I caught those *m*'s in the corner of my eye. That's how I came to feel some force in its direction. But, good lord, why? Could anything be more absurd? Would God create that way?

Look at them again: mmmmmmmmmmmmm. Hear the hum. Isn't that the purply dove? the witches' mist? It's Ella Bend in receipt of her gift. Her eyes fill.

The dove descends, says here you are, accept it and forgive. Her eyes fill.

There was nothing in her childhood to suggest it. She was pudgy. She'd worn a red coat that buttoned to her chin, scratching her neck; Sallydale highshoes, secure as a mother's love, the salesman said; thick stockings with tight elastic tops; bloomers that cut her skin; severely woven braids tied with pale fluttery bows; and wool mittens that itched when her hands began to sweat. The salesman had a case that folded out impressively. Even Ellareen had hoped he'd fold it out again. He unlidded and unpleated it. It was a polished black sample tray with shiny chrome catches—a shoes-in-the-box, Ellahen had said—and everyone had laughed, Ellareen putting her hand on Ellahen's colorless head, deciding right then to buy her a pair; and the box undid itself, legs sliding out, secret after secret coming until the shoes were there, even yellow ones, red, very vulgar and beautiful, making Ellareen feel like an Indian, covetous and primitive. The salesman was talking and smiling. He had fine hands and smooth black hair.

Let's just try this on for size, he said.

A shoehorn dangled from a chain that disappeared into his vest.

Black is useful.

Ella trembled when he held her feet. The shoes seemed cool, but they didn't feel like a mother's love.

It don't show wear.

Thomas thumped the case.

Stands up noble, Ellareen said.

It gets them all, the salesman said. They want to know how it works. They love it.

The salesman rubbed his thumb against the side of Ella's arch.

Walk on that. See how it feels.

Ella stood awkwardly, wiggling her toes, rocking as she was bid, while Thomas touched the leg-joints of the sample tray. Her mother stooped quickly, closing her thumb and finger on Ella's ankle.

Is it tight enough there?

Oh yes ma'am, you need some play.

Has to be some support, too. I like things to fit. She snapped erect. Try a pair on Ellahen.

We like to sell our shoes in the home where they're worn. That's why we come here like we do. See there, he said, holding up the mate, that's well made.

He folded the toe into his hand, then crumpled the top, and Ella felt a pang for the shoe that might be hers.

Feel that—soft and smooth.

He held it out to Ellareen, who balanced the shoe on her hand, squinting at the heel.

Has to be firm, she said.

The shoes were in tiers, one from each pair, on deep puffed velvet like valuable jewels. He had the others loose in a bag.

The salesman measured Ellahen.

Ella has weak ankles and her feet are flat, takes after Mister Bend in that. It's Ellahen who's real strong there.

The salesman smiled at Ellahen, who blinked and rubbed her nose. Well all of them lace high, he said, and Ella thought he seemed like a knight, kneeling in front of Ellahen, making his vows, and she wondered how in the world all those shoes went in. She wanted him to fold it up so she could see, and the request shaped her mouth. Then she wondered instead what the salesman thought of Ellahen, whether he'd ever seen an albino before (she supposed he had) and what he would think if he knew why Ellareen had broken her rule against men who sold from door to door to let him in.

This salesman's name is Philip Gelvin; he's a thoroughly bad hat, as the saying was then, and he hates albinos; they make his flesh crawl. He hates their pink rabbitlike eyes. His uncle saw one sunburned once. The lines in the skin were embossed on the blisters. She was helplessly sick to her stomach; terrifying white hair fell about her face; her tinted glasses lay in the grass. That was Willie Fogal—his uncle—who is ninety and who saw Pister Welcome, he says, shoot The Badman in the boot, like the rhyme says. Willie was always claiming to have seen this or that. Who could tell? He's in his dotage now and takes a dislike to death that's far too late to be sincere. But poor old man and his dissolving head. Visit him at the farm sometime, he'll tell you what he sees: gray mists, vapors, spaces, holes. Stares straight ahead. The kindly ladies keep him clean. Might as well look one way as another, he says, it's all around, just open up your eyes and *look* . . . Quite a change from the warrior days . . . Well I pity everyone his age. Anyway that's what he said: he saw Pister take his rifle down the first the pigs got loose, mad as hell naturally, and he saw him walk up the street with it under his arm until he was where The Badman was standing, where they all were standing, and then Pister says, according to Uncle Fogal, you ain't worth shooting in the head; you ain't worth shooting in the ass, whereupon the gun went off, as though, really, it was accidental, and The Badman fell on his shoulder in the mud. The boot, even with the hole through it, held the blood from The Badman's shattered foot so well it hardly stained the puddle. I never shot anybody just because of pigs, The Badman said.

Scenes like this—that's what Uncle Fogal filled his eyes with, why he lived . . . the swine.

There must be some truth to the tale, though, because you can view the boot, the shattered edges of the leather curled and the mud removed, at the Harrison County Historical Museum any hour it's unlocked. Take the stairs you'll see in front of you when you enter (mind the banister, it rocks), cross the balcony as it sweeps to the right, and you will find the boot on the first table through the door, by the spurs of The General, with a placard propped; but Mrs. Crandall keeps her schedule secret, so if you want to see it you'll have to set a watch. Try to look honest, sincere and devout. She fears thieves and anyone with a pencil. It is generally believed that wags one day arranged a number of the mounted animals in attitudes of copulation, destroying as they did so the supports and backdrop of an educational tableau, much admired over the years, which had featured a leap-

ing frog, a frightened hare, and a screaming eagle. I happen to
know that when Mrs. Crandall observed the address being paid
by a moose to a deer, a terrible weakness overcame her and she
almost fainted—not from modesty or outrage but from an
unbearably poignant recollection—sagging against the banister
I warned you about with such force it yielded, nearly spilling her
across its upper railing onto a table of fans and combs and looking glasses just below, the mirrors cleverly arranged to multiply
the combs and fans by three. (So I should, she said, have broken
more of those fine combs and illustrated fans than ever had
existence.) Instantly her weakness was replaced by indignation,
for, as she very often told me later, the decorative scene had
been created by Willard Scott Lycoming himself, and though
the foreground was mostly grass enlivened here and there with
daisies, the middle distance represented with astonishing fidelity (fidelity, alas, uncommon in the paintings of our faithless
age) a view of the Harris Creek, where the Lister Farm had been
before it burned and where the plant that folks now call the
Pork Works was, while the far ground contained the barest suggestion of a pointed mountain scarfed with purple haze of
which the artist had been vouchsafed, he had told the then
Miss Swanson, a vision in a dream (there are no mountains in
these parts, though several low hills lie along the river); a peak
which had, he said, meant a great deal to him ever since and
which the tableau had hinted was the home of the screaming
eagle, whence it came; and the violation of this lovely historical
work had filled her with such a fierce and avenging anger that
she struck an indecent squirrel from its mounting, snapping its
dry and ancient tail upon the floor. The placard was composed
by Mrs. Crandall, who ought to know the facts, and it says nothing of Uncle Fogal or Pister Welcome either. (Pister, Mrs. Crandall tells me, is a myth.) It merely identifies the owner of the
boot; relates the manner of his shooting simply and does not

fasten to his death the dignity of names; calls attention to the worn heel, the scuffed toe, the poor quality of leather; suggests that The Badman was hardly a fit object for hero worship, even though he has become a hero to our children; and closes with a bitter reference to the symbolism in his ruin, the coating of his shattered foot with clay.

What impressed me most about the boot, when I was taken as a boy to see it, was its size. It's quite small, smaller than I felt it should be, dainty almost, and in those days the top had been allowed to droop upon its stem like a flower, although now there is a stick inside to stiffen it. While I made no public boo-rah, privately I snapped my jaws together and refused to believe in it, a judgment I have since had ample reason, of course, to change. A boot so small and cheaply made could not have held The Badman's foot, I thought, and I was encouraged in this opinion by Pelcer Wilson's dad, who said the boot had been fished from the creek—the hole looked bitten through by water rats—and anyway it was a lady's style and size, look at the heel, he said, ever see a man wear a heel like that? and where was the mate if it was the boot of The Badman, a man near six foot five, he knew, and not a teeny-weeny dandy, his father having seen him kill a man with his bare hands, holding him clear of the ground at the end of his arms like a clutch of prize fish. It was Melon Yoder he killed this way, and Melon was at least six foot himself, broad in his shoulders like a steer, fat in his belly like a sow, thick through his thighs like Willie Masters' Lonesome Wife, and when The Badman loosened him he made a dent in the ground. His father told him, Pelcer Wilson said, that The Badman's boots were tall and darkly glistening; there were silver nails in the heels and silver stitching over the toe and a row of silver tassels all along the top which shook joyously when The Badman walked like wheat in an intermittent wind.

Lies, lies, lies. What can anyone believe? The Badman was a mimsy parlor-chested squit who stole small change from empty poker tables and whose most daring and most desperate act was freeing Pister Welcome's pigs to run the town. That sort of childish bullyragging jape was what he made his name by, how he lived . . . the swine. Men will always lie about the measure of their penis, you can bank on it. Sam T. Hoggart somewhere in his *History* says the same. Sam's the only historian I know who hates numbers (excepting William Frederick Kohler, of course, up on charges now for molesting his female students). Anyway, his book is a fine one, and I more than echo our friendship when I recommend it. He'd do the same for me.

Then Lycoming. I take no pleasure in inventing him. He is a negligible painter. Three names for *snob*. A man, however, as they used to say, of parts. But no dent in the history of art. It may have been his contradictions that destroyed him, teetered him insane, for he was a hollow-eyed visionary of the romantically desperate kind, cruelly devoted to the truth, afire to prophesy, full of flummoxy notions about the nature of perception, intoxicated by geometry, royally ceremonious, utterly unscrupulous, wholly mad, yet loyal, with the stupid blind loyalty of the lover, to the world he saw and felt surround him. Well it threw him down. These fanatic, jealous, brutal devotions made him so fastidious with every detail he could not manage their subordination. He gave them all his skill, painting each with a microscopic precision that shattered the unity of his canvas and created there a kind of grossly luminous horror. Obedient to the perverse demands of his creative demon, he could not paint a crowd it did not fall into an anarchy of faces (Ensor's *Christ Entering Brussels* comes to mind)—(no, it's called *The Entry of Christ Into Brussels*), while these immediately became round porous noses and converging eyes—all, mind you, at the behest of some arbitrary spatial symbol, mathematically shaped and mystically significant (like the logarithmic spiral or a chessboard, the lines of someone else's poem, and so on). Yet it is nearly true that in his work each brush stroke speaks. Well they make a godly clamor (one should confess the virtue that gives suck to every vice), but the din, I must admit, despite my love for dear Peg Crandall, who may love him still (since it was he who first put paint-stained fingers to her breasts and chewed her ear), is awful, simply awful. The foreground of that scene I mentioned, although torn by the vandals and never repaired, is marvelously rendered, and so subtle was Lycoming's genius that in its lower corner, by the signature which grime by now has nearly covered, he has broken off some blades of grass and flattened others to suggest that someone was standing there a moment ago, perhaps the artist himself, gazing across the Harris Creek to the overgrown stones of the Lister home and toward the vaguely risen dream peak in the distance.

W.S.L. You know what he asked her? To pose. What else? To pose. Oh to be a painter so to ask to pose. To pose. A request a lady's vanity will always find appealing. To pose. Nibbling on her shell-pink ear. My genius is stirred by your beauty my dear. The snake. Not nude, of course, just naked to the waist—unclothed, that is to say, undraped. So she did, she posed—despite the best upbringing, despite her years of Sunday school, despite her love of fancy clothing, her doting father, and several carnal shocks that fell together in her fifth year, none of which she could remember, though one of them had to do with Willard Scott as a little bratty boy in a Sunday tie and collar, black short pants, and urgently opened fly; despite the fact her painter had a skinny penis and a stony cod, which she could hardly have known at the time and seemed never to mind; in spite of her mother, who slept in her corset, or her marriage vows, or the laws of the state, the commands of God, or the rules of her rutty artist's maidenly college; greedily, without listening for the sound of steps on the stairs or the stealthy creak of a peeper, with laughter and with solemn lewd intent, debonair as a true gymnosophist, and, as she fancied ladies often were in Aristophanes, with a smudge of ferrous green an inch below her rosier nipple. 'Pon my honor. By my faith. And I understand that in the painting, though I've never seen it, he put the metal smudge (tenderly, with the nostalgic tip of his finger) precisely where it belonged. Poor Peg. What an unending cliché her life has been. And so badly painted. It was a sweet joke they had to nibble on between them. Of course she couldn't bear to wash it off, weeping when it flaked away. Prophetically. In the course of the fateful stars. My word as a disciple of Jesus.

To be looked at like that. Not the way the doctor did when he wasn't playing doctor. But the way the painter did whose soul admired what his loins desired. What an aureole! What an inner-thigh line! Belly button to be gently pressed. Is anyone at home? To be looked at as if it were the sun, and her blood came up under her skin like a blush a burn where the eyes gazed, where desire grazed. But the result clearly compromised her 'cause it wasn't art, it represented Lycoming's adoration OK his lust.

So she hid the painting prudently beneath her bed until her husband's hand uncovered it, fumbling for a slipper she had purchased Wednesday for the celebration of his fifty years. *N.B.* The husband and the wife made love above the oily canvas. Why not? Husband and wife. Calculate how often. Squirmed and giggled. Full orchestra for the beautiful ballad: Made Love Above the Canvas. Heedle deedle deedle. Or a cabaletta for tenor and tambourine. Ladies and gentlemen: introducing Philip and Phyllis, that inimitable pair of gymnasts, who will thrill you by making love on the giant swings—boom . . . , on the back of a galloping camel—boom, boom . . . , while riding a trike on the high wire—boom, boom, boom . . . , and as a special treat, never before attempted outside the steppes of Asia, in midair above a trampoline—boom . . . boom, boom, boom. False nose straight? Want to borrow mine? It's aquiline. Have a pink tasseled hat and a horn. Now, I hate to keep harping on this, but don't forget the significance of the slippers. Shall we play a few more games? Tromp about in the rosin box, it's slippery on the wire. Or bundle up with camera. Clothing disarrayed? Uncover to discover: your wife's image as a lover's longing. How many rents in Aphrodite's tents? Lucky guesser gets a buss upon his plucky kisser. Ah, what a rouser! Well, sheepishly he'd worn them to please her. They looked foolish and bedraggled, flopping on his feet—the sort of man he was. O wise and worldly gods, what appropriate conjunctions! But a silly sort of horns. Now. What does he say? He says very naturally what is this? what? eh? um? eh? In short, nothing. He has difficulty sliding it from under. Like the bare leg of a lover. Discovered. He tugs and hauls while Peg what? claws at her rump where she's been bitten by a spider. Unattractive patch that's not in the painting. Well, insects have no nerves. Of course it puts him in a rage. Regular. Towering. Flames flash from his steeple. His nightshirt's ashake. There follow a number of inner ticulations. So he destroys it, the iconoclast. He smashes it, rends it. Mem. must be a convenient size, consider the set. Next gesture: he takes it up in his hands and brings it down on the left post of the bed with all his excavator's strength. The canvas does not yield, though the knurl strikes her belly. Poor old Bill. It was beautifully stretched and sized. It's a problem for properties. Alarm them early. The painting springs from the post—look at those aureoles!—tears itself from his hands—the light down on her arms, what a likeness!—falls, strikes his unslippered foot, skids away, shoving the rug into waves, scratching the floor—tessellated too, what workmanship!—and so on. He nearly strangles her for that scratch, of course. Hopping, he takes her by the creamy throat.

O revengeful Italy. But his foot pains him greatly and he sits on the edge of the bed to massage it. Rough skin. Needs a regular application of Bag Balm. In any case he had his thumbs misplaced. How did Othello do it? She kneels now, mewing, to rub his footie too. *Ah, soft France.* Later he is grateful for the slippers since he cannot walk around in shoes with such a knot in his toe. Peg coughs to make him feel he's been dangerous. She may be a whore, he thinks in the freshest way he can, but at least she's clean. No doubt in his mind about that, for some reason. Thereafter, his manhood challenged, he thinks of her as cheap enough to purchase wealthy pleasures, and makes love to her with gusto and invention. Well, for him—invention. *Dark and holy Russia.* Of which the upshot is—poor Lycoming's acold. Cuckolded by the man he made a cuckold. Of. Not long after this scene whose shameful elements with zest we have provided, the husband was killed in a sewer by a slide of mud. For his sins against art. *O implacable Spain.*

Can you bear this peep show any longer? How's this for a sneak: the painter pursuing the lady, who by now is naked, through the studio with a messy palette, mainly cobalt blue, for sky, and the brush from the hair of a camel. I'll have a sweeter canvas soon, he cries, she giggling. There are jokes about Indians and sailors and circus shows. Also under canvas. And then he has her. Dirty-fingered artist. Chester the White.

Why should I complain? Our artist merely requested Peg to pose naked to the waist, and doubtless he said something about painting the delicate slope of her back or capturing the soft shadows which fell from her shoulder blades or rendering the swanlike tube of her throat. These were all lies, of course, lies; they were not meant to be believed; except the poor girl did think she had a delicate slope and that there were shadows flowing softly down her back and that her neck was tall and nobly bent, feathery smooth and white. A painter would surely want to paint such things as these if he could stand to his easel to do it and wasn't weak in the knees with lust. There must have been some excitement for her, too, in being looked at by another man, a painter, who, at least while he painted (as we've already reported), really examined his woman, consequently had to see the fine things she saw, had to touch them anyway with the soft tips of his eyes. Ah married, yet a maiden! Peg, your husband saw no further than his prick—it, elderly—and when that instrument was dangling, he was nearly blind; but a painter, even a miserable daub like Lycoming, sees too far, too dangerously far, you dare not leave an opening, he'll enter your eyes, or your mouth and ears—any of the seven portals of the head—and for god's sake tighten up your thighs. That carriageway is easy. The painter, my dear, the painter perceives as deeply as his seed. There he sends his eyes, curled like trichinae in the muscles of a pig. But never mind. It was thus, her back turned modestly, he painted her. Well, it was a fine painting, of course, though it would have been finer if the draperies, more in the classical manner, had fallen lower on the hips . . . to here, you see, creating a beautiful arabesque. Thank god that sort of flaw a little overpainting will correct. It's a wonderful medium—oil. So now he wishes to treat the splendid bones of her behind. And hasn't she, though! Her husband, bless his sewer-slid-on soul, not once hefted her there, hardly her breasts either, and his experiments at the very last were not of that kind. If you would turn please, a little, to the light . . .

There's no point in going on. The plot, which is the soul, as Aristotle says, remains the same. Only the body undergoes a change. If we could X-ray that painting, I'm sure we'd find there every level of unclothing, like the layers of Troy, beneath its radiantly naked top. Adam—wheedle by wheedle—in the same way, got existence.

Now the careful reader will have noticed—

Bless me. The careful reader. I had forgotten him.

Does anyone remember me?

Well . . . My typewriter rests on a great oak plank between two sawhorses. In the old days, when the first volume of *Vines and Memorial Porches* had appeared and I was, in a manner of speaking, famous, I had been pictured in the colored pages of a national weekly working on *Trumpet to the Dawn,* then shortly to follow *Hurst's House* as the middle of my masterpiece (and a thumping success, as it turned out), shirtless, the hair on my back, which was bleached by the sun, making quite an effect in Kodachrome, puffing at a cigarette, a bluish string of testimonial smoke wreathing my clenched eyes, hands descending roughly toward the keys, face screwed with the effort of creation and my nails trimmed, rope belt tightly cinched and tied as a pirate would with a looping bow above the hip . . . I was vain . . . god . . . it cut into my waist and raised, or rather while indenting the skin seemed to raise nevertheless, a weal, which reproduced itself in the photo as an irregular pale splotch contiguous with the top of my tan shorts . . . not a bit flattering; and as I remember, I wore clogs and had my legs spread straight as sticks, as I have since seen pregnant women spread them when they dared, and my desk in that photo was just such a desk as this, exactly the one my knees are under now, as a matter of fact, for I felt obliged by the picture to use it sometimes, though I don't wear a thing when I write but work naked and compose by staring at my cock and balls, alternatively, first one and then the other; and that sense of obligation, the sight of myself in the picture, put me under it so often that I began to compare my wooden horses to the feathered dray-pulls of the *Phaedrus:* the right-hand horse a stallion, graceful as a skipping girl, blond and clear-eyed, yet thick-maned and large like the lion, with the lion's deep throat and tubular teeth, swift and tireless, moreover, as a coasting bird, as farsighted, patient, and implacable, with a regal neck which lifted at every sound like a deer's, and with wings to satisfy an angel glowing from their passage through the air; while the left . . . oh dear, the left a shambling, drunken mare with a cropped tail and a coarse shaggy coat made of hairs with darkened ends, sore-footed, foulmouthed, fattish and nobby, with short, uneven legs and a snub face and white-webbed eyes, nervous, sly, her inner organs cruelly eaten by disease, given to rhythmic swaying like a bear, inclined to bite, her dwarfed wings so closely folded to her sides she never flew at all but fell as crudely as a stone, as brutally, as eager; and as I say, this obligation sent me back and back again until sitting to the trestle became automatic, necessary even when bitter (as now), it was a track so deeply worn; and I can reach with a pencil end the words I have carved in the wood by tracing them a hundred thousand times, my doodles too, always the same, cutting a canyon like a stream, dark at the bottom with graphite, beautifully smooth (for graphite is a handsome lubricant), in beautifully turned calligraphy: *cunt,* for instance, with many curlicues . . . (here is something funny: I had begun that particular tracing first, so it was rather permanently down when I began the final volume, and it really happened that on the day I composed its most famous scene, that tender lovers' parting on the porch of Mt. Lion, Parker kissing the tines of Carol's parasol (OK, anything sounds absurd when outlined simply, and there's a lesson for us all in that), then folding it abruptly as a sign that he is leaving the Mount forever; while I was composing this tender, sentimental scene, I say, restlessly stirring my words around and wondering how I should manage the business, my pencil was continuously, thoughtlessly, idly tracing *cunt* still more darkly in the oak—imparting a rhythm to my hand and arm, rocking my shoulder, affecting . . . what? my brain? (which reminds me of the technique of *Madame Bovary* and of Flaubert's startled whore, cigar ash on her belly, formal hat on him—the supremely cool equestrian), well . . . and Covenant, which was the name of an historic oak beneath whose boughs a treaty, depriving some Indians of land in return, I believe, for their enjoyment of an interlude of peace, was signed by some Quakers and those Indians with an X; and when the oak, having fallen prey to drought, wind, age, or some disease (I wonder was it the same disease as mine?), was cut down (bands played, doubtless; there were solemn speeches in rented hats from wooden stands while pennants snapped in the rhetorical winds), a long heart slice was sent to me, though god knows why, I hate both covenants and trees, and this accounts for the incision of *Covenant,* and for *fuck the Indians hurrah,* a bordering phrase, etched small.

I am an inveterate pencil carver and I consequently understand the qualities of wood. I know how, for instance, the grain will cause the most determined line to quake and wriggle. My first attempt to engrave the letter *c* in the plank from the Covenant tree left a very bent and shaken *l,* though you would never guess it now, the original is so overlaid with flourishes. The secret is to proceed by a series of gentle scratches, repeated often; never an impatient deep gouge, which the wood will surely put a crick in, but always the patiently light scratch. A painted surface is tricky. Oh, it's easy enough to make pencil marks on a fine enamel, but that's not the aim, you know. Get under the skin, that's the idea. You must watch that the paint doesn't flake or you will spoil the clarity and decision of your line. I'm not much interested in images myself. I always carve letters or abstract designs: five-pointed stars sometimes, the capital *L,* which in script curls its edges like a sheet of stamps, or *f* or *k,* or the word *Isabel,* or thickety black scrawls bunched like tumbleweeds, and mazes of dizzily turning lines like the spill and flow of hair, whole worlds really, the track deepening as you journey on, as if at any moment you might penetrate something, find yourself inside the sacred wood, say, or simply, like Alice, land thump in another part of the soul where a voice is exclaiming, my, my, my, as you arrive, and there is a vague flash of white from something running or a pink glow from the lobe of an animal's ear or the faint but steady ringing of a distant alarm. Then frequently: balloon.

Traveling, I've returned to stations where I've stopped for gas and found my stars still there, sometimes even darkened, or deepened, by those who love, as I do, to slip into a path and feel the rhythm of another mind, a stranger's, once sitting where you are, tracing some secret of his life on the wall or in the toilet seat, not always cheap or vulgar either, for after all it is form and not the content that matters, though there are those who scratch haphazardly, concerned to get their filthy message over (in art and life the same), but they aren't everybody, thank god, for I've seen the masculine member drawn by a genius, and a vagina rendered strangely like a daisy, and once, as high as you could reach, like the bragging claw marks of a bear, exquisitely formed, the word *lemonade,* by a divinity.

Three a.m. It's begun to snow. Could I have the time where you are? Strange. It may be morning, hot already, sweat in all your creases. Whew. Your bare legs have stuck to your chair. That time of year. In me large flakes are sailing single file. Hear the hiss? Isn't that the purply misssst?

There is a small hotel in town. I remember the dirty marble floor, cold and noisy, the nails in my worn heels clicking. I skirt bucket rings and patches of drying mop water, one in the shape of Spain, to escape the remote lamps of the lounge and keep my shadow out of corners while I flee on strips of carpet to the stairs where bumping down sedately through the door marked WOMAN I say I beg your pardon to the wielder of the mop though she is gone or not yet come and the booths are empty, idle, unobscene, unscatological. I try one out but there is nothing to it. My deeply yellow urine, like the light from those brass lamps, spills in the bowl and I leave it as a sign of my passing. Oh I am a foul left-handed fellow, Phaedrus, rarely ambidextrous. As I go I hear my feet . . . the wealthy author walks.

Did I discover much?

No, not much: stale powder, strong discharges, cheap perfume, moist hair. They write on the walls with lipstick. I've little interest in that. It's painting of a crude sort; nothing's clear. It has no permanence and lacks the shaping resistance of a decent medium. But where the women water in a public playground I did follow a track in the shape of a symbol from the Isle of Man that made my hair stand on end. There was something superb scratched in plaster with a bobby pin . . . somewhere . . . I've forgotten . . . while another time, in a roadside park, I encountered a painting, a silhouette in menstrual blood entitled *Sam*. Not much luck. Yet I keep on. Don't laugh. My god, remember I'm supposed to think and feel and see for everyone— imagine!—that's the true author's business; and all the time Christ snoozes in his chair. There's no patron for left-handed wretches. It's bottoms up, buddy, for us. All right, snicker. You've never seen your face in Leonardo's mirror. Laugh away. But poking about takes guts, all the same. Don't pay for anything less.

Some, of course I've never learned their names, anonymous Samoans maybe, saintly impersonal artisans who sit cross-legged braiding leaves to hang athwart their middles, take advantage of the natural terrain, incorporating, in the manner of collages, nails (around two such were drawn the feet of Christ, one nail for each, as though He had been hammered to the letter *H,* His hands represented in the same way except the fingers of the left were bent across a corner where a nail came through the wallboard from the other side, a shred of scarlet ribbon fluttering from the point like a trickle of blood, and I must say, though images don't excite me very much, this one gave me a turn), and every other accident and feature: bubbles in the paint, badly patterned plaster, the tracks of mounting tape, untanned squares where notices were hung, desperate old erasures and the paths of rags; flecks, picks, cracks, the heads of screws; stains, smudges, nicks, dents, pieces of paper; chips, smears, mars, knots, tears, condom and comb dispensers; scrapes, bumps, chinks, scars, furrows, burns, and the webs of spiders; clots of lifeless flies, mineral growths at the joints of pipes, even objects hung in space, dangling strings and naked bulbs and wires, for instance (in the toilet of a rural bar and billiard hall, incredibly forlorn, when I sat down to shit, the bulb blew me hugely on the wall, humped, rising out of the shadow of the stool like a giant out of granite, something by Rodin, brutish and primordial, and then I saw an outline on the wall, faint, in chalk, unsteady, often smeared, of someone else's body, bent like mine, nearly the same, but with an arm outstretched and fingers fanned, though whether as a plea for aid or in salute or benediction it was impossible to say, and strangely compelled, I reached out cautiously, enclosing my shadow in the lines, and they fit like Cinderella's slipper, they fit; that nameless idiot and myself, we fit; and when I examined the drawing more carefully I saw that the outline had been dotted in with something like the soft tip of a billiard cue, the points then joined with ordinary chalk; and so observing, I wiped myself and rose and spoke boldly to the giant as I stuffed my shirt into my trousers: but do you speak the language of the French, *mon frère?*), and, well, simply every imaginable matter: boards and pipes, hooks and other kinds of hardware, even previous compositions, whatever elements are given, just as the Aurignacian painters in their caves.

Is there a groove where I may rest my sensitive arm? I know the joke: the grave. But what selection shall I play this three a.m. in honor of the snowing? There are twenty degrees of aged light and fat young snow. A gauge grins at me through a window whose face frost is blearing. I shall play Ella Bend swaying in her shoe, a moronic look on her face. Silly fool. I hate her. I hate them all. That's not a manner of speaking. I have only to write down their names and I hate them. They make my stomach turn . . .

Except for Pister Welcome. There's a possibility there. For something new. No need to hang another doodad of a moon in the morning sky. Do Greece? do Babylon? *Of Mice and Men* again? Pister Welcome was built like Gregory Peck, only he had the head of a chicken. The irony in his name was that Pister was a hermit. He lived in the woods beneath a huge pile of brush.

Ah, thank the lord—Phil! It's you. (Phil, a friend, is knocking at the gate of my heavenly study; doubtless he wishes to come in, to see me, visit a bit.) Come in . . .

There is a film of dust on everything. It is August. The roads are dry. No. It is August. The roads are dry. There is a film of dust on everything. It settles slowly as the snow falls softly on my window. But dust is more enduring, stays the seasons, surfaces the wings of birds, persists through fiction, drifts from Ella Bend to me, and in an hour or so, though Ellareen has dusted thoroughly, I shall write my mene mene tekel upharsin on her dining room table, my fingernail like the skate of a ghost. Dust out of the dry August roads. Dust blown out of the dry August sky. It will dampen the ball of my thumb if I mark on the window. What might I write there? Heat from my hand will melt the frost. The gauge will grin through the lines. Does the shoe fit, princess? Let me feel the instep. You've an ugly ankle. Couldn't I have done any better by you? No promise in the leg either. An ungenerous thigh. Well, look at your mother. Bad blood somewhere. I mean the albino. And your father—furious for it. Shall I trouble to describe you? How shall I describe you if I trouble? Dust drawn from the dry August roads. Ah, Theaetetus, I fear I have brought forth a wind-egg. I have few positive opinions but I've opinions on that . . . somewhere . . . I've thought of it often. Don't I keep a journal? Foolish oversight. Notebook? No? It's this pain in my belly that puts me off.

Except when I hurt, this shall be your story.

Now, although the physical qualities of any lady, let's say lady for the nonce, exist as a unity and appear for the most in the same way, her description, because it must form a sequence of words, arranges these qualities for the reader's understanding, so that she comes into view like a distant ship, a bit at a time. Her description may be drawn in straight lines or in zigzags, out of curves or a scatter of unjoined dots, but whatever the geometry, the author will, as far as he comprehends the nature of his art and has capacity, compose a picture from the turns he gives to our attention that not only will possess the excitement of a moment-by-moment adventure, but will also, when the reader grasps it all as he grasps a theme in music, make a drama of the passage of the mind, even to its beginning, its middle, and its end, with recognition and reversal if the author's art requires; and what can be true of the physical description of a lady can be true of the arrangement of any set of words whatever, though the point of the arrangement may be more difficult to see, the connections more subtly joined.

End lesson one. You won't mind, will you, if I run a bit past the bell?

And. For. It? (Something's missing here, but no matter.)

It is precisely considerations of this sort that distinguish the artist's attitude toward language from others; it is the intensity of his concern that measures his devotion, the multiplication of these that reveals the grandeur of his vision; and it is the effect of such scruples, when successfully embodied, whether with the ease of an overflowing genius or by the pains of talent in team with ambition, to raise a fiction, or any other creative work, from what would be on most other grounds a commonplace, to the level of the beautiful.

When God wrote on Belshazzar's wall, the critic Daniel decided the enigmatic words were "weighed weighed counted divided," and that they meant the king's reign had been judged inadequate and that his land would be divided. But here, instead of a judgment, they are an injunction: writer, reader, weigh everything twice, make everything count, and separate yourself from your writing reading the way the snake sheds its skin, while bearing in mind, too, who you reader writer are—you are the slough, and your common text is the sly shining snake.

I wonder what disease it is I have, whether I shall die tomorrow, or sometime later. Considerations of this kind lend no urgency to my work. That only happens in stories, and the idea of death makes me nervous. It's two forty-five. And dustily snowing. Peg Crandall has gallstones. She's awake with the pain. Pister Welcome is hiding from his fate. Lycoming rots in his grave. I wish it were light. And morning.

For in the morning I shall make paths over the hills, shape five-pointed stars, draw the balls of bulls, and on a steep slope like the side of an advertising sign, I shall step off the word— *lemonade*—in a hand that's a double of the deity's.

The Clairvoyant

The spirits were not easy in the house. The cupboards, for instance. And the deep malicious grass. She would have to persuade him to move.

The spirits were uneasy, restless, tossing like a sleeper at dreams, and Ella listened, filling the empty afternoons with their concerns, her husband at his insurance, autumn at the still gray mark it makes before blowing into winter. It would be hard, he loved his grass. She pulled at her teeth and felt the beginnings of one of his corrections. He was forever making mistakes and dragging that rough long redgreen angular eraser bumpily over the error, bulging the paper.

Here's his moonlike face coming in, not a cloud or a star, shining down on a desk leafed in paper. His plump hands finalize a crease. Rings dignify his fingers. Rolls of rubber lie like defecations. There it is: tissuey, pink. First the white, then the carbon and the flimsy. Next an art gum to neaten. He'll whisk it all off in an instant, she thought, or blow the leavings in the air. That should belie him. His manner, his business, the whole of his duplicator life, should be exposed by the puff, but the poor tormented creatures whom he cheats, they cannot understand or care, they don't wish in any way to believe it. He could pee out his nose, they'd not notice, they're so frightened, so polite.

She slid one of the humps, gathering speed. OowoO. Gum left crumbs, not rolls of rubber. She felt them between her toes unpleasantly. Never need false ones live to be a hundred. Here—'way we go. OoHoO. A body could come to grief. She never understood why vocal emanations were so easy from his office or why her husband's voice, when he was there, was always captured in her coffeepot, escaping wanly out the spout. Dear me. Death and taxes. The Lord knew—bless His splendid hair—she didn't like to slide that well. Edgar's mouth was surely nothing like a spout, more like the slot in a needy box. You'll be well taken care of, Mrs. Muvvers, a policy like this. Protection against death. SpAaa. Ella cruelly scratched and stretched her legs. Hot water would steam him out. You will always be poor at spiritual analogy, you haven't the astral eye at all, Madame Betz had said. All rightie, Madame Smart, I'll read a book to pick up speed. Madame Betz had a combative head. Run over by a train, the cards had said—no—Wednesday—eleventh. That would be the Central likely since it was the only one to Stocking not a block from her. Well, she'd not live to be a hundred either, thank the recumbent Lord. Not in the cards. But she'd have a good skullful of teeth—that was a comfort. Oh sliding was indeed a pleasure. She'd have to take back all her reservations. A pleasure it was. One of the few remaining. OoHoO.

Sunk in a chair, arms and shoulders aching, Ella stared at her thin brown hands as they made the motions of cutting and dealing cards, and through the lattice of their pantomime she heard and felt and saw the bodies of the ghostly dead in the pop of contracting timber, in the smokclike grain of wood in doors, in the presence of draughts in the shut house. She put water to the coils and drew the blinds until the thinnest of its patterns marked the walls; then sank with a weary groan into the flower-covered chair and held up her weary hands to cut and deal and conjure. To be water and metal and not to mind. Then a gray waste of ease for a moment. Peculiarity of quiet. Contentment of non-being. Not a star in the sky, not an eye. Gratefully she rested, bobbing softly. The water hissed and steam plumed in the kitchen. Hushush. The spirits put their palms over Ella's ears. Through the crossing, through the interlacing of her fingers, better than any milky bowl or any smokey glass, she could hear the spirits treading the silence.

It hadn't been easy: becoming a clairvoyant. Ella'd had to refine the organs she already had past any range and tolerance printed on their ticket, create others out of nipples, belly button, warts and scars and finger ends, then even from thumbs and elbows, the most recalcitrant pieces of her body, making them receivers of signals never before known, and refining her general dialing and directional procedures, so that each hair was an antenna, whether stationed on her head or across her eyebrows, out a mole, underarm, above her pubes, down her leg, in her ear or nose; likewise her teeth were tuned, her sunken cheeks were dishier than a radar's, and her lobes turned like wary eyes.

Noises, I can see noises, she had once said to a neighbor, immediately regretting it, seeing the tremor in her neighbor's face. It was a face like her own face, a famished face: narrow, high, deeply socketed, thin. There was a soul like her own soul too, behind it. Ella's conviction was that her own had the shape and nature of molasses. Her neighbor's face, however, was not wrinkled and brown as Ella's body was all over. It was pale and transparent, and her skull lay like a quiet shadow under it. Ella could see, she thought, the world of her neighbor in her neighbor's head. She had told her friend something about the spirits, a good deal in fact, too much perhaps—yes, almost certainly too much, but it was even now necessary not to surprise her. The world rolled through her like a sea, the skin no seawall to it, and no one afloat in that tide could have guessed by a sky change or by any other that they had been swept beyond her body wall and bobbed now in the basin of her brain. Her smile would be the same, her eyes would glow with the same warmth, her head incline to the same sign of sympathy and kindliness as if nothing had passed between you but a bit of the mildly interesting and sometimes useful spew of the sea. Sympathy she had, the sympathy of the ocean: vast, unconscious, and impersonal. Nevertheless, from time to time a gesture or a grimace or a tale would disappear and not return, caught in something underneath that indifferent surge which Ella decided was her neighbor's similar soul, and then her neighbor's eyes would narrow and her lips tremble and her skin darken. For a moment there would be a real wall between them, and Ella would think, ah, now she is conscious of herself.

Ella had been wrinkled when she married. Now her edges were yellow and her hair streaked; her eyes like the holes of pebbles in the moment after striking water. Her nose was pinched and her eyes were angular and sharp, as were her chin and the bones at the base of her neck. Between her meager breasts, because of a cheap crucifix (now pitted with sweat) she had worn since a child, there was always an oblong green smudge. The skin at that place had several times become infected, raising once a lump the size and shape of a peanut in its shell, which while it stayed Ella regarded with religious awe as the mark of her talisman and thus the sign of her faith, staring down an hour a day as might a Hindu holy man to where the crucifix rubbed against the swelling and turned it successively green and pink and curd.

What Ella had said to her neighbor was true, she could see sound, and as plainly there in space and with its own distinct shape and feature as one might see an elk—antlered, hoofed, and bearded. All her senses were acute, but she could hear and see and feel most marvelously well: the tremor in her neighbor's face, the scrape of cloud, the grumble of molasses, like her soul, folding from its bottle, the rattle of smoke in a pipe, and the squeak of a suede glove fingering a chair tassel like the startled outcry of a mouse.

Cut, said Mrs. Maggies, off. Shut of her pains, if she had any, Mrs. Granley said. With the good Lord now, I hope, poor soul, said Mrs. Panishome. A sweet lady she was, so kind, though I hardly knew her she kept to herself and never returned a civil word a civil word . . .

Hush. Sugar crock. Left the lid off. How did they get in there? The cards would never tell Ella the date of Ella's demise, but Mrs. Maggies always sounded elderly. Ella'd have to live long enough for Mrs. Maggies' voice to crack. She returned to her chair with sugar in a cup, water raining in the pot. We shall simply have to move. The spirits are uneasy. It's that cupboard, to be sure, the sugar lid ajar again and they get out. She peered in the cup and shivered from the cold. The pattern on the wall grew pale. The pulse is low, she thought. They're out.

Her husband hadn't known of the smudge when he married her, although he could hardly have been blind to her drying eyes and broken lips, and, if he chose, he could have simply imagined the rest; but he was not an amorous man, easily discouraged, preferring vulgar dreams in which vague shapes performed the act at his behest; so but rarely, tired, after bowling as it happened sometimes, when sleep had stopped his senses up with nightmare and he reached out for a form within it vague enough to violate, did he roll upon her, grubbing in her nightclothes with his hands and thrashing wildly with his body, while rigid, silent, dry, Ella thrust his penis in. She became pregnant once in this way. Shortly after their baby's birth its father developed a severe condition of the back that required him to sleep on a board on the floor. Ella so cheerfully accepted this arrangement that she gave her husband, on the occasion of their tenth wedding anniversary, a wide and highly polished maple plank.

Sanding all those years like a burglar sharpening his fingers, and he squat always by the ace of swords, she was worn too finely now, her senses were so smoothly turned they seeped through locks ahead of picking them and sacked the world. How he frightened Madame Betz with his bellowing, poor trampled lady. Well, no harm to the astral body. Still all those pieces of brain about. Perhaps she should visit to say goodby, that would be friendly, but there would be that thick wintergreen odor of death she couldn't abide, it made her sneeze, and the spectral skulls jabbering and glowing, and she would almost certainly fall in the glass, as she did the last time, though the last time on the sea beach it was pleasant, like a postcard land with no wind blowing, the clouds pinned and the long white scratch on her globe showing against the sky absurdly like a long jag of thunderless lightning.

The nerves in her shoulders twitched and her eyes ached. Dangerous to shut them. She would fall back in the darkness behind the lids, soon somersaulting, and who knew how far the acrobat would take her down. When you were clairvoyant, as she was, you had to guard your entrances, but if you did not leave them open, if you fearfully closed them all, then you'd be alone in there . . . alone. It was a wet cold castle. Better to pass into any other thing, the most outlandish lampshade, and let hot bulbs beat against you, or flatten yourself in military garments, stiff as metal, or otherwise dangle in a drape or a string, feckless and loose and gentle, or ooze through a wall like the damp in the spring. Sometimes they were surprisingly sweet modes of being. In Madame's bowl upon a painted sea a pond of ducks, one tipping under, another tipping up, across the bill of the upward one a smile as silver as a fish for knowing what the mud at the bottom of the lake was like. Bite. That pain in her shoulder again. She wondered, suddenly, how a pipe felt, bent.

Sometimes her knee would begin to burn and she would think back desperately: a knee, that would be early, I was six, no, four, not the time in the gravel, it hasn't got that grated quality, I could feel the stones in the form of a square; not the ice either, the sting had a special pulse, I'd know it anywhere. It was the shape of a lake on a map, with little flurried lines around the shore. There were weeds, the bank at her back, mud on her hands. She felt the breeze against her leg, her skirt thrown up, and the sky seemed terribly far off at the end of converging trees. There were burrs in her hair. She hadn't braids then, and her scalp pulled fiendishly. I've dirtied my dress but no one will punish me, no one will care. She lay against the bank, her knee throbbing comfortably, and watched the clouds.

The past came back that way, over a bridge of pain, and she

wept for her childhood when she lived it again as she wept for all immortal things. Condemned, eternally, to be. Her eyes were full of tears and she felt herself trying to move. She wanted to roll to the water and drown. This time I know what to do, she thought. But the oat stem remained against her cheek and she heard her answer to her mother's calls and found that her voice and her answer were sweet.

At first there were only a few, the shoulder especially, but later they came in crowds, the whole lot finally, and she tracked them down, the burns and sprains and cuts and broken bones, her fingers following lines on her skin and jubilantly jabbing at scars: there—there—there it is. October 9th, 1935, I was scrubbing, and a splinter from that wideboard floor—there was fir everywhere like a forest in that April Street house—ràn under the nail of my left forefinger, piercing the skin; there's the nick of it yet, right up to the cuticle where the thing sank in—and then that doctor with the fraternity pin I went to, he drowned in the war, the fylfots got him, bless their hearts, and he was added to the sea—well, his hands were white and wrinkled as though they'd been underwater a long time already, he should have worn gloves, they would have prevented the skin from sliding off his bones, but he was so personal and there was a gap in his mouth where his death was—no, there's no pleasure in knowing—and he took my shudders for spasms of pain, saying there, there, in a filthy whisper, prodding with the dirty end of it . . . pleasure in the past? no, not for me, there's no sweetness in it, not for me, just the glistening black well in the cup, turning about the spoon, steam leaping the edge . . . the aches, the bruises, and the blows, the lacerations, pinches, pimples, sores, and my hot dung water, before I was trained, which seared my bottom raw, and I remember, in my bed, how I would whimper when I finally peed and the urine seeped around through the flannel and burned the flesh, and how sometimes Mother would come to hush me—there, there, she always said—bumping about in the room as though it weren't brightly lit, and having shampooed her hair so it hung like a fall of water from her head . . . the punctures, scrapes, smarts, scratches, tears, every sort of choking, fit of sneezing, coughing and spitting up of clots of air: they come together sometimes, strike me everywhere so I curl like burning paper, perhaps right in front of Edgar, who thought the first time—thank god, she's got epilepsy, that explains everything—but who now thinks I throw tantrums to shame him, and blood fills his face, his nose in erection, while he blocks his eyes with his palms or runs shouting to another room, except once when yelling he took me up fiercely in his arms, shouting what what what as loudly down my ear as an engine, and I managed to say, please look out I don't burn you, words which stung him like a lash—I can still see the weal on humid days—so that he jerked away, letting me go, and I fell softly like an armload of smoldering rags.

In Madame's bowl. The land lay like a magic lake. Pleasure? Those ladies came from the sugar crock, discussing my death. Mrs. Maggies, a nice old lady, is one of my Fates. That's all that's sweet, the future sometimes, but no, you only take on another role. Corpses, she knew, were eloquent, she'd hear them speak, they were never quiet, they ran on and on, even with the casket closed she could hear their steady murmuring. They ran on and on until their voices mingled with the wash and groan of burial dirt. Poor Edgar would come home angry today—drawers stuck, pencils broken, carbons smudged, and papers torn, no money made—to find her at the cards again. They're worse than alcohol, he'll bellow, sweeping them to the floor, where the eight of swords will fall face up on her foot. Why don't you drink, eh? then I'd know what to do; have a little pity, why not? do something ordinary—drink, gossip, screw—something human, goddamn it—steal, lie, nag—something ordinary—get fat, live dirty!

It would be a worn-out plea. And the speech of February 3rd was due again. They all come round like comets, soon or late. He'll have one of his terrible throwing rages, the kind Ella will find pieces of in all her bins and storage boxes later. When was the last time she'd been through this particular storm? It began before he got his coat off. He threw his hat first. It skims the table, scattering cards—the eight of swords. She listened to the slicker of their sailing. Yes, September 10th in '50 was the last time. Ella rubbed her shoulder where he'd shaken her. Everything leaves a wake. It's mostly refuse, what we've got, she thought, looking about. But it was ominous—that eight.

How was her husband to know? How was Ella? No one can be clairvoyant about clairvoyancy. For a long time as a child she'd thought that everyone could see at night, in darkness, as well and easily as she could. She'd thought that when her mother laughed, everyone saw the needles, or the dark licorice stain that spread over her chest, sometimes, when she talked. But these were isolated perceptions. It was only later, in her teens, that the world changed utterly. Slowly her senses had grown more acute, her discriminations finer. Then there was the first time—she'd been fifteen—when she'd come on a piece of astral essence lying in a neighbor's driveway. Lord—it had reeked! But how was she to know what it was, though she kept it, that smelly splinter of soul, six years in a shoebox before letting it go? Or throwing it away—most guiltily—that would be more accurate.

Philip Gelvin had come to see her father, his slick hair shiny as the shoes he sold. Her father's ears began to smoke at once, and soon a thick pall of anger lay through the house as if grease had caught fire in the kitchen. Finally Philip lifted his hand in front of her father's face, slowly forming a fist, and then he stood there—silent, declamatory, and statuesque. The next day Ella could see the dent Phil's balled-up fist had made. It was there now, so that when Edgar took her home for a visit she saw it, a little knuckled pocket of space suspended in the middle of the parlor as though it had been hung there by a spider, and she couldn't help wincing when people passed through it, for she'd learned that each time they did a portion of that fierce symbolic blow was struck again. Ella, herself, could show a matching knuckly bruise beneath her chin.

It was the same here—in their present house. They were all over the place, those people. The passions of the previous owners, not to mention Edgar's, Muffin's, hers, messed up the even drifts of atmosphere like sloppy tracks through new snow. There was, for instance, a penis in the bathroom that certainly didn't belong to her husband, and one day, driven by desires which, for a change, surprised her, she carefully closed her fingers on it. It was still warm, like a skillet handle, and the air it shaped was velvety. Well, it was true, there's nothing softer than a foreskin.

Keep off that rib, you hairy bastard, I want no further Muffer-trees, Ella shouted crossly, twisting in her chair, and the words were snapped up in the bills of black-eyed gulls who were soaring in Madame's treasure glass and laughing with their feet. It was Muffertrees again, all right; she'd caught the dirty spirit this time in its soldier clothing, walking in Berlin as of a year ago. You'll hear from him soon, Madame Betz had said, tugging her sash about her as she spoke, swollen as a red balloon; and Ella remembered it was in that moment, nearly one third in, that she became afraid of falling, of seeping through the porous rubber of that red balloon and being borne in great lofts to the arch and roll-off of the earth, where she'd be spat out in the air when it burst like the seed of a peach. Peach blossoms: how well you decorate your bones. Muffertrees! Muffertrees wore at his white belt-edge a gun in case suspended. A white helmet was a comfort to his head, and white spats were clasped to his friendly shoes. His lips were chapped from too much red wine stolen in Paris and from too much kissing of brothers. He carefully peeled the dead skin off with his front teeth and scraped it down to the end of his tongue, where he whistled it away, for he was always a tidy body and wanted a respectable entrance. How much bitten skin does a man collect in his life? Let's see. Suppose the lips were chapped one day in five, an estimate conservative enough, and on that day five flakes were commonly taken in, their normal size a thirty-second of an inch, paced off roughly; that would be approximately eleven and four-tenths square inches of skin annually. If an average life dragged on for sixty years, discounting babyhood, since the practice isn't customary at that age, the amount would come to six hundred and eighty-four square inches, or four and seven-tenths square feet, enough to carpet the average entryway. Of course that didn't count all the other kinds of skin that might have been bitten off from god knows where. Then fingernails were a covering too. The difficulty there lay in estimating the rate of chew and the amount of skin or nail swallowed on average, as opposed to the amount blown, shaken, or spat away.

Damn clattering gears and cams, dinning calculations in her ears for hours sometimes; it was worse than a buzz or a ring, and she'd felt like telling her neighbor so; that little humming her neighbor had from a defective tube was nothing compared to Ella's columns, runs, and totalizing dings. That part of the brain was a pet, but pets were a bloody nuisance; you could cut it out, who would care, though Madame Betz had said they weren't all as noisy as hers was, or as given to inventively useless computations.

Space wasn't space to Ella, it was signals. Everything was emitting: a flower its scent, a bat its ping, a file its roughness, a lemon its acidity, a girl her gorgeousness, a summer street its summer heat, each muscle its move; space has more waves than the ocean: X rays, radio and television transmissions, walkie-talkie talk, car phone messages, ultraviolets, microwaves, cosmics of all kinds, kids communicating on oatmeal phones, radiations from high-tension lines, signal boxes, transistors and transformers, gazillion pieces of electronic gear leaking information, earth tremors, jet planes, other wakes and winds; but beyond and in addition to that, the scent says sugar, the ping cries victim, the rough rasps a warning, sourness stimulates salivation, that gorgeousness deserves engorgement, or at least interest, the heat is its own threat, and movement speaks for will; meanwhile the odor that meant sugar to the bee now lays along its side a smear of pollen, every victim the bat eats means fewer insects will bite that much admired thigh; moreover it is written that one avoids one scrape only to get into another, that the lemon draws the salad through a chewing mouth into a stomach where vitamins are released like news reports and ad campaigns, the pleasured penis, presuming such a consumation, can produce an unexpected pregnancy—perhaps an unequal balance of cause with effect in that case—hot feet seek shade where struggling grass gets trodden, and the frustrated will works wearily toward one more postponed end; so that scent, surface, acidity, sound, sight, sex, the warmth of the world, the will of men, are but a sidewalk fiddler's paltry pluck among the messages, an itty-bitty fête amid such confetti; for every pit in a piece of pitted metal screams, and plants ease their juices through themselves to music, and the down of birds whispers in another register what the bird's heart holds.

Ella Bend could be called clairvoyant simply because she possessed an abnormal number of sensitive receivers. She was almost totally attention and antennae.

I'll die gladly, a girl who called herself Penny had said from the cream the other morning, when there isn't a place on me that hasn't the scar of a man's mouth. The cream had splashed over Edgar's cereal, releasing her husky voice, while the cornflakes crackled and blazed. Then Edgar's spoon began to puddle about and in a moment Edgar was chewing his wheaty cud. Ella wondered what had happened to Penny when her voice had broken in the bowl; perhaps her lover bit her then upon her . . . final skin. Where would the last spot be? That was a puzzle. Like the dipping of Achilles. Love's ultima Thule. Well, it would be none of the filthy creases, nature'd see to that. They'd be bitten first, faster than any apple. It would be a place you'd never think of, inspiring the least amorous swallow, some section of the broad expanse of back most likely, a dull plain where a portion could be easily missed, though underneath the chin was difficult to reach, just as it was no easy trick to gnaw through that hairy lather on the head. Ella had yet to receive one; she was a tabula rasa in this sense, and on this basis would live forever. First grade: a little dark knobble-crested boy, a stranger, shouting—Christians eat feet—over and over. She had wanted to say, You are wrong, they wash them. It had been a riddle to her then, but now it was clear. What was the last bite but the love bite of the spear? That blow had starred Him over all the bluegreen polar ice for near a year. Muffermuffermuffermuffertrees! Come back to be apprentice to the Doge. Well, she was always receiving loose reports like that, pieces of astral essence maybe, torn off by some disaster, like the fellow in the garden from Memphis whose tears she had heard streaking his cheeks. How short our life is, like the dew, the Japanese who love the cuckoo say. Madame had been wrong too, they'd never heard from Muffertrees' Berlin manifestation, not even when he'd taken up with that New York girl to anger her, and let Ella see how the girl's belly hair climbed swirling toward her bosom like a vine. Unless that was the message she meant.

So: Madame Betz. The sharp part in your hair will part your head. The wheel of a chair-car going sixty. Those trains try to run on schedule, are you sure of the time? And Edgar driving nearly through your trailer my last visit, the headlights roving crazily across the field and coming to rest in a ditch, blaring at the tired water, deafening mosquitos . . . I thought he might have got you then. Now Edgar looks at me and says: Are you planning to run out to Stocking? I'm sorry but I don't like men in tears, laughing or crying. All right, all right, I see you too, so bravely uniformed and purely mittened—little Muffertrees. It's hard to have a son what's born an evil spirit. He was a wraith already in my belly. Was that decent? In lengths of slippery purple rope, the doctors pulled him out. Nevertheless I wanted to take him home. Some babies begin by being dead, I said, but they come alive later. Well, how was I treated?

The coffee first darkened then swallowed the sugar as she poured. Her neighbor wasn't listening, pottering about over there, wasting her gifts. Madame Betz had her own worries and Muffertrees was up to something. When there isn't anyone to listen, Ella said, I'm in despair. Her fingernail followed the weave in a chair, a flower's stem. They should have allowed me to bring him home. Oh, I admit it wasn't a nice manifestation. It was one of his meanest. He was most unpleasant. But they should have allowed me to bring him home in a shoebox most likely, or a jar, at least for a while. I'm lonely with no one to talk to, not that Muffin was ever much company. It's no good just to be able to see, to receive. The sorrows of the radio. I'd rather be blind—god—what a relief—if the world had an ear—if it wasn't all eye really—all eye. What good does it do, just to see? Her own face stared up at her out of her cup. The coffee was black but thickly sweet. She needed her neighbor. True—her neighbor was developing. Soon she'd be quite clairvoyant, poor thing. But today she had her shades drawn and Ella couldn't get in. Look at these eyes at the tips of my fingers. I can see in pockets or under suds in the sink. My nipples could peer in the mouth of a lover and check his teeth. And my tongue, too, will light. Light lightly, like a fly. Oh, never mind. What's the use? They just bring me sorrow. Ella sniffed and sighed. Well, not quite. She could smell the sugar in the steam. Sweet was still sweet.

She'd gone first to a man who called himself Professor Logos, and seemed cheap. He didn't use a globe, he used a dictionary. What do you say to this, he said, as soon as she'd settled herself. *Vagary's* just barely ahead of *vagina* in here—he was tapping the cover—and *womb* is the word after *woman*. This, he said, lifting *Webster's New Collegiate,* is the book of the world, the one true honest holy book; it's all in here, the order of everything. Do you know what the world is, Mrs. Hess? It's *word* with an *l* in it! Now I know that doesn't sound possible, does it? Yet *low* follows loving. What do you think? And what lies so snugly between *truism* and *truly? Trull!* That's right—truth is a strumpet. What do you think? Yes, Mrs. Hess, *word* with an *l* in it. The universe, the cosmos, is simply stuck with laws all over like a billing post, and none of them makes any sense. *W* or *D*—that's the key. Why, tell me, why, when you've put two counters together on a square, are you safe in pachisi? That's just the way Parcheesi's played, right? But *peek* and *peel*, Mrs. Hess. *Evidential, evil, evil eye, evince.* So I take them hit or miss as they come, naked in their connections. *Womb* and *tomb*. What do you think? I begin with a word. I go up or down. And I construe. *Celiac, celibacy, celibate, cell.* There's a wonder in *Webster* for every wonder in the world . . . and then some. *Web* is in *Webster*, by the way. *Web* and *west*. See? *Sedulous, sedum, see,* and *seed.* Stick with me. Mrs. Hess, now, what follows you? *Hessian:* a coarse sacking of hemp or jute. Next: a two-winged fly or midge. *Hest:* a command or precept. So. A pledge. *Hester*—adultress. But goddess of the hearth—*Hestia.* What do these words tell me? What am I learning? *Hesychast:* one of a sect of mystics. Ah. *Hetaera.* Usually slaves. I lay them out as some do cards. And before *card* comes cancer—*carcinoma*. What do you think? *Ash bash cash dash gash hash lash mash nash* (OK, but the man, the car) *rash sash wash.* Convinced. Listen to what happens to the sound of *wash.* Now we're at *bosh cosh gosh nosh posh* . . . Stop. Mark this, mark this, Professor Logos said with his typical enthusiasm, notice this conjunction: *wive, wivern,* and *wizard.* Of course, there's *wive swive* too. Listen, Mrs. Hess, don't kid me, are you one of the competition? Then *wizened,* he went on, fastening her with a sharp smile. Your real name is Gelvin, Ella said. I know you. I was Ella Bend. You sell shoes and use grease on your head and like to feel feet. I know you. You're my Phil and you made a fist at my father.

Madame Betz was more proficient, there was no doubt about it. She used a crystal, but her weakness was conjuring, and as soon as Ella had stepped in the trailer, Madame Betz began the conjuration of Thursday. It went on and on: Cados, Cados, Cados, Eschereic, Eschereie, Eschereie, Hatim, Ya—name after name—Cantine, Jaym, Janic, Auie, Calbot, Sabbad, Berisay, Alnaym—until angels, stars, and planets had been invoked and Adonay Himself was called upon—Na Nim Nim Na—to bring Schiel, a great angel who was the chief ruler of Thursday, bound in a coil of greenish smoke, forcefully into her globe. The spell proved to be powerful, but Ella didn't think she could remember it all, and when she told Madame Betz that what she really wanted was to be rid of her gifts, Madame Betz was frightened and sent her away. Ella persisted, nevertheless. She came back again and again. Isn't there someone you could find who would like them—someone I could give them to, Ella begged. A Clara? My neighbor's name. No, no—no one—of course not, Madame Betz had said, your gifts aren't organs you can get dead and donate. I give them to no one—go away fast as blink.

Often Madame Betz would try to hide. Why do that, Ella told her, I always know where you are, and besides it's undignified. Then Ella suggested a charm against clairvoyancy, some spell that might work at least for a while, and be renewed when it weakened, like a treatment for cancer, but Madame Betz refused this kind of help entirely. Ninny, she said, there's no outside cure for what's inside. And this was the last wisdom which Ella could extract from her, for as Ella grew worse it became apparent, since she was so much Madame Betz's superior in every psychic thing, that if Ella were unable to assist herself, certainly poor Madame Betz, with her short refracted sight and scratched bowl and smallish magics, could do nothing for her. So she was paying Madame Betz a polite last friendly visit when Ella's husband caught up with them. He was shouting, naturally, as he always did, and there isn't much room in a trailer. Ella then slipped through the crystal. Madame Betz screamed. And Edgar began breaking her furniture.

The dark steam was beautiful, the silver spoon too, and the warm palm of the porcelain. Why don't you just pour your coffee in the sugar bowl, her husband used to ask her. Oh, a drink that sweet, she'd say, will relieve me of my teeth. Watching her dissolve still more sugar in her cup, he would groan and hide his distraught hands before his face. Madame Betz loved sweetening too. We've got to have something, haven't we lovey, she would say, stirring her cocoa pensively.

Home soon. To Ella Bend. *Bend* is *end* with a blossom on it. She slid the cards from beneath the cushion. A sip or two. After they were married and driving away, her husband said: Now you're Ella Hess, nee Bend—roaring with pleasure and rubbing the curb. You pronounce *nee* nay, she should have said, and she was still sorry. A sip or two. Do I carry the cup to the table or not? Not. It's to be broken another time. In their hotel room he'd slapped her bottom—nee Bend, he said. Nay, which means no, she should have said. She was still sorry. A vulgar whistling went through, and she thought: I've simply got to persuade him to move. Move? She shuffled expertly. I should shoo back Mrs. Maggies, she's got no business here—not yet—and with evening coming in, the damp, the chill, the wind. He's being held up by lights and traffic. A fine mood he'll be in—accelerator angry. Ella stuffed a hankie in her sleeve and sat down to the kitchen table, flicking the cards. There was no point in laying them out, of course; she knew what they'd say. At the seventh card, if she played slowly, he'd barge in. There was the king of money to start with—a very fair or very gray-haired man—yes— a protector, but easily vexed. Sorry old soul. Someday there'd be an end and he'd be dead and she'd be dead and past this kind of feeling. Perhaps they could be friends then. And the queen of swords—a very dark woman—oh that fits nicely—a false and intriguing woman—well let it be, let be—or the queen might mean a widow. What is *sword* but *word* with s on its head. The next should be the three of money—there it is, as advertised— and that's domestic trouble, quarrels, litigation. The table was glaring. Ella blinked. The cards clicked. Again a sword, the five, for bad temper. The cards are garrulous; that didn't need saying. Then still another sword—so many—worrisome, such a concentration—the three—I hadn't remembered—it's for a journey—a journey?—or for tears. It is that September fuss-up, I'm just certain. I don't weep in that one anywhere, though I get a beating. Curious. It's true my eyes are welling, things are bleary. Not a bit like me. There's no time left for this. Ella blotted with her hankie. Not now. Not now. Edgar's in the drive and I've another card to turn.

I Wish You Wouldn't

Mr. Hess said, his hat turning slowly between his knees. His wife lay sick in a chair, quite silent. Mr. Hess was leaning forward, his weight on his forearms, hat hanging from the pads of his fingers, carpet across his eyes. Um, he thought. Aah. His wife tipped back in the lounger, rigid as always, her risen feet in a V. Mr. Hess, however, sagged in contrast, his whole weight pressing against his thighs above his knees, brown hat dangling between his trousers. His missus stretched out staring at the ceiling in order not to see, and he couldn't endure that either. The canary, or whatever the hell it was, rattled its beak and then shrieked . . . shrieked and rattled its beak. Hess moved his shoes to stand inside the florals. The venetian blinds were scratched, though you couldn't see the scratches in the shade they threw. Their shadows simply said how crookedly the slats hung. What to do? although the question required no answer, hurrying after itself with furthermore of itself like a second hand. He had sucked the center from that old cliché: *and time lay heavy on his hands.* Dusk sank through the light to snow his shoes—the air so thick, the fall so fast—while whatever it was—canary bird, cuckoo—rapped its beak along the bars till Hess remembered boyhood pleasures too . . . with a pang like the smart of a stick. What? what? what to do? Thin tan lines flew parallels inside his suit no matter how he moved, but his wife could barely stretch herself about her bones. Mr. Hess was afraid she had cancer—something, at any rate, lingering and serious. Her skin was a poor color and she was wasted as an ad for famines. Maybe her mind had been affected by the illness, too; that would explain the peculiarities of her behavior. Change of life, he'd heard, often did them funny. He felt that he should get her to a doctor. A doctor—he pendulumed his hat—a doctor, yes, that was his duty. The doctor would report upon her. Smiling gently, rimless-eyed, he'd write her up as dying. Then he'd instruct Mr. Hess in the society of symptoms which his wife's disease had founded. They always turn queer in a case like this, the doctor would say; oh they go strange, sometimes very early. We suspect, the doctor would say—my science does, you understand—that there's a kind of signal to the future in it.

Poor things, he'd say, they're done for from the first: an abnormal placenta, don't you see, pressure from a pelvis that's too small, or some slight chemical disturbance, sudden stress, internal turbulence or organ tumble, a quiet slow infection, and it's all over: sizz-z-z-z until the air's out; so don't heavy your head any further with it, Mr. Hess, don't dent your hair, not even by a hat's weight, none of it's your doing, she was born at half eleven in her life . . . chew this bit of candy here to sweeten up your teeth, possess yourself in patience . . . death should follow shortly now, though her soul can only seep away, not fly, it has so little stamina. You've no young children, I suppose, Hess, have you? and I trust you're well insured. Ha ha, Mr. Hess thought. Ha ha. And he solemnly prayed for his wife's demise. Too weary for hate or even malice, he certainly didn't feel ashamed; foreign, rather, to remorse or any sorrow. She was sick enough to be lots better dead. That was a fact, god's truth. Hess wished her speedy passage o'er the great divide as he wished, weekends, for green golfing weather. It was reflexive, a wish as mild and futile as it was heartfelt and desperate, because he'd given up golf, as he'd given up bowling. Having gotten her laid to rest, he'd want the shoveling ceremony, please, run through just once again. The disappearance of her bier beneath the earth was a constant longing like the thirsty for another dram. His hat dropped softly to the carpet, quashing an edge. He slid his right arm forward to recover it. Only a doctor, only a definite "soon she must die," could give him hope, for his own heaviness was overcoming him. Every day he hung a little lower on himself. It grew more difficult to rise in the morning, lift himself from chairs or slide from the seats of cars, even stir at all, accomplish stairs or carry any trifling action to completion, and the blood which fell out of his heart was siphoned back painfully. But she would never submit herself to any sort of physical examination. It was inconceivable. She knew she had a body of extraordinary kind, and that strange gray oblong organs would be discovered swimming like sea animals in the plate of the X ray. No . . . he had to be satisfied, since it was always possible that the doctor might frighten her off from the brink of her death with a knife or a needle, whereas her present ill health, so hopefully plain, though he only conjectured it, advanced with a steadiness no one as deeply concerned as he could fail to appreciate. He would accept the uncertainty. Mr. Hess knew no more of the spirit than his hat did—that is, not directly; and if his flesh seemed to be sliding slowly from him like thick batter or heavy syrup, it did not make his bones more saintly. Nevertheless it was that realm, mysterious in its work as magnets, and moving always out of sight and underground like rivers of electricity, which was the source of his dismay and the cause of his anguish. He did feel that with ingenious instruments it probably could be seen, in some way metered or its passage mapped, for this invisible world in which his wife lived made her weary; the stream she swam in was perhaps impalpable, but it left her damp; indeed, there were times when Mr. Hess sensed, somehow, the current flowing, and knew that sallow as her skin looked, lifeless as she seemed flung down on a couch or discarded in a chair like emptied clothing, she was lit up inside and burning brightly like a lamp. Even so, the only lamp he knew which fit his image of her was the sort which smoked above a poker table; surely she had no sky inside herself to fall from, no ceiling fixture, ceiling chain, or wire burning like a worm. She had her distances, all right, but within was their one direction, and Mr. Hess could not help but wonder once again exactly why he was sitting where he was; how it had happened to him, so bodily a being, even if he were a bit baggy and had all those habits she disapproved of in her subtle aerial way, never saying a word, just exuding an odor like ripe cheese when he appeared, causing the temperature and light to alter, holding up time so that it seemed he'd been picking his nose forever, or simply sending a sigh through the house like a breeze; how had it happened he should be so fastened to this—this twig, he sometimes thought in those moments when the past seemed as though it had held a promise and he'd once been a blossom, then a fruit, full of juice and flavor; how had it happened to him? prisoners must say that, over and over, he thought, handcuffed, chained; shit, Christ even thought it, as he was hanging there, nailed; but Mr. Hess had no head for searches, he could scarcely find his slippers, answers were out of the question, as his wife said sometimes, no, only these same wonderments circled through him, wooden in their wheeling as a roundabout. I've got to slow down, Mr. Hess thought. He ran along paths in the carpet, in the tan, around the turns of leaves and flowers. She hasn't enough blood in the narrow channels of her flesh to pink a tear, while mine is like sand in a sand clock, almost wholly in my head—thick, moist, flushed, hot—or in my feet—heavy, old, cold, quiet—awaiting the tipsy-turvy to trickle out, thus I alternate a lot, don't I? she's not the only one whose spirit's like electric current, but alas I've none of the instant capacity of wires. Hang in there somehow, Hess. Hang in. But she was having her weirds now, the stiffish kind, and he wished she wouldn't. He could hit her again, of course. He could always do that. Instead he groaned and tried to spin his hat upon his finger. She was ill. She was dying. So he hoped. But she didn't have to tell fortunes. She didn't have to sit in the kitchen with the cards spread out, absorbed by the tale they were telling, bad news for Edgar when he came home. She didn't have to leave the house to squat on the front step, in the drive, where he would find her making noises like a key-wound engine. Nor did she have to disgrace his needs, throwing up her skirt quite suddenly to leave him thunderstruck. I'll be needing lawyers if I'm not careful. Not so heavy with the fall of the fists, Hess, hey? he cautioned himself. Not so quick with the kick. When the jury learns what you've been through, Mr. Hess, don't worry, they will give you sympathy; they'll put her beaten body behind bars; they'll hiss when she is carried through the court. You've heard of the victimless crime, Hess, haven't you? Well, there are crimeless victims, too. You're one of them—one of those. What's a paltry kick compared to the piteous smiles she's inflicted on you, the looks thrown heavenward with such aboriginal skill, and cunning with curves, they stone down later in your living room the whole naked length of a sofa-soft Sunday afternoon, passing through the shield of the Sunday paper, bruising your eyes; or the little whimpering moues which cower in the corner of her mouth, how about those? the glances which scuttle away like bugs to the baseboard to wait the night, all the tiny gnawing things she keeps about her: frightened knees and elbows, two flabs of breast with timorous nips, disjointed nose, latched eyes? There are laws against that, Mr. Hess, unwritten laws, the laws of common decency, laws of the spirit and the soul, what she knew best, Hess, didn't she? sure, her silences, for instance, are against the law, silence is against the law, silences are blows, and you can plead self-defense, you can plead extenuation, you can argue quite agreeably that you were driven to extremes, out of reason as out of town, by all those occasions when she struck you with inwardness—oh—withholding is wicked, refusing to respond, that's malice, Hess, you have every excuse, don't worry your warts, and when the jury hears how you have borne yourself these long weary dreadful, ladensomely heavy years, they'll set you free to cheers and to the sound of bells, though it'll help your case if you don't have young children, Mr. Hess, you haven't have you? that's best. Ha ha, Mr. Hess thought. Ha ha. Please to observe, Mr. Hess, now, that she isn't dead. She's having one of her little nervous spells, a little dab of the dizzies, so she's resting, that's all, she's merely unmoving, stiff and staring, eyes wide as a picture window, watching god knows what going on on the screen of the ceiling, some soap opera of the soul, a few new developments in the Grand Design, I shouldn't wonder—ha, Mr. Hess, hey? ha—no, it's just another quietly ordinary sagamuffin Sunday in the Hess household, and you're no stranger to it, sweat it out the same as always, lean on your knees till your thighs dent, you know how it goes, you know the routine—oh my goodness, what's to be done, Hess, what's to be done? His urine fell out of him as out of a nozzleless hose, while she was forever listening . . . listening . . . in constantly alert and continuously expectant receivership, so to speak, like a line of ears for early warning. Pamphila. Faugh. What's done is done; then done, it's done, and then it's done. So why wait any longer? when every act is over and we're filing out. Anyway . . . my wife, to picture paths and patterns in resting rocks, deep tides of feeling, vast programs of action . . . well, she became positively seismographic, and registered dirt in huge mud-bound hunks roundly wibble-slob-wobbling like a dancer's tum. Wait? Thin ass on a fat chance. Run? She said she heard his grass and claimed it was up to no good and had ungracious plans. What could he do but close his hands? She'd pick up stray transmissions even in the splash of his pee, the hum of motors, the surreptitious click of switches. Everything which entered the house, whether from above or below ground, entered her . . . entered without knocking: the wind, of course, and the rustle of leaves, sunfall as noisy as Niagara, day-mist and light spatter, they were welcome as holy water because she sensed the presence of the Sacred Word in bird whistle, rain plop—noises natural and noises not—squirrel chatter, pipe rattle, buzz, bloom, shadow; she parsed them all as easily as he read Dick and Jane—St. Francis couldn't hold a sparrow to her—and she had for each of this world's blurts a warm greeting, not for him, though, just for the holing of moles and earth-eating worms, just for the paths, traps, and caches of beetles and spiders, for ants, wasps, cicadas—veterans as jovial in their cozy halls of relaxation as members of the American Legion. She'd have an immediate sympathy for the growth of roots, too, Hess was prepared to bet, their efforts, the energy, life's task, how it was . . . like fingers struggling into gloves. Like the robin, she could hear the grub grub and the earthworm worm. It was a contradiction he couldn't countenance or fathom, because for all her foreknowledge, he still had to yoo-hoo when he came round a corner, and without that cheerful next-door warning, or the boop-boop-boop of a rubber horn he'd filched from the handlebars of a neighbor tike's bike—ha, oh lord, ha ha, ha ha—she'd startle like a sparkler, burn with indignation briefly, and darken on the wire. Otherwise she was stoical. She was patient. Rapt, she waited for erosion, rust, chip, flake, craze, settle, since slowness didn't faze her, accumulations of the gradual, the thick that gets there bit by bit the way fog sags in a hollow, little reiterations, all the overtold anecdotes of the actual, same upon same, she said, were satisfying, though her face did not betray her pleasure, if, in fact, she felt some, giving away only what a dial would, so he sometimes knew where his wife was tuned without any sense of the source or substance of the signal, and because she was a stranger to class and its consequent snobbery, she listened equally to gravel scatter or the incontinent wetting of basement walls. The further within she went, the more numerous the noises, an orchestra hot for its A couldn't compete for cacophony, and they delivered her news as diverse as the dailies. To tap drip, naturally, she bowed like a rod; to knuckle pop and cloth scrape, she was a wand . . . how do you stand it, Hess often said, with so much going on, if it's as you say, and there are vibrations in ethers as yet unimagined, sounds exceeding sound even in the customary shoe squeak and silk slither, or from drapes, morose and heavy, hanging in a skin of dust, there comes the prolonged metal shudder of a gong? Of course, it's only me who has the wonder, and who am I?—so dull, so down; but I think it's remarkable that you should be responsive to the low moan of cushions; if you ask me, it's even suspicious how warmly you are washed by every slow hydraulic sigh released by grease racks, barber chairs, and doorstops; strange that you are passionately moved—imagine—by the yearn of warping boards, the tireless cries of wood rot, thin as thread and exquisitely tangled, but perhaps it's that sadistic element in you which appreciates broken slats and tacks like teeth, screws, nails, staples with their twin penetration like the drilled wounds of eyes, the elongating pains of picture wire, the screams of burning bulbs, and although in your overburdened state it may be kind of you to regret the steady dampening of salt on humid days, still, one need not be a queen and have a palace to enjoy the sweet granular silence of sugar in its crock. Voices: they were everywhere around her like gnats. In snowfall, frost. He had his hat. To rise? to doff one final time? good day, Madame—goodby—surprise— . . . to leave? He could do that. Run under it out of the rain. How many of his dreams had flight and freedom in them? Ham and eggs. Pie and cheese. Muff and sniff. She'd hear the Southern slurs of melting custard and be . . . entranced. He had his hat. He could do that. But noises he made deliberately to set her off, stomps around the room or weights he placed on the floor to make it groan, soda he shook and swallowed, screws he gave an extra turn to, fists he left printed in the air, the pounding he gave the coverlet, or conversely the squeaks he silenced with sewing machine oil, the har har hars he swaddled in socks, the lids he glued or the many things he simply removed in the trunk of their car to cast on the dump or drop in a lake or bury: none of these acts move her because, she said, under torture matter could be made to say anything. Mud, mold, matter—what one called it didn't count—but it had neither courage, nor loyalty, nor conscience. In her husband's police state matter would moisten its tongue for its own ass, and she didn't believe that was right, she refused absolutely to consider it, matter alone meant nothing, a calf of slime, she said, not an object of experience, of piety or speech; it was a convenient carrier at best, a carton for cats, and so she thought of it the way typhoid must have thought of Mary, no more, not even as a necessary ambience or elevation or so much as a stand for music, pediment for a statue or tower with an aerial, though that was closer, and what was he, then, in his dense maleness, a series of surfaces like a stack of plates, what was he with his bowling and his beer and his business—charging the living for their life and paying off only when death was a winner— what was he with his busy pencil and greedy teeth, in the flesh of his flesh, but the purest muck, individuation driven to the point of indifference, asafetida not energy, sheer dumb disagreeable stuff, unworked, unrealized, raw, foolish in its lean and teeter, its oils, wows, and ouches, as an Evereadied dolly, yet with a prick which led him on his little trot through life like a leash held at the loop end in the Pope's fist? Butterflies leave laces in the air like a courtier's cuffs, she said. Faugh. Easy to say such, harder to prove so. Still, in order not to shit, she would refuse to eat—intolerable the sounds of devoured food: unfeathered, fried, carved, bitten, chewed—therefore why was his pissing so productive? How about a belch, he'd ask her, much message in that? How about a fart? What can you read in a sneeze or the ooze of sweat, that color of water on the toilet pipe—ha—what do you say?—what about the petulant whine and then the frightened whinny of laboring machines? leap of

light from a mirror? unkinking cock? but she would smile her
sad peacemaker's smile at his coarseness, face him with a calm
forbearing palm, explain that only the plainest idea could be
contained in such a short intemperate sound as a sneeze, bereft
of feeling and every fineness, say how often there'd be but blunt
sense in the sharpest signal, because you never can tell about
such things, Edgar, you must know that by now, surely you do,
you do, surely, and though paint slides from a brush sometimes
in a way that's purely meditative, never mind, I have heard hush!
in the batter of hammers, the clatter of cans, and please in the
rasp of a file. I know every letter of the law, Hess said: L . . .
A . . . —and I know of the awe in it, was her reply. It helped her
to hit her, Hess knew that. Surely he knew that. Who had his
hat? She hadn't his hat. He had his hat. She wanted hitting
in the worst way, although her surrender to his will was like
another conquest of China. Still, what did it matter whether she
was out from a blow or lost in her dizzy mind's movies, since she
could easily have dreams during dinner, trances during a doze?
There was no place or moment she was willing to occupy the
way Hess took over his air and hours—fully, heavily, persis-
tently—so he was unable to feel there were any outlines to
her—no weights, no volumes, no shifts—she was never anywhere. His wife might undergo visions while steaming a crease
in his office trousers, plume out a chimney and disappear,
receive visitations washing dishes, her thin hands gloved in suds
as delicate as underclothes, or entertain omens and other astral
submissions as though they were coffees set out in kitchens, as
though one's daughter or less likely one's son had come home
from a party and wanted to talk and you had perhaps pie and a
bit of cheese to go along with the midnight signs and ciphers,
the symbols and the codes, while you listened numbly dumbly
to the life you'd passed by years ago like some display in a window turntabled once again—turntabled—ha—ha ha—and your

daughter or less likely your son awkwardly dancing to it as if it were a new tune and not a revival routinely fiddled by Old Bones and his Big Band. Ha, Mr. Hess thought. Ha ha. Articles in attics: so much for her visions. Voices spoke to him too, spoke to Hess, nicknouned the Hessian by his mates—ha—ha ha— they spoke to him from out of the past as hers did out of walls, because—it was true—what has gone before goes before like a hound, peeing a path, and damn if the old days didn't dump on her, she was no different for all her fancies, because Hess knew from his own bitter history, hers too, that when today caught up with yesterday they would call it tomorrow. Visions, she said. Voices. Faugh. He had cause: cause like cotton is the cause of wounds. Blah. He knew. He had grounds. But his eyes did not step from the carpet where they were confined by stems and leaves to little curlicues. There was no need to look. Even if the room changed around him, it would be the same to his shoulders. I have cause, good cause, for what I do. My god, I've grounds, grounds like this floor here, concrete covered with fur, and beneath that earth forever and the few pipes we shit through. Listen, Father, I have cause. I do what I have to, always with cause, good cause, and only when I have to, only with cause. I've *grounds*. That's why I wait/wait till I have to/to do what I have to . . . do. I wait while the years pile up and cause after cause comes like snow in a storm, so that now I may have too many, grounds too great like a park around a puddle, because they get suspicious if you have too many, they suspect that if you have too many, you haven't any, and oh god, Father, I have many—many, many—still .

.

.

. not too many, just enough, although they may ask what are these causes which never effect?

what is this mass which never moves? but I have many—many, many, many—and who can blame me if I run past complaint now as if it were a STOP I hadn't seen? Visions. Indeed. Faugh. Blah. Visions of what, though? Never of gods and goddesses, never any angels, scarcely a cupid, beauty bare, the naked truth, not a single streak of light like the sperm of a star to pierce some window to where she was sitting, not Fate or a Fury or a vampirish mouse with a flat furry face like Bela Lugosi . . . nobodies, every one, not a name among them—Tyrone Power— not an old demon even, out of work or with an odd hour off and able to visit. No. Faugh. Don't bet the farm on Mahatma Gandhi. Nooooh-bodies, boy. Nooooo. The walls stood up around him, tan as a turkey, and the ceiling smirched along overhead as though in a day it might rain. It must be tiring to stay that stiff, he thought, for she wasn't dead, that would be restful, the stiffness, the silence, of death. This was tense, this was a bellow, a huge howl which steadily grew and now con- tained the room which contained them. Father, she's all right. I mean, she's sick, and her soul is like a Cape Cod shingle, but she's all right. Never could detect a pulse. Chest as still as a stove top. Fire's out. Sick, then. Normal. She's all right. Voices, she said. Messages. All right, messages: blah, where were they? what did they come to? sniffles and yipes from *Little Orphan Annie,* whining about lost dogs, weeping because there were boys away in the war, anxieties about men: boorish insensitive husbands like himself, brutal brothers, inconstant companions, faithless friends, lying lovers—bitching, bemoaning—nothing about the sweet thunder of the pins or the excitement of a homer, the comforting closure of a jaw in a bun, not a leaf from the tree of knowledge, not even so much as a mutter from the moral law, not even a helpful household hint—so—so much for the spiritual telegraph, for ESP, because only diseases sent messages of any length and complexity—moment-by-moment readings, hourly bulletins, daily summaries, weekly releases— every sickness seemed to be somehow a triumph of the spirit, especially stopped-up sinuses, and migraines, like static on the radio, headaches so electric they haloed your hair, and it completely flummoxed Mr. Hess, who held his own head and groaned, even whimpered, while his missus felt giddy, had a spell of dizziness, or fell softly to the floor in a faint the way clothes slide sometimes from a hanger. Then there were discharges, menstrual moans, and the whites like a fog of sound. Mr. Hess hated to think about the others and couldn't—didn't dare—ask; nevertheless, what he gathered was that the ethereal world his wife loved was nothing but the loathsomely oozy body done into jiggles and jogs like the huff and puff of someone running. The books he consulted agreed in substance, though seldom in detail: it was a school of the dance, vibrations in vapors or ripples around rocks; it was streaks in cloth, they said; it was speeding clocks; it was clouds in chambers, ozone after lightning; it was wow, ow, ouch; it was apples on vacation from their cores. And the things in nature which proved most mute were therefore most sound, were in equipoise and balance like the billiard before its score, so equal and so uniform it was impossible to guess where a lean might come from or what tilt it might topple toward. Scrape, scratch, rasp: it was this inefficiency, this illness, this grumble in the works, which caused the uproar— indigestion, for instance, arthritis, epilepsy, ulcer—so that Hess felt sometimes that if the world would fall silent, she would be silenced. The hope led him to let his watch stop, although she said it kept on keeping time, and this was yet another reason why he double-washered taps, overoiled hinges, smothered the sharpener, and carried things out of the house tightly wrapped. He had long since ceased to smoke because Ella complained of the foggy swowl in every draw, the ploan like a stormhorn in every puff. Now he went to the garage to grind his teeth. If you're all so big about the spirit, Ella, he said, why are you all so physical, hey? why so gut and head sick, so eager to hear the earth? and why are you each so ugly: you're either flat-faced or fat, thin-haired or moppy, lime-lipped, gun-gray—the lot of you—with teeth likely to be spilled in one of your mouths like a damp pan of beans; you guys ain't elegant, you're not opulent, not delicate, not shy, no ma'am, rather wart-, wen-, and liver-spotted, vein-roped, yeah, albino-eyed you bet, allergic, snivel-nerved and pukey, with tits loose and shriveled as emptied balloons, man-oh-man, or melted and sloping, uddery, why? drunk on disapproval, are you? and is every pain a blessing like a Boy Scout's badge for merit? proud—I guess so—vain as if you were a Beauty, spoiled in the same way as a Jewish Princess, still I wonder how you came to be so fuckless if so female, hey? so juiceless, dry as oatmeal overboiled, oh even your stout ones like Madame Betz have dust bowls standing in their bellies, even in July when every skin is slithery with sweat because underneath the sweat the skin is dry, cunts closed and lying buried in their also sweaty secret hair like clams in silt, hey? and you have the gall to despise me for guzzling beer at the ballpark and playing with my toes. It was the only time Ella had ever raised her fist against him, and hadn't he fetched her a good one, but there's really no use talking to her, Father, to hammer some sense, because she won't listen to me. She hears muscles jumping in my jaw; she will hear a hair gray, milli-inch by milli-inch; she covers her ears when the belly rumbles; she listens to my face flush and moistens her brow with a cloth; frequently she sings along: she hears all this, each secret part and public parcel, but she won't pay mind to *me* or to any official broadcast. Father, Mr. Hess said seriously, I have cause to believe she's committed adultery with a drainpipe. Well she raised her fist that solitary time and said something overgrand and stucco like a thirties theater. It was really rather remarkable, come to consider it, how she seemed to gather the pieces together, various panels of her clothing, a collar, a pocket, a sleeve, each moving as separately as ants yet together like clasp and tie, too, all soft and hardbody at the same time, the way a scarecrow would grow if it grew, and her mouth opening, wider than when a muffin entered or a triangle of toast, and the muscles tensing along the length of her neck, the veins enlarged, quite blue, and the cry coming slowly out atop her tongue, in scraps, in flecks, the way she'd risen from the floor—AYEEEE—"shall" the only word which seemed to have a stop to it, curling up at the end like a pair of skies—beeeeeeeeeeeeeeeeeeeee—monsters in the movies wailed like that at the threat and showing of the Cross—freeeeeeeeeeeeeeeeeeeeeeeeeeeeeeee—ha—ha ha—I shall be free. Not of me, he'd answer, automatically; not of mee, he'd said, with a depth of seriousness no dipstick was notched sufficiently to measure; not of **meee,** he'd said, shouting, and he fetched her a second and a better one. What are you at cards for, if you can hear so much? horoscoping, number-nosing, syllable counting, peering the leaves, or skittering out to consult that bubble-reading Madame Betz, all gyp, by god, no gypsy, just to show off to the competition what a better witch you are? and didn't she call you a copy-cunt right in the pleasure of my hearing? and then didn't I have to rough her up? how well you get along, you mystical ladies, pretending to concerns so delicate they can't be seen but only seen through, like a pair of seductive panties. Well, none of that's real, you hear me? I'll tell you what's real. I am. I AM REAL. And she had smiled at him from the floor, smiled a smile which spread like syrup, so full of slow sweet pity for him he could have killed her—well—and he did give her a stern toe on account of it and his foot felt as if it were entering a basket of laundry. The idea that his missus had been chaffing for something like the same thing that he, Hess—knick-nacked the Penholder by his playmates—had, was . . . infuriating, it was . . . humiliating, it was . . . intolerable. Well, no, Father, truth to tell, it's hardly been a successful union, a kind of side-by-side life, you might say, as close and on our own, each one of us, as two plants in the same row, stealing substance from one another, water and air and all the rest, what's near, what's by, that's all, yet meeting, I suppose, once in a while, like leaves meet in a pile, for breakfast or in bed—ha—ha ha—never touching except, like I've said, when I reach out and whack her, and not even then, she sees to that, I think she knows days in advance—yes siree, no mistake—why, sometimes the bruise will be there, yellow and green like a young banana, before the day before the blow. The rug rolled. Goal or threat. Perhaps a promise. Designs slid out of the rim of his eye. Something to aim at: a telepathic bull's-eye. I don't .

.

.

.

.

. know. The shriek of the bird left silence foaming behind it like a boat's wake and Mr. Hess thought of the boats he had seen in the showroom, turning slowly around and gleaming on their cradles like the girls he had ogled on the stage, paint too perfect for a world of logs and oil, and promising more escape than a plane. So. Well. Who had his hat? Mr. Hess thought he would apologize first for being so faithless—no—he wouldn't put it like that—for being so irregular in attendance, whatever it was, but it didn't matter because he hadn't come about himself, he'd say, but about his wife, Ella, who was in dreadful danger, he felt, he'd say, danger of conspiring, was it? with the Devil. She was a goddamned witch, that's what she was . . . a witch. She said sometimes her real name was Pamphila, Father, and I looked it up at the library, with a little help in the library, and it's the name of a witch—who would believe—? She said it with a small smile—true—a small smile, but in the bathroom one day he'd overheard her singing in her thin thin seldom songful singing voice: *I Conjure and Confirm upon you,* something like *ye holy Angels,* though she never encountered any, what pretensions, what a liar, *and by the name Cados, Cados, Cados,* he remembered, it was like "cadence, cadence, cadence," a birdcall, *Eschereie, Eschereie, Hatim, Ya, strong founder of the worlds,* in that direction, it filled his feet with immobility just to hear her, *Cantine, Jaym, Janic, Auie, Calbot, Sabbad, Berisay, Alnaym,* noises she accompanied by clapping, *and by the name Adonay, who created Fishes, and creeping things in the waters, and Birds upon the face of the earth, and by the names of the angels serving in the sixth host,* better she'd been masturbating, Father, when I barged in, *before Pastor,* she sang, as if undisturbed, *a holy Angel, and a great Prince,* and she said she was only trying out a conjuration of Thursday that she'd got from Madame Betz, and which amused her . . . amused her! *by all the names aforesaid, I conjure thee, Sachiel, a great Angel, who are the chief ruler of Thursday, that for me thou labor,* Father listen to that—my god! Thursday—and he'd lowered his fist like a flag at taps. A witch. A ghoul. Ha, never put a broomstick between those thighs, though, no sir, no siree, she'd ride nothing so phallic as that; she traveled in her mind, rode another wind; and he'd tell the Father how it was, and that although she was spiritual to the point of lily-wilting, she wasn't spiritual in the churchly chichi sort of way; on the contrary, she was the only cunt he ever knew to wear galoshes, the kind that buckle, that swallow your shoe, and he, Hess, who sold insurance and knew about investments in a modest, even humble fashion—money, Father, is my métier— knew she put great stock in all those lives she planned to lead beyond the grave, took great store from them, took . . . tock . . . Who had his hat? He had his hat. The feather and the felt. Then ran for fun—he could do that. Who would be missed, the missus or himself? The label and the lining: silk. There was a sign above the hooks which always warned him to watch his coat, and Hess would watch so wrathfully, on celebration Sundays, sometimes, when they went out, he could have swallowed worms and felt well fed, been none the wiser for a wedge of mud. No, no, he'd have proud pie and royal cheese. And take a poster boat to distant cities, see famous landmarks done in strident inks, shape a shy smile of gratitude for the frank solicitations of dark and unintelligible tongues. Then outdoors, what? leafy trees, new green, a breeze. Play catch as catch can there. Watch. She might have been the hook itself he'd hung his hat from, her nose in the band above the brim. Outdoors, what? not the rush and the roar of a wind but the light lift, the almost imperceptible touch, of elevating air. For if Ella looks before, I after, if I left who would replace me? the present has already gone, though in a way it lay around his wrist still, keeping tabs, perhaps more perfectly now it had no need to tick continually and mill its hands or waste its face by glowing in the darkness. Go. Though catch would come after. Either. It's just that, well, he, Hess, her husband, was worried about her chances since she lately seemed so sick and was this minute stiffer than most corpses, open and empty-eyed, and he had noticed recently (that is, in the few moments previous to his present speaking) several brief breaks in her oh-so-shallow breathing, ominous interruptions of the ceiling readings, and little lapses in reception which caused her silence to fall short of itself, toward another silence, like a broken arc, and now her pauses had a puff and stutter to them like that bird of hers when it was angry, and he thought she might be about to Kick the Habit and Cross Over, or whatever one did. Li .

.

.

.

.

. ve. Die. He couldn't settle his heart about it, couldn't get his guts to decide. The Universal Insurance Company of North America presents to Mr. Edgar Hess this Electronically Prepared Personal Proposal of . . . The blue folder contained no certificate, no diploma, no golden seal, no ribbon like a panting tongue, but a promise of protection: the Estate Builder, Econo-matic Life. Reality broke in like a burglar and stole his dreams before he could etch his name. He would raise the hue and cry. He would never be out of work. His desk was littered with electronically prepared proposals. His appointment book was black. His tie was parched, his coat was dry. Hey there, stop—stop wife, stop life. Ha ha. Hess wondered just who had his hat. The rug rose, wetting his knees. Perhaps you might sprinkle her with something, Father, water and oil, stuff like that, to snuff her evil emanations out and sail her off to heaven in a paper plane. Fold her. They were blue, with a red stripe, in soft tabbed paper, privacy assured. The last business was his business, UNICONA's deep concern, he always said, and his clients would nod submission, extend their hands, shake like canisters of ice. Now this moment she might . . . she might go Hence, cut from his face like a whisker, and Hess wondered whether it might have been otherwise, whether their life together had been so totally enformulated that they couldn't help rubbing wrongly together and consequently being in a constant state of mutual exasperation like the sawing legs and so the laughing screams of the cicada—an ill mix from the first, bad match, poor pair, punk job, odd lot, and so forth, a complete and perfect botch; but if she were oil, then he was water, and if she lay quietly in a skirt of colorful iridescence, he fell slowly into darkness and into the depths of himself, beyond all light, beyond the last fish, stonily to stony bottom, or perhaps beyond that, bottomlessly un .

.

.

.

.

.

. der . . . no, he didn't th .

.

.

.

.

. ink so;

he thought rather that they might have made it with a little counseling—right—maybe that's all it would have taken—sure—just some authority figure to tell her to **V** her legs and buck a bit, chuck his balls under her chin, to come down out of the cumulus and clown around a little, a lot of ladies like to go to the games, scream for the team, lap up a beer, some bowl, and—my gosh—many will respond to a nibble or a twiddle even, consequently square up, Missus Hess, therefore straighten around, don't endeavor to be exceptional, to see camels in clouds or become what we call cipher silly, what do you say? that's zero, the cipher, zerrr-oh, the cold, the *o* in *obliteration*.

I've known several like you in my time and practice who sought clues to the future in the daily crossword, games of that kind— the *x* in *eccentric* is a cancellation, remember—how did they fare? well, they went up, then down, across, or desperately took diagonals like last-minute shoppers at Lazarus', in the Christmas rush at Macy's or Marshall Field's, but black blocks cut them off eventually, hemmed them in on every hand like smudges on a diner's napkin—Ella, Ella—backed into byways, uneasy always, and there to remain as cats are caught at the hairs' ends of alleys, illumined by doglight—Ella, Ella, Missus, Madame—or compelled to live on a letter like *k*—what a coffin—so placidate yourself, ma'am, run for calm like a carrot, resign, accept—we know you want to know only because you're curious, but tomorrow will be along never fear . . . and Hess felt he could have been content, the conviction had grown on him—indeed was a callus—he could have been content, his length in his Barcalounger, mag open in his lap, listening for the fry of dinner, the pitpat of the cat; for what had he asked for? honey in the comb? had it been much? . . . so much? perhaps if he gave her a book of some kind, one which explained marriage and contained diagrams and pictures, anatomy and arrows, though she never had much interest in words laid to rest like that: in so many glassy-eyed rows like results of a gunning. What he wanted was calm, calm was quiet, the stillness of a world which spoke about as often as an onion. Chewing on a hard roll, for instance, the sweet work of the teeth, he thought, sufficiently contained itself. It didn't need to broadcast the news of the world, or—well—as Ella said, be a checklist of his daydreamy desires. Yes. He felt he could have been content. Ella, however . . . She never joked, never saw the funny side of life; when was the last time they'd had a good ho ho together? no, she was always, what? grim? serious at any rate, intense, anxious, fearful, pitched past every la ti do they'd so far found a line for, prim. Pris .

.

.

.

.

.

. sy. Cold. Patronizing. She gave him the length of her nose, not a hair—not a fart—from her quim. Ha. Ha ha. Flighty. Notional. Picky. Poky too. Thin. A shoe stirred ever so slightly beneath the level of the rug. Was it his? hat? Step on a slat, make your mother fat. Five, six, pull your pricks. Why did he remember that? His memory was mostly reluctance. And then she was also so sickly. Sickness in a skinny woman is particularly . . . Splaugh. What would happen? malnutrition? cancer? kidney failure, then? Cold. Consider it: ummmmmm. What could he do? Die. Live. I just don't know. Headstrong but bowelweak. Ran in the family. Distant. Cold. Hearthard but tummytender. Normal, then. Cold. While I only wanted . . . What was it I once wanted? honey in the comb? Still, I wish, Mr. Hess said . . . Anyhow, Ella, really, I wish you wou .

.

.

BED AND BREAKFAST

1

Walt Riff examined the books which, behind glass as if grand, filled the top half of the secretary. Beneath its slanting lid, the desk was empty except for one of the narrow drawers Riff had pulled out, with an accountant's curiosity, to disclose a small glass ashtray, hidden as all smoking equipment was then, discreetly out of sight. Turning the key in the door and entering the room, he had tossed his valise on the bed and gone at once to the corner where the case stood uneasily the way large things do in secondhand shops. Its fake dark mahogany finish was as embarrassed as its posture, thin and crazed like a plate. It had no companionable chair, and the lines of lead in its panels of glass appeared painted there by a hand that shook.

Traveling as frequently as he did, with an expense account so limited it would scarcely butter his breakfast toast, Riff normally stopped at budget motels. There he could enjoy a clean sheet and watch a one-watt bulb gloomily befog walls already saddened by a coating of thickly textured paint. Except for a rubber-banded stash of twenties hidden in a plastic sack beneath the spare—he didn't trust banks—Riff carried little of value in his car—what were a few cartons of yellowed ledgers to anyone?—otherwise he could have kept tabs on the car's contents

- All returned checks will incur a $15 service charge

BORDERS®

- Returns must be accompanied by receipt
- Returns must be completed within 30 days
- Merchandise must be in salable condition
- Opened videos, discs, and cassettes may be exchanged for replacement copies of the original item only
- Periodicals and newspapers may not be returned
- Items purchased by check may be returned for cash after 10 business days.
- All returned checks will incur a $15 service charge

BORDERS®

- Returns must be accompanied by receipt
- Returns must be completed within 30 days
- Merchandise must be in salable condition
- Opened videos, discs, and cassettes may be exchanged for replacement copies of the original item only
- Periodicals and newspapers may not be returned
- Items purchased by check may be returned for cash after 10 bus

through windows masked by misaligned venetian blinds and floralized drapes, curtains which had never known a breeze.

Riff would sock the middle of the bed with his fist. The blow always left the same spongy dent. There'd be a pair of skimpy pillows trapped beneath its plaid spread. Across the room—only a few steps—he saw a TV, lacking its remote, trying to remain steady on a tippy stand. Not quite centered behind the bed's shiny headboard might hang the stylized portrait of a leafless tree or, occasionally, the phiz of a happy unshaven sot said to be *The Laughing Philosopher*. Perhaps in answer to an overwhelming longing, in the middle of Iowa, or in prairie Illinois, a seascape would show up: foamy waves rolling toward a welcoming beach.

Well, what is it this time? a red-winged blackbird perilously perched on a cattail. He'd seen them—cat and bird—while driving toward town, in drainage ditches awash with weeds. Such tedious and tasteless furnishings were what he expected, and if they hadn't been there he would miss ignoring them: a desk the width of a window ledge, closet crossed by a sagging rod where three wire hangers dangled in a darkness left behind by the last guest, a lamp whose gleam was smothered by a ruffled satin shade and whose switch was nowhere to be found, neither on the cord nor by its base nor at its neck. Riff frequently stared into featureless ceiling corners until he fell asleep. A gray tarp-type rug covered the floor like a faint uncertain shadow. Suddenly he remembered how, rising early one morning, he had slid a bare foot to the floor and into someone's forgotten slipper.

What's this doing here, Riff said, as if Eleanor were sitting on the bed, rolling down her hose. He was trying to pry the glass doors open with his fingers since the knob was missing, the key was lost. Perhaps locked, perhaps stuck, the doors wouldn't budge, making the books look jailed, dim and desirable.

Riff kept a Swiss Army knife in a side pocket of his case, and because Eleanor wasn't rolling off her socks he could curse when the zipper refused to move. His bag was made of a plastic cloth pretending to be canvas, so why should the zipper's course be smooth? Using two of his long thin fingers, he fished for the knife through a bit of parted track, slid the instrument out with a modest cry of triumph. It fell on the bed without a skid. Riff unclasped one blade—wrong shape—he wanted the thin pointy one, the one you might use to bore an additional hole in your belt. He'd owned this marvel of Swiss efficiency for some time, but he had never become familiar with its workings, since he rarely used anything but the corkscrew, which was in plain view, giving the knife the barbed appearance of a fishing lure; although sometimes, after another meal of stringy beef, he'd call on the toothpick which slid out like a sliver, and once he pulled out the scissors, but only in order to pretend to cut. There the little devil is, Riff said, hiding in the backside of the knife.

He thrust a narrow mean-looking blade into the keyhole of the secretary and the doors sprang slightly apart. Open sesame, he said, returning the nasty thing to its clasp with a sound which Riff believed the glass doors would make should he shut them: a sharp snick. And that's the noise they did make when he tested his hypothesis, which meant drawing the blade from the knife case once more to pry the doors open again. This time the doors didn't budge. Oh number two all over you, Riff said. Eleanor didn't know what number two was, so she didn't object. Riff gave the frame a whack with the flat of his hand and wiggled the pick in the lock. Nope. After some fumbling he found a blade the size of a penknife's and slipped it in at the latch. Which popped. Open sesame, he said. He may have made a mar but chose not to take a closer look. Then he dropped the knife back into its place in the suitcase. Sat on the edge of the bed beside it as if winded or overcome by disinterest. Just sat. Sat.

Riff put off pleasures, even nearly invisible ones, and when interested in anything, he became extremely methodical. He liked a lot of small tasks like completing picture puzzles. They filled otherwise empty time with a satisfactory sense of healing and repair. Large chores overwhelmed him. They had no parts. They simply loomed, while Riff tended to stand and stare. Finally he tugged at the zipper and the zipper retreated over the small opening it had made. Bother, I've a ladder, Eleanor said. Let me climb it to the stars, Walt exclaimed. Eleanor's laugh was light but it had no length. Men, was all she said. Walt remembered going then and kissing her leg through one of the ladders, a square formed by threads. After that he kissed the other leg, which was bare; he kissed her hungrily, high on her thigh. Men. She pinched his left earlobe between nails she had coated with red enamel.

Riff drew out a substantial volume. It had no jacket and its spine was badly rubbed. *Barrett Wendell and His Letters,* the cover said. Barrett Wendell and his letters? Who's Barrett Wendell? Has heft. By M. A. De Wolfe Howe. My my. Hoity. Titled like his letters were his dog. Having made the comparison, Riff wondered what sort of dog. His mind had a habit of wandering off like that.

He blew along Barrett Wendell's top edge. This Wendell was a professor of law at Harvard. Well. Here's a book about his letters by a guy at Harvard Law, Riff said. Sometimes he said things out loud. Sometimes he said things under his breath. Sometimes he said things in the dark back of his head. Often he wasn't aware which. But chitchat had its comforts. The places he went he never heard birds. From 1924. Imagine. The Distant Past. He pushed the book into its slot. Out of Boston of course. Anywhere else old Wendell was doubtless not even a shade. Hoof. I thought these cabinets were supposed to protect books from dust. They don't do a damn thing concerning that, Riff said, blowing again. Here's a jazzy paper jacket. *SuperCity . . .*

SuperCity. Harry Hershfield. Um. Publish a book, you must think you're famous. Girls rub up against you like cats. Money pours in. When? 1930. Gone now. Forgotten. Never heard of, hide nor hair. There was an advertisement on its back flap for a volume by Boris de Tanko. Boris de Tanko? If there was ever a made-up moniker . . . *The World's Orphan.* Um. "Read it!" the ad commanded. "It will make a better man or woman of you!"

Better man, baloney, Riff said. They were doubtless dirty before they were racked in the cabinet. Likely they were just lifted off some stack as had been sitting on the attic floor and stuffed in the case to look solemn and pretty. But why put a big old broad like this secretary in such a dinky overnite room? Riff did fidgets with his fingers. Jeez. Grainier than graphite. Need a wash. Riff always closed the door to the bathroom, even when alone, even when his room was safely chained and double-bolted, because he was rarely really alone. He had his little tasks. He had his chat. Riff unwrapped the reconstituted chip of soap and rinsed the secretary off his hands. Then pissed and cursed because he knew he ought to wash his hands again. He had a love of order but order didn't always return the favor. Riffaterre, you can't do anything right, Walt said. You kiss good, sometimes, Eleanor said, giving the bed back to his bag.

Back on the bed, Riff sat. Picked out a ceiling corner. Caught a glimpse of himself in the distant mirror. Then, beside the bed where Riff sat, on the little table where a dead digital waited, he noticed a rose leaning out of a clear glass vase, its prominent thorns enlarged by the water in the bowl whose base made a series of semi-circular shadows on the table's varnished top. A surprise. It was accompanied by three sprays of coarse green saw-edged leaves—ah—through which aphids—likely—had eaten needle-sized holes—maybe while they were growing in the nursery's fields. So sort of secondhand. No surprise there. The dark clock hadn't a thing to say either. The punctures, through which a bit of the wall showed, had to precede the bud toward its unreachable bloom, the bud's red edges already dark, for it was dead, though it didn't appear to know it yet, as if bred to be a bud, to open like a door that's left ajar, to remain say a day in half light, half past, half night, before it's tossed into the trash by the maid, who may speak Spanish to it while her sweeper hums, who may herself be Rose by name, and who will perhaps lean a little from a little nail she stepped on when she was a kid, and then neglected till it festered a fourth of her foot off, skin a gray-green then, flesh odorous. Riff realized he'd rather put Eleanor back on her back in bed. Yet he couldn't help reflecting. Examining the motel's homey touch. The forlorn flower.

Well. Weren't they cut when kids like Christmas trees? to begin death, their big moment, alive in some water their stems'll discolor? Yes, Riff thought. Dying, they'll grow drowsy. Their features will loosen. An eyelid or a lip will be released without a signal, and by one a.m. a bare stem will stand in a shudder of petals. This didn't cheer him. Spare me your touches. Budget should be budget. Riff laughed when he realized what he'd said. And felt better.

Thought he might as well take a gander at another. Got up. Thin arty thing, title in silver on a limp chartreuse cover, but writ in a swirly hand you couldn't decipher. Inside, Riff read *Whisps of Mist*. Its gray-green letters were quite legible. Surrounded by holly leaves or some such. Hotsy-totsy. The book was a dusty green, a yellow green. A green gone or going. By . . . by Gwen Frostic. Come on. Jeez. If there was ever a fakeroo of a nom de plume . . . Lavishly illustrated by the author. Drawings of seeds, ladybugs, birds, trees, landscape, sky. On rich rough-cut paper. Everything grayed and aged, soft as wood ash. Gwen must be good. You'd love this, mom, listen. Privately printed too. Gwen must be real good to get a private printing. Likely worth a lot, this book. Listen. "On and on it goes . . ." ah . . . "each season in its glory . . ." um . . . "blinding . . ." no . . . "blending with the next." Hey, whadya think? Poems.

His mother always sat in the best chair. He saved the best for her to sit in. With her big purse on her lap she sat in the chair he had saved. Knees together under a tent-sized skirt. She sat the way sitters sit: still as the paint they would become. So tonight she'd be sitting in the nearly stuffed chair by the window, next to the air-conditioning knobs. Big white bosomy blouse she often wore for—was it midweek?—for sitting midweekly, quiet unless addressed.

I think a person ought to keep her feelings fastened to her family and not let them fly about on leafs that got, you said, bugs on them. Ladybugs, mom, the harmless ones, with the tiny black polka dots. I think a person ought to keep her feelings fastened to her family and not let them fly about on leafs that got ladybugs on them. A rose in your room though. That's nice.

How these designs did date. *SuperCity* by Harry Hershfield. I looked at this one already, Riff reminded himself. The jacket pictured a jazzy riff of buildings, shooting up like rockets yet all atumble. Riff. That's me, but me is hardly jazzy. I never heard of Elf. Some abbreviation? Published in 1930—do tell—what a year!—by The Elf. Elf? "It will make a better man or woman of you!"

Baloney. Don't need to heft *Barrett Wendell* again. But he did. It did have heft. It did. And this? *Martin Meyer's Moneybook.* Here—Riff held the book high so she could see—right on the cover—can't miss it—in redblackyellow letters like a crowd—mom—listen, the cover says, "Yes, you can earn 10.4% to 23.5% on your savings—federally insured." A subject I know something . . . I knew . . . oh well . . . What? *Once Around Lightly?* Is that a novel? No, it's travel. I get it. Around the world on small bills and a single suitcase. Just Riff's speed. These can't be leftovers, these books, which the motel has recovered from its rooms. *How I Made $2,000,000 in the Stock Market.* Oh yeah. Not likely, Mister—Mister Darvas. If you're so rich whadya writing books for? telling people how to make money too, right mom? if he's so good why isn't he still hand-over-fisting it? It was funny, Riff thought, because, in a way, Riff unmade money. He made profits take a trip. Once around lightly.

More swill than the sow can swallow—that much money— mom said, repeating a bit of wisdom from her almanac.

When Riff was a kid, *around the world* meant getting your ass kissed and your cock sucked. He had to watch the way he mouthed his thoughts. Eleanor did dirty well enough but she didn't like the dirties dirty-worded.

Walter was a traveling cut-rate accountant. He wondered what old law school prof Wendell would think of his job, because he moved from town to town and firm to firm—little loose ones mostly, like buttons about to come off—and cooked books until their figures resembled fudge. He issued statements saying all was well, which it was when he got through erasing and rewriting. Ah, but he loved account books, sheets of green-blue lines like represented rain. He loved pawing through papers, he often told himself, licking his fingers to part sheets— there was nothing lovelier than the lavender and amber and violet of faded inks—or sitting in strange offices where stamps were kept in cigar boxes and stacks of flat nubble-covered ledgers loomed and filing cases opened like fridge crispers. Where he faced row after row of drawers with brass name holders and lovely curved tugs. Where lights hung from their wires beneath green metal shades. A lot of the ledgers were dusty too, like these books. He'd had a good deal of dustpuff practice.

When he had slipped over the line and begun his itinerant practice, he had been cocky about his cut corners, his helpful little cheats. He wanted to brag in bars about it—about his legerdemain—but he knew he didn't dare, and he couldn't tell his mom of course or Kim or Miz Biz or Eleanor either. All that pride like held breath. But the breath that would have gone into boasting began to leak out after a while, because he never made much money at it, his clients stiffed him sometimes, he had to keep changing his firm's name, and sack his secretary, because he had a secretary once, he called her Miz Biz, as odd in his office as this one was here in his measly motel room, hulking up the air, with the books behind glass to pass for fancy, though Miz Biz was easy if empty under her skirt of any love, and when he fired her for financial reasons, and for safety first, of course, she wasn't willing to become even absent ash in an empty tray, to leave a pin like a shine in some dark desk drawer when she went away. She hadn't said a swear. Made no thanks. Uttered no regrets. Issued no threats. Not a single expletive was expleted. She didn't snarl, say: why don't you get fucked by a prick that's diseased, or: I hope a tornado gives you a blow job. She didn't crack a single joke of any coarse kind though she was one of the original cursing kids. No rage. No threats. No regrets. Girl her age too. Couldn't spell. Miz Biz should have read *The World's Orphan*. What do you suppose it said? Her glassy black shoes went clack, and that was that.

Maxims don't make mother happy, mom said, and I bet it was a book of maxims.

Is a book, mom. Is. Somewhere. In the maybe abandoned maybe burned out maybe demolished offices of The Elf.

Clean hands make an honest handshake.

Maxims did make his mother happy but they had to be hers.

He should shower, he thought. He'd had a tough day. All that guy did was deal in apple cider vinegar. Lots of fruit trees along the river down there. Apple cider vinegar. Yet what a mess his loan life was, his inventory. Jeez. Had to pretend he was robbed. Mister Write Off, that's me. No profit except in loss. Of this he never spoke—of course—aloud. Riff didn't sing in the shower.

He'd seen too many murder movies. Riff sang sitting on the john. He sang Neapolitans he made up as he went along: O solo meoh O Jones' cow I can't forget you Not anyhow. Maybe he should try singing something different. On and on it goes . . . each . . . something . . . season in its worry . . . yeah . . . contending with the next.

Gol'amighty, mom, don't sit so close to the AC, you'll catch a crink sure. So sit me somewhere else, sonny, she said back, as unwinking as a stuffed toy.

Catherine Carter. Pamela Hansford Johnson. What a mouthful. Which one's the author? Catherine Carter sounds canned. Like Betty Crocker. *Politics Among Nations.* Hey. Second edition. Hoo, Heavy. Hans Morganthau. There's a weighty label. Just the ticket. Germanically serious author—that's what that Hans has to be. Still, who cares? *Economics. Principles and Applications.* Another something Riff knew . . . Published in Cincinnati? He didn't know anything was published in Cincinnati. I should write a book, the know-how I know. But he couldn't tell mom its title, nor Eleanor neither. Riff had had the canny-author daydream before. *Cooking the Books,* the name would be. Or *The How to Cook Books Cookbook.* Cute. Maybe too cute. He could ask Miz Biz what she thought. Because Miz Biz knew what he was up and down to, though he couldn't speak to her shoes, couldn't tell them anything, shiny and black with big bows, or the belt about her belly, or the mole above her eyebrow, even though all were admirable and as kissable as ears. No. Let her go like a fish too big to boat.

Salute to Courage. That's the ticket. William Tyler Arms. Gives himself airs like a ritzy hotel. Signed inside: William Tyler Arms. Hey. Printed in typewriter. Riff had never seen a book like that. It said it was an historical novel. Printed by the *Enterprise and Journal* of Orange, Mass., in . . . 1966. Printed in typewriter, but how? Must be rare. What was it doing here alongside *Czar.*

Czar? As in financial tycoon. Another money book, a novel, yeah, by one of the . . . hey mom . . . Wiseman. All these different years: a volume issued in the twenties, another in the sixties, a book from the thirties, then the fifties turns up again. How come? This gathering was no reunion. They weren't related; they were never in the same class at school or found themselves frat brothers or became World War buddies. Older than the motel, most of them. Tippecanoe and Up in Arms too.

Undo her shoe—the bow's for show—undo the belt about her belly, kiss the mole above the eyebrow . . . how's one? how's two?

Men, muttered Eleanor. You still here? Girls go to reunions, not just guys go. He went to one once, Riff told her. Lost in reminder, Riff held *The Egyptian* in his hand. A small-town kid from lower Illinois—hey, nearby Cairo—so fresh even his balls were smooth, Riffaterre had attended SIU in Carbondale and studied business, economics, a bit of law, before ending up in accounting like a pinball come to rest by the binkedybank of chance in a little hole. He had had ambitions, ideals maybe, dreams. But after graduation he had drifted back into small-town life again and lost his love of study, his interest in the new and strange, anything lofty. He shortened his name, dumped earth, severed every connection with the French, ended up a gap. Gradually, as these things usually happen, he became a fixer, somebody the corner store could count on, slow as mold but sure as rust. He would carry all kinds of blank receipts in his valise, and make up expenses, their lying numbers, like words for a story. He didn't just juggle figures, he rebalanced lives, created costs and catastrophes, invented divorces, begot additional children. Wal-. Waltari. Riff laughed to think his name might have been Waltari Riffaterre before he shortened it. Pretty swish.

He went to a class reunion one time. Hardly recognized anybody, or was recognized. The whole affair, would Miz Biz have said? was flat as a sat-on sombrero. Papered tables, paper napkins, paper name tags, smiling hello buttons, happy hello hats. He found he didn't care who was wealthy, who was fat. But driving the short drive home (he'd never have gone if the reunion hadn't been near as a neighbor), he realized how backslid he'd become, how his tastes had clouded like a sky, and how he'd been sharp-eyed once, quick to retort and genuinely wide of laugh, less suspicious, less cautious, more personally akimbo, not meanjeaned and tightass thin, not closed like the cabinet he was presently pawing books from so that now he could smell the dust, and here was *Ann Lee's & Other Stories*. What the hell? That was no proper title, Ann Lee's what? Elizabeth Bow- . . . the spine was smeared, the black had run. Bowen. Bet it wasn't Ann Lee's quim. See? Here he was—playing the coarse and stupid small-town stud, mouth made for a matchstick.

The glass doors were glinting from a bit of outside light. Low sun. On the vase of his poor rose . . . raised to falsify a rented room with its pretense of friendship. Is it supposed to lead us to lengthen our stay? although we've agreed to check out tomorrow or today; which would require Rose, though footsore and weary, to wipe away our street dust once again, cleanse the mirror of our worried face, erase the traces of our restless body in the bed, straighten loose papers, replace the dead bud with another dead bud, vacuum the rug, scour the tub, and routinely carry out the other duties of beauty, so we may rest afresh in our room, in our bed, and talk to our mother as if she weren't down out of sight in the ground. Rose, dust these books, too, will you?

Riff had always had a deep suspicion of refinement. He was holding the dustiest volume of all, so visibly silted he dared not whoosh it off. He wouldn't open it either. *Adam's Breed* was on the cover. By Radclyffe Hall. But he did. Parted the pages in sudden despair. This dust goes back to '26. That's what he didn't want to grow into, a Riffaterre, a lace-cuff guy named Radclyffe. Sadly slid the book back. Closed the cabinet carefully, a pall upon him. Held his hands in the air like a surgeon beseeching gloves as he went to wash. OK, mom, OK. Keep your seat.

Such a seat as'll put a crink in my neck? Well, I got no place to go. This room ain't like your usual, with that Big Bertha sulked against the wall, sure it's not for sale? It or the books. Maybe there's a price inside each one. Have you looked? Yet a flower. Fancy.

The account books he had looked at had numbers in them right enough; told stories too, Riff supposed, of success and failure, of tragedy and triumph, of the common bollixes of life, just like, he bet, Anthony Hope's *Little Tiger* did, and just like Riff, the figure doctor, managed to write, with his long thin fingers and the fancy columns and characters they fashioned. Nice name for an author: Anthony Hope. Made you want to read, implied a happy comeuppance.

Hope you can keep your hands clean, sonny. Hope you remember life's lessons. Hope you cross at the light going home. I have. I will. I did, dear.

Tonight would he imagine his kiss burning a hole in her nightie clean to the nip? Eleanor had a nice light giggle. Men. Riff was faithful. Not like most. Her groans would grow beneath him like the spring bulbs he had never planted. But only if mom had poufed. Taking her fat lap with her. And her chin with the light white hairs. Of course he had thought a lot about Miz Biz, buxom as she was, with a Scotsman's knees. Miz Biz, though, kept verging on the real. That wasn't right, it was disconcerting, and he'd let her go like when a kite pulls free and you don't chase it into its capturing tree where its twine gets snagged on twig after twig, easy to see caught there because not a leaf is green yet, and the kite's tail made of cast-off neckties fluttering among the limbs, fluttering though fastened, therefore fluttering helplessly.

It haunted him: this meaningless gathering of meanings. He let the glass doors click. Gloom had settled in his head. That one-watt light. That's always how he thought of it. With one watt. He'd dream of creamy walls, the corners of creamy ceilings. So Riff decided he wouldn't fondle the books again. Had he been . . . had he been fondling them? Now he peered at their backs through an enclosed dusk. *The Spell of the Turf*. Two authors, Hildreth and . . . and Crowell. *Advanced Figure Skating*. Um . . . Maribel Vinson. *The Day's Play*. A. A. Milne. Wasn't he Pooh? Pooh, sure. If the case had been open, Riff would have taken the Pooh guy out, but he'd made his vow—to keep his hands clean—and held it for now. *The Little Yellow House*. *The Younger Set*. *How I Made Two Mil*—Oh yeah, I've seen through that one. *Diary of the Great War*. Wonderful. Here they all were: war, money, romance, skating, self-help, kid stuff, verse. Books which had once been open to someone's eyes. Which lay for a while on a body's bedside table. Maybe by a bud. And were held in considerate hands, propped on a welcoming tummy. Then doubtless shelved with others. Ultimately attic'd. But death had disbanded the collection. Cartons sold to a dealer for a pittance. Or given to The Good Will. Picked up by a curious browser for a quarter. *Politics Among Nations* maybe. It said second edition even on its spine. Must be important. Hans Morganthau. A popular pick no doubt—to improve the mind.

Their dispersal was easy to imagine. It was their meeting here, in his—Riff's—motel which was the toughie. Because of the room's weak light, the darkening day, he could scarcely make the titles out, and Riff regretted not having been more methodical about his inspection, making sure he took account of them one by one and row by row in the accidental order of their shelving. He knew some of the books contained fiction but now each of them (even the volumes on ice-skating and horse racing and making money) would have their own larky tales to tell: how they happened to be together here, how they went begging before they were chosen, how they came to be written in the first place, where they were in their author's family—first-born or midkid or last rite. And there'd be a story, too, or maybe just an anecdote, which would explain a jacket tear here and there, or a badly shaken spine, stretch of water damage, bit of sun fade. Bookmarks made of bobby pins revealed where a reader had ceased; dog-eared pages pointed to a pause; torn slips of paper, inserted receipts, rubber bands, postcards, indicated some interruption: however, none said why: you've reached your station; the phone is ringing; it's dinnertime; boredom has lowered its sleepy head. And the pencil underlining on page ninety-nine: what did that single sentence say, that lining signify? Should he hang his good pants and his jacket up? For just one night? Mom's face was a faint unsmiling moon, so he pulled the garments from his bag and hung them like scarves from two of the bent wires. No more click or clatter. That left a hanger for Eleanor's cocktail dress. He'd have her remove.

He'd never been read to, but he remembered some of the drawings in *Pooh*: the fat round bear, a bridge, a honey pot. Gwen whatever her silly name was did birch trees and spumes of grass. Graphs and tables, photographs were in the books on war and economics, maps when it was travel, baby pictures in the bios. He'd seen Pooh at school he supposed, and that tiger too. And the kangaroo. You'd feel real small in—wouldn't it have to be?—Gwen's large soft lap, her sleeved arms around you, holding the book in yours, the book's bright pictures as enticing as a plate of cake, enjoying the coziness of it all he supposed, the odors and textures and comforts of closeness, feeling the breath in her chest, while in his ears from the voice behind him he hears the words on and on it goes. Riff tried to wrap his arms around his head but he couldn't do it very well.

When he drew the blinds on the parking lot, he knew he was alone. He could call for Kim but she wouldn't come, only her voice sometimes like a radio's. *The World's Orphan.* Hah. So I've got to read it, have I? How, hey? He didn't have a copy, only an ad. Was that a good excuse? So he'd never be a better man. He took out toilet articles. Arranged them around the bathroom basin in the order required by natural law. Out and eat. That was the next thing. Maybe he'd just grab a candy bar from a machine. Round the world for only two mil. He'd need three quarters. Candy prices way up. Chocolate candy especially, especially with nuts. These days costs inflated like an inner tube. Kim cut two syllables from her name and it never seemed to trouble her—what she'd lost. Burly? Take a dare, why shouldn't she pare, why should she care? But he thought Kimberly Riffaterre pretty spiff. At attention now. Walt Riff! Yo! Out and Eat! Let's go! Get your ass out of traction and into action!

But Riff was unhappy. He didn't feel military. He'd eat too many fries. It was already dark, long day's end, the guy yapping at him like a pissy pup, look, there's only so much I can do for you, you've made a mess in your books. He let the ledger hit the desk like the flat of a hand. Vinegar, for Christ's sake. Sour apples from annoyed trees.

Sis in Chicago, married up to here in money, doing well like the well was deep. And what about—what about him? his one-night stands were one-night flops. Kim would never come when called, though he could sometimes tune her in, like a voice on the radio. She said her given name reminded her of Kimberly Clark Coated Papers. So she cut it down to its stump. And lost the whole of her born one when she married. Girls got a chance to be renamed, go to another family, live in a different town, lose what they'd been, begin again.

As his eye sniffed idly about, released like a dog from his thoughts, every surface which shaped the room and sheltered him seemed to be drawing aside like drapes, but their shiftiness made nothing more spacious for him. It was not as if windows streaming with rain or alive with landscape appeared when they parted. Instead, the surfaces of the walls, the napless rug, the bulk of the bed, crowded in, increasingly indifferent, any sensitivity they might have had hardening the way people, compelled into closeness, became calloused, skin pressed against skin like bolts in boxes, holes the heart of the heap. The light, he began to notice, the way it fell upon the floor like a bored sigh; and the bed, which had barely interest enough in life to squeak; his own case, no more now than a bloated sack, almost as bad as a string bag which won't even hold its own space: their bodies grew near as his clients did when it was time to consult, while their inner selves, their feelings, their natures, fled. The TV, were he to turn it on, would offer him images like packaged pie, the machine as unconcerned about its business as dessert to a diner's counter.

He heaved the remains of his valise into the closet. Sat where it had sat and tried to gather strength. This was his bedtime story. You could see the orchards from the road as you drove, the trees in long rows like disciplined entries. No Swiss army regimen in the orchard owner's brain, though. Riff's facility with figures never made anyone happy, even when he made the dishonest honest, and straightened a crooked path like a paper clip. The seeds of crime grow sour grapes. And the straightened clip was but a useless bit of phony wire.

Out and eat. He'd seen a dingy steak house near the off-ramp. Made of palisaded planks, a bad sign. But doubtless cheap. He'd eat too many fries. If Riff liked anything about himself it was that he was thin. Suddenly, out of . . . well, you couldn't say blue here . . . he realized there was a row of books he hadn't handled. So what. Why realize? He shoved "so what?" aside, and rose with a reluctance overcome by what he'd call curiosity but what he knew was fate. No light reached the low row. He tried to pry the secretary open with his fingers. Failing that, he was inspired to push up from the bottom where the door was a bit warped and offered a meager purchase. Open sesame.

Satisfaction settled over him. Success. It was a sign, and now he was holding *The San Felipians* by someone called Roger Cowles. A society novel from 1932. About the successful, Riff bet. *Diary of the Great War*. Dates didn't interest him anymore, even if they dated a diary. He'd been over the date business and it led to a mystery. Henry Williamson. There was the Radclyffe Hall again. So he had looked at the last row—a little bit anyway. What a slip. Now he was nervous. Luck had lost its luster. That quick—turn of card. Rad Hall would be a tough guy's name. But Clyffe. Shit. *Guide to Illinois Bed and Breakfasts*. Also to *Country Inns*. A book called *Six of Them*. What? Like *Five Little Peppers? Fireweed. The Younger Set. The Golden Door. The Little Yellow House. An American in Italy*. Yes, he'd seen some of these; he'd been here before. The last one, a mystery—*Jink*. Jink?

But he didn't riffle through the books. He held them gingerly, glancing at the jackets, sampling a bit of the flap copy sometimes, but less and less, nervous without any recognizable reason, drawn and repelled by all these—well—former volumes—books no more now that they were never read. There was something about them—abandonment maybe—which resembled him, alone in his dowdy room, and wasn't his face covered with little crinkles like the lacquered surface of the secretary? His hands were soiled. He put the last book back but left the doors ajar. Went without washing to curl up on the bed while neglecting to remove his low-topped boots. He didn't wish for his sis. He didn't call out for mom or undress Eleanor or anymore miss his gorgeous girl Friday, Miz Biz. His fingers still felt the paper of the pamphlet, very lightly, very slightly textured, soft though, despite some sense of soil, his tips the fingertips of a typist.

2

Riff held the *Guide to Illinois Bed and Breakfasts* in one hand while he chased cream around through his coffee with the other. A night ago in Chester, where he'd been skewing the vinegar man's books, he could have stayed at Betsy's Sugar Wood and enjoyed a view of the Mississippi from the inn's perch on a bluff. If it was still there of course. And this morning he could be having coffee with Vennard and Norma at the Dowd house instead of sitting at the counter of this dingy Moweaqua diner. If his work was going to take him the entire day, he might still sleep in the "Cats and Hats" room after rocking for a few meditative moments on the front porch, though it was getting a bit chilly along toward evening now. Maybe there'd be a plant in his window. At any rate Rock Island, where he was due to dock tomorrow, had a large listing. Phone ahead, the IBBA booklet said. There was even a central reservation service. In the living room there'd be a TV to warm your eyes by, books in cases and magazines in racks. Anyway, there was a chance. Of course, his information was ten . . . eleven years out of date. Hey, in Mendota, where he was headed after he left the Rock, one place boasted balconies.

How'd you like a view like that, mom, Riff said, balcony by gosh. You want somethun else besides pie, the counterman asked. Riff wagged his spoon and put it down wet by the coffee mug. Amenities were what was needed: fireplaces, porches which ran around the house like a large dog, armchairs, woodsy settings, antiques, artworks even. A large dog, that would be nice, a woolly one, friendly and smart. He read that down in

Marion there was a collection of original log cabins collectively called Olde Squat Inn. Gee, he'd been many a time in that vicinity, and missed out. In his past, there was not a single squat to brag of. Probably built by river people on land nobody wanted. In Lincoln, the booklet said, you could snuggle into an antique walnut bed covered by a homemade quilt; then in Maeystown you could rent a rig. He envisioned Eleanor stretched out under a loopy canopy and it stirred him like a spoon chasing a cloud of Cremora.

Amenities, yes. Here was a B&B that boasted six fireplaces, a player piano, stained-glass windows, and embossed-leather wall coverings. Riff's shadow always fell so wanly on the motel's creamy partitions, through which quarrels could be heard as though broadcast, he felt he was his own ghost . . . and a ghost barely ghostly, too. A glass case on the counter nearby contained a single piece of cherry pie looking like a lost red mouth. How had he managed to eat the apple? . . . tranquil porches, shaded yards, riverboats, eagles . . . hickory trees with woodland paths . . . Victorian furnishings, organic gardens, wrought-iron gates. Mom? In Olney, Olneys had white squirrels scampering through their oaks, free of earth, but as though the oaks were roads. A milky morning light glowed in the glassware like a low-watt bulb. The counterman's rag moved through it as if it were a spill. Lit his spoon too, sitting in its wan brown sop. A little leftover reflection touched Riff's cheek. Outside, gravel complained, crushed by the wheels of a truck. Riff was like a stool on his stool, his head like a seat turning slowly round. Like a hurt bird. He was.

Riff read that Quincy's streets, away from the highway, were shady and spacious, with Victorian homes of every style flaunting their porches and celebrating their dormers and chimneys. He read that Elsah's Landing was largely made of village homes built before 1900. In Navoo, there was a house put up by Icarian wine makers. Icarian? Was he supposed to recognize their role in history? He hadn't known much about his odd-lot book collection either. Icarus was faintly familiar. Flew too close to the sun. Didn't he wear wax wings like the bird? Well . . . Navoo was a Mormon hangout. Would he ever have time to stroll around in these towns? Bedded in a B&B, maybe he'd want to. How long ago, though, since he'd seen a waxwing? Riff lined coins for his coffee alongside the handle of the spoon. Prices always higher. Birds fewer. Would one of those economics books he'd entertained last night explain that? Riff slid his bottom slowly from the stool, stuffed the booklet safely in a back pants pocket. Up and attum. Antique toy store in tiny tons of trouble. Time to tip the scales.

Riff decided to phone around.

But in the phone booth, the booklet held awkwardly open in his dialing hand, he had second thoughts. It would be like going to another country. He would probably encounter a smothering gentility. Old people and oddballs made up most guests. He'd feel uncomfortable, as if the room weren't his, especially when he'd only be staying overnight; it would be someone else's place, full of foreign things, personal and uncommercial; it might be inhibiting to have Eleanor in such a proper bed, and he couldn't risk imitating her coarse cries in an old house where sounds must carry like kites; moreover his valise was shabby, he wasn't much for dandy dressing himself, with his cowpoke's florid silver buckle, his satiny shirt, a long row of white buttons descending it like berries on a bush, its open throat, and, below the steer's-horn decoration on his belt, jeans as snug as a banana's skin. They could refuse to take him in.

Hither and dither, darling, Kim might have chided. She was always so sure of herself, her views, her choices, her plans. Riff had to admit she'd done well by herself, and he could certainly use her advice right now. So he'd be late for his date at The

Wooden Soldier if he didn't shake a leg. Only a kid himself, he'd try to hold her up in the air in his arms so she could fondle the earlobes she liked. Until his ears heard their own tingle . . . He began to dial, and as he did the booklet fell from his fingers. In a rage whose reason he'd never realize, Riff stomped upon its flop-open side with his half-boot, stomped again and again, pursuing an obnoxious insect. I didn't need that, he shouted at its bent flat pages, angry as though all morning he'd been put upon, and now angry at his anger. Recovering the pamphlet, which had a heel print across the antique teapot pictured on its cover and a streak of dirt on its drawing of a gingerbread house, Riff dialed Rock Island, fear fueling the rage which urged him on.

Walter Riffaterre, Riff replied to the voice in his embarrassed ear. One night. Yes, by six. He'd be driving in. Yes, alone. He'd be by himself, so a single. They weren't booked? No, he didn't smoke. Oh yes, cash. He didn't say he had no credit, that he avoided records, that his income resembled a series of modest tips. Did he like what? scones? Riff was standing by a pole in a parking lot of gray gravel. Maybe he should have called himself Barrett Wendell. Hoity-up the Toity. Still, Walter Riffaterre was pretty good. He turned to stare at the white sky. Gee, mom, they're baking me some sort of biscuit, and I'm not even there yet. He felt a warm feeling which was just the morning sun, he supposed.

Rock Island and Mendota were as far north as his travels normally took him. Most of the time he hung around Carlyle and Nashville, or Belle Rive and Du Quoin. Got to Oblong on occasion. He remembered, from the booklet, there were homey places there. That is, if they were still in the bed-and-breakfast business, because the very hardships which gave Walt Riff employment would work against any profitable custom and any lodging's continued life. In Du Quoin he'd been to the fair. Maybe he would again, and Riff pulled out the pamphlet to verify his memory. Yes, only five blocks from the grounds, Francie's Inn, a restored orphanage, it said, with yard games, what would those be? croquet, he bet, he'd never played, too genteel, kick the can was more his speed, and, sure thing, credit cards accepted. Even back then? Well, it made no never mind to him, he was on nobody's books, he was invisible, hidden in his figures, shading the truth, yes, shading it a shade.

Since he'd sacked Miz Biz (because she wouldn't put out, he was sure she thought), he had acquired an answering service, so he was free to move about, his office in his auto, rootless as the wind. He would simply phone in to find out about new jobs. The Rock wouldn't be rural, so where would his B&B be? He was promised a view of the Mississippi. Davenport more likely. Garbage scows, coal and gravel barges. Over the river and I-oh-way. Nice roll to that region. He longed for an anonymous motel alongside 80, no more memorable than its vacancy sign. He was sure he'd done a dumb thing. Well . . . only a night, he could survive that.

Wooden Soldier, here I come. In Du Quoin, another balcony, mom. Perhaps from there, just five blocks, you could hear the holler of the crowd, or the horse's hoofs, or the whirr of the sulky's wheels. Someday. Rock Island, right now. Well, Rock Island would be a bit of a drive. On 121? Out of here on some slow back road. Maybe he could manage to go by Vennard and Norma Dowd's place. Everything took time: the smallest, the simplest step. He'd better look alive.

3

The walk was made of evenly laid brick and marched straight to the house like a battalion on the move. On the porch there were a swing and hanging pots. Its nicely spindled railing curled round a corner out of sight. Up on the second floor façade, dark green shutters were folded back against a wall of bright red bricks like a photograph for Christmas. Riff was going to be knocking on someone's front door, a salesman hoping to get in, as shamefaced as his dubious product. He held his valise up close to his chest, concealing the belt buckle, of which he had suddenly become very aware. But his case was scratched and crummy. A button on his shirt was a bit pulled. Welcome. Please ring. Riff rang, though only after carefully inspecting the card above the bell. Then a very square-jawed man of some age stood before him in a vested suit. Oh dear. I'm Riff—Walt Riff—Riff said. I have an appointment. Riffaterre, that is. I called this morning. I've a reserv— . . . room reserved.

I guessed you'd be he, the square-jawed man said in a surprisingly light high voice, artificial even, with a wheeze. The screen remained between them. Mother, the man called in a loud whisper as if winded by just standing there. Riff lifted his valise a little higher. For the night, he said. You've rooms? No more empties now that you're here, the man said. Two rears taken. Nice folks. But don't like tea. Neither did Riff, Riff realized. Was this bad? He bet it was bad. His—what? host?—was a big blocky figure except for his putty-shaped nose. When he spoke, he puffed something awful. Then a white apron and black dress materialized in the sliver of the doorway that remained. You'll be Mister Riffytear, the woman who'd been called mother said pleasantly, a slight but genuine smile on her long face.

They managed to get the screen unhooked after some fumbling. Mr. Vest pulled Riff's case out of the arms in which it was wrapped. This all? This trip . . . yes. You'll be wanting to wash up, mother said, standing aside. The entry had a table which held a sign-in book. Riff remembered to write Riffaterre, but he forgot to put Walter. What sort of home address? He did what he often did to smear his tracks when checking into motels, and wrote Richmond, which was a speck of a place at the edge of the state way north. In front of him, Mr. Vest was puffing Riff's valise up bare polished stairs. Hauling his own weight seemed to be the trouble. I can do that, Riff said. Mister Ambrose does it, mother said in a low not quite conspiratorial voice. I am Missus Ambrose. Welcome to our house, your home now, for this night. Thank you, Riff said. You have the nice front room with your own bath. I've turned out towels for you. Come along after me, and then we'll show you around, so you'll feel comfy. One needs to feel comfy, don't you agree? Riff did. Richmond, Indiana, Missus Ambrose asked. No, not Indiana. Ah, then Virginia, she said with a finality which shut him up, I'll just add that to the book . . . but in a minute. This staircase is over one hundred years old, yet do you hear a creak? quiet as a quilt it is, the way they built then, with blessed wood. Missus Ambrose went lightly up as fizz. The stairs curved after they reached a strange little landing. That window there depicts Ruth out of the dear Book. They stayed on the landing for a moment to admire it. Ruth's hair was yellow as a lemon. Why not? Who knew?

There was a chest at the end of the bed against which his valise leaned as if on one foot. Vest had vanished as well as his wheeze. Door to bathroom—mother says, pointing—door to closet—another gesture—and then that connecting door, that one over there, is locked, so don't rattle the knob—might disturb the folks on the other side. Those front windows overlook the street but the street is quiet. Just come down to the parlor, Mister Riffytear, after you've had a wash, and we'll—smiling—take you on a little tour. Pulling a pencil out of her apron pocket, she turned toward the deep upstairs hall and disappeared into her dark dress. We have many things, many wonderful things, she said, her voice floating back to him. Riff stood in the doorway for a moment, looking in at his new one-nighter life.

Mother or Missus Ambrose seemed certain he would approve of his circumstances, and he guessed he did. Actually, he was overwhelmed by the opulence which now enveloped him, a plenty which made him feel secure, embowered even—pillowed, draped, laced—though he noticed, as he closed it, that his door had no lock, no catch, no latch, no hook. Still, what a place. Actually he had a little entry of his own. Very lahdeedah. And a bath . . . to his right . . . of where he stood. Once he ventured farther into the room, he first saw, still to his right, a radiator white as polished teeth, then the closet door which the Missus had already pointed out, and a catercornered sofa—a couch, geez—with a low oval table in front of it; all this before his examination reached the far wall and its three tall front-facing windows, each magnificently draped from floor to ceiling in pleated ivory with a valance which matched the wallpaper concealing the curtain tops. Riff stared. Matched perfectly. On the broad board between each window a small electric candle was fastened, while a single paper dove dangled from the lower sash, the birds aglow in the late light. In front of the central window a fern of some sort in a shiny white pot rose up from a wooden-legged plant stand. Below the pot, on a small shelf held between the spindles, a tiny hurricane lamp sat in a saucer ringed by a lacy border of cutout hearts.

Riff shook his eyes as if they were full of pool water. To his left, and opposite the sofa and the closet where he was, the great bed and chest stood, tables on both flanks. In addition, there was a small chair caught in a corner. No, that wasn't a table but a cabinet on the left side of the bed, next to another window which he realized, when he came near, overlooked a side yard and garden, in addition to holding the air conditioner in its grip. He peered out between the curtains: flower beds, a little lawn, walk, patio edge—a walk, yes, more bricks—low evergreens, flowers in tubs. The interior wall, where he knew there was at least one door which fastened, had a dresser with fancy pulls and spindled feet placed midway between his entry and the allegedly locked opening to the adjoining room (for underwear, shirts, socks, he supposed); then, returning to the lawn-side window after a futile peek through a keyhole blocked, Riff guessed, by a key, there was a nice desk with its proper chair just before the corner was reached. Gee. His own desk. A chair with a fat round embroidered pillow on it. A secretary here too. But this one . . . so fine . . . so ornate . . . like a tower . . . tiered.

How many of these things could be declared a business expense? Riff realized he didn't know how you depreciated antiques. Because they were being used, not simply shelved, cased, admired. How about insurance, too? How much risk? He tried to study the scene economically, but his heart wasn't in it.

Doors go both ways. They always have. So if there was a key . . . well . . . other guests could enter his room although he couldn't even peek in theirs. Which wasn't fair. A bit unnerved, Riff felt the wood of the desk, then turned slowly around in a state of perplexed wonder like a kid in the toy store where he'd worked this morning. The shop was full of wooden antique trains and trucks and blocks and birds. Wooden dolls, he remembered, with faded faces. When he left he said . . . If you want my advice, well, you've got that shed out back, right? well, I'd pretend it was full of new stock, that's right, that shed, I'd pack it with woodsy amusements, then I'd burn it down and claim a loss. Create a bundle of old receipts. Make those receipts claim you bought a cigar-store Indian in March of nineteen ninety-two for a hundred ninety-two and change. No round numbers. On stale paper. Violet aged ink. Then—pouf! Gone with the wind. Up in smoke. And your business—from rotten to rosy. All those expensive toys gone to god in a cloud. Overseas buys are hard to trace. The marionettes from Prague—now not even a cinder. Who would know? Mute, the man, the manager, nodded. When Riff left Riff said don't take any wooden nickels.

He'd better wash up and get below. They'll begin to wonder what was keeping him, and he didn't want them wondering. The same carpet that lay thick as an animal's pelt across the floor of the bedroom continued into the bath, although there was in addition to its thick nap and foamy edging a green mat afloat like a rubber raft beside the deep antique tub whose leonine paws sank beneath the pile. Leaping lizards! Riff's eyes became comic circles. Well, he was limber. He'd get his leg over. Next to the bath, and perhaps now upon a second glance its not pawed but more prehistoric feet, a modern john had been installed, gleaming like a scrubbed face. He'd never dare sit there and sing o solo mio, I come from reo. No jakes this, but commodiously Roman, his bathroom had its own closet, its own radiator too, covered in aluminum paint, a window with indoor shutters, and between the window and the radiator an oak washstand from whose top rose a tall pale candle held in an equally high . . . what? dicky doodad . . . which looked to Riff like an oversized wooden spool. Against the spool's base, if that was what it was, a board bearing the charred image of nuzzling horses leaned like something momentarily left behind. Beneath the dark scar of the design was a message from R. L. Stevenson about the value of friends, shakily handwritten with the same burning tool, while beside the candle and its holder was a purple pitcher and two plaster-pale figures in fancy French court costumes, Riff guessed, along with a commercial blue-and-white mustard pot. Odd mix. Just piss. But how could he not notice the crocheted doilies that had been carefully drooped over each edge of the stand. Just piss and get in the game.

Those plaster figures were a puzzle because the clothes, not the figures, looked naked. Ah . . . he had it—the pair were part of an abandoned art project. They were modules and were meant to be painted. Then baked, he bet. Mannikins. What color would he have chosen for the collar and the wide lapel? Mock-ups. Could be fun. Ma-. Ma-. Market. He knew he hadn't yet found the right word.

On top of the toilet tank he saw, as he aimed, tubes and jars of oils and salves: Potter & Moore Rose Hand & Body Lotion, Hydrox Fresh Tearless Shampoo. My goodness. Hey, don't miss. He could lie in the tub and luxuriate. Or were these objects, like so much else, here only to be admired? Higher still, on a shelf, a bowl of shaped soaps had been placed: rosettes, butterflies, turtles. Who could be so cruel as to wash those slender wings into flightless lumps? Hey, careful about flopping drops. In among the baby bars he saw a small card. Hope and prayer are the soul's soaps, it said. Next to the john and its roll of florid paper was a dotted blue enamel sink, as oval as a trotting track. Riff had never seen a thing like that. Its faucets looked normal enough. Perched on the wide ledge that ran around it was, incredibly, a glass swan whose wings were mirrored. Hope and prayer were . . . were they? . . . that was mighty wise. Off the end of the cabinet in which the sink was recessed, and at its base, lay a large black cushion with pink cloth ribbons and fabric-formed roses pinned to it with big bright pins, nuzzled by a basket containing an extra roll of pale orange paper—tangerine?—and a jug of foamy bath salts.

Riff retreated, nearly forgetting to flush, forgetting to wash his hands, as he realized (though there was no soap he dared use), descending the stairs with a look he hoped would show he was ready to receive his welcome. At the landing lemon-haired Ruth was still standing in front of a field of something not quite wheat, not quite corn. But a rusty orange. On a path or road of brown. There was another faraway figure in the composition which Riff would have moved to a more prominent place. Imagine owning your own stained-glass window. And a landing alive with church light. The glass looked scrubbed. Missus Ambrose kept a deeply clean house. Not like the three-sweep, four-swipe dumps he was used to.

The parlor, as he guessed it was, was full of chairs in which no one was sitting. A small TV screen stared out into the hallway and into failing light. Riff bet it picked up only test patterns. A long narrow oak table held wax fruit and magazines—magazines at least, as he saw upon inspection, fifty years old. *The Delineator*. Whazzat? De-line-eater? The newspaper rolled up by the fireplace tongs would probably contain news of the Civil War. The arms of the chairs ended in paws, the feet of the chairs in claws, and hard black leather pads had been hammered into their seats with button-headed nails. Heralded by his wheeze, Mr. Vest appeared. Mother will be right out, he said in his high aerated voice, she's pothering about in the kitchen. You can see—his gesture was vague—we have a wonderful collection. Quite—yes—impressive, Riff said, uncertain what it was he was supposed to admire. Maybe the pictures in acorn-addled frames.

Come into the Family Memorial Dining Room. Missus Ambrose beckoned. She hadn't her apron on now, her bust and hips sloped like land seen from a high hill—smoothly and without a wrinkle. Her face remained pale and long. She had itty-bitty eyes, Riff suddenly noticed. Itty-bitty. Like lookouts. The skin of her cheeks seemed drawn, and shone in better light like tile. Here is the Ambrose family, she said with pride, and there is mine, the Meyerhoffs. Across the wall in irregular ranks were photographs and portraits, most small, some oval, one square, many in sepia: solemn faces, hairdos severe, a few beards, carefully combed, ladies in foams of clothing sitting before painted backgrounds in photographers' chairs, gentlemen standing stiff as death, elbows resting on a cut-off Grecian column or posing beside a cardboard fireplace or in front of shelves of uniformly solemn black frock-coated books.

This is where I serve breakfast from seven to nine. There'll be fruit and fresh scones. You can have eggs and sausage if you like. Toast too, of course. There's always butter and warm toast. Mister Ambrose and I dine here in the evening, where we can see our ancestors, all those who brought us to this dear earth, and allowed us to live in the light of the Lord. Missus Ambrose said this last in a tone so matter-of-fact and unaccented Riff felt the strength of her belief like a firm hand on his arm.

You were certainly surrounded here by furniture and family, the old house itself, old oaks too, he shouldn't wonder, planted by pioneers, knickknacks of every kind, souvenirs and snaps, and memories of when and where you'd acquired this or that, of an aunt . . . Missus Ambrose said, the one wearing the bonnet and swinging in the swing, even as a child she would rise quite high, it was a somewhat scary sight, though Missus Ambrose smiled at the memory, and Grandfather Meyerhoff, there in the military suit, was actually dressed up for a costume ball where they took your picture after the dancing. Of course Grandfather didn't dance, he felt it was wicked. He was a most virtuous, most upright man. Riff saw a wooden soldier. I am a man of peace but not a pacifist, his bearing managed to suggest. Missus Ambrose faced her lodger formally. The Lord is a light sleeper, she said, and can rise and make day whenever He wishes. Riff understood that this was an answer without understanding why. On a finely filigreed wooden stand, its supporting legs curving as though outlining a lyre, a decorated glass oil lamp bubbled up into a gulp-sized globe, a globe a lot like the world. Ah, Riff enthused. Missus Ambrose approved. It still glows, she said, not offering to demonstrate, while including the patio he could see through the room's row of windows in a sweeping gesture of pride and ownership.

Out of sight, the Vest, as Riff preferred to think of him, was coughing violently, putting upon Missus Ambrose's face a faint frown, more of annoyance than concern, he thought, before he started at the sight of a huge cushion bristling with hat pins, pearly beaded and roundly knobbed, one headed by an *M* and another topped off with a metal leaf and still another by a glass marble the size of a shooter. There was a sideboard with a large mirror above it which reflected Riff and, distantly, several parlor chairs, barely bulks in the parlor twilight. Nearby, a china cabinet, crammed with plates in stacks and cups on hooks, held on its architecturally ornamented roof a collection of blue, violet, and sea-green bud vases at the same height as the plate rail which ran like a road along the brow of the room's inner wall, and down which paraded objects of all kinds, not just plates leaning as though into a heavy wind, but salt and pepper shakers, relish dishes, salvers, cheese trays, china-handled fruit knives vased by a tumbler, oval cut-glass bowls propped precariously like pigeons about to poop, Riff disrespectfully thought, surprising himself at the same time by feeling some shame at entertaining the idea.

In the gloom of a small adjoining alcove, dresses on dressmaker's dummies huddled like a group in conversation. Riff made out hats: laced, furred, rimmed with roses, of velvet and cloth and straw, feathered and figured, hanging from—it had to be—strings which, almost invisible themselves, disappeared in an upper darkness. There were grand gowns, long skirts, and flouncy jackets in styles he had no name for. The wheezing and the coughing no longer seemed so distant. Concentrate, kiddo, don't come across as a snooze. So clothes like these would have to be meant for large buxom women. My dear mother was a seamstress, Missus Ambrose informed Mister Riffytear in a manner which expected him, as a cow-handed country male, to take no further interest.

But he did take an interest (following Missus Ambrose around as he once had a paid guide in Mammoth Cave, afraid of getting lost), in the innumerable number of objects, ornaments, and endearments she had amassed. Mottoes educated every foot of every wall. Riff delayed the tour to read a poem in a more than modest green frame, the words already surrounded by fat watercolor robins who nevertheless failed to weigh down their slim brown flower stems, sturdily upright as wire. Said the Robin, Riff read, to the Sparrow, "I should really like to know Why these anxious human beings Rush about and worry so!" Yes, well, good question. Said the Sparrow, Riff read, to the Robin, "Friend, I think that it must be That they have no Heavenly Father Such as cares for you and me." Where was the sparrow? Ah, there he was in a cloud of leaves lower left.

There were so many many many things. Riff was quite overwhelmed. He had no idea. We cohabit with microbes and insects, too—in the billions. Without feeling crowded.

Oh dear, excuse me, Mister Riffytear, Mister Ambrose will need a moment of mine. Please to wait in the parlor and we'll finish our tour from there. I want to show you what porch is reserved for guests and what chairs are safe to sit in. Riff soon stood in the parlor's gloom like a dummy himself, but unlike the dummies was amazed that so much attention, time, and taste had been lavished on little decorative things, at how many napkins had been needled by diligent fingers, how many pieces of wood had been bent or carved or otherwise teased into imitative shapes, how much glass had been artfully blown, what a number of fanciful forms had been contrived for iron and brass and silver, how many pictures had been painted of birches hanging over streams, how many men in beards and women in flounces had posed for photographers against pasteboard props like solemn-faced politicians or famous singers.

More than fifty years old—jeez. He held *The Delineator, An Illustrated Magazine of Literature and Fashion,* up to his eyes, searching for its date . . . below a mother and her two sweet children . . . framed in a frame . . . January 1903 . . . as long ago as that. On the other side of the cover was an ad for . . . for Cottolene . . . what? The Perfect Shortening. A woman, dressed like a nurse at the front, was holding toward him a plate piled with fat biscuits. Below, in print so fine he could scarcely find it, his eye made old by evening, Riff made out the product's pitch: How can you expect the purest, most palatable, most healthful food to be made of ingredients obtained from swine? Well, that's right. How could you? Cottolene is preferable because made from refined vegetable oil and choice beef suet. Suet? Come on. Riff laughed. It is white, it said, and odorless. It is purer, more healthful, more economical than hog lard. Hey, pretty blunt.

Missus Ambrose's chuckle wasn't one of amusement. It was an announcement. We shall seem as silly someday, she said. Let's take a look at our wicker. Riff lay the magazine carefully on the top of its short stack. His hostess nodded toward the pile. My mother's, she said, and Riff realized that comedy was not on the bill. He'd had a glimpse of the ad on the page facing Cottolene's come-on: Holiday Gifts for Whist Players. He bet grandfather didn't approve of cards. For shortening—Cottolene—a name nice as Caroline. He asked: is Mister Ambrose better? There's just time to see the yard. We'll go out this way, Missus Ambrose said, leading him toward what he took to be the kitchen. In this house, she said over her shoulder, but for Mister Ambrose and his ailments, we'd be surrounded and kept safe by a better time. Yes, I guess it was a better time, Riff managed. Mister Ambrose pays the price. He has asthma, emphysema, and an artificial larynx. Oh . . . Oh dear. For every vice you pay a price, she recited, not quite loudly, holding open the screen door for him. And Mister Ambrose had three—three he pays for every day—with weakness, pain, and coughing—with a pitiful shortness of breath—and one more, I guess, I hadn't known about, she said, letting the screen slam. Because I smell another cancer coming. There's your chair.

4

Light conceived in etched and painted globes danced through ruffled shades to bring its comfort to the room and all the room's arrangements. The pale blue tweedy carpet seemed to soak it up. There was a name for the sort of rug it was, but Riff couldn't summon it. Here was a whole world to which he was a stranger. Silk and satin stuffs, wood and glass, shapes and services, he didn't understand: had never used, had never seen, had never touched. Riff couldn't believe he had his own sofa. When had he had his own sofa? A three-cushioned sofa, too. No dinky divan for Walter Riffaterre. Covered in green mohair, it canted across one corner of the bedroom. Its half-sleeved arms were upholstered in the same mohairy cloth, and the wooden feet concluded in claws like the relics downstairs. Two pillows puffed the sofa's luxury to the world, one wrapped in the wallpaper's pattern and the other in something white and cleansing with embroidered hearts. Snugly set among these pillows as if all along they meant to make a nest for it was a small anonymous felt-formed bird whose body, though white, had bright red wings, while out of its back ran a fine green string for fastening the bird, Riff saw, to the branches of a Christmas tree, where it would pretend to be in exultant flight.

He gave himself a start. It was a real pang he felt, as on a roller coaster. The valances—he had that word—the valances which masked the rods for the drapes, this pillow he'd now picked up so the bird flopped to its side, and the wallpaper— just as he'd thought—shared the same design, quite a trick; but what gave him the pang, as if a road had dipped, was the fact that the paper went up the wall only about a yard to reach a . . . wain . . . a rail . . . a bit of molding, while the rest of it was plaster painted in robin's-egg blue, plain as a baby blanket. And he hadn't noticed that till now. He did notice the two pink-and-white crocheted throws draped over one end of the sofa, and the easel tucked into the corner out of reach behind it, which held, as if it were a work in progress, an oil, amateur even to his eyes. But jeez. Riff plumped the pillow and put the bird back in its nest.

He knew why one normally didn't look. There were too many things to see. Every feature was a forest where you'd get lost in leaves, in their serrated edges, their dim red veins, to fall through the small holes eaten by insects.

In front of his couch sat the oval glass-topped coffee table he'd leaned over while replacing the pillow, its color a light green like some goblets he'd seen, but partially covered by a white cloth with many tiny sewn-on flowers. A good-sized green glass vase containing real lilies and leaves and wearing a white ribbon wrapped around it like a string for remembrance—the girdle of the Queen of the May?—was, for all its considerable presence, not the predominant element, because it was clear that tabletops in this house were there to bear objects up to the eye, to serve as surfaces for the display of collections, and this table was no exception, since Riff would have had to have more adeptness with coffee cups than he felt he presently possessed in order to find a ready place to put such a cup down, or to pick one up, without dipping his fingers perilously between spires of vase and candle glass, like the steam shovel's claw in its transparent case which he tried to get to grab novelties and candies for a dime when he was a kid.

So around the base of a pair of white art-glass sticks, holding pale green twisted candles, with forever unlit wicks, Riff saw twined a bunch of white plastic roses. Next to them sat a large seashell containing smaller though similar shells in its maw, while nearby a stuffed russet bird with a tan breast and long dark tail appeared to be approaching a basket basin'd with white lace and filled with . . . he knew this one . . . poe . . . pose . . . poury . . . and piles of the burnt purple petals of roses.

Where had the petals of his own rose ended? Ended.

Whew, said the soul of Walter Riffaterre. Aromas. He'd better put his things away. This room seemed to call for order. Try to be somebody for a change, his soul said. At the end of the bed, where his case lay, was a trunk painted to look paneled. It had a humpbacked lid like one of those French roofs. Across the top sailed a wooden representation of Noah's ark. At one end a plant sat in the center of a doily like a cat; at the other lay two Siamese candles joined by one wick.

Curiosity bit him like a snake. What was in the chest? But the objects which stood upon it said: do not move me or open this lid. Did they mean that? He felt the venom tingle at his finger ends. Not exactly to ransack, just to peek.

Next to his closet (from whose door hung a huge puffy tablecloth-covered wreath, wrapped with a narrow white ribbon that nevertheless managed to be dotted down its middle by a row of dinky red roses, the wreath sorrowful as though resting from a funeral) stood the familiar suitcase sling with its crossed legs and standard straps, as out of place as Riff was, who had lit here like some bird blown off course. But it was also a busy place— what wall wasn't?—because in the space above the radiator a wide round mirror reflected Riff and many of the room's wonders. Next to it was nailed a bird in a hoop of needlepoint, then a bamboo oval surrounding a rose, and on brackets a wooden tray which contained another candle lying at length and—wait a minute—a note—it looked—it looks like a . . . Riff read: "Thank you for being considerate. You are welcome to smoke on the porch or on the patio." From a corner of the tray, which was decorated with wood strips, two further candles were suspended from the loop of their common wick. Candles came in pairs like twins who shared the same cord. A lone candle—like a sentry, say—signified some family catastrophe, and a fallen candle? . . .

The door knocked. Riff was entranced. There was a straight walking cane with a knurly knob squeezed between the wall and the radiator, and leaning against them both at an angle on either side were two decorated panels, the first of a gaggle of geese honking away at a boy (in the other) who was carrying a gosling off in his arms. The radiator was topped by a white embroidered runner and a basket full of weed fluff and maybe Christmas cards. Coming. Yes.

It was Mister Vest. Only he wasn't sporting it. He had on a cabled cardigan sweater instead, which Walter recognized immediately because it was the kind his father used to wear before everything went blooey, the wool worming its way up his front to where his tie would tuck. He'd come home from peddling his atlases and change from his suit coat to that sweater, stained with pipe ash or darkened by washless wear—who knew what else?—over years. So Walter inferred that Mister Ambrose was off-duty, though not quite. Not to pry, but if you're going out to dine and intend to be a while, please pick up a door key before going out. All these words were slowly whiskelated in phrases parted by puffs and wheezes. Ah, sure, Walter said. So you won't need to wake us when you come in. Ah, sure thing. We gets early to bed 'cause we're early to rise. Walter bet that his host had cranked out this sentence on many other occasions. Mister Ambrose coughed, but delicately this time, fist to his lips.

How are you feeling, Walter heard himself ask, holding open his door as if wide.

Punished. Punished, Mister Ambrose repeated after a pause. As mother says, he says, turning as if on a spindle, justice gets done whether Tuesday or Doomsday.

Walter returned immediately to the basket where a card with a button sewn on it lay among others which, he discovered, all carried religious messages of the sort one was awarded at Sunday school, always accompanied by bright-colored images in thematic harmony. He picked up the button-bearing card and read: "There is a message inside." Indeed, it did unfold. Inside he found a handwritten note dated 6-16-92. Walter became terribly excited. He couldn't peekaboo the keyhole, he didn't dare open the chest . . . yet . . . Once he had watched a woman widdle in the woods . . . still . . .

Dear Bettie,

    Just a little thank you for letting me share the Thursday Bible Study. It has been a blessed time for me this year as you have shared so many special things from God's word. I've enjoyed *all* the gals who come and will miss you and them and the support you all have been.

    I've just enjoyed getting to know you & love the Bed and Breakfast. It was such fun helping you out.

    Emery is special, too! I wish we had had more time, time just gets away doesn't it! Your thoughtfulness to us has meant a lot and so has knowing you! Pray for us! Thank you!

    Keep us in your prayers and thanks for being a special friend.

Love,
Alma

This took some digesting, this did. Emery? Was the Vest— Mister Ambrose—Emery? Walter tried it: Emery Ambrose. Had a certain ring. Then, on the back of the folded sheets, he saw the rest:

> When with my note you are through,
> you will still have this button to pin on you.

Filled with admiration for the cleverness of this couplet, Riffaterre looked up to see, then to remember, finally to realize, that the back of every door—closet, bath, bedroom—had been rendered useful by the addition of a milk glass coat hook—heavens—how could he have missed it?

And did this mean that Missus Ambrose was a . . . a Bettie? Bettie and Breakfast? Come on . . . come on. On top of a plastic rose, and tented beside the basket full of cards, its spiral on high like a roof tree, was a friendship sampler. Picking the notebook up, Riff read a message about the holiness of friendship written by another guest. The thought didn't sink in, however. Walter had become distracted by events. There'd been some lines on friendship from whatzhizname—Stevenson. Who wrote—right?—*Treasure Island*. Emery . . . was his tinny mechanical voice the result of some vice? suppose he smoked or chewed tobacco? but if he paid the price now maybe he'd have a clean slate ready for the hereafter? was that the idea? Not bad. In that case, life was purgatory. You'd better use it wisely.

But what of Walter Riffaterre? What about his sleazy little sins, his slippery inks both out and in? His worried eyes on the street-side wall, more objects he hadn't noticed when he'd first come in began to solicit his attention. But God, he said sort of seriously, hadn't he led a life of minor-league misery for as long—well, almost—as he could remember? No one would shout "fun!" while Riff went round from town to town tarnishing his already tarnished reputation with winks. Don't let it get you down. But it had . . . it had got him down. Hey, he had a breakfast-in-bed tray made of bamboo—that must have come from far away—Samoa, Singapore, Stevenson, someplace east—and sitting on it waiting for morning were an egg-blue candle in a brass holder, a teapot shaped like some sort of fall gourd in company with three gold-rimmed, so very frail looking white teacups you could see the shadow of your fingers through, all on a crocheted circular doily with a sunburst border, boy!

The tray and its appointments were only for show, though, because he was expected to eat breakfast downstairs, in the Memorial Room. Scones. No . . . Heritage Room. Boiled eggs. Balanced atop a holder. Unless he had a temperature. And were confined. Then in bed: coffee and cream, berries and cream, rolls and butter. Maybe jam. Sliced bananas covered with cream the same color.

Weren't these wonders a sign? Near the last window stood a small dark wooden table rugged by yet another doily, and topped by a phonograph in a portable case with its crank—yes, let's dance—still in operative place and a record ready on the platter. Player is a Superphone, record is a Supertone. He felt better. Performed on a pipe organ, "The World Is Waiting for the Sunrise" by Ralph Waldo Emerson. Walter carefully lifted the record to examine the flip side: "Indian Love Call." Below, on a shelf, there was an odd selection of out-of-date contemporary magazines like *Victoria,* and leaning against the legs of the table was the image of an owl protected by bubble glass in a round wooden frame. Grandfather disapproved of dancing. Excuse to get close, I'm sure, he thought. Or to wiggle and shake and rub. Eleanor.

He couldn't sit on his sofa, the coffee table was too close. No leg room. Instead he was supposed to contemplate the composition of white cloth and green glass, of flowers, feathers, wax, and ribbons, Bettie had arranged. Bettie. And learn what? About the luxuriance of life. About shades of gray and grades of cloth and twists of glass and candle wax and ribbon. About spices and herbs. God's plenty. Yes, Walter thought, looking around at all his wealth: God creates, and then man creates, in God's image, things of love and harmony and service. A leaf, a seed, the wood of trees, the metals of the earth, which God made and placed where God wished to put them, were taken up by devoted and skillful hands and transformed into frames and stands and cloths and lamps, and put in their place in their turn: chests in rooms, drawers in bureaus, china in closets, beads in boxes. And on the clay the potter incised lines and painted flowers, and on a petal put a drop of translucent dew after the manner of the morning. Walter's mind had at last managed to move his emotions.

History was here, too. History. Not a life lost, not a thought gone, not a feeling faded, but retained by these things, in the memories they continually encourage, the actions they record, the emotions they represent, not once upon a time, but in the precious present, where the eye sees and the heart beats, and where you clear gutters of leaves whose trees you know and recognize, and you furthermore remember when the soldered copper shone and the roof's slates were reset and how the kitchen will any moment smell of bread like the brightness of the day and where the ladder's shadow falls as though it were a sun clock striking three. Not the work-weary world Walter went around in: his old roads and weedy berms hadn't a single memory pressed in the macadam, or reflected from the splotchy counters of greasy spoons or sensed like an odor out of dirty-bowled gas stations where, in back, bent tin signs in cast-off heaps collected—Mail Pouch Tobacco and Royal Crown Cola and Black Jack Gum—or down the dim smeary halls of his motels had some imagination passed like a worried ghost . . . no . . . where he was it was never how it ought to be: redolent . . . relaxed . . . reflective . . . rich . . . Where one dined or supped. Where one, of a p.m., tea'd. Where one went to bed early and read.

Walter's hungers were of another kind; he had no desire for dinner; and the idea of putting on some loud pomade to drive about looking for familiar logos, or even of crossing into Davenport, where there were doubtless decent places, upset him. His appetite was in his eyes. In the morning—he remembered with a smug smile one of his mirrors immediately made him appreciate—he'd breakfast on scones. But then he thought he'd have to pay his bill and leave. Perhaps he could prolong his stay one day, those bozos in Mendota wouldn't cop the diff. He could call ahead for another B&B. Where was his book?

On the seat of his car. These were really painful thoughts . . . painful thoughts should be put behind him, but the fact was there was no place appropriate for pain here, it hurt to have hurts in this—sure, material—sure, commercial—although transient—heaven. Well, haven, anyway. On his way to pee he wandered a few steps, drawn to the connecting door, and noticed nearby it a white ceramic birdhouse with two green ceramic birds. Around the neck of one was hung a "Sweet Bouquet Calendar for 1994." All the months, printed in a bell which pretended to be suspended from a nosegay of violets, were laid out on one flat sheet, each day as small then as real days must be. A key continued to block any view.

In the bath he might choose to sit, not on the john, but in a rocking chair placed almost facing it. Made of maple, shellacked for a high shine, with a brown seat and backing for comfort that was all of a piece and tied on like a straightjacket. At the end of the tub, a wine basket which he hadn't seen. In the holes where the bottles would normally be, Bettie had stuffed rolled washcloths and small towels. Walter bent down near the swan's reflective wings and saw his face in slivers. Attached to the wall above the washstand was a wooden rack with hand towels and odd magazines in it: the magazines are *Readers' Digests*, the towels are draped. With the door closed to do his business, he could see a strange basket made of spent buckshot casings glued together, and into each hole some cloth has been stuffed so the whole thing looked like a sick creature's furry tongue. In his head, Walter praised human ingenuity. What could beat it? But were there any towels you'd dare to dry your hands on?

About now, he bet, Bettie and Emery were having supper in the Family Heritage Room, the table set with splendid china from his or her grandma's stock. Candlelight, he thought. Covered dishes leaking the scent of sweet potatoes and ham, a nice mess of greens. It was harder for Walter to imagine what they'd be saying to one another, although the character of Emery's voice box wouldn't alter. And the dents at the ends of Bettie's small mouth would fill with shadow, and the narrow eyes in that long face would seem even more intense in the glow of the candles. Then her teeth, so small they seemed set in multiple rows: they'd be intermittently bright too. Flatware from the old country, cider in mugs. Well, maybe not mugs for supper, just for luncheon. Walter would have rolled out the ornate lace cloth over the walnut table, the wood shining like a snowed-on lake through the filigreed cloth.

What he could do: he could ask to stay on, and commute to Mendota, it wasn't so far, a drive of what? maybe seventy miles, out of here on 80, easy, up on 34. He'd want the same room though. He'd have to have the same room. He'd have to make that plain. Where were all the other guests? those in the back? not a creak of course on account of workmanship and devotion.

Walter was careful on the stairs, its steps were a bit variable, and the light was low, Ruth's window as dark and featureless as a paneled wall. He saw Missus Ambrose—Bettie—but he mustn't let on—in the dining room in a small pool of electric, reading a book while eating alone. He began his apologies in the parlor and let them precede him to her table. She looked up at last. It'll be available, she said, but at a weekend rate. Walter said he didn't mind paying a mite more. It's lower—the rent is— for weekends, Missus Ambrose said rather severely as if he ought to have known. Less custom, fewer traveling men, on ends. I see, Walter said, I should have known. Going out now, Bettie inquired brightly, as if a change of subject required a change of expression. Ah, nah, I thought I'd just stay in. Well, sit and have a bite with me if you like, Bettie said, a second grace goes well in God's ear. Walter made sounds which suggested second thoughts without any coming first. Mister Ambrose didn't feel up to eating this evening. His evils were at him, so he's in his room resting. Walter, after some hesitation, and a glimpse of chicken breast and cooked spinach, slid into Emery's seat with a grateful sigh. Emery's plate did not reflect a face. The fork and knife had bamboo handles. Bettie selected a piece of chicken from a platter. So, she said, with as wide a smile as she was willing, tell me about yourself. Only—was that a chuckle?—be truthful, the Lord is always listening. Ah . . . well . . . me? ah . . . The tines of Walter's fork went deeply into his piece of chicken. He saw, with appetite, a bit of juice ooze.

5

Early to bed. Early to rise. Early on the road. Out 80. Up 34. Above a headboard of old oak, Walter read a cross-stitched saying borne by a wide pine frame which was peppered with pin-sized wormholes: God grant me the serenity to accept my lot in life. The pinworms did their job; they accepted their lot in life, he was sure; and a piece of pine which might have passed from mill to floorboard to kindling was given character, even charm, and saved for a saying. A nightcap hung from one bedpost, a bed jacket from the other. They weren't meant to be worn. He hadn't lied to Missus Bettie exactly, but he had left out a lot. He'd asked what she was reading, and she'd replied, thumb to mark her place, the *Life of Pastor Kneemiller,* something similar. Very edifying. Brave noble man. You know him. When the priests were cowering in their coops like pigeons, Missus Bettie said with some heat, he stood up, he stood firm. Ah, yes, admirable, I'm sure he did, Walter agreed, and the spinach is perfect, so fresh, a second crop is it? plant your own? how wonderful! iron up to here, and good for the blood's color, makes it red as ripe tomato.

Missus Bettie removed her thumb and the volume fanned slowly open to the place she'd been reading as if she meant to go on. I'm an accountant, Walter said. I travel about between businesses, like now, and help them with their figuring. Helping is a holy thing, Missus Bettie said. Saint Peter keeps God's. His keys? His accounts. Saint Peter has God's list of ins and outs. Income and outgo, Walter joked, is what I watch. We are all accountable, Missus Bettie said, not a fork of food goes unnoticed, how it's chewed, how it's swallowed. The chicken's very good, tender as— Tea? Tea, oh, well, thank you, very kind, just a spot, it hits it though, the spot, I mean. How do you keep accounts, Mister Riffytear, Bettie asked, fixing him in her look as if holding both his ears. I look at lists, Walter managed, receipts and bills of sale and lading and such. Overhead, you know. Well, I'm sure it's over mine, what you do, Mister Riffytear, she said, wholly unaware of any witticism. Do you know a book, he said, do you know a book by Boris de Tanko called *The World's Orphan?* Bettie's head drew back into the dark. It made a better man of me. It made a better man.

Oh dear. What he'd said, how he'd let on. Oh dear. His bed was fitted with white sheets trimmed with ruffled eyelet. There were two bolsters matching the eyelet but decorated with a pink crocheted ribbon containing another oval in rose velvet with an oval panel inset and on its ivory ground, trimmed in gold braid, a tiny pink needlepoint rose like a gift at the end of a journey. His second set of pillows was embroidered with a multicolored flower pattern—spring things, hyacinths and crocuses. Did he dare climb in? Layer after layer like cake: an ivory woven coverlet with puffy balls at bottom, then between sheet and coverlet a rose-colored knit blanket, and under the sheet, he could see where it hung down, the dust cover with still more ruffles. You didn't want to dent it.

You have a family, Mister Riffytear? what do you do when you're not fixing figures? It was just an expression but he felt chilled, so held his teacup with both hands. He hoped for another helping. The gravy was thin and clear and pure and perfectly delicious. He'd never cared for spinach much but he cared for this spinach as if the plants were plants of his own. Nutmeg, she answered when he asked. Ah. Where did you learn to fix figures? . . . cook? . . . They laughed at the way their questions had run together. But had she said fix? My mother. My mother was a minister's daughter. Did socials and picnics most her life. Could cook for a company. I bet she could. She stood by her stove like a sentry. I bet she did. No children, then, Mister Riffytear, love's gift to life? No, sorry, no, no wife. Yes, if it's so, then you should be sorry, oh, I too am left at the end of my line, though there must be a meaning, mustn't there be, Mister Riffytear, a meaning to being barren? I always wanted a boy, Walter confessed, to take— Not hunting, I hope, not killing in the leftover fields, Bettie said sharply. Oh, no . . . ah . . . bowling, he answered with a stupidity which made him blush, but she seemed not to have heard him, staring into the dark remainder of the room, speaking as though to a corner.

We must bear up under much, Mister Riffytear, she was saying. We are barely here, so short a time, yet there is much to endure while we are here. For if you're spared the pain of chil-dren—the pain of their appearance, the pain of their growing up, the pain of their pains, the pain of their going away, the pain of their eventual indifference—well, you must, it's only fair, now, isn't it, Mister Riffytear, fair that you should have another burden, because what would we do if we had no burden, no weight upon our chests, we'd fly, wouldn't we? fly like fluff, up and away to nowhere, for we're nothing but our burdens, so that's why, one way or other, we were meant to labor.

And make things, Walter added, with our hands. Like all these lovely things you have here, and have taken such loving care of, as though they were your children. Oh, as if the house, she said in a melt, were.

Bettie held her hand to her mouth, Walter supposed, to stifle a sob, and got up swiftly, turning her back to him. You'll be stay-ing another night then? His yes ma'am ran after her disappear-ing ears.

Walter thought he might as well toss a shirt and a sock in his dresser if he was going to stay another night. Settle in, even somewhat. And see what he could see in all these things, learn what he could of their names, he stumbled so, as if they were ahead of him, running away nimbly over rough stones. There was a circular doily on its oak top in the center of which stood still another candle—this one pink—in a glass tray. Around the circumference of the cloth like a crowd Bettie had collected was a decorative vase in gold and ivory shaped like a slim and elegant pitcher, a long low dish full of po . . . that porry flakey stuff, and a huddle of white bone china: sugar bowl—he found out when he lifted its lid—chock-full of fresh peanuts, such a nifty touch, then a soup-sized bowl which was empty, and another with a round hole in the middle of its cover, what was that for? He had this need for names. His eye, when it had finally begun to look at things, had become literal.

Two harp-shaped arms embraced the mirror, which, he supposed, was supposed to make the dresser into a dressing table.
On either side, the crocheted outline of two hearts. Next to the
dresser, but leaning against the wall, as so many things had to,
was a satiny white hatbox topped by a wreath of what looked
like pale gray weeds and tied on with a wide white bow.

Pulling out a drawer, Walter found it lined with embroidered
white linen the size of the space and held down at the front and
most observable corners by two cherubs cut out of soft white
stone. Maybe he'd leave well enough alone.

But even this modest bit of embroidery . . . a loop of thread
which looks nothing like a rose . . . and this loop, too, which is
like another loop, another and another, anonymous all . . . each
thread pulled through and started over . . . with the patience of
the spider . . . nothing shows, yet, moment by moment, and in
another minute—wait—one more loop or two indistinguishable
from the others . . . and suddenly a small pink petal, the first of
the rose, lines up on the canvas of the cloth. This accumulation
was a miracle. Such work required (Walter was awed) . . . it was a
sign of (he ransacked his head for a simile) . . . care, concern,
devotion, a considerable degree of skill . . . gained over how many
years of application? and what for? that was what was most amazing . . . after all, did tatting or carving or sanding or shellacking
abolish war? did framing some of our often foolish, former faces
in windows made of twigs or bark or knotwood boards redeem
past time? All this, he waved his arm with histrionic vigor, was
clutter unless you saw the composition. Without much ardent
uncompromising dedication, there wouldn't be this comfort.

The nervous excitement which had sustained him most of the
day, and carried him through his tasks at The Wooden Soldier in
record time—a few sums here, a few charges there, a little loss,
some creative debt, nothing to it—was finally gone, and though
he felt full and good he also felt weary, weak, stupid; for

instance, that chair in the corner—what kind was it? all he knew to say was Windsor, and if you just said chair—hell—the kiddiest kid knew that much—dog, cat, table, chair—he'd sat in a memorable pool of light with Bettie, fending off her questions with his famished fork, and dipping the tip of his reluctant tongue into her tea, while she wondered what sort of man he was, he was sure, with his silly western shirt and buckle, geez, buttons and belt would have to go, yet feeling no real fear from the quiz like one day he'd be frightened when they caught him—couldn't he quit?—how would he live?—go back to school? on what? at his age?—could he recover himself and rest in a room like this, in a house full of fine things, things and images and signs you could obey, enjoy, respect? no . . . not when he was a bottom dealer and low roller and only a guy who made the vacancy sign go off. Good chicken. God. That too.

The chair, which he couldn't call a Windsor even if it was the only name he knew, was . . . well . . . sumptuous . . . upholstered in gold velvet with a braided trim. On its seat a cotton pillow, printed with narcissus and tulips, lay in a cuddle like a cat. Between it and the bed was a small round table with a long green skirt, the green cloth overlaid by white linen like a snowflake on grass. A symphony of green, Walter marveled. Small white matching napkins were fanned like a neatly folded hand of cards. Then on a metal tray shaped like a leaf floated a glass coaster, green plastic clock and flashlight, and a stack of four candies wrapped in silver paper, objects which might have looked as out of place as workers at a social function if it were not for Bettie's thoughtfulness about every detail. The tray's metal edge nudged a milk glass candlestick out of which a bright red candle erupted.

If, for instance, he were to move, say, the stuffed long-tailed bird from its place on the coffee table next to the basket filled with pohpuff and petals and put it on top of the glass-enclosed cabinet on the other side of his bed by the desk, it would dwarf the male and female figurines already there, as well as the miniature porcelain boat and little glass coaster. Even the coaster, if it were shifted, would find competition everywhere; besides, such a thing belongs by the bed, where you might want to set a drinking glass. No higgle-piggle in this house—thoughtful planning, care—for instance, the linen hand towel draped over the back rail of the glass cabinet. Four small shelves were sheltered behind the cabinet doors, the only doors or drawers he'd found which were locked. Inside he'd seen three souvenir teacups and two mugs stuffed with dried weeds. Walt only for a moment remembered and rejected the use of his knife.

At last, Walter slid naked between the cool sheets, as careful as if he were a layer himself, and felt their cool calming touch, the touch of an other who wanted nothing from him but would grow warm when he relaxed and went to sleep in his skin. It seemed a shame to be asleep so many of the hours he'd have in this room, though all these things would quietly remain for him to realize again come morning. When he shifted his bolster to settle his head, Walter discovered another pillow, shorter, flatter, heavily embroidered—he could feel it—from which came a subtle sweet scent as if from long loose hair. In a bed like this he would never need to curl or clench—not beneath his rose-colored knit blanket. On and on it goes . . . each season in its glory . . .

6

Walter drew a bath a Roman would have waded in, and lay in it pretending to be at the end of his day, and that he was about to put on a warm robe and go down to the kitchen for a light snack. His belly button stared up through swirling suds, its eye half shut with pleasure, and warm steam scented with something unfamiliar moistened his military hair. It was fortunate he habitually shaved with a throwaway piece of plastic, because he hadn't seen a proper plug for anything electric. He even enjoyed brushing his teeth and, with twin brushes, his hair. He'd wear his best shirt, a proper tie, a thin brown belt, as modest as small change. And he had a choice of mirrors. Nothing could be done about his accounting books or the cowboy cut of his trousers. Not just now. And Ruth would be blazing on the landing. But— think a moment—would she? because—he had to persuade himself to remember—it was morning, and the morning sun would be on the other side of the house, coming in the dining room windows like Niagara Falls.

The room *was* full of light, and a place had been set for him facing the garden. a napkin in a numbered silver hoop, which meant he was expected to stay, an etched juice glass and a plate for fruit, his own jam pot, covered with little green leaves and little red strawberries, cup and saucer for coffee in a pattern so fancy the saucer's rim was as full of holes as lace, then silver that seemed to smile, knife and fork gleaming with greetings, tiny spoon for the jam, he supposed, cut-glass bowl of butter cooled by cubes of ice, a napkin'd breadbasket, cloth white as white, so all was well, and here he was: Walter cleared his throat, sat as softly as a cat.

Mister Riffytear, is it? Be right out. Sleep tight did you? He heard a knife go chop. Yes . . . well . . . very well . . . yes, he called back. Good. In a moment. And in a moment she put a plate of fruit upon his plate, fluted rounds of orange and kiwi, geez, its face like a peppered flower. Juice? In her other hand, a pitcher, poised. Please. He smiled at Bettie as only happiness can, but saw her face get stern as he lay a fork against a slice of orange. Oh . . . he knew, put down his knife, withdrew the fork, looked apprehensively solemn. We like to have a little prayer before the duties of the day begin, Mister Riffytear, if that's not displeasing to you, Bettie said, in tones that had never heard another answer than the one he gratefully gave her.

Normally, had Walter been asked this question in the abstract, he would have answered in words short and coarse, because displays of belief always made him uncomfortable, whether it was his father railing against the Republicans, or his mother rebuking the flower children, or his sister standing to sing hymns in that soprano of which she was so proud. Right now, he would have had to admit he was apprehensive, but not entirely disconcerted; after all, when had anyone ever prayed over him? except when he imagined he was dead.

Lord, I want to welcome Mister Riffytear, here, to our bed and breakfast, a stranger who's come a ways from Virginia to stay in a home where every dish we own, and stick that makes our walls, and swatch of cloth that clothes, and bite of toast that warms us to our tasks, is dedicated to your cause, and where your name is praised not merely mouthed the way they do down the street. And I'd like to ask for you to bless this—I believe— dear man as he goes about today's work, because, although he hasn't really told us what he does, it's righteous service I'm sure that he's about. Bettie seemed to glow with goodwill and Walter went warm, though he would have said it was the morning sun.

Bettie flipped a corner of the napkin. Scones, she said, fresh. Warm as my cheek, I promise, Mister Riffytear. Ah, so nice, I'm sure, your cheek, too. Bettie's short mouth tried a wide smile. Her small eyes drew her skin into a pucker. We know, she then said to the ceiling so that Walter's finger had to scuttle from his fork, that it doesn't matter how you come to God. And any road which leads here is a good one. Coffee? Will you be wanting eggs, a bit of bacon?

Walter ate slowly, which wasn't his way, cutting the scones carefully in half, buttering their centers with even swipes, taking a mannerly modest bite, and then letting the cake melt away from its currants. The coffee had a dark rich hearty zing, and his eggs were like suns beneath soft clouds. Bettie mostly stayed out of his way and let Walter seem to sleep inside sensation.

Only as he started up the stairs, returning to his room, his appreciation in a wake behind him, did Walter realize that Bettie had asked the Lord to bless him, but had neglected to ask for God's approval of the food. It would be all right. A natural oversight. You could take it as asked. Mister Ambrose puffed into view on the landing, suitcases lengthening his arms, breathless and in apparent pain. Walter bounded up the stairs and unburdened him. Here, let me help, Walter said to Emery's fallen face. And was immediately away, even out through the screen, which he unhooked with the fore edge of a bag, stopping only at the steps to the front porch. A young man and woman were murmuring about their bill. Walter bet Bettie accepted only cash, which certainly suited Walter . . . to a T, he thought, drinking in the early fall sky, blue as new jeans. Bye bye, said Bettie, now on the scene and following the couple out. Where's your car, Walter asked. Next to the red wagon in back, the man replied. That was Walter's car. Walter shot away and put the bags down by their tailpipe. Many thanks, the man said when the couple arrived, having said their farewells and made their thank yous. Not to mention, Walter said, helping him load the trunk. Safe journey. Bye. Bye bye.

Walter was actually pleased that Bettie and Emery were nowhere to be seen when he returned to the house. He had dawdled. The path along the west side of the house was lined with cheeky yellow pansies: thirty-seven blooms. Among his forms, there were no receipts for thanks. Nor did he wish to put his present impulses on parade. Come to think of it, he had a few yellow tablets but their yellow was paler than beer, no match for the egg-yolk yellow of the pansies. Walter thought

Bettie must find it hard to live alongside such noisy ill health. It might have been the beginning of fall, but Walter had spring in his step, so if he was dawdling, he was dawdling at high speed. He also had to consider what he'd need for his trip to Mendota, a chastening thought. Most of his equipment was in the car: a few calculators, files in boxes, pads of forms, records and other books in the trunk. The drive would eat up hours. Walter drove carefully because his license had expired. At least he knew what to expect. He had cleaned up a mess or two for that Karmel Korn Kompany in years past. They weren't krooks, they were just klumsy, and were feeding too much popcorn to the birds. That kute KKK on their box didn't help either. He told them as much. Kan it, he said. We already do, and showed him a tin. All concerned had what used to be called a good laugh.

What would he need? damn near just his jacket. Which he'd put away like a gent. A porcelain orange studded with cloves hung from a string in the closet where a row of wooden hangers swayed and clicked like some Eastern musical instrument. A sachet a day keeps Bee Oh away, he hummed, glancing about his bedroom and its possessions with a fondness he knew was a little sappy, before closing the door quietly on his domain. It seemed a shame to leave them here alone, to lose a whole day . . . They will be here when you get back, his father always promised when he pulled him from his play to do chores. Bettie was beneath, stirring the stagnant parlor. Her long face sure had plenty of space for cheeks. And when he went away she waved out a window.

7

Mr. Vest was there to greet him again and to fumble with the hook. It was nearly seven and shadows followed Walter in.

His day had been long and arduously dull. Through every moment, he had yearned to be away from where he was, an enamel-topped table at the back of the Karmel Korn Kompany, more sugar than oxygen in an atmosphere jittery with poppety pop, a box like a trash can full of loose papers, and an absence of records so complete the Kompany might as well not exist. Later in the day, while he was putting the triple-K popcorn people back on the map, Walter made the comparison: these rosy-cheeked happy-haired young weirdos might as well have been selling lemonade from a card table on the corner. They bought corn and corn syrup and sugar and popped it and cooked it and colored it and put the poppings in plastic packages and then in pasteboard boxes and shipped some and sold some over the counter under names like Hawaiian Pineapple Surprise, hired an old man to sweep up at day's end, and paid kids about their age and education to answer the phone and collect money from customers, while managing to meet the rent each month; yet nobody knew how much of Cinnamon Sensation had been bought or sold or barely where and certainly not why; all they knew was they were still in business—hadn't run out of lemons or the strength to squeeze them—but of what their business had been and done or might do tomorrow, there was scarcely a hint, only the faintest trace like a puff of distant dust . . . dust of the sort Walter's red wagon made going fast on fineline back roads.

The loose Kash Kids, that's what he called them. You've got to make deposits. You've got to write checks. You've got to establish a line of credit. You've got to know what your costs are, what your volume is, the favored flavor, what's up. You've got to keep accounts: hire a bookkeeper, buy her a pencil, find her some silence to have thoughts in and a little sugarless air to breathe: let her straighten you out. And the moppets said fine, they would do that, good advice—just what the artless tykes had said the last time he'd bawled them out—then paid him in small bills like a tout at the track. His last words were: try not to get robbed. And don't sleep in the shop. They laughed.

Miles down the road, Walter sat in his car and consumed a steak sandwich, a shake, and french fries, with a swiftness which seemed to cancel the occasion, and wondered why had he scolded the Karmel Korn Kids? They were a perfect client. They'd laughed—all right, giggled—but their giggles were not on record.

Walter bet Bettie kept clean accounts. He bet she knew the date on every penny. Not that she was grasping or cheap. The room rate was more than reasonable, and her breakfasts were as sumptuous as her bed, scented with more sophistication than those guys their caramel corn. But she would sweep and scrub her figures the way she scrubbed and swept her house; not a spot of dirt was allowed to smirch, not a speck of dust permitted to mote, not a fly allowed to light, not in her house; and not a transaction, a purchase, or a profit, would be permitted to go astray and leave its inscription in her records to sneak errantly off. Every knickknack knew its place and had felt her rag. Table-tops shone with good health, pillows were plump, drapes were vacuumed on both sides. He felt certain that sachets lay in her handkerchief drawers; that small scented pillows were being flattened by mattresses in all her beds; that she kept tussie-mussies too, deep in her purse; and that flexible stalks of laven-der, plaited into dollies like his mother had once done corn, were tossed among her underthings like herbs in a salad.

How are you feeling, Walter said again, because he couldn't think of anything else to say, but wanted to show concern. Bet-ter in the evening when I can watch TV, Emery whistled. Though it's hard to find anything funny when you don't dare laugh. It hurts to laugh, Walter wondered. Life is nothing to make light of, Emery said, as if his sentiment had been memorized.

Walter understood that, and said so, but thought that maybe that's just what he'd been doing, for what did he own? what debts weighed down his pockets, what pets or family held him fast? ah . . . but on his conscience—or was it the fear of getting caught—there was a weight and a worry darker than an attic closet and heavier than a highboy. There's a TV in the parlor, Emery offered, if you'd like to catch a game show. Thank you, no, Walter found himself saying, at night I like to keep my windows closed.

And of course his door, though Walter remembered it didn't latch. He stood in the darkness for a moment realizing he could feel his room's presence, he could smell it faintly of course, but he knew his many things were there, as his father had said about his toys, waiting: the wooden soldier, the teddy bear, the paper horn. He only had to fumble for a moment turning on a lamp. Its glass shade burned pink and green and clear. Next to the desk a flat-headed brass floor lamp stood a little unsteadily, and Walter went to turn that on as well. Beside it was a painted metal wastebasket with a kind of Grecian frieze around its oval top. On the side of the desk near the air conditioner he had to admire a long-stemmed green plant which graced—yes, graced, that's how he felt—a wooden stand with a marble top. *Philodendron* was the only word he knew.

There were so many many things, yet they didn't seem to menace. That was because small lives lived their lives inside or on top of larger lives, nested and arranged themselves, their folds folded in like fans, as nature intended; because the dresser's bulk functioned the way an apartment did, since the families the building contained did not enlarge it any, make it invade the street or the park next door. However, his motel drawers and closets were empty, tabletops and windowsills were bare and simply shiny, beds were scarcely covered, walls unmirrored and neglected, floors a stretch of patternless carpet as arid as a desert. But inside that misplaced secretary there were all those books, each compressing hundreds of pages into something as simple as a brick, while upon those pages lines of words were layered the way beneath a quilt there was a blanket, beneath the blanket, an embroidered sheet; and the words were several sounds as leaves and blooms and maybe a boat upon a pond were threaded together, making better environments for one another; thus with the cabinet shut, book covers closed, you couldn't hear any talking going on, the shouting and the singing, yes, quiet as a reading room, though in each reading head there'd be a booming world: that was why his empire was so wide and full, both few and many, near and far.

The world was flooded with ruck. And these things had made their way here, sometimes, like the corded candles, even two by two, to Bettie's Bed and Breakfast, where they might be borne away in safety, surrounded by peace and solicitude. And one day, when the ruck has receded, they will march out of these rooms, this house, into the world again, to replenish it with properly realized things, and set an example for excellence to strive for, and history to enrich.

With some nervousness, Walter sat himself down at the desk. It had a pull-down writing surface and was made of oak. The desk was open and behind the lid were pigeonholes surmounted by a pair of pillars bearing a pediment decorated with hand-carved leaves and flowers. This section, which backed up behind and above the pigeonholes, held a mirror set directly in its center. There was another level above that where a further frieze of leaves and petals crowned the entire ensemble. He'd seen pictures of Italian hill towns less impressive. Walter felt he was to sleep tonight in an opulent garden, and he planned to revisit all its flowers, but only after exploring this desk, this plot and planting, which he had saved to enliven his evening.

A book lay on the lid like a Bible. Walter realized he hadn't seen a Bible. *The Collected Poetry of Robert Frost.* Everybody knew Robert Frost, and his great white head of hair. Or was that Carl Sandburg who had the great white head of hair? No dust to blow, not this time. The jacket—on which were pictured dark woods and shadowy water—bravely boasted that all eleven of Frost's books were snuggled under its covers—see, Walter said to himself, see—and he saw a stack of blurbs on the back by a lot of literary politicians. Walter leafed through lazily, his mind on how nice it was to have a room with a desk like this in it, with a book full of poems like this on it, serious and dark and heavy in the hand. Lots of words here. Lots of poems. "There Are Roughly Zones." Strange title. Zones? *We sit indoors,* Walt dared to read aloud, *and talk of the cold outside.* Well, it wasn't cold yet but it would be surely. *And every gust that gathers strength and heaves is a threat to the house.* That seemed a bit strong. Every one? *But the house has long been tried.* True. And the stairs don't even creak. Go up and down them—not a sound. A poem about a tree? *What comes over a man, is it soul or mind—that to no limits and bounds he can stay confined?* Odd word order, but poetry was poetry, odd as it got. Oh, the zones, Walter now saw, looking ahead, were climates. That's why the—peach—tree was in trouble. *That though there is no fixed line between right and wrong . . .* whoops . . . *wrong and right*—fooled me—*there are roughly zones whose laws must be obeyed.* Hum. Walter didn't finish, just held the book on its back for a moment. John F. Kennedy, he saw, had said something. Jeez . . . *a body of imperishable verse . . . we'll gain joy and understanding.* Well, that was poetry for you. Its whole point. To remind you to plant hardies.

Consulting the front flap before putting the book down, Walter saw a lot of writing on a flyleaf. *Sorrow overtakes the hour.* His glance fell to the conclusion. The poem was signed

B. Meyerhoff. Walter put the book carefully down on the desk—to steady it—and read:

> Sorrow overtakes the hour
>   And leaves me befit
>   of the power
>   To claim yet peace
>   While I cower
> Should sorrow have grace to soften sod
> With its ever-heavy rod
>   And bruise the heart
>   That so loved God?
> Yes—there is answer in the rain
> For lo, I shall come again
> And touch sorrow's cloak
>   "Be gone—O pain."

The matter of the poem did not appear to be entirely clear. Poor B. Meyerhoff nevertheless. Bettie, who else? *Befit . . . befit . . .* Walter didn't get *befit*. And *sad* didn't make sense where it was, though the poem was sad enough, so it had a right to be in it somewhere. Wait. Should sorrow have grace to soften sod! sod with its ever-heavy rod. But then the rain was going to do that. The heart wasn't buried, was it? Under the sod. Maybe . . . maybe *bereft*! that's it! He felt like he did when he got a cross-word puzzle definition. *Bereft of the power* was perfect. Walter thought, poor Bettie, what had gone wrong, what had happened to weaken this strong woman? One of Emery's punishments perhaps, another illness added on to all the others?

Walter was moved. He stood up. It eased his sudden anxiety. How long ago had the poem been written? He faced a mug which contained a shaving brush and said Williams Mug Shaving Soap. No poem there. At the other end of the desk's crown sat a kerosene lamp in a bowl around which was wrapped a lace skirt. His chest, which he realized lacked character (it looked weak in the sort of shirt he was wearing), appeared in the mirror. You could sit here and powder your nose. Or shave. In front of the mirror, on a ledge formed by the top of the pigeonholes below, leaned a stiff white card bordered with tiny flowers and tinier leaves. Walter loved the hidden messages the room provided. And the open, even welcoming, complexity of its many things. Attached to one side of the card was a piece of lace as from a sleeve, and a stuffed heart made of a black cloth which had blooms printed on it in blue. Very odd, but an unmenacing mystery. On the other side, at the top, was fastened a cluster of buttons like a bunch of acorns—nuts of some kind—from which dangled several very short strings of miniature pearls. Below these baubles was a handwritten message dated 1993:

> I've collected these bits and pieces with care. Just like friendships, some are old, some are new. Like friends, all are one of a kind and some are unique treasures. When you look at this, think of me.
>
> Charlyene DeWett   Pequa, Ohio

Walter tried to do as advised but found he could only say her name. No image magically materialized, as he had, for a moment, hoped. Next to the card, on another white doily with a pink string fringe—boy—upside down and open in a **V** like a Boy Scout tent, was propped a wedding booklet. On the cover, which was decorated with pale roses and paler leaves, were the words "Our Wedding Day" in silvered Gothic letters—oh boy. Walter held the booklet in his hand while walking about the bedroom in a kind of trance of possession. The desk was a wedding monument . . . that's what it was. It was a museum of memory. And maybe this was a bridal bed and maybe this space was the same space as the space of the First Night. The Vows. Yes. I will. I do.

·

Not Charlyene DeWett of Pequa, Ohio, surely. Something borrowed? something blue? the black blue-blossomed heart? Walter did a loop about the end of his bed and sat in the chair which was cornered there. Truly, his fingers trembled as he opened the booklet. He wasn't a Paul Pry. These things had been put here purposely to be inspected—admired and enjoyed. And he did admire and enjoy them. What guest, he bet, had ever appreciated these . . . these appointments as he had . . . as he was . . . and as he would? . . . no one, yes.

Inside were several prefatory pages of poems printed in Gothic again, though silver had been replaced with common black. One was authored by Anonymous and called "Wedding Bells." Another was by Paul Hamilton Hayne—"Our Wedding Day." There were a couple of short and sort of silly sayings by Sidney Lanier and Winthrop Praed. Then a bridal prayer by a person named Rankin. Following these sentiments was a page posing as a certificate to assure the world that on this day, which turned out to be the Eighth of October, Nineteen Hundred and Twenty-Five, he—the preacher—Guy Holmes of Camp Point, Illinois—had married Harry H. Meyers and Fae Arline Elliott in the bridegroom's home. Was this . . . was this that home? Had to be. Camp Point? Camp Point? little place, near Quincy, wasn't it? he'd only driven through.

Now—see, you see—Walter said to himself, Camp Point is a place I'll pay attention to. I won't just drive blindly by, no, I'll go slowly up and down the side streets, maybe have a cup of something in the local chuck. My, 1925. Back as far as the books had gone. Circumstances were fortuitous. Yes. That was the word. Listed on the certificate, beneath the parson's warrant, were the signatures of fifteen guests, ten with the name of Meyers. Missus Holmes was also present, no doubt to help out with the service as she so often had.

On the next page, the bridal gifts were noted in a hurried hand.

Aunt Mary—money and spoons
Mother—clock
Clarence & Lily—casserole
Virgil & Gladys—fruit picture
Ella—money & cow

Cow?

Willis & Hobart—money
May, Edna, Nona & Margaret—gas iron & rug

Gas iron? Wonderful . . . the names were . . . the bride's especially, Fae . . . Fae . . . Ar - line. Not Arlene. My.

Louise—pickle fork

Hah. An essential. Good old Louise.

Wilbur—alarm clock
Florence & Aunt Celena—silver set

A whole set! More likely a silver tray with silver cream and silver sugar, maybe some of those cute small spoons in a tasteful fan.

Aunt Stella—table cloth and napkins
Cousin Clella—hand painted salt and pepper set

Clella and Stella . . . could that be believed? Had he ever heard . . . well . . . no Fae either, in his experience, or a Nona. Still . . . Clella. Walter laughed. And what about that cow?

Uncle Tom and Aunt Lula—table cloth & towels
Aunt Julia—silver butter knife
Olive Spenser, Ruth & Lois—lace buffet set

More damn doilies. Of all the stuff about him, Walter had least affection for the doilies. They were too protective, too inhibiting, stood between things and their use. He mused. Holding the booklet open like a hymnal. Maybe it didn't mean more doilies, maybe it meant more napkins. He didn't really know what a buffet set would be.

Glenn Spenser—silver bread tray
Miss Leach—picture

Of what? Well, of course, Fae would remember and could drop its description.

Mina & Agnes—copper tray
Mrs. Hayer—serving tray

A few too many trays.

Winifred Priest—pillow cases
Mertis Sturtevant—table scarf

Mertis . . . man . . . another one. Made the mind imagine.

Gertrude Overholser—ditto

Table scarves were runners, weren't they? elongated doilies.

Wilbur & Lydia—hand painted plate

Were any of these things hereabouts, Walter wondered. Wouldn't that be wonderful. How could he tell? Perhaps those pillowcases there. Perhaps where his head had slumbered.

Uncle Charlie & Aunt Sophia—2 vegetable dishes
Uncle Charlie Elliott—bed spread

And perhaps that gift was this—the cover of his bed, still doing duty.

Maude—dresser scarf
Bertha—towel

Sort of a letdown—towel.

Walter was exhausted. He lay the book with great considera-tion in his lap and closed his eyes and entered a world of won-dering . . . wondering who these people were with their plain strange names, old country names, small-town names, and what the hand-painted plate looked like or what the pictures repre-sented; what the cow was, it couldn't be a real one, a china cow with a penny slot? and how everyone felt about the wedding and were they all from that town—Camp Point—a practical name, that was for sure—and who loved whom, who hated whom, and how it went with each of them; were they pretty, handsome, or old and bent and ailing, were Mina and Agnes sisters, unwed, awkward of movement, slow of talk; and then whose eyes strayed from calf to bosom, and whose fingers itched to have the loot themselves; which ones had lives that had fully fruited and which ones had withered leaves like Walter's had; oh, who knew whose secrets, all of it, all, who farmed, who fixed cars, who waited tables, who nursed aged parents; because the past was real, he knew—he knew it—and were these wedding guests gone now; had they become bone and tomb and stone and attic'd objects, gone into the past which filled this room? remaining as a little list of names, souvenirs of a night, so many years ago, when Harry had claimed Fae right here, maybe, in this very place where he . . .

Which he would have to leave tomorrow. He couldn't stay another day, could he? The booklet felt as heavy as Frost's verse. He could say he had more work in the region. But suppose he couldn't have this room; suppose he had to go to a room in the back, and someone slept here in his stead, some salesman with samples and slick hair asleep on his pillow, which Walter reached out to pat feebly, full of sorrow for himself; for the fact was, he slowly realized, he didn't want to go on another hour the way he was, the way he had been going on; he knew he would toss like an ill child all night and no longer enjoy his bed or chest or sofa and its laden coffee table or the messages sewn on pillows or the smell of the soaps; not if he knew he would have to leave and drive off down the road to—still—still, he had nothing scheduled tomorrow, no book to cook—and could he afford to stay in such a place?—not *such* a place—here, right here—could he afford to remain in this house—as reasonable as the rent was, when he often pulled behind a highway sign for cover and slept in his car, out of cash, and parked in parks like a hobo; so where would he go? so alone his pockets felt foreign, so alone his bones hurt from being bunched, and his throat was sore from talking to himself and to his sis and mom and to the figments of his hand.

Maybe he could strike a bargain. Walter opened one eye. They were still here: his things, his home, his history. He had new friends, how could he leave Uncle Charlie and Aunt Sophia, or May, Edna . . . Nona . . . or . . . or Cousin Clella, Miss Leach? . . . He bet the lace buffet set was still around. And Bertha's towel. A deal. He could offer to stay long-term, at a reduced rate, which Bettie would be happy for, since then there'd never be a vacancy, and always someone who could be counted on, quiet and regular, and helpful even here and there, bringing wood in or taking bags to the car or picking up a few things in town, someone who wouldn't mind being prayed over in the morning, who would look forward to it, who would fold his hands if it pleased her to see them folded, who'd believe, who'd cherish what she cherished, her family history would be half his, he'd ask after her husband's health, he'd listen to her stories, he'd relish her food—she'd like that—and the table . . .

and the table would be set for the morning light every morning, the wood shining up through the lace like a winter river through ice . . . ah . . . the pain was dreadful; he could offer to help survey the household accounts; it was dreadful; he could offer advice on improving efficiency; it was dreadful; with his one eye he saw a slice of kiwi gleaming like a green coin dug from a trove of treasure . . .

It would have to be. It would simply have to be. Walter stood up. He pretended to be vigorous and hardy. He would be . . . what? . . . well, worthy. Like a summer coat, he would put on an optimistic outlook. He would make his soul work out as though it was some fatty in the gym. He would make himself measure up. Hadn't he stood in a doorway as a kid to have a line marked on the jamb where his head reached? It was his last chance to be Walter Riffaterre. Steamy soaks in the tub would soften his hardest thoughts. And Bettie's wholesome big breakfasts would warm and thicken the cold thin wire he was. Think of a life lived alongside . . . no . . . lived *at* this desk, so full of marvels he hadn't yet catalogued them all. He had to make it happen. He'd be so sweet his teeth would melt. And the wedding guests— dear people—would line up to shake his hand: Maude and Virgil and Gladys, Mertis Sturtevant especially. Each would hand him a present: a silver butter knife, thank you kindly, an alarm clock, needed that, a picture whose frame was made of fruit, how original, a pickle fork, so thoughtful. It would be like being a groom. No more checkered shirts and dumb belts and tight pants. Money and spoons.

Walter put the booklet back where he had found it, open and tented. Next to it was a wedding crèche with tiny toy figures of a bride and groom—standing together of course—at the edge of a puddle of Everlastings in the middle of which was a small glass dome enclosing a captured cotton bird and two—wasn't it?—two twigs interwoven with a pink-and-blue ribbon. Of course. These were figures from the cake. How clever. Then pink and blue for babies. And there's a piece of stiff paper the size of a playing card propped against the glass. I see it. I am sitting here at my desk and I see it, I pick it up. "Blessings on you for not smoking here." Back of the ensemble is a yellow candle. There was—there is—there is certainly no concern for fire.

Yet who would blacken these wicks by lighting them? who would risk wax on the glass, the doilies, the polished wood below. Candle stumps are so spoiled, runny and irregular. They were here—pure, unlit and unharmed—so he could recollect light, its flicker, and remember romance.

Walter held his breath. Should he look now in the holes below? Or should he save that for another night? Would there be another night, any other night? Well, there wasn't much: a spare candle, a small Bible (here it was), an even smaller book on the language of flowers, a greeting card, a clear glass bowl of poh . . . that stuff . . . against which was propped a reproduction of a religious painting in a really dinky wooden frame (he'd study that later), then a sort of silver basket holding a pincushion impaled with pins, and finally a green glass pill jar, empty of everything but its air. Walter let the jar revolve in his eye. Admired for its shape? its color? its screw glass lid? why?

There was more. Indeed, he had the desktop to inspect, as well as the drawers underneath, and the cabinet which served as a nightstand, next to the bed. But he was totally tired. How long would the little cash he had concealed in his car last? He pulled his shirt off, let his pants drop. In the hopeful hereafter, he'd never let his pants puddle. Soon Walter was lying languidly across the coverlet. He was considering the feasibility of returning to the Karmel Korn Kompany and stealing the stash of cash the Karmel Korn Kids left lying about as carelessly as a pulled-off sock. Of course he couldn't. He was too tired. There wouldn't be much in any case. Even stretching the dough like a loaf, it wouldn't last. What he wanted, what he needed, was a miracle, a kind of sign. What he didn't need was to be one of the thieves. Bettie's Lord wouldn't in the least like it: a silly idea born of desperation and desire.

Walter slid between the sheets, sheets cool as a caress, and chewed a corner of his childhood pillow on his way to sleep.

8

Walter heard unfamiliar voices in the dining room. Bettie was serving other guests. He retreated to his bed, moving soundlessly up the solid stairs and sitting where he had smoothed the covers back. Nervous, anxious, disappointed, Walter stared at the short ladderback which served the desk, and at its woven seat. He had no proper plan. Certainly he'd be wise to pay for his two nights. It wouldn't do to run up a big bill, or make Bettie uneasy. Beyond that . . .

Walter wanted Bettie's Bed & Breakfast to prosper but he didn't want her to have any customers. He had no smile for the contradiction. Or for the creamy blotter covering the desk's writing surface. He heard Emery laboring on the landing and rushed out to rescue him from the baggage. The offer, the protest, the capture, the capitulation rapidly followed one another, and then Walter was rushing down the remaining stairs toward the porch, the outdoors, the trunk of an out-of-state car. He couldn't pass himself off as a handyman, could he? Who was it who was always happy to be of service? In some film. He put the bags between two strange cars and escaped into the garden, which he'd hardly looked at. The air felt as it should feel: early on an autumn morning. The light was lean. There were a few roses in wan bloom, the pansies of course, crysants, ah . . . cushion mums, yes—what was that? a weed? a hedge which looked like the original burning bush—and lots of plants which seemed simply to be waiting around much as he was.

After a few minutes on the garden's bench, he felt the cool damp concrete through his pants. He would have to wait out the concluding coffee, the obligatory brief exchange of small talk, the awkwardness of paying and checking out, a few flattering remarks would be flourished at that time, and then everyone would take their leave as if they were family or invited guests, and all this, he feared, would take a while; meanwhile his rump was growing cold, the patch was precise. He tried to take an interest in the plants, but they were so clearly in transit toward their last legs.

Walter ended up sidling around everybody in the entry, pretending not to be there like a draft, but disappointed he was ignored by the two men who were tossing hearty goodbys back and forth like a ball, and by Bettie as well, who had her hands clasped and every fold under control. Mister Ambrose was sitting on a step past the turn of the landing at the top of the stairs. Ah . . . not feeling well, Mister Ambrose, Walter asked, keeping his voice low. The screen banged at that moment, and he relished the little click of the hook going home. Phlegm in my nose and mechanism, Emery burbled, can't breathe. Oh dear, said Walter, getting behind him. You'll breathe better standing. He put his arms under Emery's and lifted. Emery unkinked slowly like a hose. Mother, he managed.

Bettie appeared on the stairs in a dark dress and wide white collar like a Pilgrim. Just go on down to breakfast, Mister Riffytear, I'll join you in a tick or two. Walter unhooked himself and came out from behind Emery, who suddenly seemed huge. Like the sun from behind a cloud, he unaccountably thought, feeling a sudden warmth. They passed on the stairway without further word. I'll steam a kettle for you, dear, she said, drop in a little Mentholatum. Hoof, went Emery. Yes, the screen was hooked, and a car was backing cautiously out the drive. A streak of soothing sun brightened the railing of the porch. The fall air was cool and clean. Walter filled his lungs, pleased it was easy as filling cups.

In the entry hall at the foot of the stairs, sitting on the radiator cover as if it had always been there, though its presence was a surprise to Walter's eyes, was a little wooden schoolhouse some amateurish hand had glued together. What brought Walter near to inspect it further was its weather vane. Sorely overscale, it topped the dormer where the school bell lurked, one rod ending in wooden N and S, another, naturally, in E and W, still a third tipped with arrow and feather. Perched above this was a jigsawed rooster as large as the school's door. The whole thing had been put together, it looked like, from a kit of precut parts. Bettie's arm, white as the sleeve of a nurse, reached past him to pick the little house up. Carefully, she wound the key sticking from its rear. The school's bell began to ping. Bettie returned the music box, as Walter now realized it was, to a place so familiar the shadow of its occupancy showed, a faint stain from the wood remaining on the radiator cover. The pingadings performed a delicate, somehow familiar, tune. Rooster, compass, arrow turned hesitant and wobbly turns. "Idlewise," Bettie finally said, after she'd let Walter listen for a puzzled and searching moment. What a strange combination of concepts, Walter thought. Austrian, she explained, as the pauses between pings and dings lengthened and the melody unwound like a twisted string. The last note arrived so long after all the others it seemed in despair at being left behind, bringing Walter close to heartbreak.

Some breakfast now, Mister Riffytear? . . . come along.

In a bit Bettie set a bowl of bananas and cream before him. Walter moaned gratefully. Haven't had this since— A little visit to childhood, Bettie said. But first— Walter nodded, folded his hands, lowered his head, his features solemn as her dark dress. Lord, I know you're listening because you always are, keeping kindly track of us down here where sometimes things are hard—and the kettle whistled in the kitchen. Get under the cloth now, Mister Ambrose, Bettie shouted, get your head the whole way under. I'll see how you're fixed after Mister Riffytear and I have talked to the Lord. Poor Mister Ambrose needs the help of the Holy Ghost to breathe on days like these, Bettie said to Walter rather grimly, before raising her voice to God again. As I said, some times are hard, here in the world where we must all work and sweat our brows to prosper at all. And I hope you'll take special care with our good guest here, who leaves us today, and goes out to work in harmony with your will, as I know he does.

Ah . . . about today, Walter began, but Bettie was not through asking for things. Lord, Mister Ambrose is very poor off today, which is not fair, because he already has so many former evils eating at him. He doesn't need his nose not to work, or his machine to fill up with snot. Walter flinched. This woman was someone to be feared. At least let the steam ease him. Amen. Thank you for letting Mister Ambrose into your blessing, Bettie said, motioning Walter to eat, although Walter couldn't determine where his permission might have figured. I made pancakes for those other gentlemen. Walter felt his head whirling as if it were a seed in the wind. About today— But Bettie was gone to see about Emery and whether his head was altogether under.

The pancakes came slathered in butter and syrup. The coffee was dark as a well and reflected his face as he leaned his nose into it. Walter remembered to cut one bite at a time out of his stack of cakes, instead of slicing everything up at once; and he ate almost without chewing, the sweet becoming mush, then melt, and sliding away down his throat as a liquid. He'd have to sit as still as a cushion until she returned. I've had a very pleasant stay, he'd say. And I mean to settle up today. But I'd like to delay my departure . . . ah, there's more work for me in the Quad Cities than I counted on, he'd say, but he mustn't claim that business was brisk, because Bettie might think he was flush then, and besides it wasn't true, he'd have to call his service and hope for the best, not something downstate, though, something mid which he might easily reach, if, that is, an arrangement could be made.

Mister Ambrose is eased, thanks to God, Bettie announced, his nose is breathing, so a cup more coffee while I rest my feet, Mister Riffytear? She sent a long sluice of it streaming from the spout, and sat herself and the pot down. Walter almost called her Bettie (don't do that!), she seemed suddenly so forlorn, sitting where one of the young gents had sat, the place empty of gent's plate and nap but surrounded still by butter, jam, and bread. Walter's arm reached across the table and fetched her a fresh cup and saucer from another setting. May I? Gently, he filled her cup. And nudged the sugar. Poor Emery, she said, stirring two sugars in. He led a loose life once, drank and smoked and talked a lot, but he's paid his debt in misery and disappointment, I should think, by now. He was always somewhat a good sort in spite of being sinful as they come. Helped out without my having to be cross. Didn't author any public disgraces. Bears up best he can. But it is hard to have to depend on so armless a man to lend a hand. She lifted the cup like a chalice. Delicately inhaled its odor. Gazed into the parlor in a meditative mood.

I'd like to stay a while longer, Walter blurted. Quite a while. You see, my work it seems is not yet finished here and I rather like . . . I like more than much, Missus Ambrose, my room here, and your breakfast, and I admire, I do, your many things, the history they have, the care that's gone into them, and the care you've given them, too—

The front room is the best, Bettie said, giving him a look he couldn't translate. I'm sure, Walter replied, worried. It's certainly splendid. The street is quiet most times. Oh, I've noticed. Can't see the river, some complain. Only barges anyway, Walter said sincerely. The wind doesn't winter up front, Bettie promised, but it can be beastly in the back bedroom, that northwest corner calls up quite a howl. In front, however, Walter attempted to agree, it behaves, I'm sure; however, I can't afford the full fee, not right now at any rate; however I'm convinced that in time business will pick up—not the wind, I don't mean—however now what I hoped was that maybe the longer stay—you see—would make possible a lesser price. Bettie sipped, keeping her lip inside her cup, warming her fingers and her face. And I could always lend a hand around the house, happy to. I'd be here when most needed in the morning and again in the late afternoon. Bettie lowered her cup but Walter saw her hand was shaking slightly, a tremble like a plant's leaf in a hidden draft. Her gaze had grown watery. Was she well?

In any case, Missus Ambrose, I'd be obliged if you'd recommend a house of worship to me, since of Sundays on the road I've missed devotions.

Well Mister Riffytear, that's a fine thought, since the season's slowing. And Mister could certainly use some help with the walk come snowtime. Let's just say a week for trial and if you still want, and we want, we'll do the Lord's bidding, and continue on as we've been doing, does that suit? It was fine, most fair, most considerate. Walter tried to keep his composure, spread calm across his face like he was painting a porch, but Bettie could see he was happy . . . happy . . . and he could see his happiness didn't displease her, though her small smile came and went like a bird past a window. Good for a man to find some fellowship too, a few friends, hear the Holy Word; it would be a proper show of substance if you'd think of coming to my and Mister Ambrose's church, not too far down the street, though not everybody, you understand, Mister Riffytear, is really there for God's good or that of their soul either. I must admit, too, our minister is young, a mite new, a bit green, and I detect a loss of strictness in his point of view; it's the times.

Walter was willing to agree about the times, the times were a terror; but he couldn't remove relief and pleasure from his voice. He heard himself beginning to babble so he said he must away; there was much to be done, he said, full day. He'd have to leave as if for work and stay well out of reach for a while to make it look like he was substantial and had some business. He could check out Davenport, the city was abustle, and Moline maybe. Returning to his room, he realized he felt a little like a modest book on maybe managing one's affairs which finds itself tucked between serious great tomes on history or the mysteries of the universe, grateful for the company, although a little overawed, spiritually somewhat squashed. This wasn't a crowd of gawkers, however, attracted to an accident, in which he found himself; it was a choir of voices, and the song was soothing and melodious, and its words spoke of peace and of peace's perfections. He— Walter Riffaterre—merely had to learn to behave, blend in, and sing along.

But today he'd have to grab the old belt by the horns and take some steps toward a better future. He'd comb the phone book, collect a few names and addresses, buy a Sunday suit, ring his service. Beneath the desktop was a drawer, which he hoped might contain a pad of writing paper. It was hard to see what was there with the desk down. Walter groped about. His hand found nothing, which was surprising—wait—a piece of soft cloth, which he drew out and held up. What in the world! Between his two hands he had a . . . a white satin swimsuit? . . . a bikini? was it what they called a thong? Skimpy as could be. But it was filmy. It was underwear.

Walter wadded the G-string in his fist as if to conceal it from himself, his face hot with shame and shock. This lascivious thing, he thought, in the matrimonial temple. And in this proper . . . this perfectly appointed, well-kept house. It would have surprised him less to see a mouse. The cloth was slick, satiny, tiny . . . so brief . . . it could scarcely cover a— Rough blunt words which came so quickly to his tongue when he was working in the world were unthinkable here, just as this piece of . . . clothing was. Angry at his discovery, Walter threw the G-string onto the bed. I'd like to gander you in that, he said, though he couldn't see Eleanor anywhere. Not a chance, Eleanor's voice replied; it's pretty, but you don't know who's been wearing it and having a high time, strutting and making out like this room was a runway.

The news that the world was ending would not have disturbed him half so much. In front of his face the figures of the bride and groom, fifty years from their cake, mocked his hopes. The tented book with its holy homilies, its sentiments of blessedness and joyful union, its list of celebrants, seemed nothing more than an embodied wink. Emery called Bettie mother. Mother, he always called, and she came. So she'd had a child or children sometime. So why was he surprised by that? Sorrow overtakes the hour. Perhaps she'd lost a little girl and that was the reason for her poem, and its ending: be gone—O pain. Begone, was how he felt.

But now his thoughts began to sort themselves out. He'd found it where it had been left, with all the other mementos, all the bridal things. No veil. Wait, that's what one of those doilies was, right there. And suppose some of the petals in the pohs were from roses that . . . of course. This then—he held the garment in his hands again, displayed it for himself—this was a part of the bride's wedding outfit. Brides didn't just wear ruffles and wide skirts. What was a wedding after all but the legalization of . . . of course. And so this would mean, when she wore it, that she was willing, waiting for her husband, wanting him to want her, but at the same time saying—for the thing was white as— Well, it wasn't quite . . . for at the bottom of its widest part, where it would wrap around the—he wasn't sure—was a lacy edging marked off and on with delicate rosettes and small white pearls. Wow. . . . at the same time saying I am a virgin. I am untouched, pure.

Panting but pure. He thrust the thought away. Lascivious yet innocent. He thrust the thought away. Beneath the cloth of God the thong of Satan? Walter found the joke hidden in his own words and laughed at himself. He had it figured, however. The husband was reassured: this part of me, his fair bride said to her husband, is no one's part but yours. Even this . . . Walter's eyes and mind took a loving inventory of the room: the front bedroom, where the wind wouldn't whistle; his bath, where towels were packed in wine baskets; his home, where candles were everywhere like spires of a holy town; where little messages were secreted among mingled scents, in lace-bottomed baskets, beneath loving fingerwork, and spoke through every detail, even in the deep corners of drawers, where some gesture shows up to say: the heart's been here and cared for even this little lost place; nothing has been neglected; nothing has been overlooked, nothing rejected. Even this, Walter said in amazement, his face in the satin. Ummm . . . this. This too.

EMMA ENTERS
A SENTENCE OF
ELIZABETH BISHOP'S

The slow fall of ash

Emma was afraid of Elizabeth Bishop. Emma imagined Elizabeth Bishop lying naked next to a naked Marianne Moore, the tips of their noses and their nipples touching; and Emma imagined that every feeling either poet had ever had in their spare and spirited lives was present there in the two nips, just where the nips kissed. Emma, herself, was ethereally thin, and had been admired for the translucency of her skin. You could see her bones like shadows of trees, shadows without leaves.

Perhaps she should have been afraid of Miss Moore instead of Miss Bishop, because Emma felt threatened by resemblance—mirrors, metaphors, clouds, twins—and Miss Moore was a tight-thighed old maid like herself; wore a halo of ropey hair and those low-cut patent leather shoes with the one black strap which Emma favored, as well as a hat as cockeyed as an English captain's, though not in the house, as was Emma's habit; and wrote similitudes which Emma much admired but could not in all conscience approve: that the mind's enchantment was like Gieseking playing Scarlatti . . . what a snob Miss Moore was; that the sounds of a swiftly strummed guitar were—

in effect—as if Palestrina had scored the three rows of seeds in a halved banana . . . an image as precious as a ceramic egg. Anyway, Gieseking was at his best playing a depedaled Mozart. Her ears weren't all wax, despite what her father'd said.

When you sat in the shadow of a window, and let your not-Miss-Moore's-mind move like a slow spoon through a second coffee, thoughts would float to view, carried by the current in the way Miss Bishop's river barges were, and they would sail by slowly too, so their cargoes could be inspected, as when father yelled "wax ear" at her, his mouth loud as a loud engine, revving to a roar. All you've done is grow tall, he'd say. Why didn't you grow breasts? You grew a nose, that long thin chisel chin. Why not a big pair of milkers?

Emma'd scratch her scalp until it bled and dandruff would settle in the sink or clot her comb; the scurf of cats caused asthma attacks; Elizabeth Bishop was short of breath most of the time; she cuddled cats and other people's children; she was so often suffocated by circumstance, since a kid, and so was soon on her back in bed; that's where likeness led, like the path into the woods where the witch lived.

Perhaps Emma was afraid of Elizabeth Bishop because she also bore Bishop as her old maid name. Emma Bishop—one half of her a fiction, she felt, the other half a poet. Neither half an adulteress, let alone a lover of women. She imagined Elizabeth Bishop's head being sick in Emma's kitchen sink. Poets ought not to puke. Or injure themselves by falling off curbs. It was something which should have been forbidden any friend of Marianne Moore. Lying there, Emma dreamed of being in a drunken stupe, of wetting her eraser, promising herself she'd be sick later, after conceiving one more lean line, writing it with the eraser drawn through a small spill of whiskey like the trail . . . the trail . . .

In dawn dew, she thought, wiping the line out with an

invented palm, for she knew nothing about the body of Elizabeth Bishop, except that she had been a small woman, round-
faced, wide-headed, later inclined to be a bit stout, certainly not
as thin as Emma—an Emma whose veins hid from the nurse's
needle. So it was no specific palm which smeared the thought
of the snail into indistinctness on the tabletop, and it was a
vague damp, too, which wet Miss Bishop's skin.

Emma was afraid of Elizabeth Bishop because Emma had
desperately desired to be a poet, but had been unable to make a
list, did not know how to cut cloth to match a pattern, or lay out
night things, clean her comb, where to plant the yet-to-be-
dismantled ash, deal with geese. She looked out her window,
saw a pigeon clinging to a tree limb, oddly, ill, unmoving, she.
the cloud

Certain signs, certain facts, certain sorts of ordering, maybe,
made her fearful, and such kinds were common in the poetry of
Elizabeth Bishop; consequently most of Elizabeth Bishop's
poems lay unseen, unsaid, in her volume of Bishop's collected
verse. Emma's eye swerved in front of the first rhyme she
reached, then hopped ahead, all nerves, fell from the page, fled.
the bird

So she really couldn't claim to have understood Elizabeth
Bishop, or to have read Elizabeth Bishop's poems properly, or
fathomed her friend Marianne Moore either, who believed she
was better than Bishop, Emma was sure, for that was the way
the world went, friend overshading friend as though one
woman's skin had been drawn across the other's winter trees. a
cloud

Yes, it was because the lines did seem like her own bones, not
lines of transit or lines of breathing, which was the way lines
were in fine poems normally, lines which led the nurse to try to
thump them, pink them to draw blood—no, the violet veins
were only bone; so when death announces itself to birds they, as

if, freeze on the branches where the wind whiffles their finer feathers, though they stay stiller there, stiffer than they will decay.

When, idly skimming (or so she would make her skimming seem), Emma's eye would light upon a phrase like "deep from raw throats," her skin would grow paler as if on a gray walk a light snow had sifted, whereupon the couplet would close on her stifled cry, stifled by a small fist she placed inside her in congruously wide, wide-open mouth. ". . . a senseless order floats . . ." Emma felt she was following each line's leafless example by clearing her skin of cloud so anyone might see the bird there on her bone like a bump, a swollen bruise. She was fearful for she felt the hawk's eye on her. She was fearful of the weasel 'tween her knees. fearful

Emma owned an Iowa house, empty and large and cool in the fall. Otherwise inhospitable. It had thin windows with wide views, a kitchen with counters of scrubbed wood, a woodshed built of now wan boards, a weakly sagging veranda, weedy yard. At the kitchen table, crossed with cracks and scarred by knives, Emma Bishop sat in the betraying light of a bare bulb, and saw both poets, breasted and breastless, touching the tips of their outstretched fingers together, whereas really the pigeon, like a feathered stone, died in her eye.

Emma was living off her body the way some folks were once said to live off the land, and there was little of her left. Elizabeth Bishop's rivers ran across Emma's country, lay like laminate, created her geography: cape, bay, lake, strait . . . snow in no hills

She would grow thin enough, she thought, to slip into a sentence of the poet's like a spring frock. She wondered whether, when large portions of your pleasure touch, you felt anything really regional, or was it all a rush of warmth to the head or somewhere else? When Marianne Moore's blue pencil canceled a word of Elizabeth Bishop's—a word of hers hers only because of where it was, words were no one's possession, words were the matter of the mind—was the mark a motherly rebuke or a motherly gesture of love? Thou shalt not use spit in a poem, my dear, or puke in a sink.

There'd been a tin one once, long ago replaced by a basin of shallow enamel. It looked as if you could lift it out like a tray. It was blackly pitted but not by the bodies of flies. A tear ran down one side, grainy with tap drip, dried and redried.

How had she arrived here, on a drift? to sit still as pigeon on a kitchen stool and stare the window while no thoughts came or went but one of Moore or two of Bishop and the hard buds of their breasts and what it must have meant to have been tongued by a genius.

She would grow thin enough to say "I am no longer fastened to this world; I do not partake of it; its furniture ignores me; I eat per day a bit of plainsong and spoon of common word; I do not, consequently, shit, or relieve my lungs much, and I weigh on others little more than shade on lawn, and on memory even less." She was, in fact, some several months past faint.

Consequently, on occasion, she would swoon as softly as a toppled roll of Christmas tissue, dressed in her green chemise, to wake later, after sunset, lighter than the dark, a tad chilly, unmarked, bones beyond brittle, not knowing where

or how she had arrived at her decision to lie down in a line of verse and be buried there; that is to say, be born again as a simple set of words, "the bubble in the spirit-level." So, said she to her remaining self, which words were they to be? grave behaving words, map signs

That became Miss Emma Bishop's project: to find another body for her bones, bones she could at first scarcely see, but which now were ridgy, forming W's, Y's, and Z's, their presence more than circumstantial, their presence more than letters lying overleaf.

She would be buried in a book. Mourners would peer past its open cover. A made-up lady wipes her dark tears on a tissue. Feel the pressure of her foot at the edge of the page? see her inhale her sorrow slowly as though smelling mint? she never looked better, someone will say. heaven sent

Denial was her duty, and she did it, her duty; she denied herself; she refused numbering, refused funds, refused greeting, refused hugs, rejected cards of printed feeling; fasted till the drapes diaphanated and furniture could no longer sit a spell; said, "I shall not draw my next breath." Glass held more heaviness than she had. Not the energy of steam, nor the wet of mist, but indeed like that cloud we float against our specs when we breathe to clean them. Yet she was all care, all

Because now, because she was free of phlegm, air, spit, tears, wax, sweat, snot, blood, chewed food, the least drool of excrement—the tip of the sugar spoon had been her last bite—her whole self saw, the skin saw, the thin gray yellow hair saw, even the deep teeth were tuned, her pores received, out came in, the light left bruises where it landed, the edge of the stool as she sat cut limb from thigh the way a wire passes the flesh of cheese, and pain passed through her too like a cry through a rented room. Because she had denied herself everything—life itself—life knew she was a friend, came near, brought all

Ask nothing. you shall receive

She was looking at the circular pull on the window's shade, her skin was drawn, her fingers felt for it, her nose knew, and it was that round hole the world used to trickle into her. With Emma down to her *E*, there was plenty of room, and then she, she would, she would slip into a sentence, her snoot full of substance, not just smell, not just of coffee she hadn't cupped in a coon's age, or fresh bread from back when, or a bit of peony from beside a broken walk, but how fingers felt when they pushed a needle through a hoop of cloth, or the roughness of unspread toast, between her toes a memory of being a kid, the summer's sunshine, hearty as a hug, flecks of red paper blown from a firecracker to petal a bush, the voices of boys, water running from a hose, laughter, taunts, fear they would show her something she didn't want to know

red rows the clapboard shells her reading eye slid swallowing solemnly as if she'd just been told of someone's love, not for her, no, for the sea nearby in Bishop's poems, a slow wash of words on a beach hissing like fat in the flame, brief flare-up before final smoke

Aunts trying hats on, paper plates in their laps—no—dog next door barking in his sleep, how about that? the flute, the knife, the shrivelled shoes I spell against my will with two *l*'s, how about that? her ear on the pull, the thread-wrapped ring, swell of sea along sunsetted shore, Maine chance, I'm now the longing that will fill that line when I lie down inside it, me, my eye, my nips, fingertips, yes, ribs and lips alined with Moore's, whose hats, maybe, were meant in the poem, the poem, the poem about the anandrous aunts, exemplary and slim, avernal eyed, shaded by brim, caring for their cares, protecting their skin. a cloud

Now I am the ex of ist I am the am I always should have been. Now I am this hiss this thin this brisk I'm rich in vital signs, in lists I in my time could not make, the life I missed because I was afraid, the hawk's eye, owl's too, weasel's greed, the banter of boys, bang, bleeding paper blown into a bush, now I urinate like them against the world's spray-canned designs and feel relief know pride puff up for their circle jerk fellowship and spit on spiders step on ants pull apart peel back brag grope, since it is easy for me now, like sailing boats, making pies, my hair hearing through the ring the rumble of coastal water, rock torn, far from any Iowa window, now I am an ab, a dis, pre's fix, hop's line.

Out there by the bare yard the woodshed stood in a saucer of sun where she once went to practice screaming her cries and the light like two cyclists passing on a narrow road, the light coming in through cracks between the shed's warped boards, the ax she wouldn't handle, its blade buried in an ash tree's stump the shed had been built around so the stump would still be of service though its tree had had to come down, dad said, it would have a life like an anvil or a butcher's block because as long as you had a use you were alive, birds flew at the first blow, consequently not to cry that the tree'd been cut, groaning when it fell its long fall, limbs of leaves brushing limbs of leaves as though driven by a wind, with plenty of twig crackle, too, like a sparky fire, the heavy trunk crashing through its own bones to groan against the ground, scattering nests of birds and squirrels, but now she was screamed out, thinned of that, or the thought of the noble the slow the patiently wrought, how the tree converted dirt into aspiration, the beautiful brought down, branches lofty now low and broken, the nests of birds and squirrels thrown as you'd throw a small cap, its dispelled shade like soil still, at toppled tiptop a worm's web resembling a scrap of cloud, it should have been allowed to die in the sky its standing death, she'd read whatever there is of love let it be obeyed, well, a fist of twigs and leaves and birdspit rolled away, the leaves of the tree shaking a bit yet, and the web

whisperating
what was left

A fat cloud, white as a pillow of steam, hung above the tree, motionless, as if drawn, as if all wind were gone, the earth still, entirely of stone, while the tree alone fell, after the last blow had been withdrawn, and the weeds which had tried and failed to be a lawn waited their bruise.

The house, like herself, was nowhere now. It was the reason why she fled facts when she came upon them, words like

"Worcester, Massachusetts," dates like "February, 1918." Em had decided not to seek her fate but to await it. Still, suppose a line like that came to claim her. It was a risk.

I have lost this, lost that, am I not an expert at it? I lost more than love. I lost even its glimpse. Treefall. Branchcrash. That's all. Gave. Gave. Gave away. Watched while they took the world asunder. Now even my all is smal. So I am ready. Not I hope the brown enormous odor . . . rather a calm cloud, up the beach a slowing run of water

wait

far from the flame,

They were women. They were poets. But Miss Bishop proba-bly knew a man or two, had him inner, while Miss Moore drew another pair of bloomers on. Hardly a match. Miss Bishop smoked, drank, wheezed, stood in the surf, barefooted about, fished. Miss Moore hunted for odd words. Exercised her fancy at the track. My father would stare at my bony body. Shake his head sadly. Nothing there to raise a dick. I'd be bare. Stand there. Bedsided. Scared. Oh yes mortified. Ashamed. All my blood in two lines below my eyes. Streaked with rose like twilit clouds. I'd stand. Before the great glass. It would be to see as he saw the then smooth skin, rose lit, cheek to lay a cheek against, smooth to smooth I suppose, or wipe a weeping eye.

They were women. They were poets. But Miss Bishop lusted after love. Miss Moore cooled like a pie on a sill. Hardly a match. Not my wish to be Elizabeth Bishop. Not for me, either, to be Miss Moore. Yet alike as a pod houses its peas.

Unfit for fooling around. Like those Emmas before me, I read of love in the light of a half-life, and the shadow of its absent half gives depth to the page. My made-up romances are proba-bly better, probably worse than reality. I am a fire at which my swain warms his hands. I am a fire quenched by a shower of scorn. Tenderness and longing alternate with cruelty and aversion. I study how to endure monsoons of driving snow.

Let's see how you're coming along. I'd have to slip out of my dress. Why are you wearing a bra? what's there to bra about. After he left I'd stand in the cold puddle of my clothes, step to the mirror to see for himself myself and my vaginal lips clasped like devout hands, praying to God to let me die before another day.

There was nothing to see, he said, so why did he inspect me as if I were going to receive a seal from the FDA? Elizabeth Bishop's father died of Bright's disease when she was still a child, and her mother went mad in Elizabeth's teens. My mother took her sturdy time dying. The day she died in her bed in this house, she had washed the windows of her room, though she could scarcely stand, and fluttered the curtains with arms weak with disease. Bustling about like a bee but without a buzz. Keeping out of reach, I now know. Wiping mirrors free from any image. Staying away by pretending to care and tend and tidy and clean and sweep and mend and scour and polish. Married to a gangplank of a guy. She scarcely spoke to me. I think she was ashamed of the way she let him make me live.

I learned to read on the sly. I failed my grades, though in this dinky town you were advanced so your puberty would not contaminate the kiddies. Despite the fact that I hadn't any puberty, my father said. But I read on the sly the way some kids smoked or stroked one another through their clothes. I read in fear of interruption. So I learned to read fast. I also read mostly first verses, first chapters, and careened through the rest, since my ear, when it turned to catch a distant tread, swung my eyes away with my brow toward the sound.

The ash came down but I never believed why. The shed was built around the stump to become an altar where my father chopped firewood or severed chickens from their heads. Slowly the stump was crisscrossed with cuts, darkened by layers of absorbed blood, and covered with milling crowds of tiny tiny ants. Traditionally, kids went to the woodshed for a whaling. Although once upon a time I stood still as a stick by the edge of my tot-wide bed, I now went to the shed to get undressed under my father's disappointed eye. Staring at hairs. And had he said something lewd, had he laid a hand, had he bent to breathe upon my chest, had his dick distended his pants, his point would have been disproved. I'd have elicited some interest.

He watched me grow like a gardener follows the fortunes of his plants, and what he wanted was normalcy. I dimly remember, when a child, how my father would hold me in his lap and examine my teeth. Something coming in there. He would push his finger down upon the spot. This tooth is loose, he'd say, with some semblance of pleasure, wiggling it painfully back and forth. Well, he was a farmer. And I was crop. Why not?

Getting a man was the great thing. My mother had got a man and what had that got her? Knocked up. With me. That's what. Maybe my father hoped he'd see, when I stripped, a penis lifting its shy self from the slot between my legs. Flat as I was, he may have thought there was a chance. There was no chance either way.

I might have been a boy in his balls but I was dismantled in her womb.

a residue of rain

Emma Bishop let the light on the table tell her about the weather. Sadness was the subject. Disappointment. Regret. The recipe? a bit of emptiness like that of winter fields when the fierce wind washes them; acceptance, yes, some of that, the handshake of a stranger; resignation, for what can the field do about the wind but freeze? what can the hand do but grasp the offered other? and a soupçon of apprehension, like clods of earth huddled against the frost they know will knock someday, or an envelope's vexation about the letter it will enclose; then a weariness of the slow and gentle variety, a touch of ennui, an appreciation of repetition. This sadness had the quality of a bouquet garni discreetly added to the sauce; it offered a whiff of melancholy, subtle, just enough to make the petals of plants curl at their tips. A day of drizzle in the depths of November. Not definite enough yet? All right: the quiet hour after . . . the nearly negligible remains . . . an almost echo.

The theme: leave-taking. Bidding adieu to a familiar misery. So . . . long . . . . . . The house was empty. The light was late, pale, even wan. The table lay in the light as though dampened by a rag. Emma Bishop saw her fingers fold up like a fan. Her life-like light. So . . . long . . . . . . Nothing stays the ancients said but the cloud stood above the treetop while it toppled, still as painted, her father murdering her tree's long limbs before they had loosened their leaves. Why then should anything be loved if it was going to be so brutally taken away? He had seen the tree *be* in Emma Bishop's bright eyes. Beneath it, weeds where she rested and read. When she no longer had to hide her occupation.

It had been of some interest to Emma that her father had ceased his inspection of her bared body after her mother died. As if . . . As if it had been to distress her mother he undressed her, had walked around her like a car he might buy, had a list of factors to check for flight safety, to justify his then saying: see what you've given me, what you've grown, you are a patch of arid earth, your child is spindly, awkward, chestless, wedge-chinned and large-eyed, stooped too, not as though gangly but as though old.

She had been a ten-month kid, she'd been told. Maybe during that tenth month her weenie had withered.

Over time Emma began to perceive her parental world for what it was. Her father farmed by tearing at the earth, seeding soy with steel sticks, interested in neither the soil nor the beans, but only in what the beans would bring; interested in the sky for the same reason, in the wind, in rain. The creek overflowed once and flooded a meadow. He saw only a flooded field. He didn't see a sheet of bright light lying like a banner over the ploughed ground. And the light darkened where the lumps neared the surface. Emma watched the wind roughen the water so that sometimes the top of a clod would emerge like new land. Crusoe in England? in Iowa. She imagined.

And her mother scrubbed their clothes to remove the dirt, not to restore the garments; and wiped up dust to displace it, not to release the reflection in the mirror or the view through the glass or the gleam from the wood. She pinned wash to its line as if she were handcuffing a criminal. Emma saw dislike run down her arms like sweat and transform the task. She didn't say to the pan, "Let me free you from this grease." She said to the grease, "Get thee away, you snot of Satan."

Emma ultimately preferred her furniture tongued and grooved, glued rather than nailed, for the nail had not only fixed Christ's hands to the Cross, it had driven Eve into labor and a life of grief. Her mother wouldn't cry over spilled milk, but she would silently curse, her lips retreating from a taste. Emma learned to see the spatter as a demonstration of the laws of nature and as a whimsical arrangement of pale gray-blue splotches. When she read that infants sometimes played with their stools, she knew why.

Maybe her father stopped inspecting her when he saw her watching, simply watching him; when his naked face and naked gaze were gazed at, gazed at like urine in the pot, yellow and pearly; when his hard remarks were heard like chamber music.

He wore boots on account of the manure, he said, though they hadn't had horses or any other sort of animal in Emma's time. Except the chickens. The rooster's crude proud cry rose from the roof of the coop and from the peak of Bishop's poem. Perhaps it had a line that would do. He'd pull the boots off and leave them on the back porch, where Emma would find his handprints on their dusty sides. The handprints, thought Emma, were nice. There were prehistoric handprints placed in caves. Her father's boots were four hands high. Maybe five.

As a young girl, Emma had run around barefoot until she began to loathe any part of her that was uncovered, her face and hands first, her feet finally; and she realized her toughened undersoles had little to no sensation. Now her feet were both bony and tender and could feel the floor tremble when the train passed, three fields and one small woods away.

She herself was a residue, her life light as the light in her inherited house. Emma's mother had died in the bed she had no doubt grown to loathe, a bed full of him every night until her illness drove him out, lying there in a knot, staring up through the dark at death—who would not want it to come quick? Emma wondered whether her mother had ever had a moment of . . . exultation. Little cruelties cut her down. The rubadubdub of every day's labor, always going on as long as there was light. Same old cheap china on the table. The same old dust seeping in to shadow the mirrors and coat the sills. The same old rhubarb brought from the patch, the stored carrots and apples and sprouting potatoes. The same unrelenting sun in the summer. Then deep cold and blowing snow. The three of them in different corners of the house. Emma would sit on the floor of her room, reading, her back against a faintly warm radiator, afghan over her knees, squinting at the page through inadequate glasses. She would occasionally hear her mother sweeping or washing, or the rhythmic treadling of her sewing machine. Her father would be busy with his figures, rearranging, recalculating, hoping to improve the columns' bleak assessments, since outgo regularly threatened to overtake income. But they sewed their own sacklike dresses; they ate their cold stored root crops; they killed and plucked and cooked their own chickens, though Emma didn't eat dinner those nights, not since she'd fainted in front of a fistful of freshly withdrawn innards; they scavenged pieces of firewood out of their neighbor's woods; they picked berries and crabapples and dandelion greens, and jarred elderberry and made apple jelly and canned beans and tomatoes, and even fed the chickens homegrown corn: so what did this outgo come to? Not much, her father allowed. But they were eating from their kitchen garden like squirrels and rabbits, out of the nut-and-berried woods like the deer. The soybeans weren't fertilized and they couldn't afford those newfangled chemicals. The only machine still working was her dad's arms and legs and cursing mouth.

on morning grass,

I've died too late into your life, her mother said to Emma, who was rocking slowly in the rocker by her bed. Emma wondered what she meant, it sounded like a summing up; but she knew an explanation wouldn't be agreeable to hear so she didn't ask for one; she didn't want to wonder either, but she was haunted by what seemed a sentence of some sort, and kept on wondering. Her rocking was not a rocking really. It was a little nervous jiggle transmitted to the chair. Emma would never have a husband to stare at her body, she had her father for that; she'd never have to do for anybody, never have to sew buttons on a shirt or open her thighs or get him off in time to church. But her life would be like her mother's just the same. They'd endure until they died. That would be it. Over the world, as far as she could see, that was it.

The dying had enormous power. Emma wondered whether her mother knew it. Everything the dying said was said "deathbed." Everything the dying said was an accusation, a summation, a distillation, a confession. "I died too late into your life." Which was it? confession, distillation, delusion, summation, provocation?

Her mother tried to get God to take her part against her disease, but churchgoing did no good; prayers went as unanswered as most mail; the days came and went and weren't appreciated. She couldn't keep anything in her stomach. She was in the bathroom longer than she was in bed. "Maybe I should be like Emma and not eat," she said. Was it a gift, to have been given a life like that? Close to no one. Never to see delight rise in another's eyes when they saw you. Dear Heavenly Father, let me suffer a little while longer. Let me linger in this vale of tears and torment. I have potatoes to fork and rinse, windows to wipe, dishes to do, rips to mend.

Her father fell over in a field. Nose down in the dirt. A dog found him.

At his funeral somebody said well, he died with his boots on, and some mourners appeared confounded by the remark, some looked puzzled, and some smiled as much as was seemly, but none of the mourners mourned.

The world was a mist and black figures slowly emerged from the mist as they had in one of the few movies she'd seen, when the townsfolk were burying a family who'd been murdered by the Indians. It was a moist gray day and most people wore a dark coat against the chill. Emma in her horror held herself and stood far away from the hole so she wouldn't see them lower the man who'd brought her into the world and made her ashamed to be seen and hacked her ash to bits and cut the heads off chickens and left her a few acres of unkempt land and a dilapidated house. There was a hole in her memory now almost exactly his shape.

Emma sat on the front porch and greeted darkly dressed unaproned women while the men stood about the yard in awkward clumps waiting the decent interval. A few wives had brought casseroles of some kind. Emma never lifted the lids until she realized they'd expect their dishes to be returned. Then she dumped the spoiled contents in the meadow—smelling of mayonnaise and tuna—and wiped the bowls with grass. Forgot about them again. Only to come upon the little collection on a walk a week later. Now she couldn't remember to whom the bowls belonged. Emma huddled the crockery in a plastic sack and tottered the mile and a half she had to totter to reach the house of a neighbor she knew had brought something, and left the sack on the front steps. They had been trying to be helpful, she supposed, but what a trouble people were.

During the evening the air grew damper. Moonlight and mist, as Bishop wrote, were caught in the thickety woods like lamb's wool on pasture bushes. Except there was very little moonlight. It was the headlamp of the late train which allowed her to see the fog like gray hair in a comb, but only for a moment before all were gone: woods, fog, trainbeam, lamb's wool, gray hair, comb.

She sat in the same chair she'd sat in to greet grieving company, sat through an evening in which only the sky cared to snivel, and sat on after they'd left into the deep night's drizzle, hoping to catch her death; but in the morning when the sun finally got through the fog to find her sitting in the same chair, as fixed as the leaves and flowers burned into the slats of its back, it flooded her cold wet lonely frightened immobile face impersonally, as though she were a bit of broken statue, and moved on to the pillars of the porch, knurled a bit to be fancy but picked out of a pattern book to be cheap, and then found a grimy windowpane to stain as if the grayed flush of dawn were drawn there. The sun made her open eyes close.

snow in still air,

The art of losing isn't hard to master. Emma remembered with gratitude that lesson. But she took it a step further. She lost the sense of loss. She learned to ask nothing of the world. She learned to long for nothing. She didn't require her knives to be sharp. Her knives weren't her knives anyway. She gave up property. She didn't demand dawn. When the snow came she didn't sigh at the thought of shoveling. There was no need for shoveling. Let the snow seal her inside. She'd take her totter about the house instead of the narrow path around the woods. She moved as a draft might from room to room. She ascended and descended the stairs as silently as a smell. Not to keep in trim. Not as if bored, caged, desperate. To visit things and bring them her silent regard.

Emma made her rounds among the mantises. Tending the garden in her teenage days when she'd been put in charge of it, she would find a mantis at its deadly devotions. And she discovered that the mantis rarely ventured far from its holy place. *Mantis religiosa.* It slowly turned the color of its circumstances. There was one on the roof of the shed the shade of a shingle. Another among the squash as green as most weeds. Motionless, she watched the mantis watching, and now Emma understood the difference between its immobility and hers. The mantis was looking for a victim, her father was making his assessments, her mother was doing her chores, while Emma was watching . . . why? . . . she was letting the world in; and that could be done, she learned, anywhere, at any time, from any position, any opening—the circle of the shade's pull. She ate her fill of the full world.

No wider than a toothpick, a mantis would rest on a leaf so lightly it never stirred from the weight of the insect. The mantis rose and fell as the leaf did, a bit of leaf itself, its eye on the shiny line a little spider was lowering. Emma Bishop rose and fell as well, soft as a shadow shifting across the floor, weightless as a gaze, but as wide as a rug, as good underfoot, as trustworthy in the pot as tea.

Large snowflakes slid slowly out of a gray sky. A lot like a winged seed, they wavered as they came and lit on grass or late leaves still whole and white as doilies. They fell on her hair, clung to an eyelash, melted upon Emma's extended tongue so a thrill shivered through her and she blushed. She also tottered out in the rain when the rain was warm and fell in fat drops. Her cheeks would run and ears drip. And her hair would very slowly fill with wet, and whiten gradually the way her hair had grayed, till it became a bonnet, not her hair at all. Her outheld hands cooled until, like butterflies did a few times, the crystals lay peacefully on her palms.

Her father found out that, though Emma tended the garden, she didn't pull weeds or kill bugs. So he removed her from that duty and made her hold the guts he pulled from plucked chickens.

Elizabeth Bishop was a tougher type. She caught fish, for instance, and held their burdened-down bodies out at arm's length to study the white sea lice which infested them. She lived near water in Nova Scotia and the Keys and hung around fishhouses to note the glistening condition of the fish tubs, coated with herring scales, and the tiny iridescent flies that hover over them. Her father's slimed-on arm slid out of the cavity, his fist full of the chicken's life. He didn't look at Emma. He said: here, hold this. Could she now have enjoyed the mucous and the membranes, the chocolate and the rufous red of the liver and the . . . the white patches of fat like small snow on brick. The word was *gizzzzzzzzardzzzs.*

Maybe not. But who had really reached sainthood in this life, and was willing to look on all things with equanimity?

Her totter took her along a lane where she'd dumped the funeral food, and there she found the cookware in an untidy pile like stones. "There's stillstuffstuck on the sides of the Corning Ware. I don't care. Leave it there." The grass grows high at the side of the meadow. Already it's popping up between them. Let them lie. The life I missed because I was afraid. That's where we buried him. A dark day. Twilit from dawn to twilight, then at twilight it was night. These dishes remain to be done. His remains, his fists, are encased in a cheap box six feet in the earth, crabgrass over dirt, fog over grass, night sky over fog, blackest space. I'll take one home this time to soak in the sink. Where my thought of the poet had her sick. I alone know how glorious grime is. Go it alone. God. Go it alone.

I vowed I'd get good at it. Going alonely. Holding the bowl, with blades of grass fastened to its sides where I'd wiped it weeks past, I promised myself a betterment. They were both gone. I was free of ma's forlorn face, dad's rage. The house was mine, I reminded myself. And so it could stand nearly free of me. Stand and be. Recognized. Because I relinquished whatever had been mine. My thoughts I let go like lovebirds caged. One dish a day. I'll return them like pills. There was a nest-shaped dent in the grass where the bowl had lain. What an amazing thing! that such a shape should be at the side of a path between meadow and wood—the basin of a heatproof bowl like a footstep from the funeral.

Emma remembered, in the middle of that moment, while she was making a solemn promise to herself to do better, be better, become none, no one, of the spring day she'd run into the woods to find bluebells and found instead the dogwood in bloom at the edge of a glade, each petal burned as if by a cigarette exactly as her poet, only that day discovered, had written in a poem, only that day read, in lines only that far reached and realized, before Emma's eye rose like a frightened fly from the dinner cloth.

So when the bowls were relatively rinsed she stacked them in a string sack, all six, with lids, so she tilted more than normally when she walked so many fields so many meadows to the nearest neighbor, and with a sigh and a sore arm set the sack down on the porch just so, so they'd find them soon enough, some wife and mother named not Nellie no Agatha, was that so? who would no doubt wash them all again and find good homes for them as if they were orphan kids. A tale they'd tell too to the ladies who had lent the dishes to Emma, foisted their food, their indifferent good will, their efforts of affection upon her. Yes, the ladies would laugh at least grin at the way they'd been returned, lumped in one sack like spuds, their pots, after so many weeks of wondering what . . . what was going on . . . and would . . . would they ever get them back.

The snow sidled out of a gray sky, and fell like ash, that slowly, that lightly, and lay on the cold grass, the limbs of trees, while the woods went hush and her quiet place grew quieter, as peaceful as dust; and soon everything was changed, black trunks became blacker, a dump of leaves disappeared, the roof of the shed was afloat in the air, the pump stuck up out of nowhere and its faint-handled shadow seemed the only thing the snow couldn't cover.

wounds we have had,

Emma Bishop had not been born on the farm but in a nearby town where five thousand people found themselves eating and sleeping and working, meeting and greeting, cooking and cleaning, going up and down, and selling and signing, licensing and opining, because it was the county seat. The farm was in the family. It belonged to Emma's great-aunt, Winnie, but when she died the farm, already run-down, fell further, and into her father's stubby unskilled mechanic's hands. Her father, when her mother met him, repaired tractors. Beneath the nail, his nails were black with green grease. Lo and behold, beyond Emma Bishop's richest imagining, her parents met, married, coupled, whereupon her mother bore, and brought a baby naked into the world, the way, it would later appear, Emma's father wanted her. Because the baby was inspected for flaws. No one found any.

Emma's mother was short slender wan, while her father was broad and flat across the front, knotty too, a pine board kind of person. Emma, contrary to the core, was thin as a scarf and twice as tall, angular to contradict her father's bunchiness, given to swaying even when standing still, swaying like a tall stalk of corn in a field full of wind. It made her difficult to talk to, to follow her face, especially if you had to look up a little as her parents both did. Emma didn't have Marianne Moore's recessive features. Hers resembled Edith Sitwell's in being craggy.

Nevertheless Marianne Moore saw into things, saw seeds in fruit, and saw how a tendril born of grape would wind itself like hair around a finger, cling to anything; or she would wonder what sort of sap went through the cherry stem to make the cherry red. Emma Bishop practiced by watching a worm walking, how it drew its hind end up into its middle, and then accordioned forward from the front. A rubber band could not do better. Leaving a small moist trail soon a light dry line lost on the limestone.

Her tree, where Emma went to read, was a tree of seed. It

bore them in clumps, in clusters, in clouds. They were tapered like boat paddles. Her tree was very late to leaf, and every year her father would declare the ash had died, and indeed it was nothing but a flourish of sticks until, at last, fresh shoots appeared and the squirrels crept out on its branches to eat the tender stemtips. The ground around her tree would be littered with their leavings. While still small and green, seeds would begin to fall, and her father would say the ash was sick, because the seeds were so immature; but there were crowds, mobs of them left, dangling from every new twig like hands full of fingers. Moore called apple seeds the fruit within the fruit, but here the ash seeds hung in the air without the lure or protection of peel or pulp, just a thin tough husk which turned the color of straw and flew from the tree in the fall like shoutfuls of startled locusts.

The ash sucked all the water from the ground and shaded a wide round circle too where nothing much grew, a few baby ash of course, a weed or two, plantain principally, pushing up from the claygray earth to stand defiantly green between the roots. Its trunk was deeply furrowed, the bark itself barky, as if rain had eroded it. "This is the tree Satan's snake spoke from," Emma's father would say, his tone as certain as gospel. "It is the dirtiest tree on God's earth." The risen emblem of a fallen world.

The seeds would settle first, whirling up from the dry ground at a breath, stirred as the air stirred, and encircling the trunk with pods which curved gracefully from an oval head back to a needle-sized point, to lie in warm ochre layers like the tiniest of leaves. Her father cursed the tree as if it were littering a street against the law.

And quite a lot of little branches would break off and break a bit more when they hit the ground, causing her father still more annoyance, because the dead branches of this ash were dead in a thorough and severe way, dried as they were by the sky. Finally the five-leaflet leaves would begin to fall, the tree's seeds would come down in bunches, and everyone then knew autumn was over and that the sun always withdrew through the now bare branches, and so did the moon.

Her father said it was a moose maple and not an ash at all. Its wood is spongy, but brittle as briars. Emma protested. It was a green ash. She had made the identification. There was no moose maple in the book. That's what we call it hereabouts—a box elder, big weed, dirtiest tree. A true ash don't fall apart like that.

Despite her father's annoyance, Emma would sit upon a smooth bare root, her back against the trunk, surrounded by seeds and leaves, twigs and weeds, and read poetry books. If she'd been a boy, he might have beaten her. She could feel his eye on her, hard as a bird's. She weathered his rage as the tree weathered the wind. Then one day a branch, broken in a previous storm but caught by other branches, slipped out of their grasp and fell like a spear, stabbing her ankle with such a suddenness she screamed, feeling snake-bit. She saw blood ooze from the wound in astonishment, the stick lying near, stiff and dry, sharp where it had snapped. Emma bawled, not from pain or even shock, but because she'd been betrayed.

dust on the sill there,

Marianne Moore liked to use words like *apteryx* in her poems. Very mannered, her style. Edith Sitwell liked to too. Emma would suddenly say "One fantee wave is grave and tall . . ." and suddenly sing "The hot muscatelle siesta time fell . . ." Her mother would hear her with astonishment, for Emma very rarely laughed let alone sang. Even in church she just mouthed.

Now that she hadn't had to poison her mother or strike her father down in the field with the blade of a shovel, but was so alone even the chickens unfed had wandered off, she could have sung without surprising anyone, or sworn without shocking her father with unladylike language. She did sing sometimes inside herself. "In the cold cold parlor my mother laid out Arthur . . ." She didn't remember any more of that brutally beautiful poem. Words drifted into her eyes. When she was reading, it was always summer under the ash, and words fell softly through her pupils like ash soot pollen dust settling ever so slowly over hours over summer days a season even an entire lifetime that their accumulation was another cover. Solace for the skin.

She bore books out to the tree and made a pile. Her father glared. Why so many? Stick with one. One is plenty. But Emma couldn't stick to one. She'd begin "When night came, sounding like the growth of trees . . ." or "In the cold cold parlor . . ." and she'd feel herself becoming tense, was it her legs folding as if up into her bottom like the worm, and her arms canting outward like the mantis that worried her? Emma had these flyaway eyes, and after a bit she'd skip to another page, or have to drop one book in order to pick up another. Edith would take Emma aback with beauty "sounding like the growth of trees." Emma'd have to stop, to repeat, to savor, to—in her head—praise, to wonder at the wonder of it, why was that Nova Scotia wake so devastating? not simply because it was being seen by a kid. "His breast was deep and white, cold and caressable." The way the boxed boy and the stuffed duck went into one another: that was making love the way she imagined it would be if it were properly done. Everyone was entered. No one was under.

A poem like the Nova Scotia poem—brief as it was—would sometimes take her weeks to read, or, rather, weeks to register all its words, and never in their printed order. That ordering would come later. One day, finally, she'd straighten the lines and march them as printed across her gaze. She could not say to her father when he glared at her, angry she knew because the books, the tree, her intense posture, the searing summer sky, were each an accusation, a reminder of another failure, that the words she read and fled from were all that kept her alive. "The mind is an enchanted thing like the glaze on a katydid-wing . . ." Words redeemed the world. Imagine! Like the glaze on a katydid-wing, sub . . . subdivided . . . sub . . . by the sun until the nettings were legion . . . the nettings were legion . . . Her father really should have kept the grease beneath his nails and never replaced it with plant smutch and field dirt. His world was mechanical, not organic. It was cause followed by effect, not higgledy followed by piggledy and the poke.

Her father's figure would appear to her, dark and distant, wading through beans. Emma tried to unresent her mother's failures too. Why hadn't her mother protested her father's cruel scrutinies? Even the browbeatings her mother received she endured in silence, though with drooping head. Why had Emma herself stood so still in his stare, less naked later with pubic hair? Skimpy. No fur there. She could have refused. Fled. Cried. She stood in the shed and screamed. She shrieked. She shrilled. But they were in the ground less likely than seeds to volunteer, to rebreed, pop up in a pot or rise from beneath bed-clothes sheeted and disheveled, hearing her scream. That's all she did in the shed. And she went there less and less, needed that silly release less and less. She was even proud she could be so loud, slight and without a chest, weak and out of touch with speech.

Edith Sitwell had a lilt. She went ding dong. Did her verses breathe, Emily Dickinson wanted to know. "Safe in their alabaster chambers . . ." Hoo. "Untouched by morning . . ." Emma was untouched. No man had ever laid a hand. Hardly her own, but once, curious, experimentally, secretive, ashamed, she felt herself as she supposed men did, and then withdrew in disbelief. To never again. "The meek members of the resurrection . . ." Emma stood in the center of herself and slowly turned her attention. There were windows, sills, shades, beyond the windows a world, fields, the silhouettes of firs and oaks, a dark quick bird, and then a wall a corner crack and peel of plaster pattern of leaf and stem and flower, too, counter of hardwood, wooden cabinets, one door ajar, dark as eyebrow, at the glass knob stop the little light left was captured there and the glass knob gleamed and its faint faint shadow, made light now not light's interruption, touched the soiled unpainted pine.

Mom and dad she never had await their resurrection, according to Emily. Grand go the years . . . ages . . . eons . . . empires . . . but only the words will arise, will outwear every weakness. Emma knew. That was why she waited for a line. Not an alabaster chamber or a boy's box—Arthur's coffin was a little frosted cake—but *Arthur's coffin.*

That was what the soul was, like the floor of a forest, foot of great tree, earth on which seeds leaves twiglets fell and lay a season for another season, all the eyelighted earheard words piled up there year after year from the first *no* to final *never.*

Her mother died of the chronics, her father of a fell swoop. Emma would become a certain set of words, wed, you might say, finally, and her flat chest with their warty nips placed next to Bishop's where Moore's had been. Her mother's face was closed as a nut, but you might say the same of Emma's too, who learned, as her mother doubtless had, to conceal her feelings for so long she forgot she had any.

Scream. The shed would seem to shiver with the sound. It was an awful makeshift, built of cast-off wood and some tin. Perhaps it was the tin that trembled. Hummed. Windows were unnecessary. There were parts between boards. A chicken might cluck till it was thwacked. Their bodies rocked on after.

Upon her tree's stump, the tree of knowledge, blood was bled. She screamed because there was a world which contained such scenes though she also knew there was worse worse worse sorts of wickedness frequent in it.

dew, snowflake, scab:

Conversations, for instance, Emma never had. She didn't believe she could sustain one now even if the opportunity were offered, but at one time she thought she missed chatter, the sound of talk, laughter, banter, chaff. Her family exchanged grimaces sometimes; there'd be an occasional outburst of complaint; but mostly words were orders, warnings, wishes—stenographed. Emma thought her father often talked to himself. He'd sort of growl, his head would bob or wag, his lips tremble. Her mother had an impressive repertoire of sighs, a few gestures of resignation, frowns and sucked cheeks. No word of praise was ever passed, a grunt of approval perhaps, a nod, and either no shows of affection were allowed, or there was no affection to be displayed.

So Emma talked to the page. It became a kind of paper face and full of paper speech. "The conversations are simple: about food." "When my mother combs my hair it hurts." Emma, however, couldn't speak well about food. She no longer grew it. She couldn't cook it. She didn't eat it. And how could she respond to remarks about her hair. Emma unkinked her hair herself. So she at least knew what the pain of hair pulling was and how carrots felt. Wherever you are the whole world is with you. A nice motto. Emma Bishop applied herself. She worked hard, but without success at first. Her life's small space had no place for stars. A dusty boot, a mixing bowl, a backyard plot. Judge not. Another maxim. But the boot was her father's where his foot went and was shaped by how he walked; booted because of the manure, he said, though the pigeons didn't even shit on Bishop soil. The earth is dirt. That was his judgment of it, hers of him. "Illuminated, solemn." The fact was, Emma Bishop hated her mother for being weak, for giving in to her husband's minor tyrannies. Take the flat of the shovel to him when his back is turned. Instead, Emma's mother turned her own and disappeared into a chore as though on movie horseback. The spoon spun in the bowl like a captured bird.

When snow and cold kept them cooped, each of them managed most marvelously to avoid one another. If she heard her father climbing the front stairs, Emma used the back one. If her mother and father threatened to meet in the upstairs hall, one ducked into a bedroom until the other had passed. Her father would always appear to be preoccupied, his thoughts elsewhere, a posture and a look which discouraged interruption. The three of them really wanted to live alone, and Emma at last had her wish. Each of them hungered for the others' deaths. Now Emma was fed.

However the habits of a life remained. Emma was haunted by them, and repeatedly found herself behaving as if she might any minute have to strip or encounter her mother like a rat on the cellar steps.

At more than one point, Emma pondered their acts of avoidance. And she concluded that each was afraid of the anger pent up inside like intestinal gas whose release would be an expression of noisy and embarrassingly bad manners. They also supposed that this swampy rage was equally fierce in others, and feared its public presence. With so few satisfactions, the pleasure of violence would be piercing, as if the removal of any player might redeem a dismal past, or create new and liberating opportunities, which of course it wouldn't . . . hadn't . . . couldn't . . .

Occasionally they would have to go to town for various provisions. The tractor, their only vehicle, and very old, nevertheless purred. Emma and her mother rode in an old hay trailer, most unceremoniously, Emma with her legs dangling from the open end, which made her mother nervous. For these occasions, Emma would wear what her mother called "her frock." A piece of dirty burlap was thought to be her frock's protection from the soiled bed of the wagon, so she sat on that. And watched the dust rise languidly behind the wagon's wheels, and the countryside pass them on both sides like something on a screen. The nearby weeds were white as though floured.

For her birthday—twice—she'd been taken to a movie. The town had a small badly ventilated hall, poor sound, and a cranky projector. Actually, since they couldn't afford more than one ticket, you'd have to say Emma was sent to the movie. Both times her mother had warned her—both times to Emma's surprise—"Don't let anyone feel your knee." To Emma's nonplussed face her mother would reply: "It'll be dark, you see." Darkness and desire were, for Emma then, forever wed. The films impressed her mightily. Gaudy, exotic, splendid, they didn't at all resemble her daily life, but they were additional experience nevertheless, and showed that the strange and far away was as inexplicable as the common and nearby. Words on her pages, on the other hand, even when mysteriously conjoined, explained themselves. Moonlight and mist were mute. But a line of verse which described moonlight and mist caught in pasture bushes like lamb's wool, for instance, offered her understanding. A film might capture the fog as it crawled across the pasture, but there'd be no lamb's wool clinging to its images.

The movies weren't her world for another reason. The pictures, the figures, the scenes, the horses, the traffic, passed like a parade. Highways ran into mountains, streams rattled over rocks and fell in foam. Clouds scudded across the sky, and their shadows dappled the ground. The sun set like a glowing stone.

Emma's well went weeks without a lick of light, and the yard lay motionless under its dust and seeds, disturbed only by an occasional burst of breeze. The mantis waited, head kinked, hard-eyed. Her mother occupied a room as if she were household help. But Randolph Scott was out of sight in a thrice. And all the sounds . . . the sounds were bright.

All the while she sat in this strange dark room with a few strange dark shapes, none of whom offered to touch her knee, and watched these grainy gaudy imaginary movements, Emma was aware that her father and her mother were out in the town's drab daylight, their shopping soon completed, waiting for the picture to be over so they could go home. They'd be stared at, their tractor and its wagon watched. As time and the film wore on, Emma became increasingly anxious. If she had any enjoyment from the show, it was soon gone. On the drive home, her mother would cover her sullenness with another coat.

Emma sat shaded from the hot summer sun by her ash–moose maple and went in her head to New Brunswick to board a bus for a brief—in the poem—trip, and view her favorite fog once again. By far her favorite fog. Yet it rendered for her her Iowa snow most perfectly. "Its cold, round crystals form and light and settle . . ." Here was at last the change: the flat close sky, the large flakes falling more softly than a whisper. Yet the snow would stay to crust and glare and deepen, to capture colors like lilac and violet because of all of the cold in those blues, and repeat them every day like her bread and breakfast oats. Settle in what? "In the white hens' feathers . . ." ". . . in gray glazed cabbages . . ." She couldn't get enough of that. ". . . in gray glazed . . . in gray glazed cabbages . . ." "on the cabbage roses . . ." The repetition enchanted her. So she repeated it.

As temporary as dew was, so they said—more meltable than oleo—the snow nevertheless stayed for months, covering the seeds which had lain for months on the hard dry monthslong ground. Then there'd be mud for months, oozy as oatmeal; whereas Randolph Scott would scoot from frame to frame like a scalded cat. Dew could be counted on to disappear by mid-morning. But you'd never sense when. What sort of change was changeless change—imperceptibly to dry the weeping world's eye—when Ann Richards rode through outfits faster than Randolph mounted his horse? And when Emma was wounded by her faithless moose maple, the scab formed so slowly it never seemed to.

By the shaded road, at the edge of a glade, in open woods, the mayapples rose, their leaves kept in tight fists until the stems reached the height of a boot and a bit, when each fist unfolded slowly to open a double umbrella a foot wide—hundreds of the round leaves soon concealing the forest floor. This was the rate of change Emma understood. Differences appeared after days of gray rain and a softening wind. As predictable as the train though. Then glossy white flowers would show up like tipped cups. Bluebells were bolder and would spread a blue haze over the muckier places. Cowslips her mother called them. But the mayapple's flower hung from a fork in the stem and well under the plant's big deep green leaves. Finally a little jaundiced lemon-shaped fruit the size of an egg would form. At her father's insistence they'd gather a few peck-sized baskets and boil the nubbins into an insipid jellylike spread for bread.

Her father claimed the mayapple was rightly called a mandrake, but the plant didn't scream when Emma pulled a few from the ground, nor were its roots man-shaped; it grew far from the woodshed, their only gallows, and she doubted it had the power to transform men into beasts. Instead it left some toilsome fruits to enlarge and encumber their larder.

Her father prowled the meadows and woods looking for edibles, herbs and barks he said were medicinal when turned into tea, vegetable dyes her mother would never use. Since these lands didn't belong to them, Emma felt uneasy about what she thought was a kind of theft: of nuts and berries, wild grapes and greens. Emma put no stock in her father's claim to understand nature, because he was at home and happy only around machines. His tractor was his honey.

Nor did her mind change much. It was like a little local museum. The exhibits sat in their cases year after year. Possibly the stuffed squirrel would begin to shed. The portraits continued to be stiff and grim. Until her poetry taught her to pay attention. And then she saw a small shadow—she supposed shame—pass across her father's face when he looked at her nakedness. Because she was hairing up, she supposed. And found grief beneath her mother's eye in a wrinkle. A hard blue sun-swept sky became a landscape. Even now, when they were both dead, it was still impossible to go in the shed except to scream, and, through the greater part of her growing up and getting old, from most things she still fled.

Was she screaming for the chickens or the tree?

As slowly as her scab, her father's resolution formed. The moose had wounded his daughter. It had to come down. After all, he enjoyed the solemn parental right of riddance.

light, linger, leave

Poets were supposed to know and love nature. "Nature, the gentlest mother is." Purely urban or industrial poets were suspicious freaks. "Bumblebees creep inside the foxgloves and the evening commences." She had taken the knowledge and the love for granted. "Carrots form mandrakes or a ram's-horn root sometimes." But then she learned that it was not good to be "a nature poet," and that descriptions were what girls did, while guys narrated and pondered and plumbed. Ladies looked on. Gentlemen intervened. "Nature is what we see—the hill—the afternoon—squirrel—eclipse—the bumblebee." Surely she was seeing herself as a gazer and seeking her salvation in sight. She was seeking to see with a purposeless purity, her intent always to let Being be, and become what it meant to become without worry, want, or meddlesome intervention. If anything were to alter, she must allow it to alter of itself; if anything were to freeze, even new-budded buds, she had to be grateful for that decision; if anything were to die, she'd delight in their death. For all is lawful process.

When Emma had reached such serenity, such selfless uncon- cern, she would be ready to disappear into her memorial dress, lie down in a sublime line of verse, a line by Elizabeth Bishop. Since she hadn't the art necessary to express the dehumanized high ground she aspired to, she would have to turn to someone who had that skill, if not such a successfully pursued imperson- ality. For who had? She

And the tree groaned and crashed with a noise of much paper being angrily wadded, as if God were crumpling the Contract. A cloud stood above the tree like the suggestion of a shroud to mark the spot and evidence the deed.

Miss Moore, in her silly round black hat, looking like the *Monitor,* or was it the *Merrimack,* her hands half-stuffed in a huge muff made of the fur of some poor beast, stared with con- summate calm out of her jacket image at Emma. Not a mirror. Not naked but smothered in overcoat except for her pale face and pale throat. No sign of nips the size of dimes, or barely there breasts or bony hips or hair trying to hide itself in shame inside its cleft. A slight smile, calm demeanor, self-possessed. Light is speech, her poem like the camera said. "Free frank impartial sunlight, moonlight, starlight, lighthouse light, are language." But not firelight, candlelight, lamplight, flickergiven, waver- lovers. The firefly's spark, but not an ember's glow, not match flare or flashlight. Stood there. Aren't lies, deceptions, misgivings, reluctances, unforthcomings, language? Stood there. Stood there. Could one ever recover?

Chainsaws her father understood. They wore like a watch a little engine.

The Bishops would dodge one another for days. Occasionally, Emma would catch a glimpse of her mother sitting in the kitchen drinking a little medicinal tea her husband had brewed to soothe her sick stomach. From her window she might see the tractor's burnt orange figure chewing in a far field. She'd imagine cows they never had, stable a horse in their bit of barn, with a little lettuce and a carrot visit her hutch of rabbits, when a paste-white chicken would emerge from between piles of scrap wood and scrap metal as if squeezed from a tube.

Emma's eye would light; it would linger; it would leave. Life too, she was avoiding. There were days she knew the truth and was oppressed by her knowledge. These were days of discouragement, during which, almost as a penance, she would sew odd objects she had carefully collected to squares of china white cardboard, and then inscribe in a calligrapher's hand a saying or a motto, a bit of buckup or advice about life, which seemed to express the message inherent in her arrangement of button or bead or bright glass with a star shape of glued seeds, dry grass or pressed petal, then, sometimes, hung from a thin chain or lace of leather, a very small brass key, with colored rice to resemble a fall tree, and a length of red silk thread like something slit.

Forget-me-not was a frequent sentiment.

These she would put in little handmade envelopes and leave in the postbox by the road for the postman to mail to the customers who answered her modest ad in *Farm Life*. Emma did not in the least enjoy this activity, which required her to look out for and gather tiny oddities of every tiny kind, to select from her lot those which would prove to be proper companions, envision their arrangement as if thrusting stems into a vase of flowers, and finally to compose a poem, a maxim, an epigram that suited their unlikely confluence. So on really down days she would do it, on days of rueful truth, which may account for the cruel turns her verses would sometimes take, veering from the saccharine path of moralizing admonitions into the wet depths of the ditch where the lilies and the cattails flourished, just to point out—because she couldn't help herself, because she had no prospects, no good looks, no pleasures herself—that the pretty was perilous, pleasure a snare, success a delusion, that beneath the bright bloom and attractive fruit grew a poisonous root.

Emma's sentiment cards were, however, a means to a greater good, for it was with the small sums her sales produced that she purchased her poetry: books by Bishop, Moore, Sitwell, and Dickinson, on order volumes of Elinor Wylie and Louise Bogan, which, she would regularly realize, unaccountably hadn't come.

She shared grass-of-Parnassus with Elizabeth Bishop because it grew near the bluebell's sog, and in Nova Scotia too. It was a part of the inherent poetry of names: lady's slipper, sundew, jack-in-the-pulpit, forget-me-not, goldthread, buttercup, buttonbush, goldenrod, moonshine, honeysuckle, star grass, jewelweed, milkwort, butter-and-eggs, lion's heart, Solomon's seal, Venus's looking-glass, with some names based on likeness, plant character, or human attitude, such as virgin's bower, crowfoot, Queen Anne's lace, Quaker lady, wake-robin, love vine, bellwort, moneywort, richweed, moccasin flower, snakemouth, ladies' tresses, blue curls, lizard's tail, goosefoot, ragged robin, hairy beardtongue, turtlehead, Dutchman's-breeches, calico, thimbleweed, and finally bishop's cap; or because they were critter-connected much as mad-dog was, hog peanut, gopherberry, goose tansy, butterfly weed, bee balm, moth mullen, cowwheat, deer vine, fleabane, horseheal, goat's-rue, dogberry; or were based on location and function and friendliness like

clammy ground cherry, water willow, stone clover, swamp candle, shinleaf, seedbox, eyebright, bedstraw, firewood, stonecrop,
Indian physic, heal all, pitcher plant, purple boneset, agueweed,
pleurisy root, toothwort, feverfew; or were simply borrowed
from their fruiting season like the mayapple, or taken from root
or stem or stalk or fruit or bloom or leaf, like arrowhead, spider-
wort, seven-angled pipewort, foamflower, liverleaf, shrubby five-
finger, bloodroot; while sometimes they gained their name
principally through their growth habit, as the staggerbush did,
the sidesaddle flower, prostrate tick trefoil, loosestrife, spatter-
dock, steeplebush, Jacob's ladder; although often the names
served as warnings about a plant's hostility or shyness the way
poison ivy or touch-me-not did, wild sensitive pea, lambkill,
adder's tongue, poison flagroot, tearthumb, king devil, needle-
grass, skunk cabbage, chokeberry, scorpion grass, viper's
bugloss, bitter nightshade, and lance-leaved tickseed; or they
were meant to be sarcastic and cutting like New Jersey tea, bastard toadflax, false vervain, mouse-eared chickweed, swamp
lousewort, monkey flower, corpse plant, pickerelweed, Indiana
poke, and the parasitic naked broom rape, or, finally, gall-of-the-
earth—few of which Emma knew personally, since her father
had made edibility a necessary condition for growth in the family garden, and had stepped upon her nasturtium although she'd
argued for its use in salads. But peas, beans, and roots were
what he wanted. Salads don't make or move a muscle, he said.
So instead of cultivating or observing weeds and flowers in the
field, Emma collected and admired and smelled their names
and looked at their pictures in books.

   "Pity should begin at home," Crusoe said, enisled as utterly as
Emma was. Sometimes Emma tried to feel sorry for herself, but
she scarcely had a self left or the energy available or what she
thought was a good reason. Yes, she had barely made a mark on
the world, her life was a waste, and she'd had little enjoyment;

but on balance she had to admit she'd rather have read the word *boobs* than have them. A moose comes out of the woods and stands in the middle of the road. When the bus stops, it approaches to sniff the hot hood. "Towering, antlerless, high as a church, homely as a house . . ." Well, there were so many things she hadn't seen, a moose included, but she had envisioned that large heavy head sniffing the hot hood of the bus, there on that forest-enclosed road, at night, and understood the deep dignity in all things. "All things," she knew, embraced Emma Bishop's homely bare body standing in the middle of her room. Antlerless . . . boobless . . . with hairless pubes . . .

like a swatted fly,

Her Iowa summers were long and hot and dusty and full of flies. Ants and flies . . . In the early days, before unconcern had become endemic, her mother had insisted that the dinner table wear a white linenlike cover. Even dime-store glasses gleamed, cheap white plates shone, and tinny silverware glittered when they sat on the starchy bleached cloth amid their puddles of light blue shadow and pale gray curves. But through the ill-fit and punctured screens the flies came not in clouds but in whining streams. At breakfast it wasn't so bad. One or two or three had to be waved away from the oatmeal. Maybe, though, that's when Emma's aversion to food began. Flies. Raisins for the oats, her father said, waving his spoon. Sugar brings them. They love sweets, her mother said. They did seem to, and crumbs, on which they tried to stand.

These weren't manure breeders and the curse of cattle, but common bluebottles, persistent and numerous in the peaceful sunshine. Emma would have to shake the cloth from the back porch before they'd fly. They seemed to like sugar, salt, bread crumbs, cereal, leavings of any kind, jam, and Emma learned to loathe them, their soft buzz and their small walk, their numbers and their fearless greed.

The deep dignity in all things—phoo—not in flies, not in roaches, not in fathers, not in dandelion greens.

"Nature is what we see—the hill—the afternoon—squirrel— eclipse—the bumble bee—nay—nature is heaven." Not a word about flies. There was a song about a fly, and that rhyme about the old woman who swallowed one, who knew why, but Emma could not recollect ever reading a poem about or even including a fly. Miss Moore wrote about horses, skunks, lizards, but not about flies. Emily D's little list included the bobolink, the sea, thunder, the cricket, but left out ants, mosquitos, and of course flies. Good reason. Because she wanted to say that Nature was Heaven, was Harmony. Poetry, Emma would have to admit, later, recalling all those flies, poetry was sometimes blather. Her noble resolutions would also falter in front of the phenomenon of the fly. How could she honor anything that would lay its eggs in a wound? They carried diseases with more regularity than the postman mail, and they lived on leavings, on carrion, horse droppings, dirt. Like sparrows and pigeons. Phoo indeed.

Hadn't she lived on leavings too?

The mantis would close her forelegs like a pocketknife and eat a wasp a fly a lacewing in a trice. She'd rise up to frighten the wasp to a standstill, giving it her triangulating stare, and then strike so swiftly her claws could be scarcely seen, nails on all sides, the hug of the iron maiden.

Nature was rats and mice, briars and insect bites, cow plop and poisonous plants, chickens with severed heads and minute red ants swarming over a stump soaked in blood. It was the bodies of swatted flies collected in a paper bag.

The swatter, an efficient instrument, was made of clothes-hanger wire and window screen trimmed with a narrow band of cloth which bore the name of a hardware store. Emma became an expert, finally, at something. Sometimes she would hit them while they were still in the air and knock them into the wall, where she'd smack their slightly stunned selves into mush. Even so, they were clever little devils and could sense the swatter's approach, even though it was designed to pass without a wake or any sound through the air. They knew a blow was coming and would almost always be taking off when the screen broke their wings.

Emma killed many on the kitchen table, sliding the carcasses into a paper sack with the side of the swatter. It occurred to her that there was no word for the crushed corpse of a swatted fly. Her father liked to swing his right hand across the cloth and catch one in his closing fist, a slight smile slowly widening on his face like the circle of a pebble's plop. Where's your sack, he'd say, and when Emma held it out he'd shake the body from his palm where it was stuck. Once in a while, with that tiny smile, he'd try to hold his fist to Emma's ear so she could hear the buzz, but she would leave the room with a short cry of fear, her father's chuckle following like a fly itself.

After they'd eaten, Emma would clear the dishes away and wait a bit while the flies settled in apparent safety on the crumbed and sugared cloth. Her mother sweetened her tea with a careless spoon. Even the herbals her husband sometimes brewed for her she honeyed up one way or other. The flies would land as softly as soot. They'd walk about boldly on their sticky little feet with their proboscises extended as though requiring a cane. Her father was pleased to explain that flies softened their food with spit so they could suck it up.

Emma liked to get two at once. Each swat would bestir some of the others and they'd whiz in a bothered zigzag for a while before trying to feed again, no lesson learned, the carnage of their comrades of little concern, although a few would remain at work even when a whack fell within a yard of their grazing.

Flies seemed to flock like starlings, but the truth was they had no comrades, no sense of community. Occasionally, a crippled one would buzz and bumble without causing a stir, or a green-bottle arrive in their midst to be met by colossal indifference. Standing across from the center of the table, Emma would slap rapidly at each end in succession while uttering quiet but heart-felt *theres* each time: there and there and there.

Oh she hated the creatures, perhaps because they treated the world as she was treated. It was certainly out of character for Emma to enjoy bloodshed. However, her father approved of her zeal, and her mother didn't seem to mind, except

trace to be grieved,

for the little red dots their deaths left on the tablecloth. They'd accumulate, those spots, until their presence became quite intolerable to her mother, and she would remind Emma how hard it was to get those spots out, and about the cost of bleach, and how she hated that bag with its countless contents, she felt she heard a rustle from it now and then, it gave her the creeps. Emma wondered what, in her mother, creeps were. Later, when her mother was ill always, and vomiting a lot, Emma thought that perhaps the creeps had won out.

When the fly was flipped from the table into her sack, it would almost always leave that reminder behind, a red speck as bright as the red spider mite though larger by a little. And after the evening meal, Emma would enter a dozen specks and some-times more into her register.

Where were they coming from? the compost heap? Her father said he saw no evidence of it. Her mother shook her head. Somewhere was there something dead? Her father hadn't encountered anything, and he walked the land pretty thor-oughly. From as far away as the woods? Her mother shook her head. Well, Emma wondered, if the breeding of these flies was a miracle, God was certainly wasting his gifts. God is giving you something to do, her father said.

There was something in Emma which made her want to keep count, and other things in Emma which were horrified by the thought.

Days drew on, mostly with a monotony which mingled them, so that time seemed not slow, not fast, just not about. And she failed grades and advanced anyway, and grew like a skinny tree to be stared at, and became increasingly useless, as if uselessness were an aim. Why, her father complained, wouldn't Emma attack those bugs in the garden when she was so murderous about flies. As if he'd failed to notice that Emma had stopped swatting them many months, years, failed grades ago. Things went on in their minds, Emma imagined, out of inertia. Memory was maybe more than a lot of little red dots. The swats were still there, swatting. The paper sack still sat in a kitchen chair like a visitor. And Emma stayed on the page even when all her books were closed. The cloud

The shed got built about the ash stump. Emma could hear the hammering. Built of limbs and logs, it leaned to one side, then another. Had her father any interest in the number of nails he'd hammered while the ash shack was going up? Did he know how long the walk to the mailbox was? how many yards? Without books, Emma couldn't disappear into them. So she began to make and mail her memory cards, her versified objects, receiving for them a few dollars, and then, with this slim income, to order books of poetry by Elizabeth Bishop from an Iowa City shop. It was a great day when

POEMS
North & South
A Cold Spring

arrived, the title typed on a chartreuse ginkolike leaf lying across the join of two fields, one white for northern snow, she supposed, the other blue for southern seas. The flap copy was typed, too, and there were warm recommendations from Marianne Moore and Louise Bogan as well as the usual guys. Emma opened the book and saw a poem on a page like treasure in a chest and closed the book again and opened it and closed it many times. She held it in her two hands. Finally, it seemed to open of its own accord. She began "The Monument." Page 25. Yes, she remembered. Even the brackets [25]. "Now can you see the monument?" She could. She could see it. "It is of wood built somewhat like a box." Yes, Emma saw it. Her eyes flew flylike to the yard where the shed stood. It was a revelation.

Later on there would be others.

She turned the page and read the conclusion. "It is the beginning of a painting," the poem said, "a piece of sculpture, or poem, or monument, and all of wood." All of ash. "Watch it closely."

Emma's father probably didn't care whether she found out or not. He probably neglected to tell her he was intercepting her mail, whether going in or going out, just because he didn't care, one way or the other. He simply piled it up—the square envelopes with their cards of sewn- and glued- and inked-on sentiments and emblems, those with a few customer requests, some with simple sums inside them, a bookstore order—higgledy-piggledy on a small oak table in the room he was sleeping in now that his wife was ill and vomitous. That's where, through an open door, Emma saw her envelopes, looking otherwise innocent and unopened, and said aloud in complete surprise: that's why I never got my May Sarton.

She did not try to retrieve them. To her, they were dead as flies, leftovers from a past life. They almost puzzled her, they seemed so remote from the suspended condition she was presently in, although not that many weeks had passed, she guessed, since she'd composed her last card: four hard green pea gravels placed like buttonholes inside a wreath of mottled mahonia leaves, stained as though by iodine and flame. In a kind of waking dream, Emma tottered the hundred and more yards to where the postbox leaned from a tuft of weed at the roadside, and opened it on empty. She held on to the lid as though it might fly up, and stared hard into the empty tin, more interested in the space where the confiscation had taken place than in the so-called contraband. Empty. Its emptiness was shaped from zinc. zzzzzz . . . in . . . cckkkk. Emma knew at last something for certain: her father was poisoning her mother.

Well, it was no business of hers.

She closed the mailbox carefully so none of its emptiness would leak out.

Indeed her mother rasped to her rest in a week's time. Her father rolled her mother in the sheets and then the blanket from her bed and laid her at length, though somewhat folded—well, knees a good ways up—in a wooden footlocker. He poured a lot of mothballs in the crannies. We won't be needing those, he said, fastening the lid with roofing nails. He slid the locker down the front stairs and lugged the box, cursing because it was heavier than he expected and awkward to carry, to the back of the wagon—lucky the wagon was small-wheeled and low— where he propped one end and lifted the other, then pushed the locker in. He never expected Emma to help. At helping she was hopeless. That's enough for one day, he said. I got to scout out a good place.

He went inside and washed all the household dishes. Grief, Emma decided, was the only explanation.

The next day she saw her father's distant figure digging in a far field. He appeared to be digging slowly because he dug for a long time.

Emma's head was as empty of thoughts as the mailbox. There was no reason to stand or sit or walk.

Got my exercise today, he said.

Marianne Moore and Elizabeth Bishop were both dead. Edith Sitwell too. Elizabeth Bishop just keeled over in her kitchen. Nobody knew. Her poems couldn't purchase her another hour.

I've got to figure how to get her in, her father said. Can't just roll her over. A fall like that might break the box open. We'll do it tomorrow.

Her father found an egg, which he had for breakfast. Emma rode in the back of the wagon with the coffin and an ironing board. The tractor dragged the wagon roughly over the ploughed ground. Then reluctantly through the marshy meadow. Smoother movement steadied her horizon. Emma remembered the Randolph Scott movie. Her father had chosen a spot near the trees which appeared to have no distinction. Earth was heaped neatly on both wide sides. Emma looked in the hole. "Cold dark deep and absolutely clear."

Her father backed the wagon up to an open end of the pit. Then he pried the box up with a crowbar and forced the ironing board under it. He never expected Emma to help. He steadied the box on the board as it slid down the board from the wagon. It was, Emma realized, a mechanical problem. The board then was lowered into the grave, and the box once more sent on its skiddy way. In a cant at the bottom, her father wiggled the board out from beneath the box so at last it lay there, as settled as it was going to get. The zinc-headed nails reflected a little light.

Supposed to say a few words, her father said, so why don't you?

Poetry doesn't redeem, Emma thought. Saintliness doesn't redeem. Evening doesn't redeem the day, it just ends it.

Her father waited with a fistful of dirt ready to fling in the hole.

She was small and thin and bitter, my mother. No one could

cheer her up. A dress, a drink, a roast chicken were all the same to her. She went about her house without hope, without air. Her face was closed as a nut, closed as a careful snail's. I saw her smile once but it was not nice, more like a crack in a plate. What on earth had she done to have so little done for her? She sewed my clothes but the hems were crooked.

While Emma was silent a moment, trying to remember something more to say, to recite, her father released his fistful of earth and he went for the shovel. He shoveled slowly as if his back hurt. Dirt disappeared into dirt. The morning was cloudy but the grave was cold and dark and not so deep as it had been. The nails went out—animal eyes in a cave. Layer after layer: sheet blanket mothballs board, earth on earth on earth. Too bad we couldn't afford to do better by her, her father said, but we didn't do too bad. Emma realized he hadn't cared what her words were, probably hadn't heard. Words were one of the layers—to ward off what?

They hadn't any prayers. Emma hated hymns. Hymns weren't private enough. And you were told which one to sing. This morning, please turn to [25]. The grave filled and a little mound rose over it, the soil looking less raw, more friable. Emma rode back to the house alongside the ironing board which was quite dirty and bedraggled. The board bounced as it hadn't bounced coming out, when it was wedged. Emma tottered to the mailbox and looked in. That was how it was inside the box, she supposed. Empty, even though

In the days, the weeks, the month which followed, Emma disappeared almost completely into her unattachments. She freed herself of food, of feeling, father. The fellow was a wraith. She was a shadow no one cast. He no longer farmed, though he often stood like a scarecrow in the field. Grief, Emma decided, was the explanation. But his grief was no concern of hers. She thought about freeing herself from verse when she realized she always had been free, for she had never respected, never followed, the form or been obedient to type.

She waited for the world, unasked, to flow into her, but she hadn't yet received its fine full flood. What if it weren't a liquid, didn't flow, but stood as if painted in its frame? What if it were like a fly indifferent to its own death? No matter. She was freeing herself of reflection. All of a sudden, she believed, the lethal line would come: "The dead birds fell, but no one had seen them fly . . ." Perhaps it would be that one. So what if it was shot from a sonnet. The only way flies could get into a poem would be as a word. "They were black, their eyes were shut. No one knew what kind of birds they were." Each night, night fell in huge drops like rain and ran down the eaves and sheeted across the pane. He'd move somewhere in the house. He'd move. She'd hear. "Quick as dew off leaves." The sound will be gone in the morning.

Mother beneath the earth. Others are, why not she? He waits in the soybean field for me. I must carry the shovel out to him. It is thin as I am. Almost as worn, as hard. Mother has no marker. Many lie unknown in unsigned graves. Might we hear mother rustling under all her covers, trying to straighten her knees? To spend death with bended knee. He'll never mark her. The mound will sink like syrup into the soil. Weeds will walk. Perhaps black wood-berries will grow there as they do in Bishop's poem. My steps are soundless on the soft earth.

Emma struck her father between his shoulder blades with the flat of the spade. She hit him as hard as she could, but we can't suppose her blow would have amounted to much. She heard his lungs hoof and he fell forward on his face. Emma flung the spade away as far as she could a few feet. What can you see now, she wondered. Or did you always see dirt?

She hadn't considered that a blow meant as a remonstrance might have monstrous consequences. She bounced floatily back to the house somewhat like a blown balloon. That's it: rage redeems. What does? evening.

And evening came. The dead birds fell. Found in the field. She hadn't missed him a minute. She hadn't for a moment worried about how angry he would be, or how he might take his anger out on her, so uppity a child as to strike her grieving father in the back. Found facedown. After a rainstorm. Heartburst. Creamed corn is a universal favorite. Dark drops fell. The field was runneled and puddlesome. Emma peered more and more through the round thread-wound shade pull. And felt the flow. The world was a fluid. Weights have been lifted off of me. I am lonely am I? as a cloud

Emma was afraid of Elizabeth Bishop. Emma imagined Elizabeth Bishop lying naked next to a naked Marianne Moore, the tips of their noses and their nipples touching; and Emma imagined that every feeling either poet had ever had in their spare and spirited lives was present there in the two nips, just where the nips kissed. Emma, herself, was ethereally thin, and had been admired for the translucency of her skin. You could see her bones like shadows of trees, shadows without leaves.

Some dreams they forgot. But Emma Bishop remembered them now with a happy smile. Berry picking in the woods, seeing shiny black wood-berries hanging from a bough, and thinking, don't pick these, they may be poison . . . a word thrilling to say . . . *poison* . . . us. Elizabeth Bishop used the phrase *loaded trees*, as if they might like a gun go off. At last . . . at last . . . at last, she thought: "What flowers shrink to seeds like these?"

dot where it died.

THE MASTER OF
SECRET REVENGES

Luther Penner, after many years, had perfected the art of secret revenges. They were pallid, to be sure, these revenges; they were thin; they were trivial and mild compared to the muscular and hearty recoveries of honor that brighten history and make it bearable to read; yet they were revenges so secretly conceived and so deftly executed that the spider might have learned a more entangling web, the wasp a surer sting, by studying them. It was Luther Penner's solemn purpose to improve on Nature and prefigure Providence, and to this end he had, during the time of which I write, become a master of the art of his invention. Completely conscious of his powers, he did not hesitate to address himself in his journal as *cher maître et ami,* taking care to compose each entry in the third person and to invest it with all the featureless precision of analytical philosophy. There was no affectation in this formula of greeting, for he had come to regard the creative part of himself with astonishment and awe as having separate existence and richly independent means. Always himself a modest, humble man, he knew his genius had not only discovered an art and carried it to perfection, it had also seized upon the idea of the transcendental revenge itself and, like Descartes, had come into possession of its essence in one searing afternoon of vision. While he felt he could ascribe the necessary preparation for this moment to his lifelong study of revenge—a study which had till then resulted only in a catalogue of every kind of offended honor with its appropriate requital—he could not honestly suppose that from these studies, by themselves, had come such a revolutionary notion as The Pure Revenge *en soi;* never, without the aid of the Upper Air, could he have realized the secrecy essential to it, or discovered the subjective ground of its satisfaction, or understood so well its immeasurable moral power. Indeed, the idea of The Pure Revenge puts within the reach of every ordinary man and woman a truly formidable weapon, a weapon which balances at once the forces of the weakling with the bully's, and one which must, in time, surely tip the scales to the nobler side; for despite the fact that these revenges are in figure pale and wasted, and regardless of the measures which a man may take to guard himself against the vigorous antique kinds, there is no safety for him from L. T. Penner's invisible reprisals; no man may sleep securely who has sinned against his neighbor; and I feel confident now, as I have never dared to feel before, that our most pious hopes shall be fulfilled, and thanks to Luther Penner, we shall see this unjust comedy of life justly concluded, and the meek come into the legacy that long ago was promised them.

It is my intention here to lead this modest genius gently before the public, and to acquaint it with the doctrines which will one day fasten his name to every soul like a maker's mark. I have no doubt that when my account reaches print, and when his journals (all of them frank, unfettered, and green as a meadow's grass) are set in type, Luther Penner will be hailed as another Copernicus, turning our view of the universe around. No one has dreamed as incessantly, as deeply, as madly, as he. Like his famous namesake, Luther would reform us in everything, and surely nothing is more evident than our need for reformation, since even Nature, not to mention Man, has fallen from its former place in our regard, and now lies smashed in fragments, in a scatter of meaningless shards. From earliest childhood this disagreeable state of affairs had impressed itself on Luther Penner, and through the sight that seems to be given in secret to those destined by the gods for glorious things, he saw into the "dirty persons" of his small companions, as passages in his childhood diaries prove, with a terrifying penetration and clarity, while his commerce with them sounded in his thoughts the first note of his music, an aria of revenge and vindication.

Lest the reader imagine that I am letting my fancy free to infer Penner's early attitudes from his later and more rounded nature, I shall quote here some of the first scrawly-handed entries to be found in his diaries. He began his records early and continued them until his unfortunate demise. There is an astonishing continuity of content and tone to them over the years, despite the changes of style we might expect, along with Penner's mounting maturity and enlargement of learning. The late journals of his middle (and last) years are increasingly devoted to philosophical reflections. What Luther Penner always wants to know is "why?" "why?"

April 1. Got a wagon for my birthday. No red wheels.

April 18. Pushed out of my wagon—my! wagon—three times! this morning Millicent said I was a . . . meezy peezy.

May 4. What is a meezy peezy. Millicent calls me. Why. Her pants were dirty. I didn't say so. Look out, Millicent.

May 25. Andy pulled up all of Mrs. Putnam's flowers. I was tripped by Sully while I was running! Still a sore on my arm! Cried in front of his father. Craig is going on a picnic tomorrow. Hope it rains! Marsh is a sneak.

May 26. It! Did! Hard! Is! I can hear it! hitting on my window. Good! G!o!o!d! I have to stay in my room. I don't care.

May 30. Millicent pushed me! More than once! Why.

June 11. We went to the farm. Saw horses, cows, plop, and chickens. Like geese least. Hissers and honkers. Just like Millicent! I fell down a lot. Daddy drove in a ditch driving home! I put my hankie in my mouth so as not to make ha ha.

June 17. Red faced fat boy moved next door. Picks his nose on his front porch. Why.

June 19. Maybe because he knows nobody likes it.

Luther was never a strong child, as he was a weak and timorous man, forever saying "I agree," as he ruefully admits, "undoubtedly," "of course," "how clever," "very true," "quite nice," and showing the soft, uneven edges of his teeth in a continuous, shy, abasing grin until his fellows grew suspicious of him and he no longer was appointed to committees or assigned to sections of the major courses but put where there was no one over him to whom he had to play the poodle, and where, at first with difficulty but later with increasing calm and forceful execution, he ruled himself like a lord, turning his soul to steel in his wretchedness, beginning to gather the significant acts of his past together in a pattern which cried its moral aloud; for it was during these days that he remembered, for instance, how, in a playground as a child, he had many times spat vengefully on the slide to moisten the pants of an enemy, or, older, dropped a fly in the soft drink of a burly, overbearing girl, or at the commencement of his teens, dried his aunt's silverware upon his desocked feet.

Obvious as the principle may seem to us now, Penner did not immediately perceive it, and it was only when he widened his data with the whole of history, at the end of a life of labor, that the truth was plain; so it was a particularly important moment when, shortly following another recollection of how the silver felt between his toes one sweaty August afternoon (fork tine between toe tine, as his diary reports it), in a book of Italian history, he made the acquaintance of that redoubtable cardinal Ippolito d'Este, a man of singular directness and moral purpose. Learning that his brother Don Giulio was preferred to him by Angela Borgia because that babbling whore admired, as she had imprudently said, the tint and lashes of her Giulio's eyes more than Ippolito's very serviceable body, the cardinal pointed to his brother when he chanced to meet him on the road (seeing that his brother rode with pride, in ornament, and was poorly attended), and cried out to his grooms impulsively, "Kill that man, gouge out his eyes." Important, I say, for on reading this, Penner put his finger to his lips and sucked upon his breath as if a secret were about to be released from his lungs. He describes the occasion vividly in his journal. Then he says, "I suddenly realized that the real distance between the way I chose to dry my Auntie Spatz's sterling service and the jealous cardinal's fierce command lay not in what I and Ippolito differently desired, but in what we differently dared."

Penner's family was in no way remarkable, and it is difficult to see in it the soil that was to send so great a tree aloft. Penner notes only, in a letter he wrote to me during those sad last days, his father's habit of swearing constantly under his breath at absolutely everybody, his wife and son in particular, but also at stair treads and stuck doors, the broken points of pencils, dead batteries, bent nails, coffee spills, shirt stains, car horns, newspaper articles, market reports, his son Luther's frequent colds with their accompanying coughs, sniffles, and whining, cold cuts too (baloney on bread, Spam with spinach), cold coffee, cold days, his slippers on such mornings, and the morning floor.

He had it in for radio commentators especially: Kaltenborn, you caponized cockadoodle, what do you know about machinists? he would say to the radio, his head nonetheless hidden behind his newspaper, as if the announcer might be looking through the Philco at him; what mental illness, *Scheisskopf*, makes you think you know what the workers at Chrysler are going to do? (Penner's father particularly hated the AFL and the CIO.) These sneaky labor organizers hiss and coil and crawl about because they're snakes, he'd grumble somewhat redundantly, and will strike at anything in their path. His father would fork his fingers like fangs. Did you call upon your fat *Boche* brains to figure that out, he'd growl at one of Kaltenborn's pronouncements. Too bad, because, Kalty, your brains are too soft to even rattle. His father's swearing rarely rose above a mutter, but it was nearly always there, accompanying the damn dumb morning paper, the damn dumb cantaloupe which was difficult to spoon, the damn dumb honey which leaked on his fingers, the damn tough toast which scraped raw the roof of his mouth.

Luther's father was a muscular and massive man, which made his timidity even more than customarily unendurable. It was his mother, though slight of figure and dainty of manner, who would chastise workmen for poor performance, or return mislabeled goods, or complain to the waiter that her cutlet was overcooked. Secure in his car, the windows rolled up, behind the covers of a book, in movie darkness, then father would freely comment, for he, Jerome Penner, was never taken in, no sir, no illegal allurements, no bites from the hated apple for him, he already knew what John L. Lewis was up to, that Bette Davis hadn't a decent bone in her body, that Father Coughlin was a fascist.

It is possible—one must not idly discount such simple solutions—that Penner's conception of a pure revenge reflected his father's habit of swearing in secret, damning images, and cursing a commentator who existed only as a voice. It would not be the first time that a father's habit had lodged itself in a son's psyche in some transformed yet symbolic fashion.

But the true source of Penner's inspiration, I think, is not to be found in such familiar family failings, from which we have all received our own wounds, but from his observation of the habits of his playmates and his school companions; an investigation which led to the disclosure of their "dirty persons," and a revelation, as he remarks himself in a rare moment of candor, equal in importance, though not in dignity, to the discovery by Socrates of the soul.

We must set aside, with the greatest respect, of course, Descartes' overly linear view of rational explanation, because revelations are rarely the result of the mind's climbing a ladder, each clear and definitely placed rung surmounted foot after foothold like a fireman performing a rescue; they are achieved more in the devious way cream rises to the top of its container: everywhere the thin milk is sinking while simultaneously countless globules of fat are floating free and slipping upward, each alone and as independent of one another as Leibniz' monads, until gradually, nearly unnoticed, the globs form a mass which forces the blue milk beneath, whereupon the sweet cream crowns the carton, waiting to be skimmed.

When young Luther Penner, in all innocence of theory, was wiping his aunt's sterling with the socks he had taken from his tennis shoes and removed from his feet (actually running pieces between his toes came later, and was, you might say, *le coup de patte*), he was acting with heedless enthusiasm. As a result he did not count on his prank having consequences which might discomfit him later. His aunt, he ought to have remembered, did not entertain often, and then only relatives, of whom Penner's family was nearest and dearest, so there was a distinct possibility that the silver Luther found himself using a few months later had lain unmolested in its velvet chest while a more plebeian plate performed daily duties, hence he might have then been buttering his bread, as he wryly noted, with his own toe jam.

Luther Penner filed away this lesson with the many others he would learn, either from experience, as in this case, or from his extensive reading. Each was like a little blob of butterfat rising to meet the others. For instance, he realized that, although his childish prank had been, for him, impulsive, it had nevertheless been in its own way appropriate, because his Aunt Spatz was a fanatical housekeeper. She walked about with a rag in her hand, sweeping it over sills and the seats of chairs, caressing the globes of lamps, and rubbing the light out of small panes of window glass, of which her house had many. She had nurtured this virtue so successfully it had become a vice, and she felt she was improving Luther's character by delegating her authority and enlisting his assistance in washing up and putting away the dishes and the silver after dinner (a service which was given reluctantly at the signal of his mother's glare). Luther particularly remembered disliking the floury white apron little larger than a loincloth his aunt wore around her waist over the severe dark dresses she fancied, protection more symbolic than practical and giving her the appearance of a maid in the movies—a comparison wholly cultural in origin since Penner had never seen a maid anywhere else.

He also realized in due course how risky running knives and forks between your toes was, and how vulnerable to apprehension he had become, barefoot in the butler's pantry.

The punishment should be suitable to the crime—like an iron maiden, cut to fit—that was the ancient principle, and properly interpreted, it would certainly prove itself over and over again. If Aunt Spatz was pretty twitty about dirt and germs, she nevertheless had not deserved Luther's mean and unclean joke, since she had never, by look, or word, or deed, dishonored her nephew, nor did she call him "nephew" or treat him with the usual familial contempt. In sum, and on account of his ignorance and youth, Luther had been unjust; he had put himself at risk in more than one way; he had been careless in his employment of the powers he now saw were his; and consequently he had stained the shirt of the self well above the cuff.

Later, when Penner read George Orwell's *Down and Out in Paris and London,* he would recognize many of the tricks cooks and waiters played on their customers as belonging to the same dubious class of requitals as his sock-wiping did: cooks would spit in the soup, handle raw steak with dirty fingers, and lick its juice with their lascivious tongues. Waiters were worse, using gravy to grease their hair, because a proper revenge was supposed to be a response to some dishonor, and what honor did waiters have, who were expected to "sir" and "ma'am" and bow to anyone who could pay the tab? The waiter, when treating his wife and kids to an ice on a Sunday, could be haughty to the help without concern, since, on Sunday, in the company of his kids, and with Louise on his arm like a fancy cane, he was a customer, and therefore a king; but on work nights, in the diner or the café, he was worse than dirt on the floor, earning tips by showing his teeth, groveling by bending his backbone, sucking up to customers with his solicitous-servant's voice, not even in a whore's place to give pleasure with her person, but in the pimp's position of one who merely conveys the goose to the table.

Looking clean, Penner remembers Orwell writing, was dirty work.

Thomas Hobbes insisted that the state of nature was a state of war, of every man against every man; however, with due respect, this statement was true of the schoolyard too. At recess, Penner would run to a corner of the yard and try to hide behind a bush or a tree, sometimes one, sometimes the other, but it was no use, his tormentors would be hot on his heels, taunting and snickering and threatening till finally they did pinch his arm and pull his ear, singing horrid songs like Suck my dick, it is so thick; I'll come quick, and you'll be sick—stuff like that—while Luther tried to keep the trunk of the tree at his back, though that never worked because Cy would wrap his long arms around both Luther's trunk and the tree's, and then some sneak, bearing the name of little fairy Larry, would punch him in the stomach until Luther (who had, as he told them, a real religious name, unlike Cy and Syph and Larry, names of diseases) learned to take a drink from the fountain just before recess and hold his cheeksful so he could pretend to upchuck when struck, spewing his amalgamated spit all over Larry's surprised face, because by gagging and pretending to an involuntary vomit, it would not appear to be an act of purposeful aggression but a slavish response to pain and fear, and therefore wouldn't stimulate retaliation.

My name ain't the name of a disease. Syph is too the name of a disease. It's the name of a disease you catch by fucking. But my name ain't Syph. That's what everybody calls you: Syph Syph Syph. You break out in pimples, Luther assured him, which was an appropriate improvisation because Syph suffered from acne. Eventually you go mad because those pimples have covered your brain.

Cy is short like Syph is short and it's short for Cybernetics, a disease of the balls. They swell. Like balloons. You can't stop them. Aaah, that's just what you say. It's in all the books. Aaah. The books about bad things. Eventually your balls burst. These cybers, see, they grow inside, get thicker and bigger till bang. Naah. They grow like potatoes in their hidden hills. Cy waved a dismissive paw and said naah, but Cy wasn't so sure anymore.

While you were tormenting me, I prayed to Lord Jesus to forgive you. That's what little Rainer the Rilke says he said when he was bullied at military school. And earned a further beating.

Because turning the other cheek is a first-class revenge, and wholly infuriating.

Larry is so a sickness. Oh yeah. Larrygitis. You get it and you stop making any noise. You can't talk, you can't burp, you can't snivel, your knuckles won't crack, your farts don't blat or hiss or burble, you can't snore, your body, when it moves, doesn't make a single sound, like you were overoiled, your teeth, when you eat, are like colliding cottons. Ah nuts, I ain't named for that. You are though, Larry—larrygitis—you are.

Larry complained to his pa, who was more than firm in denial—loud and long—ridiculing his own kid for being such a stupid, which made Larry exceedingly wroth, so that the next time Cy grabbed Luther, suddenly and from behind, but without including the tree, Larry kicked Luther once in the shins, kneed him twice in the groin, and punched him three quick ones to the stomach. Syph, Cy, and Larry were at last observed by a teacher administering this beating, and all four were hauled before the principal and asked for explanations. Cy couldn't bring himself to talk about ballooning balls to a person of such dignity, and since he was commanded to speak first, his reluctance put a damper on the others, who decided it was going to be manly to say nothing no matter what. The "what" was that they were all roundly paddled, including Luther, whom the principal (one Horace McDill) felt must have done something to provoke the attack.

And what had Luther done, what was Penner doing, to deserve such a series of injustices? He led a superior existence. That was his crime. Though this was Luther's first thought, he soon faced up to the fact that he did not lead a superior existence. His existence was inferior in almost every way. Which accounted for his many smirks of superiority, and his delight in words which rarely had a use, like *tantamount* and *parse* and *diapason*. His studied aloofness didn't help either, especially when it had to be expressed through hasty concealments behind the leaves and branches of a bush. The correct formula would have it that Luther Penner was a superior person forced to lead an inferior life. That was his crime.

The next day, still sore in so many ways, Luther had his first vision. He saw a white splotch, about the size of Aunt Spatz's apron, appear on Cy's apple-red shirtfront. That meant it was more pink than white, the apparition, but Luther's impression was he was seeing something white behind or under or immersed in something red . . . apple red. John Locke had mistakenly argued, although with the best of intentions—not to gainsay such a noble if boring thinker—that the human mind, at birth, was a tabula rasa, and that experience wrote, like chalk taken to a slate, upon it. Locke had, however, got hold of the wrong spiritual organ. It was not the mind that was blank at birth, but the moral soul, white as bond paper, bleached as desert bone, and it was this that Luther saw, of a sudden. He must have looked at Cy very strangely, for Cy was struck dumb, as if by larygitis, and merely returned Luther's stare, a stare in his case without significance.

The splotch moved a little like a flag—undulant. And on that white area there were small droplets, black as India's ink, flecks scattered like pollen might be from a poisonous plant. Luther's vision, as we know now, was of Cy's dirty interior person, already dotted with a bully's dark deeds and secret fears. We are born morally pure, Luther Penner realized, but life dirties us, and we darken over time, so a self that might have been once radiant within, lightening our skin and shining through our eyes, becomes besmirched by anger, fright, and pride, by pettiness and mean designs. Over time our inner sun will dim, we shall be less and less morally alive, and one day night will pull down its blind, we shall do a Dirty which leaves us at last with no more guilt or remorse than a squirrel feels for stealing the birds' seed, and we shall find ourselves finally without humor or indignation or passion or desire or any inner heat whatever. It was what was meant by "the dark night of the soul." We shall be zombies of the spirit. Like politicians too cynical to bother feeling the cynic's superiority or even showing the cynic's sneer.

You have beshat your soul's shirt, Luther cried, quite involuntarily. No one knew what *beshat* meant, or *soul's shirt* either, so no one took umbrage.

Yet it was not clear, then, as it is not clear now, whether those spots were like dark stars, present all the time but obscured by clouds which opened now and then to reveal them, or whether over time the soul became soiled like a shirt, as Penner initially believed, tattered like a battle flag.

In one case, it would mean that the white area Luther had seen was hypocrisy's fog, concealing a constant and continuing deep meanness, while in the other it would suggest we earn our bad characters and bear them like bruises. Healing, cleansing, might then be possible.

Beyond his single exclamation, Luther Penner told no one of his vision, which he wanted to believe was an aberration anyway, because the sight of the sheet or shirt had unnerved him. Blake, as a boy, had seen angels in the trees, but Blake had made the mistake of mentioning his vision to his father, who promptly beat him for telling lies. Neither of Penner's parents would have beaten him. They weren't the beating kind. But his father's heavy eyebrows would have risen like a pair of startled birds, and absence would have occupied his face. His mother's mouth would have become pursed as if glued shut and her eyes would have fixed him fiercely, as if to see from where inside him this silliness was coming.

I found out you get the syph from toilet seats, Syph said, so you're a liar, Luther. Luther saw Syph's soul show like a long white scarf worn through a snowfall of soot. His jaw dropped as jaws are supposed to do, but Syph misunderstood the reaction. Yeah, caught you out, lout, you lying Luther. It wasn't as if Luther were seeing through them like Superman by exercising moral X-ray vision; it was as if their natures were rising to the surface like hungry carp. The sheets, shirts—whatever they were—were in motion, flags in a wind, mufflers in a breeze, towels on a line. They didn't resemble ghostly stage smoke; there were no ethical ethers here either; but what Luther saw each time had a linenlike character. Even silk. Nor were the shapes the same, or their sizes either. A few were ragged, one as rectangular as a room, Syph's was shawly, and then, as Luther was registering these differences—between Clarence Pewly's "conscience" caught coming down the school stairs like a pattern woven in his sweater, and Brownie Burks', holding his books to his chest (his soul shone though the covers like something laid on by the sun)—two questions rose: had he noticed how long the images lasted? and were there any manifestations from the girls?

It caused Luther Penner considerable distress to realize that although the dirty persons of his schoolmates came and went, he had little idea of how they did—they were there, they were not there. He supposed that adults were too darkly dyed by sin to be clearly seen or too weighed down by evil to materialize (or immaterialize, who knew?), but what about those girls? And then he realized to his shame that he rarely stared at the girls on account of their breasts, whose presence made him blush, and caused his eyes to misfocus. In short, he wasn't looking in the right place. Neither knee, back, arm, nor face would do. The soul liked the strike zone.

He decided he'd gaze at Gilda, she had no breasts, at least not yet. He tried to address her during recess about algebra (she was a whiz), however she kept standing at an angle to him. Perhaps he was too obviously addressing her, and that was the problem. Anyway, it wasn't working out. Furthermore, he was teased for talking to a girl. The goons. He'd have called them the Three Stooges, but they liked the Three Stooges.

Meanwhile, Penner was walking with a spiritual limp. The principal (the aforenamed Horace McDill) had treated him unjustly, lumping him in with those bumpkins and giving him, as though he deserved it, an equal set of swats. There was no redress. And Luther knew he would continue to stumble about, injured by everybody, until he'd taken his revenge, for revenge was necessary in the absence of justice, and in distasteful equal-itarian societies where the quiet merits of the meek were given but fat lip service.

The lady with the scales wore bandaged eyes. That symbol-ized the fact, Luther had been told, that justice was ideally indifferent to the person you were: male or female, rich or poor, black or white, Chicano or Jap. The unsymbolic fact—the actual matter of fact—however was that justice paid every attention to just that: who you were—it cheated, it peeked—because it wanted to know precisely whose donkey it was pin-ning a tail to. Which Penner thought was proper. Who you were ought to count. But only on the basis of an inner measure. Character ought to matter. Intelligence. Talent. Perhaps not looks. Certainly not wealth or parentage or nationality or color. Or health. The lady's bandaged eyes ought honestly to mean what would in fact factually happen: justice would arrive unseen, unexpectedly, deal you your deserts, steal you blind, and then scoot.

Luther put on his best pair of downcast eyes and slipped into a contrite grovel (his self-deprecating language in a letter to me reflecting an adult's opinion), and inserted himself slyly into Principal McDill's office in order to confess that those boys had beaten him because he didn't want to participate in—he'd bet-ter say "go along with"—their plan to steal the ditto masters of the final exams, memorize or copy the questions, and return them undetected to the drums of the machines. Luther hinted that the gang had already made experimental forays to test their chances. Despite a performance (in Luther Penner's opinion) that merited three stars and a round of applause, Principal McPickle seemed skeptical, as if feeling his leg pulled; however Syph's inky fingers, Cy's shirt stain, and the blue dirt beneath Larry's nails convinced him of their guilt immediately he began his inquiries: when he saw those finger ends, that shirt splotch, and the dyed dirt.

Penner had simply soaked some marbles in Quink, a water-soluble ink popular then; allowed his three bullies to wrest the glassies from him (temptingly displayed in a cellophane sack); and waited for the marbles to mark the thieves and send them to their reward, which was a brief suspension from classes, nothing they would have minded if their parents hadn't. The Master was never particularly proud of this revenge, since it was early and full of errors, but he understood perfectly well that its success depended first upon the predictable mendacity of his tormentors, second upon Principal McPickle's penchant for rushing to judgment, and third upon that same Pickle's suspicion of all kids, including, initially, Penner, based on a professional experience of twenty years. But the revenge was reinforced by circumstances Penner had not taken fully into account: namely that the ditto room was found to be insecure, so that the plot he had dreamed up would have been easy to perform, rendering his tale more plausible; and because his three dupes had joked wishfully on numerous occasions about how great it would be to "get aholt" of the test questions by one bit of magic or other (giving Luther the "germ" of his plan when he overheard), they were not as prompt and determined in their denials as they might have been. They *had* wanted the answers. They knew that. They *had* made plans, however imaginary. They knew that too. In their heart of hearts, they knew they were guilty.

From Penner's point of view, since his gulls had been innocent of conspiracy, the requital had been unjust; however they had bullied him badly, and had stolen his marbles, and had, like so many boys, failed to wash their hands with Aunt Spatz's saving promptness. The stains on their moral souls would not be so simple a washday project. Penner's revenge, of course, could not remain secret, at least the schoolboy side of it, and he paid the price of a good pummeling after; nevertheless there was a hidden and favorable facet to the affair: McPickle had been persuaded to revisit his poor judgment and repeat his previous error. And that constituted a secret revenge by any standard.

Socrates had wondered why you would want to make your enemies worse than they already were by punishing them. So noble himself, Socrates refused to accept the fact that making people worse than you are is one of the world's true pleasures, one to be pursued even at the price of future pain. Socrates, wise as always, argued that justice was a harmony. Unfortunately, he accepted the least appropriate sense of that word. Justice is doing whatever it takes to restore the world's moral balance. It is evening up, defending one's honor, requiting wrongs.

If a robber had pointed a gun at Luther Penner's boyhood head and demanded he hand over his marbles, Luther would not have been dishonored. His marbles would have been stolen, but the robber would have thought enough of his marbles and of him to have taken them at gunpoint. Penner need never feel ashamed. When they are laughingly snatched from his grasp, however, by a set of stupid boys, in front of the entire school, too, with even the teachers watching; when Syph shouts, "Loothie hath lost hith marbles!" and a crowd laughs, then such a humiliation needs to be paid for, and in kind. Like the dye that gilds bank robbers by exploding onto their faces and their clothes, as well as over their stolen money, the marbles did them in.

An eye for an eye is the only moral law, Luther Penner wrote in his little-known though, for that few, notorious pamphlet "The Moral Self Wears a White Shirt." Suppose we made, using Kant's own rule, the law of the talon into a universally operative physical principle. Let us imagine a world in which, if I strike my brother, I am that moment struck; if I cheat on my wife, she fucks my father; if I rob a neighbor, the neighbor breaks open my money box; if I kill an enemy, I am a suicide, for I shall die in his instant, and in the same way, cut for cut, outcry for outcry, and bleed for bleed. Another merit of the code is that the instant retaliation ends the affair. It both inhibits crime and supplies society with an appropriate reply. The law of the talon won't fuel a feud.

Consequently, capital punishment *is* a deterrent, if the punishment proceeds promptly and falls with certainty upon its subject. Society, which frowns on individual vengeance (with good reason), and instead takes revenge on miscreants for their victims' sakes, pretends to be improving them when it imprisons; when it puts youthful felons with lifers so they may learn buggery and burglary at the same time; when it allows jails to reflect the very corrupt and prejudicial social order of the world at large—debauchery, bribery, corruption, racism, tyranny, there as well as here—when it sends its criminals to schools for scoundrels; but it is at bottom lying to its citizens. The honest efficiency of Hammurabi's code must be admired—all thirty-six hundred characters of it. Makeshift imitations—I steal from the poor box so the state cuts off my hand, or I lose my dick if I am guilty of rape—are certainly better than incarcerations, so inefficient, so ineffective, so costly, but having lost one hand I will steal with the other, and like Popeye, Faulkner's nasty bit of business, I will continue to rape, though now, perhaps, with a corncob, no significant loss, since sexual pleasure was never a motive. Pause, Mister Rapist, Penner writes, to imagine that corncob up your own ass. Penner put it that way to remind us that there will always be a few who will choose murder as their suicide; who will want pain enough to pain others to receive it; who will enjoy theft so completely they are willing to pay with an equal loss for the pleasure; who will molest boys as they would love to be molested. No principle is perfect.

The only problem with the code is that it isn't one. Society is naturally nervous, too, about making mistakes, castrating the wrong fellow, or executing someone guilty only of a forced confession. Nevertheless, the best way to cure crime is to scare the criminals so badly they desist ahead of time.

Gilda is our next case. In the succeeding year, Gilda grew into a properly appealing girl while remaining a genius at algebra and adding solid geometry. Their first encounters were contrived. Luther Penner wanted to test his perceptions. As if she suspected something, she stood to one side or behind things. However, when her breasts appeared, she grew noticeably less shy, and Penner had to conclude that she had been embarrassed by her flat chest, but was proud of her hilly one, which she rather liked having admired. She accepted his stares as her bosom's just deserts. And moved on to uplift bras.

Although Luther was now allowed to gaze at Gilda as if she were a work of art, his look had become impure, and he saw nothing but her "suckle centers," as he termed them in those desperate journal entries. Puberty threw Penner some strong punches, none of which he managed to dodge. He had no charm to begin with; now he had acne, and longings, and ejaculations so embarrassing he dreaded sleep. Nature itself was humiliating him. How did you get back at Nature? He wasn't sure about girls, maybe they deserved their fluxions, but a boy was born naked with a nasty character, required to live and grow up with strangers who would then believe they had an understanding of him as well as rights over his every thought. Before he knew it his balls would be aching because some sweet little girl had allowed him to pet her leg in a movie. Oh but it does feel fully magical, that soft stretch of inner thigh, the low highway of lust and longing. Then life snaps its sex shut and he is captured like an animal. Must he chew his own cock off in order to escape?

Monks surely had the right idea: to retire behind walls and eat roots; but more than likely it was the root of another brother they ate, or they climaxed between chosen pages of their missals, or dreamt of ravishments so total they were, in effect, tossed off all night. Later, Luther would lecture me about the virtues of the Shaker way of life. Instead of making love, they made cupboards. Lovingly. And lots of perfectly fitting, smoothly sliding drawers.

Penner's reformatory plans would have to become metaphysical, no less than his namesake, Martin Luther's, had. Abetted by their parents (like father one son, like mother the other), Larry and Syph had connected him with some long lost comedian of the Penner name whose tag had apparently been "Wanna buy a duck?" Thusly he was now greeted. Well, it was better than being pinched in the ass and pounded on the arm, although by this time Luther had perfected his defense against his tormentors, which was to become another person while being bullied: either the Joey Penner the comedian was called, or Millicent Peezy, after his earliest enemy. It was as if she, then, suffered the sore arm, and it served her right.

Penner confesses that he now passed through a period of delinquency. He felt out of sorts with everyone and everything. Pretending he could drive, he got a Christmas job as a delivery boy. He figured he'd learn by doing. Fired for caving in a fender on his first day, he got even so promptly it elevated his attitudes. He'd suffer many blows in life. He certainly knew that by now. His meekness had grown worse as though in tune with his acne. He felt lower than the worm and less wiggly. In those days, gas caps weren't locked as they are in our more suspicious age. When Luther left the company's parking lot he pissed profusely into the pipe of the offending van. He buttoned his pants. He screwed the car's cap tight. He strode happily away. But Luther then returned every day at first light to inoculate all four of the Philander Brothers' trucks, one morning at a time.

He was almost caught by a kid who was driving for the same store, and then chased from the place, which was certainly humiliating. It cast him down again. To revive his spirits, he asked himself: do what? Wait until the cars wheezed to a halt in huge drifts and the drivers were fired for incompetence? In the holiday snow, by the side of each car, he'd left his prints. That realization threw him into a cold sweat. Merderation. He'd failed to think things through. Again. He didn't even know how many gallons of urine he'd need to pump into those machines before they'd feel any marked lowering of octane and begin to cough. Of course, he argued with himself, what mattered was, he'd done it, and he at least knew it: he'd pissed in Philander's tank. It was a revenge so secret, its consequences were a secret even to himself.

He could have sugared the gas, had he known of that trick; he could have thrust a banana into the tailpipe, but he was ignorant of the chemistry of machinery; however he did consider smearing honey on the steering wheel and waxing the side mirrors with soap. Still, wasn't that Halloween stuff, and beneath the level of skill he'd reached? What acumen could he really claim, though, when he'd left a trail like a moose in the snow, and probably his fingerprints on the cap like the most ordinary criminal, and chilled his instrument once to the point of pain when the glans had brushed frozen metal.

There was, when younger, the time he got even with a bratty little boy who often came with his parents to visit. The kid was supposed to be bright, but he was a handful, darting into rooms whose doors were closed, shrieking for no noticeable reason, picking his nose and wiping his boogers on the curtains if they were curtaining nearby, or the rug if he were playing there, cutting anything innocently flat and cardboardly stiff with sewing scissors, throwing blocks, and making faces at Luther when no one else was looking, thrusting his tongue rapidly in and out of his cupped hand, a gesture Luther didn't even understand at the time, so it was very unlikely the whiz kid did.

Luther's father had just painted the downstairs bathroom a glistening white, and the wall under its little diamond-leaded window now called out for a sign. So, with a big black crayon, Luther drew an asshole there. The asshole, which he puckered, was accompanied by an arrow pointing toward the toilet, and by the message: put it there. Then—Luther smiled at this early display of his cleverness—in lighter smaller print he put "looser did this" under the drawing way down by the baseboard.

As if sent by heaven, Jerome Penner discovered the graffiti first and let out an incontinent howl, but to Luther's surprise it was his mother who shook the brat back and forth like a mop in front of his parents, screaming at him so angrily it sounded like Hungarian (indeed, it could have been, since that was her parents' native tongue). Luther had to admire the way his mother's hair flew about her face, and how her arm was working away like a connecting rod. Visible annoyance, even yelling, might have been acceptable to the Penners' shocked and dismayed visitors, but playing yo-yo with their future Edison was not, nor did they enjoy being ordered into the bathroom to observe its desecration.

The realization that the crayon marks could be scrubbed off was slow in coming, but when that recognition did arrive, it could not save the situation, since the outrage of the image and the spiteful cowardice of its feeble attempt to shift the blame to Luther were fuel enough to make and sustain considerable steam. The little vandal's father (as Luther jocularly describes him) protested that his boy was too smart to misspell *Luther,* and Luther for a moment feared exposure: what if the kid were asked, or were to offer up a proper spelling on the spot? But there was too much anger in the air for that, and the visit ended abruptly amid the protests and accusations of windmilling wives, and the strutting glares of their spouses, sufficient to peel walls.

This revenge could not have had a better outcome, except that Luther was, though innocent and terribly put upon, still required to scrub the scurrilous drawing from the wall. It turned out that, beneath the more explicit hairy orifice, a gray ghost lurked, and that the arrow also palely remained, pointing its faint way, suggesting a rule of life.

What was the difference between revenge and vandalism? between restoring your damaged honor and behaving like a little prick? Sure, he could put pinholes in ripe fruit, place an earthworm on a deli plate, soak his aunt's Aspergum in alum, and he could read with pleasure about the dishonored queen who served her husband his mistress' heart. Poisoning loved ones over long periods held his interest, as well as wars of recovery like that of the Greeks against the Trojans. Sing, goddess, the *Iliad* should have begun, of the revenge of Chryses, the priest of Apollo whose daughter was taken to be Agamemnon's whore; and of the revenge of Apollo then, who sent a plague to punish the Greeks; and finally of the revenge of Achilleus, who sulked in his tent because his concubine had been taken away to replace Agamemnon's mistress, since the king had had to give up his new pussy (unentered, he argued, unpetted, unbussed) to fend off Apollo's anger; and sing too of how Achilleus remained there, covered with canvas, to play every violet evening with the penis of his pal Patroklos, until Patroklos met death in daytime while hiding in the armor of Achilleus; whereupon the sulker went forth in a rage to revenge the loss of his pal; and how, at last, Hector's corpse was dragged around the walls of Troy to ensure that the Trojans' hero would live his afterlife in bruised bits and tattered pieces.

Penner learned that great historical epochs were characterized by an advanced sense of individual honor, the pursuit of *gloire,* and were consequently marked by many imaginative acts of revenge. The Classical Greek, the High Roman, both the English and the Italian Renaissance, were packed with such self-justifying hijinks.

Late in Luther Penner's senior year, Syph suddenly stopped asking him whether he wanted to buy a duck, and began calling Luther "Mary the fairy!" in the loudest voice he could muster. This required a reply, but it could not be one which would cause more name-calling or earn Penner further blows. Shielded by traffic and safely across the street, Penner shouted: I've a riddle for you, Syph. Why is your mother like a police station? The answer to this riddle doubtless perplexed Syph considerably. He was not clever enough to guess the answer, but bright enough to understand that its arrival would not make him happy. To inflict perplexity upon your dishonorer is sometimes enough.

Learning from this success, when he's called a bad name now, Penner told me, he replies by flaring his nose and saying *"Jou moer!"* in a venomous tone—an expression he picked up out of Afrikaans like a bag lady dips a dainty from the trash. Luther went so far as to memorize several sentences of invincible vileness in a language he said was Cushitic. One expression, he claimed, asserted that your enemy broke wind without pause. I couldn't tell whether the sounds he made were in a language or not. He has also invented gestures of which no one else knows the meaning, such as putting a fisted thumb in his ear or lifting his left leg slowly from the ground.

The revenge Penner came to admire most was that of Alcibiades, once a ward of Pericles, called by all the beautiful, a lovelorn lover of Socrates according to Plato, and, as a general and statesman, extolled by Thucydides for intelligence, skill, and courage. Chosen to lead the Athenian fleet against Syracuse, Alcibiades was accused, just before the armada was to sail, of obscenely mutilating the phallic statues of Hermes, and thus outraging the god of crossways and travel. Unjustly removed from his command, Alcibiades defected to Sparta, since only the defeat of the Athenian invasion could satisfy the sort of dishonor he had suffered. There he advised the Spartan king, Agis I, as to strategy, with such success that Athens was brought down like a last-act curtain.

After a falling-out with Agis, Alcibiades did some braintrusting for the Persian satrap Tissaphernes, urging him to enter the war on the Spartan side (thereby doubling his revenge quotient). He was even able to return to Athens and earn more military triumphs there because the Athenians knew he had been unjustly disgraced, and understood his treason as an appropriately proportional response. When that scheming brute, the Spartan commander Lysander, defeated the Athenians at sea, Alcibiades, though far away on another mission, was blamed for the disaster, and exiled once more for his excellence. Luther Penner regarded this as an insult sufficient to justify an entire life bent on revenge. Alcibiades' days were numbered, however. Seeking safety with still another satrap, this time the Persian pig Pharnabazus (whose name Penner could never bear to pronounce, and whom he referred to always with disgust as that Persian pig, popping the p's needed to produce the phrase like others do bubble gum), Alcibiades was murdered by his host, the aforementioned Persian pig, at the behest of Lysander, to whom the Persian pig wished to suck up.

What was a man like Luther Penner to do? He hadn't a fleet to lead, estates to patrol, daughters to guard. He hadn't been thrown from his home by an angry parent, or falsely accused, or wrongly jailed. He had never been the friend of a revolutionary so he might enjoy a little guilt by association. Even when fired from this or that small job, Penner had in all fairness frankly to admit he deserved to be canned.

Movies were not helpful. Many of them were rituals of revenge, of course; however, rarely did these celluloid reenactments add anything to its understanding. Penner quite liked *Hang 'em High,* a flick in which Clint Eastwood stars as an innocent strung up by a vengeful posse. He escapes that fate in order to do the dirty on the vigilantes, one by one. The venge-film always begins with a crime against the hero: his daughter is raped or kidnapped or killed, wife and child are murdered, his house is burned, a community is terrorized, worse yet, the hero's horse is stolen, his dog is kicked. The greater the injury, the more violence the hero will be allowed later; and the more painful, cruel, and horrific the eventual recompense is, the better. Individuals may be speared by a harpoon gun, consumed by burning gasoline, plunged into a vat of acid, pulled through a jet engine or torn apart by tractors revved in opposite directions, stabbed in the eye by an icicle, simply beaten and kicked to death, buried in the sand to their neck by Apaches, or by symbolic circumstance the way poor old Winnie is in *Happy Days,* without a trace of guilt appearing on the actor's murdering hands or any evident darkening of his vengeful character, while applause can be heard coming from an approving, pleasured, and heartened audience. The well-deserved death of Indians can be numbered in terms of burned villages and sabered encampments; red-legged marauding comancheros can be Gatling'd by the dozens; over-the-border towns are often burned so entirely to the ground the graveyard goes up in smoke and ashes—it's all quite OK and great fun—we are soaked in satisfaction.

Not everything is permitted. The avenging angel may not bugger the bastard who raped his sister, wife, or daughter. He may not kill anybody's cow, and he has to keep his hands off kids. But he can shoot the rapist's cock into kingdom come and then cauterize the wound with a hot iron; he can carve up the cow if his wagon train is starving; he can teach the kids how to set traps and aim guns.

He must not cut the whore's nose, scald the cat, spill milk, or fail to relish simple greens and homemade biscuits.

Plays, poems, tales, and images of vengeance have pleasured the human heart since God set the standard by sending Adam and Eve out to labor in the dust, snow, and rain. There can be no doubt of that. The reason? because there are way too many wrongs in this world and far too little justice. In any after-world, Hell would have to be hellish to stay even with Heaven. Moreover, the meek who were not merely meek beneath their meekness, but mighty inside it, were hourly humiliated by an unfeeling multitude.

And by Nature. Which filled them with longings. With bestir-rings. And left them in despair. In his journals Penner complained of having naked bodies on the brain. All the temptations of Saint Anthony were paraded past him: he was offered a book of blank checks signed by the Persian pig Pharnabazus; a peach in the shape of a schoolboy's testicle was then held out to him, into which he sunk his tangle of teeth; next a lectern of teak appeared, behind which he was urged to speak his piece; suddenly he stood in the air above an arena where his tormentors were being eaten by large lizards or strangled by squids, then equally suddenly he's tripped up by bird wake and falls forty feet upon his face; a book of beliefs is opened in front of that flattened face, suggesting he subscribe to the tenets of the Paternians, the Marcosians, or the Montanists *tout de suite;* he is beset by daydreams of the Annunciation—not of Mary being entered by God's angel, but of the winged phallus itself, dew tipped, its wings pulsing like a butterfly feeding from a flower; at last, lifted up again, he becomes a constellation of falling stars. Penner would hit his head with his hands, with a fist strike his thigh, once again be required to tame his member. It occurred to him, finally, that the only way to get even with Nature would be to formulate and propagate fallacious descriptions of it. Philosophers had been engaged in this felicitous enterprise for ages. But at the time Penner came to this conclusion, he did not know what new illusion to promote.

Like someone drowning, Penner flailed away at his world. Always anonymously, he posted envelopes to his enemies (the list grew almost hourly) on which he printed: *how much you mean to me.* Inside, the recipient would find a carefully folded blank sheet. To mail-order houses which had begun cramming his box with their gaudy catalogues, he packaged dried dog turds tied together like small logs with a ribbon and a message which read: *you send me shit I don't want; I send you shit you don't want.* The pleasure he felt when he imagined his victims opening their presents was considerable, and he did dwell on the scenes, filling them with appropriate details: the dog dung falling from frightened fingers, yelps of distaste, groans of disgust, each in a cartoon balloon; or he pictured a puzzled gaze flung at the empty page followed by slow recognition and a gradual increase of anger; however, he also understood the inherent crudity of it all, the cowardice too, for the anonymity he had to insist on was not altogether noble; it was, in a way, downright demeaning. To lower yourself in order to get even, he realized, was not an ideal procedure. He was also probably breaking some federal law.

Luther eventually replaced his scatalogical rejoinders with an adaptive one: he figured out a method of getting his marks on the mailing lists of sleazy novelty hawkers, lingerie manufacturers, the floggers of erotic toys and devices, and he brought their addresses to the greasy attention of plain-wrapper pornography peddlers and no-exam insurance companies. The way Penner got a person's name put on these mailing lists is neat and ingenious, but I don't wish to encourage this practice, so I'll not divulge it here. For the few who he judged might be pleased to be placed in the way of such sludge, Penner arranged for them to be solicited by the Knights of Columbus, or hectored by the Seventh Day Adventists, or threatened by the Nation of Islam instead, and, in addition, to receive with menacing regularity the *Mormon Monthly, The Jewish Daily Forward,* the *American Legion Magazine,* or the *Christian Science Sentinal* on a regular basis. It was one of these latter little revenges which provided me with the program by which I might follow in my master's footsteps.

Luther Penner was in a desperate and despairing mood when I first met him. We were both going to night school. I was studying history in preparation for the law, and he was taking literature courses with the idea of becoming an English teacher. Our bikes were one night parked next to one another in the rack. Penner had a soft tire and borrowed my pump. I'm like this tire, he said to me. Every morning I pump myself up only to leak slowly away all day—sssssssss—so by evening I'm soft like this—flat, and unable to function. I made no memorable reply, but the way Penner had hissed—with soft insistence—remained in my mind. I joked that perhaps he should carry a pump around with him as I was doing, and he laughed, turning from his task to gaze at me with disconcerting fullness. Ah . . . by evening I've run out of lies.

He greeted me with a smile and nod next night, and proposed

we wheel our bikes to a nearby coffee shop for talk. I was pleased to agree, as he'd been pleased to hear I was presently studying the Renaissance. The perfect period, he said. *Then,* he said, *then* there were ghosts and gods; *then* there were men. And Italian, the language of the mafioso, of opera, of revenge, of *maledizione,* was in the process of freeing itself from Latin. Had I much knowledge yet of Caterina Sforza, that dear and devoted woman whose memory he cherished? I said I thought "dear and devoted" were hardly the right words for a will as unbending as hers, and Penner stopped stirring his coffee to hold up a damp spoon. Oh, dear and devoted, she was, he exclaimed, devoted to *la vendetta!* When her second husband, Giacomo Feo—to whom, by the way, she was also dearly devoted—when he was murdered on the road, set upon by assassins at the rear of her own cortège—it was returning from a hunt—and Caterina had to scamper to her castle like a rodent—much in grief, more in rage—you remember?—she returned like a tiger, putting scores of conspirators, their friends and families, to death, and many others to torture and imprisonment. She had the wife and children of the principal plotter thrown down a well previously appointed with spikes. And her own firstborn—a weakling like me—because she had observed the child's jealousy of his stepfather, Feo—she incarcerated just in case.

Luther Penner's speech, punctuated by pauses, and conducted with his spoon, though itself not normally vehement, was accompanied by an intensity in the set of the jaw and a squint to the eyes which was quite striking. Soft-spoken and deferential with strangers, he held forth confidently, candidly, at length, when he felt he was among friends, a state he sensed existed between the two of us from the first. Near the end, he told me that he believed he'd seen a white flag flutter across my person that first night. If so, it was the last of those early envisionments.

We sat, that night, in the middle of a brightly waxed and Formica'd room with the traditional clunky white diner mugs in front of us, and talked of history and my interest in politics (a concern of which Penner jokingly disapproved). His fingers raised hell with a paper napkin, and he tended to stare into his coffee while he talked. When he listened, though, his head came up, and his eyes tried to lock on yours. He seemed wholly oblivious to everyone else in the place.

His spoon—in this sort of "joint" his spoon had to be pale, short, and plastic—his spoon could become quite aerially active, but his spoon was not employed to whirlpool cream or encourage sugar to dissolve, because he liked his coffee black and strong (caffeine was the only drug he could tolerate); still it might flick droplets on your person or lightly tattoo the table or illustrate the fast passage of an idea from one context to another. He drove his spoon through the air like a taxi in traffic.

Since my aim here is to elucidate Penner's ideas and describe their development, I shall omit what I told him about myself and what I was then thinking; these omissions will unfortunately make our conversations seem one-sided, as if Penner were wholly preoccupied with his own notions and given to extended monologues and nervous stirrings of his coffee. Although it is true that Luther Penner rarely strayed from his single subject, it is also true that he questioned me frequently about my own life and about my plans and opportunities, and that he listened with a diligent attention to what I said, and furthermore remembered it, reintroducing one of my memories into our conversation as if it were one of his, and frequently finding food for his thought in dishes I had set out, saying "I can make a meal of that" when I had uttered some opinion or concluded some story.

Naturally, it would not be sensible to reproduce the repetitions, backtrackings, or hems and haws of our conversations (which were normal, I think, in these respects), let alone observe the frequent silences which fell between us while I waited for him to complete a thought.

He told me that first night only that he was building a theology based on the idea of vengeance, but, he said, he didn't know me well enough yet to risk my laughter. I denied all possibility of mirth. Naturally you protest, he said, but if the cock crows to discomfit Paul, it will crow and discomfit anybody. Then he surprised me by asking, as we prepared to leave: do you know what Seneca says about retribution? I said I thought not. If you think not, you know not, Penner said, smiling so there'd be no reproof.

Well, Seneca says: *Scelera non ulciseris, nisi vincis.* I had no idea, I reply, honestly enough. And you still haven't, have you, Penner said, a bit peevishly. You can't be a lawyer and not know Latin.

After a bit, it became our habit to meet after class, wheel our bikes along the walk out of the college while talking about what had just taken place on Saint Bartholomew's Eve or about "the fair field of folke" Penner was ploughing through, according to the schoolboy joke. At Cow's Lick Café (so called because its owner had one), we would center ourselves as we had that first night, smack in the middle of the glare, where Luther would stir his coffee almost out of the mug and gradually admit me to his universe.

God said "Lucifer" first. Penner pointed his dripping spoon at one of the blazing overhead lights and then at their reflection from cabinets and counters and floors, from fat mugs and white faces. So Lucifer thought he was . . . was first, was foremost, was of all created things . . . the boss. He was the angel of clarity, regardless of the cost, of purity and unconcealment, of everything naked and shining—the bare breast, the fishes' scales—and of immediacy, too, he flew so fast—here to there in only a *t*. Indeed, he was the first sun of God (Luther's grin slowed him down so I could catch up with his puns), and he revealed himself in the morning as a star.

You might say it was a case of hubris in the highest which brought Lucifer down, but he had cause to be confused. All seemed clear to him, for he was clarity itself, he was light. Though he was not consubstantial with the Deity, he was still first in form and fact below that rank. He went anywhere and everywhere with amazing immediacy. And in each everywhere he was the cause of sight, of understanding, of life. I'd have forgiven him his pride. But God kicked him out of the sky for his presumption. Lucifer's light became fire as he fell, as though he were a meteor entering the atmosphere. The pale spoon spun out of control into the cup.

So he burned into the core of the earth, melting it like lead in a smelter, and now and then he shakes it, or it erupts, for he is still boiling mad after a zillion years. God dishonored His first creation, His son's shine, and made him hide in the ground, where he lurked like a locust. When Lucifer flew into the caverns which became Hell, the universe went dark once more, chaos returned, reasoning was impossible. God had to do many things over again. This time He made a lot of little lights like Gabriel, who has to polish his armor to achieve a gleam, and who is dim as a grimy dime when he's not wearing it.

But if "Let there be Light" was a mistake, "Let there be lights to the number of the bugs" was a catastrophe.

Except for the occasional smile to bemedal an especially smart remark, what Penner said was said with simple seriousness, even gravely, particularly when he drew consequences, like lengths of knotted hankies, from the sleeves of sacred texts.

The soul is that inner gleam which enables us to see, to understand, to reason as I am doing now, to shine from one thought to another. It used to be called "the candle of the Lord."

You won't believe it, but I have seen that light. Our little Lucifer. Yes, yours too, I think. That first night.

Reason, you know, is the one real enemy of God. Reason is the Great Satan.

Penner had a disorderly jam of teeth like flotsam on a beach, but he did not hide his mouth behind his hand, and his smile was broad and his grin wide. They gave a certain meaning to his words which his words by themselves never had, as if his sentences had seeped through several openings—as if they had been sieved. He was already losing the hair on the top of his head, and would soon look tonsured, which seemed suitable to me—to wear a halo of hair.

Lucifer insisted on behaving like a Lord of Hosts, and many of the lesser, later angels followed his lead. He was, after all, the first word, the first deed, the seed of all sense. God really wanted Lucifer to deceive himself and accept a lesser station. Yet how could Light pretend to Darkness? Well, many angels went with him when he fell. There was a shower of them like a torrent of stars. The tormented flutter which came from the descending host created a great wind. Planets were blown from their orbits. Mountains lost their tops and through these holes the angels fell like thrown stones. The resulting winds ran like rivers through the universe, and are still the source of all streaming air—the breath of beating wings. Angels kept arriving in hell for eons after, plashing down into lakes of fire like tardy geese.

This was revealed to you too? along with the sight of the soul's inner light?

And you said you'd be more reliable than Peter.

I didn't say I doubted or denied.

You im......plied.

During the ensuing weeks we discussed such oddly assorted

subjects as the Wife of Bath and the machinations of Pope Six-
tus IV, the idea of a pilgrimage, and the Pazzi conspiracy, *The
Rape of Lucrece* and the siege of Siena. Shakespeare, Penner
claimed, takes a revenge upon his readers which is so subtle and
so artfully wrought they never feel its bite. "To take arms against
a sea of troubles" was an idiot's activity, and not likely to end
anything, and a line like "To stamp the seal of time in aged
things" was pompous, repetitive, and empty beyond belief, yet
readers were led by his art to fancy the music such lines made,
to repeat them for pleasure, and feel them profound, which
demonstrated the readers' own shallow standards instead, and
how easily led down the rhetorical path their ears and minds
and hearts were. It was a revenge by the great writer of the
sweetest sort.

  After our coffees, we would push our bikes back to the rack,
and go our separate ways from there, so our conversations
tended to have a tripartite structure: first Chaucer or Pazzi, then
Lucifer and treason, finally worries, hurts, and hopes. Penner
was planning something in regard to his English instructor,
who, he said, had resisted certain of Luther's interpretations in
a publicly scornful way. As the term's end neared, I asked him
what he'd done to redeem his honor. Oh, he exclaimed, it was
easy. Always count on the weaknesses of your prey, for that is
what makes them fair game. He had simply cited, in his final
paper, a number of nonexistent sources to support his views,
and the instructor, one Claude Hoch, had failed to challenge
any of them. Surely, Luther said to me with his toothy smile and
syrupy tone, surely you have read that splendid book on *The
Canterbury Tales* by Nikki Quay D'Orsay? Sugar gave way to
gravel. The ignoramus who is supposed to be teaching me
Chaucer didn't bat an eye at so openly outrageous a fabrication.
Well, a snook for his snoot.

  Under ordinary conditions, Penner was a truth teller, but he was inclined to let rhetoric enlarge his assertions. I noticed this for the first time when we were discussing the Pazzi conspiracy, interesting mainly because the Pope was the principal plotter of that miserable enterprise. It failed and two subsequent attempts on Lorenzo the Magnificent, like fading rings around the tread of a water bug, were equally inept. Frescobaldi and his hired assassins were hanged from the windows of the Bargello, two to a window, Penner said, like drapes.

I tried to envision it. Unfortunately, I was able; sadly, it was easy.

During these days my mind was a jumble of examples, Luther supplying most, but I stirred in my share. I saw designs in the scud of clouds, underhandedness in every hello, a widespread scheme in the smallest exchange.

Lucifer, Luther said, as he elaborated his Genesis for me, may have been guilty, but he has, ever since, felt unjustly punished, and has nursed his grudge like a sucking calf. Good and Evil are like the family feuds between the Hatfields and McCoys, or the Montagues and the Capulets. Rejected, tossed aside, light began to burn, to consume instead of illuminate, and Lucifer became Satan, the Prince for those who would even the score—or go beyond the game the way the Duc de Guise did, who felt, like *Hamlet*'s Claudius, that "revenge should have no bounds." That's Seneca again. But by overstepping the bounds, by unevening things, as vendettas are inclined to do, the dreadful Duc earned and deserved the same fate as those he had massacred. Still, few retributions have been so thorough and carried out on such a scale as that of Saint Bartholomew's Day, when, according to Lord Acton, whom we must believe, over two thousand Prots were piked or otherwise killed in Paris. Isn't it Sully who says no person ever exacted as severe a vengeance as the Duc de Guise for his father's murder?

Light was so redundant in this place I thought of it as light's last stand. The café echoed and my eyes heard. So you believe the Biblical account? I believe the Bible as semaphore—as encoded poetry—and what deep signals it sends—Penner replied. It's written in wonderful "as it weres"—in brilliant *als obs*. The Big Book depicts—doesn't it?—*the* moral world—I mean a world where every enterprise has its ethical price and every stone and bone and grommet its moral worth. In the same way the stage mocks our ordinary life. In front of painted flats, fakes in costume mimic our dreadful deeds, yet the moment the deed is done, the deed redounds; it replicates itself like a shout in a canyon; it bounces back upon the doer like a serve returned. Penner's spoon ticks metronomically. Is that the way it happens here among us commoners? Remember Uzzah's fate? a lowly soldier, unsanctified, touches the Ark of the Covenant while preventing that most sacred of symbols from falling off the rear of a rocking cart into the mud and dust of a rutted road. Uzzah, the salvator, is struck dead in thrice less twice. He broke a rule. Lightning, all fire and light, is ignorant and indifferent about what it fingers. The spoon points and spears.

Do you know an Elizabethan play called *A Warning for Fair Women*? Luther, I know it not. Gooood. You've learned to light up your areas of ignorance. Actually, one can practice being proud of not knowing some things: how to bowl, for instance. Such an attitude is very disconcerting to those who had thought themselves superior on account of their lime Jell-O salad or the size of their stamp collection. Not having read the book or seen the movie everybody is talking about. Not being natty. Not owning a car though you know how to drive. Not being there.

Anyway, in this characteristic drama a ghost comes whining and crying to be avenged. *Vindicta,* it asks. Like Hamlet's father's ghost, though less manfully. I'm impressed at the amount of vengeance that was hired out in former times. Not very honorable. But even the honorable thing has its mean and cheaty side. Remember the moment when Hamlet, prompted by his father to avenge his murder, comes upon the usurper, Claudius, kneeling and praying to his no-doubt forgetful and forgiving God. Now might I do it easily, Hamlet thinks. Now. Why not now? Because then we wouldn't have a play, I brightly say . . . delay, delay. Quite, Penner responds with dry politeness. The Inquisition gave a different answer. I was supposed to be confounded by this shift of venue, and I was. Hamlet would seem cowardly, I offer. Quite so, yes. But . . . Luther is silent until I say what? You've forgotten. Hamlet has a splendid excuse. If he kills the king while the king is praying, the king's soul might take flight to heaven, and Hamlet wants to send that soul straight to perdition. *There* . . . there is a secret revenge indeed. The Inquisition, with an opposite intention, used to torture its heretics until they confessed and were shriven. Then it *auto da fé'*d them (as if Hell were here) before they could relapse into sin again, saving their souls in the bargain. Clever, these Jesuits. Good fellows all: by this means they had their vindictive pleasure, scared their fellow believers into even finer conformity, redeemed a whole bunch of lapsed coupons, and got in good with their God by one turn of the rack and scratch of the match.

I waited through a long silence. Then: scratch of the match, Luther repeated, as if deep in meditation. I wonder how many cases of arson . . . are . . . Easy to do. Hard to halt. Hellfire. Fun to watch. Difficult to detect.

The maddened postal clerk . . . The low put-upon person . . . Snap . . . but now not like a twig . . . a grenade . . . Become a gun and go off . . . Remember Faulkner's annoyance when he worked as a postal clerk: being at the beck and call of any asshole with three cents for a stamp. Spray the office . . . shoot from a campanile . . . tick tock . . . tick tock . . . Luther's gaze would cloud, voice drift away.

The whore who adores giving sailors syphilis, the guy with

AIDS who adores making whores HIV poz. Luther's spoon draws the plus, as if on the end of his nose. Typhoid Mary, on the other hand, was an innocent carrier. Like the transmitter of bad genes. But these cases teach us—see?—to see the difference between the specific victim of some revenge such as Ippolito's brother was, with its focus on Don Giulio's eyes, and the generic subject of a retribution like Alcibiades' move against Athens, or an impersonal disdain for some Universal like Swift's dislike of Man.

These distinctions, which might have been subheaded and neatly numbered, I found drawn out in detail in Penner's journals. There, revenges which were carried out against substitutes the way Satan tempted Eve to get back at God are carefully distinguished from hostage situations, scapegoats, and random misplacements. The measurements for appropriate requitals are taken with a tailor's care. Symbolic revenges (burning the flag, for instance) are duly noted and evaluated. Sports and other games are rated for their revenge factor: hockey gets the highest marks. Throwing at a batter's head is seen to be very complex, since the pitcher who is carrying out the revenge is rarely the one who was earlier hit, but is retaliating for the team, and the batter about to be hit is seldom the initial villain either.

Luther made immense lists of massacres carried out to teach towns and/or countries a lesson, and these lists were accompanied by careful evaluations of the results, usually futile. Tribal feuds, racial hatreds, ritual retributions: they were all present and accounted for.

There is the verbal vengeance of the quick-witted, who take people down from their pegs, like meat-lockered pigs, and cut them up, and the presumably acceptable revenge we call the practical joke: whoopee cushions, eh? Penner blows burbles through his lips. Drinking glasses guaranteed to spill something on your tie. Plastic turds. Rubber snakes. An industry.

Then suddenly Luther returned to Hamlet, as, I discovered, he so often did. Why didn't the king's ghost go fright Claudius out of his widow's bed? throw a baleful glow on the usurper's gonads as they incesticated the sheets? say in the ear that had his own ear poisoned: remember me . . . Remember me? The handle of Luther's utensil reamed his right ear. The gesture lacked class. It resembled the thumb in the . . . as I've already reported.

I'm sure there is a reason, I say. Penner nods. You're learning. Maybe a lawyer yet. A reason. At least a cause. Yes. Probably because the ghost can walk only at certain hours and in certain lacks of light, for when the cock crows to warn of the arrival of rosy-fingered dawn, the ghost feels summoned, and fades away as mist does. Or it is angered into absence because the crowing is a signal that Claudius' cock is coming in the cunt of the queen, where the ghost once came, so that now it must go away in shame. The ghost wears armor like Gabriel, remember. I wonder whether he has ghostly private parts as well as ghostly shield and buckler. Penner's look had withdrawn as if to another room. My spoon, my baton, has beat a bad tune and must be disciplined. He snapped the plastic handle from its plastic bowl and dropped them both in his nearly empty thick white china cup. So the interesting question is—beside the cock's crowing to remind us of Peter's denials and . . . yours of me—is whether Hamlet is to revenge his father's murder because he is his father's son, or whether he is to do it because he is the Prince and has royal obligations. In only the latter sense is his requitaling Christian according to Saint Thomas.

How so, I say, but I am in a quandary, or a daze, because I had never heard such language from Penner, nor would I hear it again. He was never a foulmouth despite his crooked, occasionally green teeth. Moreover, his violent gesture was not customary either, as far as I knew. I didn't understand its rhetorical intent, though I knew there must be one.

A reason. Or cause. A reason.

Luther Penner was no stranger to coarseness, no more than his namesake, who used to curse the Devil in the Devil's tongue. Yet he confined it to his journals, notes, and letters, which, as I've said, are frank to the point of painfulness, and to one public pronouncement—the notorious "Immodest Proposal"—a publication which led to the culminating catastrophe.

Whoever takes vengeance on the wicked, when it is done on behalf and with the sanction of the state, does so with God's blessing, because God, busy with other things, and with his hands full of wretches who deserve whipping, delegates his sacred powers to the princes; and the princes (who are more devoted to hunting) pass it on to judges and policemen. It is really the Mighty Mikado who is doing the revenging after all. Only by remote control. From beyond a cloud. Through anointed orders.

Oops. Hamlet runs Polonius through through the curtain, the arras too, and through Polonius in consequence, but the punctures he makes in cloth, place, and Polonius he makes as a private person. It was, of course, an accident as well, and an oops of the most careless kind. On Laertes falls the burden of revenge, but it is an onus which is politically and religiously unsanctioned. Even if it is his dad. Penner poked at the plastic pieces and then rose to go. You didn't drink your coffee, he noticed. I let it get cold. Good idea.

Throughout these after-class meetings, which were about to end, I had always been painfully aware of our surroundings, not just of the bright polished plastic interior of The Cow's Lick Café, but of our central seating—open, unprotected, obvious— and of Penner's not loud but penetrating voice, and certainly of his expansive gesturing and Stukka-diving spoon. Our conversation was not something others would overhear with any understanding. On the contrary, I thought. Consequently I snuck peeks at our company while Penner's eyes fished in the dark void which existed before the first word. There were a few regulars and one or two solitaries nearby who had obviously taken note of us, but that seemed to be it. I longed for wood paneling and low light and red vinyl banquettes, high-backed booths and a bit of privacy.

It was not to be. The last evening of class it rained rather ferociously and Penner pedaled home through the downpour tented in a dark tarp like a waning ghost himself with hardly the sort of lengthy adieu I'd hoped for. I got goodby but no address, no "it's been good," no "let's get together sometime," no number for a phone. Upon reflection, I realized I hadn't given him my address or phone number either, or said it's been a pleasure, let's get together, cuddle up to a cup of java in a cozy dark place I know . . . no, I had ridden away in the watermelon weather, watching the ground, hunched in my slicker like someone homeless, as, in a way, I was.

I had time to ponder Penner's incipient Manichaeanism, but I mainly wondered why anyone would be rehashing such an ancient heresy in our time. It also seemed to me easily misunderstood and mistaken for Satanism. This was a feeling which proved unhappily prophetic. If anyone had overheard him say (and it would have been easy) "God hated Lucifer's intelligence; He always preferred faith": what would they have thought? And I'd had hints of Penner's growing fear of women. He simply would not talk to or look at them.

Which is perhaps why he got in such trouble with his landlady, Mrs. Ollie Sowers. Luther, at this time, was living in three attic rooms of Mrs. Sowers' tall bluff-built house on Peak Street. When I went to visit him I had a lot of steps to climb. There was a wide wood-railed stairway which led to the front door, since the main floor was already half a story in the air. The stairs to the second were naturally narrower but commodious enough. However, Luther was obliged to use the former servants' staircase all the way to the attic, which he didn't mind, privacy was important to him, although the passage was narrow and dark, the steps steep, and Mrs. Sowers had the annoying habit of stashing cleaning equipment and stacks of mags on various treads, pretty much catch-as-catch, so you couldn't even predict where obstacles might be and prepare to avoid them. Luther pointed out to Mrs. Sowers that when he was carrying a fat package or a sack of groceries he couldn't see his feet or spot the dangers, and that it would be better all round if she could find another place to put the mop bucket or her out-of-date *Woman's Days*.

Luther said he spoke most politely to her about it, and I believe him, since he wasn't a forceful sort, but Mrs. Sowers got snappish, and continued to clutter his climb with her cleaning compounds. So Luther kicked a stack of *Liberty Magazines* into a slither. Unfortunately, they simply stayed where they'd slid, making the stairway even more treacherous. "Watch where you're going and you'll get by," she told him, using a haughty contemptuous tone which simply asked to be repaid. Penner, with the simplicity of solution, and the self-sacrifice characteristic of genius, fearlessly flung himself from a top step one morning, a buttered English muffin in his fist—what an inspired touch—and lay on the first floor landing in broken-legged pain an hour before his howls were heard.

It was, oddly enough, because of this feat that I saw him again, for there was a small note about the accident and the ensuing lawsuit in the neighborhood freebie sheet which mentioned the hospital where Luther was recuperating. I took myself, as they say, to his side. He was surprised and not undelighted to see me, and soon we were talking as freely as before. Penner had repeated one of his previous mistakes: failing to consider all the consequences. He had not counted on having quite so many injuries: a cracked rib, a cracked—was it?—shin, lots of bruises, and a swollen nose. Not to worry, even though he'd been let go by his most recent employers the day before, because he had been given the customary ten days' notice and was therefore still covered by the company's insurance, which certainly served them right.

My area of study enabled me to counsel him on a few legal matters, and I did a bit of fact checking for his case. The Widow Sowers told me she couldn't bear the boy, as she called him, because he was untidy and smelled bad and stood sideways to her when she talked to him. Odd as last apples, she said he was. Luther had at least one leg to stand on, and that should have been sufficient. The Widow Sowers hadn't that much, so her insurance company paid up pretty promptly, though Penner wouldn't tell me to the penny how much. It was still enough to install him in a building with an elevator—he had to use a cane for quite a while—though Luther did regret losing the widow's bluffside view, which gave him a long look over the tracks to a ribbon of river he could occasionally see between the leaves of a few scrubby trees.

While on the mend, with me seated by his bed, Luther spoke bitterly about his behavior. Revenge ruled the world. That he knew. That was his creed. Alas, he had not been able to live up to his ideal, partly because it wasn't formulated yet. Mrs. Ollie Sowers suspected something, he was sure, and he'd had to pay a price in pain and disability he shouldn't have had to pay if he'd played his cards right.

During his hospital stay, Penner had apparently decided to let his beard grow. He sported (if I dare use so predictable a word) a small though poorly trimmed moustache and an equally modest and badly barbered goatee. These were joined to one another by a thin line of hair along the sides of his mouth, so that it was now surrounded by a gentle growth of whisker—a den in which his teeth lay like a heap of wet stones.

After Penner had gotten installed in his new apartment, he invited me over—yes—it was for coffee. We sat in his kitchenette at a little enamel-topped table whose dropped ends he'd awkwardly lift to make room for my knees. He appeared tired, in an interior sort of way. There was so much to do, he said, every day. At the bicycle shop, where he'd taken his tires once again to be repaired, a young lad had sneered at their condition. At the Healthy Harvest store where he'd stopped to purchase some organic and unchemical'd pretzels, an elderly woman had held up the line of customers who were checking out by examining every fold in her purse with nearshot eyes, searching for those pennies which would provide her with exact change, thereby placing her nerdy little need over the patience of others. And the checkout girl (for a girl she was) had assumed he—Penner—was a vegetarian. What an unnecessary insult. And in the mail this morning he'd received a dun for a debt only one week overdue! While Luther was crossing the street, a mere moment behind the light, one of the local yokels had honked at him. He had the car's description. Penner held up a list. It was long, I could see that much, and was written on paper taken from a roll of cash register tape. Some items had been crossed out. This is just one week's worth of slights and requitals. The tape, it turned out, was one of the latter.

I know where that bleeper parks his car, where that bleeper lives, but I don't know yet how to make his horn stick. To learn how to blare a horn will take research. Isn't it sort of dangerous, I said, tinkering with the fellow's car. Your intentions might be misunderstood. Chance you take, Luther said briskly. Maybe marshmallow will work. It works on boom boxes. Remember the Tylenol scare? Can't risk random damage or even inconvenience. Not fair. Have to pinpoint the particular. Have to balance the account. Have to carry it out promptly. Otherwise, he waved the list at me, you get backlogged and overwhelmed. You could stay home more, I offered, to lessen the chances of receiving slights.

A shadow—yes—as from a passing cloud on a summer day— passed over Luther Penner's face, and I feared my insufficiently serious suggestion had offended him and got me on the list. Then he said: television insults the intelligence. It is so obviously true, and we've been told it so often, that repeating the proposition is another insult. He began tightly pleating his paper until it was very small and then he put it away in his shirt pocket. Girls who paint their toes . . . I almost exclaimed, had he noticed?girls?paint?toes? Those toes affront anyone with discrimination. Well, I said, after a pause, perhaps they're not aimed at you. Another cloud. Another shadow. People who pierce their ears, he went on finally. People who wear string ties, silver buckles, boots; people who bleach or tease or dye their hair; women who walk about in curlers; people who paint their house purple, keep noisy dogs, don't scoop their poop; people who try to run cyclists off the road; noisy bikers, nosey landlords, pushy people . . . This was a mood I hadn't seen him in: wholly petty, consumed by trivial and commonplace complaints. Yet Penner was dreamy-eyed. All those false product choices we're offered, the silly ads, the promises, the lotteries and sweepstakes . . . We are treated, you know, treated . . . like children . . . like fools . . . all the time . . . It's not just this or that assumption about us that offends. It's the entire atmosphere of life. One drop does not make a downpour. It's the constant con. The torrent of lies. Coming from every corner. Molesting every sense. How to resist?

Despite living in a society made of insult and shame, Penner was a fountain of data during those days. He was no longer working at wretched little jobs; he was back in school studying poetry, and planned to take a master's, if he could, after catching up at the community college. What do you suppose Proust was up to, he asked me in mock-heroic tones. What crime had he committed so serious it required all those froggy words to obscure? I remember looking nonplussed . . . because I was nonplussed. Proust confessed to his desk, not to a priest. He knew his novel would console him, and his art forgive.

Confession. Penner made as if to bare his breast. Confession. What a sweet revenge it can be. Honesty and openness. Isn't it lovely how honesty hides the wickedest of intentions? If I mention Proust, I should mention Gide. What does the rascal do, this Gide? He discovers his homosexual leanings. Like many a Frenchman, he goes to the Islamites in North Africa to verify the diagnosis. Knowing how much he loves boys, Gide nevertheless marries his cousin Madeleine. Then what? After a proper time has passed—to make matters most bitter—he writes *Corydon,* and confesses to the world his so-called wound. But who's been wounded?

Luther Penner stages a wail. The woman . . . the wife . . . the woman . . . the wife . . . Ah, Gide and his Protestant conscience. The bounder can't admire Proust's book because the fags in it give buggery—all boy-and-baby-love—a bad name. Proust's people are all perverts of power and pain. Well . . . isn't the world wonderful. Wait . . . it gets better. Gide scoots off to Africa again with his fourteen-year-old concubine Marc . . . Marc Allégret. How is his wife to understand this? Easy. Gide has gonads for brains, and they tell him to separate lust from love, and having done so, he can confer his love, pure as perfumed fingers, on his cousin, Mme. Gide, while directing his licentiousness safely toward Marc of the lithe thighs.

Despite a past as checkered as the game, Luther was getting

on splendidly at school. He was impressing his professors. He was doing the work, keeping up, managing to stay out of trouble. Well, most of the time. Once, he regressed, and everything he'd been aiming at was almost lost. Claude Hoch . . . Claude Hoch . . . that instructorless instructor of mine . . . you know what he said, Penner said to me . . . no, first . . . you know what he did? I went to see him about a paper . . . OK? . . . and the whole time I was standing there at his desk . . . standing, mind you, not invited to sit down . . . Hoch was laying out a solitaire . . . he looked to put a six on a seven . . . then . . . then he says, somewhat apropos of my project, yes, admittedly . . . doesn't matter . . . Hoch maintains to my face that Hopkins . . . Gerard Manley Hopkins, mind, the priest . . . was a homo. He said Hopkins was a homo. This man . . . with a name which sounds like a cleared throat . . . In mid-my-sentence! I said I was seeing sprung rhythm as a kind of revenge, you know, against the practices of the past, a move against previously ruling meters. And he said, right after that, Hopkins is a homo, he says. Well, the Higher Powers helped me. In the middle of everything, just after he has said that Hopkins is a homo, he says he has to answer a call of nature, and he puts . . . he slaps a card down on a run of reds, gets up and goes out past me into the hall as if I were invisible . . . invisible . . . as if I had no feelings, no soul . . . so . . . taking my cue from Claude the Sod, I answered a call of nature too: I pissed in his desk drawer. Copiously. I simply pulled it open and let his clips and bands and pencils and notecards and stamps have it. Then I shut the drawer, zipped up my fly, and lit out. I said to myself: that winsome wee widdle was for Hopkins. I was on air. High there! But now I know . . . I have touchdown . . . Now I am ashamed at how far back through childhood I've regressed, how little control I have over my lower nature.

Luther went into mourning over the character of his crude

kidney-shaped backslid soul, and I didn't see him for about a month. During that month there was quite a to-do at the community college. Claude Hoch hadn't immediately discovered Penner's little prank, but when he did so it was the smell which alerted him. He must have relived the hours which lay between the drawer's condition of dry and ordered normalcy and its withdrawal into one of smelly contamination—perhaps he even appreciated the pretty pun the act involved—in order to select a couple of likely culprits—those with opportunity, maybe motive, and malicious wit. It was a matter of access, most likely. It was not easy, however, to confront a suspect or broadcast the bad news, given its odoriferous and shameful character. There was a similar quality of embarrassment in the revenge which, earlier, had made Syph shut up. So a memo was sent out advising the innocent, warning the predisposed, and threatening the perpetrator of this unspecified yet jejeune bit of cheapjack lowjinks with exposure, dishonor, and suspension. Luther Penner's posture, as I've pointed out, was normally so passive and humble and servantlike, so modest and discreet, that it made people uncomfortable (its intent, of course); consequently it was difficult for Hoch to believe Luther would have the vulgar gumption which he imagined the deed required; however Penner had been about during the likely time, and so Hoch had Luther in for a little chat. There was no card game in progress, Luther noted with some satisfaction. The desk drawer had been removed to receive some healing rays and enjoy the cleansing air, he supposed. He wondered how much of his urine had leaked from the drawer, and how much had puddled, rusting clips and soaking cards.

This was the real revenge, Luther told me, the happy occasion: listening to the man squirm and turn a pusillanimous phrase, hinting and hiding and hating his own caution, while

Luther played deferentially dumb, and dutifully though igno-rantly concerned. As their interview was about to conclude, Luther remarked, after a slight shy laugh, that he'd thought Pro-fessor Hoch had asked to see him in order to take back his remark about Gerard Manley Hopkins. Penner proudly con-fessed that he couldn't help himself. Now Hoch knew. Knew why and who. And was helpless as a pinned bug.

Luther collared me at the college cafeteria, after the month of mourning was up, and kept me cornered for an entire afternoon to talk about literary revenges; not just the kind that occur in movies, plays, and stories as the basis of the plot, but rather about the way women writers in particular wrote their former lovers and ex-husbands into fictions that skewered them, showed them up, righted old wrongs, evened scores, and squared, quite literally, accounts. Not much of that is done by poets, I ventured, perhaps the medium isn't agreeable. Oh you're wrong, Penner responded warmly. How about—just to consult a recent instance—how about Lowell's *Dolphin* son-nets, the ones in which he actually quotes passages from his wife's letters? Kids embarrass their parents by failing, by doing stupid things and getting caught. Poets do that too. Dylan Thomas was an expert at it. Until Caitlin no longer felt any dis-may for him when he fell in the street or sympathized when he vomited, compelling him to fall and vomit where she could hear and see and smell and suffer. Afterward, he puked for any pub-lic. Lowell wrote to the world of his titled English mistress while his wife took nips from his hidden whiskey I suppose. He shamelessly pursued women as if he had a right—as a poet—to be a penis.

Lowell has this manuscript that's full of purloined lines and indecent endearments, which he shows about as if it were a pet pony. To Stanley Kunitz, for instance. You know Stanley Kunitz?

No? You *have* learned. Well, he's also a poet. And Kunitz writes Lowell. Tells him some of the poems are repellent. They are— hey—heartless—cruel, he says. Lowell, of course, has been pretending all along to be as morally concerned as all get out about this. What does the dear man do? He offers to dedicate a book to Kunitz, not *The Dolphin* of course—not Lowell's banquet of confessional ingredients in some self-serving stew—that dedication goes to Lady Caroline, where it belongs—but another called *History*—a maneuver to ponder and praise—well, Kunitz accepts with polite pleasure, thank you, and, I presume, calms down, as disarmed as a defeated nation. "Cal" for Caligula, some say, but a "Calvin" all the same. Maybe he was my true precursor. Though a Calvin can't precede a Luther, can he?

Luther is radiant. He is swimming in an ocean of proof. It is clear that, while his language might not seem to support the feeling, he actually admires Gide's morally merdish cruelty, and Lowell's arty hypocrisies. And who, Luther asks, is this Marc? this Allégret? He is the son of a Calvinist pastor, Gide's tutor for a time, think of that, and the best man at Gide's wedding. Gide debauches the boy. Gide. Gide. Wonderful Gide. Lowell . . . Lowell . . . Cal again . . . lovely. Penner grasps my arm. A final note. I am startled by his touch. Touching is not customary. What next, he wonders, then what? Gide's wife burns all of his precious letters to her, letters which go back through his youth to the summers they first, as relatives, met; letters which describe his spiritual, high-minded, mustn't-touch love for her; and Gide weeps for a week when he learns of her revenge. Penner applauds. What a beautiful affair, eh? Not the Medici or the Borgias, but pretty good in its minor way.

My smile was genuine, but it was for Penner's appreciation of his own antics rather than the case itself. Proust too, Penner says. Proust was busy justifying his queer ways to his queer friends and their queer world: his sycophancy, his snobbery, his sadism, his sickness, his shyness too, his dependency, his jealousies. The spoon, now stainless, made a right turn. Suddenly I remembered flying toy planes when I was a kid. The feeling and the flight path were the same.

I want to call attention to this episode and these remarks of Luther Penner's because doing so should defuse the charges of misogyny planted on my friend. Over and over again, I heard him take the woman's side. Catherine de' Medici, Medea, Charlotte Corday . . . And the slander that he was queer is certainly far from true. He didn't like fairies much. But he did believe every homosexual was getting even with a parent or two. The gay guy has got his father's balls in a basket and is carrying them to grandmother's house to wait for the wolf, he said.

He spoke glowingly of widows who censored their husbands' letters after their death, thereby misguiding the future, and those who sequestered documents or trashed laboratories or burned papers or hacked apart works of art. It's also true that he admired such people only because they proved his point. He liked to cite the ungrateful children of presidents and other VIPs, who wrote character assassinations and crippled dadmum careers with their exposés. Maybe it's the way we raise them, but kids in our society seem required to disappoint their parents by failing to "live up" to this or that expectation, by going off in an undesired direction, or by embracing obnoxious values and opinions.

So many Chattertons, so many Romeos and Juliets, Penner said, youngsters in our society love suicide. Daily, dozens do themselves in. But what a revenge—as a penalty it is perfect. Penner made a gesture I couldn't understand and allowed his spoon simply to sit still and glint. Penner talked to the table as if mesmerized by the shine. You'd have to dream about doing it— dream and redream—in order to receive death's pleasure. Have a plan . . . Luther had a limited repertoire of gestures. The spoon took off. Elizabeth Bishop's Brazilian lover, Lota, flies all the way to New York to overdose herself in Elizabeth's fotch-on apartment. Comas herself practically on the front stoop. Dies in due course, causing Bishop not only the pain of her loss and the guilt of her going, but the gossip of friends. Penner looks up, meets my eye, fixes his gaze to my face as though fastened by paste. Neat, eh?

We then began to meet rather regularly in cafés and occasionally had dinner in some modest Italian bistro. But he wouldn't eat meatballs because you never knew what had been hidden in them. Pretending he was merely mixing in the Parmesan, he'd totally retoss his bowl of pasta. I don't like my food "filled" or my rice "hilled" or my potatoes "piled." With his fork he'd lift up lettuce leaves before proceeding. It was discreetly done, but done, nevertheless. I seriously considered introducing Penner into my circle of friends, since I took him to be lonely and in search of an audience, but he refused my initial invitation. I don't want to complicate our relationship, he said. I didn't quite understand what that meant, or how his joining us would complicate anything, but Penner had a plot afoot, and didn't wish to dilute his attention. He was writing "An Immodest Proposal."

Aside from "The Moral Self Wears a White Shirt," written earlier, this was to be Luther Penner's only other public and published document. The remainder of his writing was confined to his journals and letters. Swift was of course its explicit inspiration, but I know from our conversations that his mind was filled with Dante, the supreme master of literary revenge, and in particular it focused upon that canto of the *Inferno* which describes Malbolge, the pit where flatterers and sycophants swim in shit.

It is one thing to *be* a Uriah Heep, Penner said, but quite another to play the part so wholesomely you seem a Heep, for flattery is insulting when undeserved, and especially satisfying when it is humbly—ha—humbly accepted as the dope's due. I learned that much of Luther's success at school was the result of his ass-kissing. He has a brown nose as long as Pinocchio's, Professor Hoch, not one of his champions, told me.

I no longer regretted Luther's rejection of my friends, for we often—my circle—met at my house, and I didn't want him contaminating my toothbrush or switching pills in my medicine bottles, as Mrs. Sowers said she felt sure Penner had when he'd been her roomer. Or losing one of my crystal goblets by simply putting it in an odd place, as he admitted doing to others on occasion. If matters warranted. Depending on how the party had gone. Let's say that after washing up, an empty place in the rows of crystal becomes evident. A wineglass is missing, leaving puzzlement and mystery in its place, until the thought that it was secretly broken or even stolen appears. These worries will occur well before the thing is stumbled on, because the goblet has been slipped so slyly out of place only chance can recover it; and because the puzzled victim gives up the search to embrace a hypothesis made of suspicion, as the host wonders which one of the guests quondam friends—has done the deed. Penner laughed. Once the prodigal returns there is more puzzlement and mystery: how could a flute have been put away among the tumblers? Preoccupying parts of people's minds can make for fine requitals. The secret to secret revenges is the sowing of uncertainty.

. Related to the revenge of disordered order is one whose lengthy description I found in the journals, although, oddly enough, Penner never spoke of what he called there "the implanted or time-bomb revenge." It is a favorite of secretaries and accountants. What could be more natural than for such folks slowly to invade and erode the powers of their bosses by doing more and more for them, but inevitably in their own way, so that in time a business or an office is ensnared in the secretary's system. Nothing can be found unless she finds it; nothing can be invoiced, nothing commanded, unless it passes her eye and receives her OK. Then if the company decides to fire her or their figure man, they soon find themselves unable to function. The inventory, the billings, the filing system, the mailing lists—everything—hours worked, bonuses earned—is in code. She was indispensable after all. Profits and losses, income and outgo, grosses and nets, overheads and payoffs, are figured in Arcane. Yes, that quiet little squit learned how to make himself essential.

About this time, as if I knew a calamity was coming, I began to draw up a list of people I'd need to interview to complete the very account you are presently reading.

I've been pondering the problems of punishment and the nature of the vengeance society exacts from its criminals, Luther told me, rather portentously. We were in the college cafeteria. I think we treat one another like fools because we have become, by repeated practice, quite accomplished at both being fools and treating others in the same way, so we deserve the insults which fall like hail upon us. Penner paused. What size? he asked archly, what size should the hail that falls upon us be? rice size? pea? pearly onion? chunk of stew meat? baked potato? Luther was mocking his use of a cliché with a list of available items from the steam tables. I hated the cafeteria. It was one more place whose surfaces were so permeated with plastic the light sterilized the eyes, and there was no relief from noise.

Penner showed me his wrist, which bore, where one might wear a watch, a bruise which was passing purple and fading on to yellow. Hat gave me that. Hattie? the librarian? at the college? Yes. That mountain of fat. How? drop a dictionary? hit you with her stamp? Penner gave me an intensely angry look. Hattie—yes—Hattie the Fattie thought it necessary to tell me how to pronounce *slough*—you know—the *slough* in "slough of despond." With a weenie little smile in her immense face, she started to explain Meaning—to me!—I threw up my hands to cover my ears, and this happened—this bruise—the result of her condescension. Imagine if I had heard her clearly how my ears would ache. I don't understand, I said . . . the bruise? Penner shook his head as if flicking water, like a dog, from his hair. I call—you know—that little superior pucker of hers—I call it a pook, he said. A pook in a pig. Luther's laugh stood for a complete absence of good humor. Well, our exchange—Fat and me—(pook)—was as freighted with irony as a train. I cupped my ear, a gesture I don't think Luther approved of, but it was clatterous—clatterous and sordid—the cafeteria—full of loud talky kids and clinking trays. Penner was oblivious. Hattie the Fattie . . . (pook) Hattie the Fattie . . . Luther crooned, ignoring the students who were sitting around us, chanting himself back to childhood—and carrying me with him. Hattie the Fattie was complaining to me about her boss—that guy Serkin—Ferkin?—Forkin?—she was going on and on about Serkin/Ferkin/Forkin's mistreatment of her—well—I made a bad joke but still—I told her to just slew him off, and she looked at me, laughed, not at my pun but at my ignorance—and proceeded to explain to me the difference between *slew* and *sluff.* (pook pook pook) An awful moment. An awful moment . . . After I had done her the honor of supposing she would understand my little witticism and respond appropriately. Terrible—to be talked down to like that—terrible—to appear to have given cause, to be pooked. Are all fat people like that? eager to suck finally on any thumb that will signal their superiority?

Then Luther laughed a happy laugh. But good came of it.

Good? Good. I suddenly saw the solution. To what? what about the brew— ? Well, I wasn't immediately there—at the solution—but I thought . . . I thought: you'd look pretty funny, Miss Hattie, in the stocks, only the stocks I had in mind had holes for her boobs, not her head. Yes. Laughed. Saw her in the stocks. Big laugh. Large as life. (pookedy pook)

I, however, wasn't following. I was still puzzled by the origin of his injury. I had misheard. Or had he left out a key part of his story?

The Chinese do a lot of this sort of thing. What? wait—I don't get—what—? Penner was impatient with me. Public humiliation. They'll parade people they are going to execute through the street. They'll box an official's ears. We ought to go back to that. I'm sorry, I said, back to what? But he stood up, grabbed his books, and huffed out.

Weeks passed. Not a note, not a call, not a chance encounter. Of course I didn't drop him a line or phone either. We were remote and apart as the two poles.

It was then I began my own research in earnest, and learned that my fears for my toothbrushes were well founded, for Luther had apparently been accused of polluting whole bunches of them when he was at scout camp as a kid. His scoutmaster told me that Luther had then pretended to have been the scoutmaster's concubine, and gotten him into trouble from which he had never recovered. Luther was a horror, he alleged. Did he do a lot of practical jokes, I asked, like giving hot foots or tying shoelaces together or immersing sleeping fingers in lukey water? Not as far as he knew, the former scoutmaster said, but Luther had come to camp with the three-day measles, dipped other boys' brushes in the toilet, and performed a shadow play in the leader's tent one night which outdid Salome. Luther was furious because the scoutmaster had rejected

Luther's advances, the dishonored scoutmaster told me. Who would want to make love to such a mouthful of teeth?

I am of the opinion, however, that Luther Penner had no sex, and was as neuter as *das des dem das.* Being accused of tainting toothbrushes would have been enough to provoke his revenge, I think. It didn't take a lot. Luther could be as venomously reformist as his namesake, Martin.

I also discovered that Luther had been holding out on me, because the former scoutmaster told me that he had received a number of envelopes in the mail containing cutouts of young boys in bathing suits—nothing more. But with local postmarks, and addressed in smeary ink.

Miss Hat's version of the *slough* slip was somewhat different than the one Penner had put to me (and I write the phrase *put to me* on purpose, because that's how it felt: put to me). She had responded properly to the pun, she said, and had laughed, perhaps rather too politely, but she'd never complained about Lorkin, she said, who, although he was a bit of a stick, was still decent enough. Mr. Penner likes to show off his languages, Miss Hat told me, and likes to quote Latin mottoes or French and German poets. A few lines in each language are all he knows, though: *mais ou sont les neiges d'antan,* indeed. But when I went on, I thought, in my jolly way, to quote the next refrain: *autant en emporte ly vens* (after all, I've had a little French, anyway it's not a poem that's hidden itself in some lost volume, because the line is everywhere these days, blowing in the wind), he looked at me like a snowman, with a pitifully frozen expression, made of coals and a carrot, you know, before bustling off like he was late for something.

Miss Hat confirmed a suspicion I'd had for some time: that Luther Penner memorized lines and sayings from all types of texts and all sorts of languages; phrases and catchwords he thought would be of use in his rationales of revenge; but of the languages and their literatures as a whole he was woefully ignorant.

Single fat chocolates, wrapped in ruby, gold, and deep green foil, began to show up on Miss Hat's desk, one at a time, by the phone, in the raffia sack in which she carried books home from the library, at the cloudy bottom of a vase of flowers which decorated her cubicle, unnervingly shoved in an open pack of cigarettes, an especially vexing event, since, by smoking, she was trying to lose weight. As tempting as they looked, except for the one she fished from several inches of stem-slimy water, she didn't dare eat any, because, well, why were they there? what did they mean? were they undoctored? or had they been inoculated with an embarrassing jolt of Ex-Lax? They lay in an open ashtray like jewels for weeks, unwrapped, until they had to be too stale to be beheld, whereupon, with what she described to me as a sniffle, Miss Hat slid them into a bin of used paper towels when she visited the ladies'.

The pamphlet, "An Immodest Proposal," appeared on the giveaway racks of supermarkets and drugstores, and on the outdoor tables of bookstores, as suddenly and as unexpectedly as toadstools pop up in the morning yard and garden. They were ignored at first. Finally a few readers were reached. Soon slow word of mouth was like a shout. Then there was outrage; there was laughter; there was suspicion. Copies were confiscated and removed, but it was too late, the shouted word of mouth became the outcry of a crowd; shortly the pamphlet was being eagerly sought by those for whom scandal and shock were necessities. The pamphlet had been crudely printed on the cheapest newsprint, and was the modest size of those booklets which advertise houses for sale and rooms for rent. It occasionally used the color yellow, as if the paper were already sulphurized.

The pamphlet contained a proposal to cut down the population of prisons, and hence to reduce the expense of maintaining them, as well as simultaneously creating an effective deterrent against crime, a deterrent which would also be vindictive enough to satisfy society and crime's victims while avoiding barbarism and the chance that corporal and capital punishments would be inflicted on innocent persons.

Closely supervised groups of criminals would be employed in the construction of what Luther Penner coarsely called "pisspits." Some would hold a single person as though in a tube, others would be more ample and might have half a dozen occupants. They were to be built like large sunken urinals: slick, well-drained holes which would be topped by a grid through which any citizen so minded—or bladdered (it was Penner's joke)—might pee upon the deserving wretch below. The principal ones would be located in parks, airports, and stadiums, where use could be expected to be frequent and urination copious, and where the outcries (as Penner supposed) of those thus urinated on would be muffled by aircraft engines or crowd noise.

For those who required privacy for their peeing (and Penner, I think shrewdly, believed many men, as well as adolescent boys and surly punks of all kinds, would take to relieving themselves in public with a kind of eager bravado), tents resembling old-fashioned bathing machines would be pitched on the mesh at appropriate places. Penner was clearly not concerned with details that any bureaucrat could work out in an afternoon. I shall restore the pissoir to power, he said, raising an admonitory hand. I found him holding forth in our town's only sidewalk café, surrounded by supporters (in numbers which surprised me) and by obstreperous opponents, hugely enjoying himself. Depending upon the time of year, prisoners would be placed in the pisspits naked or lightly clothed in sackcloth, he responded, in answer to questions. When their period of punishment was up, they would be drenched with antiseptics, hosed and scrubbed like cars in a Wash, before being released (in the same way as they'd been condemned) in a public ceremony.

How would the prisoners be fed? Unpleasantly, Penner replied, and the group laughed, even those who were obviously in opposition. From time to time the pit would be flushed, just as an ordinary urinal is, to cut down on a stench which might disturb the public. Mightn't numerous nasty people throw swill and dump excrement into these pits as well? Yes, Penner replied, all to the good. Would women be inclined to participate in what one man called "these festivals of urination"? and Penner answered with a serious smile that the pleasure for a woman who'd been raped in peeing directly on the prick who'd raped her, for instance, or the gratification of those who'd had their handbags snatched, would be more satisfying than sex. There was more laughter, and Penner looked puffed and red and pleased in a rare way.

The pamphlet contained crude drawings which showed how the pits were to be built, and suggested lengths and limits of penitence which lasted for hours and went on through day after day after day after day up to a month. The runoff could be processed to produce urea, he argued. Meters might be installed, because people were interested in statistics, like: More pee has been pissed upon prisoner P than on any previous occupant of these Johns of Justice. Although there'd be a few who, experiencing the shame and pain of the pit, would come out of it bent upon their own revenge, this was a possible consequence of any form of punishment, including executions, which might infect clans or families like an inherited hatred.

Take a punk kid from a gang—say—put him in a pisspit—well—what's he going to do next—how's he going to like getting showered by his rivals? Or by his own pals? And suppose when he's out he gets even. To land in the pit again for—what?—for good? forever? till he dies of acid rain? The fact was, Penner claimed, his plan would avoid the huge loss of useful labor which confinement involved, eliminate most prisons (a few would be continued for bloodletters or other dangerous incorrigibles), and ease the need for guards (a job which created its own brutes). The courts could act quickly because errors in judgment wouldn't cost years of life, and apart from psychological consequences, punishments in pits were disgraces, like being stuck in the stocks, which intended no physical harm. Penner proposed the latter's revival, as well as the custom of shaving the hair of miscreant women and parading them naked through the streets, including other practices perfected during the Cultural Revolution, not omitting many social humiliations: wearing the dunce's hat, having one's ears boxed or emblems of rank removed, a swagger stick snapped over an outraged knee, ceremonial robes ceremonially ripped, or being forced to march in a parade of shame—mooned by a multitude—to endure catcalls and jeering, to suffer even the dunking stool, or be compelled to perform various acts of contrition, to crawl as the snake was condemned to in the dust, to wear sackcloth and ashes, the horns of the cuckold, the crown of the king of fools. There are precedents of every kind: Jesus was jeered.

The belief that the physical character of the pisspit was basically benign was disputed, I remember, because there were many who argued that even a few hours in such a poisonous environment would lead to injuries to the eyes, the mouth, the lungs, and so on, and to diseases which might show up much later.

So stay out of the pisspits, Luther sternly replied. And people *will* stay out. I promise. He extended a hand which held a spoon. The pits are pragmatically perfect. The pits will work.

Several tables had been shoved together and Penner sat in

the middle of a group—a few homely young women, but mostly men—and waved his spoon, rapping the table with the bowl when he made a point. Just as the body is soiled by the excrement it makes and carries, so the soul, you see, is blackened by its dirty deeds, hence the appropriateness of using bodily fluids as punishments—spitting on faces fastened in the stocks, for instance—because punishment is always levied against the body, isn't it, even when it is the inner character—the spirit—that commits the crime. He turned to a rather pudding-faced young woman and wondered which would be more satisfying to her: to know that the punk who'd snatched her purse was going to see jail for a few months, or to be given the opportunity to spit in the punk's eye, even though he'd be collared in the city square only for the working day. Or ... or kiss him on the mouth despite his tendency to bite? The girl's smile faded. Suppose he'd cut the screen on a summer eve and entered your bedroom and entered you as you tried to sleep—suppose—and he's now in a hole below you, and you can defile him with the same organ he defiled—how would that feel? Finally, clearly embarrassed, she covered a small smile and half a giggle behind a warding hand. What, I wondered, had she done earlier to deserve her present little penalty. Perhaps she had tried to attach herself. Penner had said, as if warning me, that to affirm yourself as a disciple was already to have betrayed your master.

Suppose, the Master grimly concluded, we really forced society's enemies to eat shit. How many crooks would be willing to risk the perpetration of a seven-spoon crime?

The evening over, Penner left for his apartment. I caught up with him after leaving an excessive tip at my table for inattentive service, as I'd been taught, and we talked off and on while we walked, although he was clearly still unhappy with me. I surprised him by chatting at first about nothing in particular: I asked how he was, what he was presently studying, what his plans were—that sort of thing. Finally, in front of his digs, he asked me if I admired his secret revenge. Well, I said, it's hardly secret, Luther, everybody knows you wrote that pamphlet, after all you signed it at the end. He sneered. I'd have to say—he sneered at length. My "Immodest Proposal," if accepted—if acted on—would signify society's intention to take revenge against those who offended it; such aims would not resemble mine. Penner's look annoyed me, so I stood my ground though my head was blank about his meaning. He continued his sneer into his tone as if it were a second feature. You don't enjoy the paradox? Most people—right?—who've read or heard about my suggestion are outraged. Disgusting, they call it; repulsive, they call me. These are people comfortable with long penal terms and with cruel executions. These are people who raise no great outcry about chain gangs or prison rape or the common corruptions of prolonged confinement, the brutalities of guards, the laxity of parole boards, the happiness that fills impoverished small towns when they learn a prison will be built nearby and the citizens can furnish it food and guards and the blackest of markets.

Yes, I said. And? Well, their complaints about my "Immodest Proposal" reveal them to be hypocrites of the deepest dye. The dye and its depth is there for those—like me—who see—to see, he said with satisfaction smearing his face like jam. This evening, I talked with a guy who was willing for the state to emasculate rapists, yet he was furious with me for my proposal, and called me an anarchist and an un-Christian creep. Think of that. These Christians would renail Christ if they thought it meant a second chance at salvation.

One of the immense moral advantages of my pisspits is that—well—they don't bring you face-to-face with the person you aim to punish exactly—but they do require a kind of confrontation, and some people don't like that, they prefer to hire executioners and have their vengeance done at a distance.

Well, Luther, the idea isn't exactly new, I remember I replied. The visitor can still see, in the dungeon of the castle in Regensburg, the deep hole where the Elector put his enemies, and where, as the guide euphemistically puts it, guards enjoyed reposing their relief. But people may not wish to return to such medieval practices in a world which is supposed to be modern.

I had committed a calamitous offense. No, two. It was instantly obvious. Penner's grin was a grate made of nails.

Are you hanging out at the Sidewalk Café these days? Most evenings, Penner said. I'm holding court. Tomorrow the subject is suicide. Have you discussed the revenge of the unearned windfall or the calamity of sudden celebrity yet? (No reply.) No time for tête-à-têtes then? You can come if you want, Penner replied with a shrug. I'm being sloughed, I thought, but merely said good night. It was our last conversation.

Journal entries suggest it was about the same time as the foofaraw caused by the pamphlet that Luther Penner was roped into Harriet Hamlin Garland's sordid little social circle. I know of her only secondhand, though it may indeed have been she— the pud-faced girl—maybe really a woman, the light was inconclusive—whom Luther had embarrassed in the café. Anyway, she bore some relation to Hannibal Hamlin Garland, a writer of modest attainments whose autobiography, *A Son of the Middle Border*, is sometimes remembered, and her name certainly celebrates that relation, if perhaps too raucously.

Luther's notoriety drew her to him like blood draws the shark, and soon he was a fixture in her salon, a salon he despised, as his journal entries amply attest, but one he suffered because he sensed in her total self-absorption and stubborn persistence a type ripe for his instruction. In this he was not mistaken. From what he writes of her, Harriet Hamlin Garland was a lady fashioned, it seemed, entirely of library paste and venomous malice;

she possessed, he wrote, a soapy denseness of mind ideal for persistence and self-deception, because not only would she never take no for an answer, she rebounded from every snub with a resilience rubber might envy, and oozed on the course of her self-promotion like pus from a perfectly infected wound. It was not that she did not notice she was being ignored or insulted, waved away like an annoying gnat, for if the persons who did not render her sufficient devotion were deemed to be of no further use, she would turn on them like a hole card from a winning hand, and show her true nature; but if use were there still to be found, she would swallow every distasteful scrap she was thrown like a camp dog, snarling only at strangers, biting only the dying or the dead.

All gall, Penner concluded, was divided into three parts: Harriet, Hamlin, and Garland.

In short, she'd never know—because she couldn't comprehend—well, she'd understand, all right, and be angrier than ever—when she'd been the object of someone's revenge, but the pain would have to be pushed past—ignored—if there were still profit to be seen in the relationship.

Her circle was made of incompetents and designed to contain outcasts—Luther understood himself to have the latter quality—so that they would finally feel they had a home: a lesbian or two, excessively fat people, several who blew horns in bad bands, poets so wretched they could hardly stand to hear each other's voices, as Penner observed it, but people nevertheless of numerous hues who understood the considerable advantage of their handicaps. She practiced yoga herself like a child beginning piano, read about Buddha with hush in her eyes, and used mysticism like smelling salts. Kerouac had inserted his fingers into her early youth (that was Penner's phrase), but her views now reflected the Beats only distantly. She was a soured visionary. One had to admire her, and Luther Penner did, because Harriet Hamlin Garland picked up every rebuff the way Sisyphus did his rock, and soldiered on.

Harriet Hamlin Garland has become as valuable to me as a laboratory to a scientist, Penner wrote. Her resentments mirror mine, invert them, give them a new and novel look. "Here is a woman who deserves to be dumped, who is dumped, and who won't take dump for an answer."

A year later, after Luther was made an instructor at the college, so well had his wooing of the faculty obtained him advancement (over the weak opposition of poor Professor Hoch, who feared another inundation, and despite the notoriety of Penner's pamphlet, whose force faded like red in the wash), Harriet Hamlin Garland enrolled in one of his classes, to sit at his feet, she said, but only "to pour water on their clay," Luther wryly concluded.

Yet from Harriet Hamlin Garland, for instance, Luther learned how to systematically misunderstand whatever was said to him by those he had determined were his enemies. If an opponent argued for Y, Penner would congratulate him for defending Z. He turned out laudatory reviews of works in his field which distorted them beyond repair or recognition, and condescended to his betters with a suave show of politeness which they had to accept, and which left them furious. "I do by dint of careful design what HHG does by thoughtless instinct."

Fulsome in his praise of someone in a private moment, Penner would lamely laud that same gull at a public one. His journals are replete with derisions of this kind, and encounters of which he gives detailed descriptions. Casting aside pooks as no longer relevant, he soon stole Harriet Hamlin Garland's smile, which was small, quick as a twitch, and entirely symbolic. It resembled a smirk but was too short to signify satisfaction. He called it a "smill." This adopted tic Penner would insert like punctuation between pieces of his speech where it warned his auditors that something witty, cute, or clever was coming: "After some study [smill] I have come to the conclusion [smill] that people actually approve of crime [smill] so long as they can feel sure that others will be its victims." (Here he would raise his eyebrows quizzically as if doubting his own declaration.) "Since comics, crime, and sports [smill] are all they want to read about in the newspapers [rising eyebrows]." The entire performance was quite unnerving. "Without crime life would be too boring to be borne; without scandal there'd be nothing to discuss."

So why was he trying to prevent it, I wondered when I saw this observation. Was that to be the revenge whose profit would be the pleasure of starting a Bring Back Crime movement?

It occurred to Luther at last to use his hostess as an implement in one of his secret revenges. He would draw the deserving victim into Harriet's circle, where the mark would sail in slow orbits through a sea of fatuous expressions (Penner meant both phiz and phrase) which the gull would at first find flattering (another of Penner's alliterations), "blown by a breeze made of self-congratulation and other pufferies." The Garland group so leaned against one another, it was like adding a fresh face to a house of cards, and once properly propped, the new knave was indispensable.

Yet Luther liked the fawning, it appears. He had at last a respectable position; in his narrow world he was widely, if not always happily, known; there were, for his pleasure, devotees, acolytes, faithful followers. From parlor to pub, from couch to café, he carried his coterie and broadcast his message.

Then suddenly, he left them all in a lurch so extreme the house came down as if its table had been tipped. Penner publicly—as publicly as he could manage—repudiated his opinions in a letter to the editor of the freebee press, attacked his own pamphlet as poisonous, the poetry of his pals as putrid, and the basis of their previous association as hypocritical and self-serving. "Mallarmé has canceled his Tuesdays. Nor will there be any more coffee served me on pink plastic trays." "The old days are dead, the old ways are over, past wrongs must be righted," he wrote. "The pits will prevent nothing, although they will make punishing dumb bunnies more fun." The result of this recantation was to make "An Immodest Proposal" momentarily an item of interest again. "It's like a bubble of spit at the tip of everybody's tongue," one critic complained.

When taken to task by those who perceived this *volte-face* as an act of treachery, Luther Penner is reported to have replied that Ludwig Wittgenstein had done no differently when he rejected the *Tractatus,* confounding his copycats—who knew only how to meow as he had taught them—by setting off in a diametrically opposite direction, gathering a group of new strays as he went along—whom he would train to bark instead of mew, and piss on posts instead of scratch.

I perceived Penner's new tack as a masterstroke (the preemptive betrayal of those who would certainly have betrayed him before long), because most people naturally, if naively, believed he had come to his senses, as sometimes happens, and would now embrace imprisonment, favor capital punishment where appropriate, encourage neighbors to spy on one another, and support the other humane measures—such as dog patrols, wiretaps, sting operations, search and seizure—which are commonly urged in order to reduce crime in communities. Nevertheless, though his letter had achieved a . . . well, mostly secret revenge . . . it was not yet a transcendental one, since for that even the revenger must be unconscious of what he's done, and unaware, while reaping it, of any reward.

Harriet Hamlin Garland did do things by thoughtless instinct. That is: her self was her narcotic and put itself to sleep.

Which placed her above Penner on any scale measuring tran-
scendence. She was of course surprised and hurt by his recantation, but that only meant his doctrines were all hers now; and
the fact that it was a woman who was spreading such proposals
through the state—that she had, in effect, embraced what were
popularly believed to be venereal views—simply enlarged her,
increased for some the attractiveness of her circle (such are
our times); so if Penner's clique had flown the farm when he
chucked his recantation at them (as one wit remarked), Harriet
Hamlin Garland soon had recooped, gathering a new group she
deemed worthy by—as it were—crowing mightily every morn;
and after a few months not many remembered that it was Penner's pamphlet she was preaching from. She merely gave his
views a new (rather appropriate) name: the Justice Restoration
Movement. The eagerness with which some women took to
these ideas and staunchly served under the banner of victim-
hood unnerved not a small number of husbands. They forgot
that there have always been furies.

I don't believe Luther Penner had calculated that Harriet
Garland would simply steal his proposals and stump the state
with them, but there she was, on the road, leading a picket line
in front of the capitol. "Make Pits Happen," the placards said.
"It's the Pits," they avowed. "The Pits Shall Be Our Pendulum,"
they sang. And got plenty of TV coverage. And were the lucky
butt of anchorperson puns. Which spread her message like mar-
garine. I saw a bumper sticker which read: Your John or Mine.
Less public, though popular, were the cardboard coasters which
encircled a black hole with the pointedly censored injunction:
"Put the . . . its in the Pits." The worst by far was: "I Pit Out." At
least, I thought so. And of course the entire brouhaha was
called—doubtless deservedly—the piss war.

I have always wondered who the writer of these dubious slo-
gans was. It could not have been Harriet Hamlin Garland. She

hadn't a bawdy brain cell, she wasn't a cutup, and had no wit in her longer than the word. It occurred to me that maybe—just maybe—Penner had been planning some sort of campaign, and that Harriet had appropriated his publicity propaganda too.

Whatever the reason—whether Penner was discouraged and disgruntled, or had another aim—he disappeared from more eyes than mine; and when, at last, I mustered the courage to approach his parents for an interview, I learned that they knew nothing of his whereabouts, nothing of his reputation, still less about the pamphlet "An Immodest Proposal," with which I made bold to acquaint them. They were quite predictably horrified. Father's eyebrows rose like a pair of startled birds. Mother's mouth painfully pursed. I tried to put their son's project in the best possible light; that is, find a place for them from where they might be most likely to perceive it favorably.

Penner's father, who cursed Kaltenborn with such quiet gusto, had no trouble understanding the basic tenets of his son's philosophy. His mother followed lamely along. But neither grasped the beauty of the pure revenge, which I was left to explain as best I could. I cast about for examples they would understand. I cast about and cast about. The cowbird. "The cowbird," I said. The cowbird's revenge is pure because the cardinal, in whose nest he lays his eggs, raises the cowbird's brood in ignorance of the interloper's true nature. The revenge in question becomes transcendental when we realize that the cowbird hasn't a clue either. The cowbird is simply being cowbirdy, and cannot boast of his success because he doesn't know that he's succeeding.

So, after a bit, Penner's mother says, "What had the cardinal done to the cowbird?"

They were comforted only after I showed them Luther's letter to the freebee press. "It's where you end up that counts, sane and settled," his father said, "but some of those ideas were pretty good really," a certain disappointment showing in his voice.

I shall relate the next part of Penner's story with some reluctance, since I have misgivings about my own part in it, but I feel that honesty with respect to the historical record requires me to fess up. My concern for Luther's whereabouts had drawn, as it naturally might, a favorable response from his family, and after several visits I was able to offer my services, not exactly as a private eye, but as a worried friend, to help locate him, and inquire as to his condition and state of mind. I pointed out that I had performed certain services for Luther in the past, and was quite willing to do so again. With this intention, then, I was allowed access to Luther's boyhood room, where, with no difficulty at all, I found journals and letters in a desk drawer, as if waiting for me, just as I had retrieved two, formatted like account books, from his former landlady. These freshly discovered treasures I took away with me to peruse at length, and, as the reader will surmise, I have based much of this study on their remarkable contents.

Here, I found, early on, the difference between the pure and the transcendental revenge spelled out in no uncertain terms. What surprised me was the major source for the method of its achievement, since Penner had said not a word about this part of his reading. One could see how a pure revenge might be achieved, so that its victim might remain in ignorance of—not his plight, certainly, of which he would, no doubt, be painfully aware—but its cause. It is well known, for instance, that those who come suddenly into undeserved wealth by winning the lottery or growing seven feet tall are frequently ruined by it. They become the object of thieving sycophants, predatory agents, packs of hungry relatives. They invest unwisely, quit their jobs, reject former friends, overspend, take to drugs or loose women, permit their character to be corrupted, and end—so much for good luck—in the gutter, alone and unmourned. Fairy tales are fond of achieving the same results by granting wishes to greedy people. Thus the general "kill with kindness" principle can be confidently embraced. Supply the jealous with fragile treasures. In front of the envious flaunt advantage. By means of overindulgence and generosity, by encouraging stupid endeavors, by feeding the fat and offering another drink to a drunk, much damage can be discreetly done. Unconsciously unwanted, a child receives *Liebestod* for a lifetime.

Penner reports that he had heard of a woman whose rich sister had been seduced by a painter unhappy at home and momentarily on the prowl; and how she had captured the painter for herself (with great economy getting even with her sister, whose wealth she envied), then succeeding to second-wifehood by repairing the painter's sexual insufficiencies; and in that way, then, she had proceeded to become his muse as well as his wife and mistress; but an evil muse, praising his weaknesses and poohpoohing his strengths, surrounding him with her poisonous worship, while encouraging his for her breasts, which he drew and redrew, nippled and renippled, as if in a whirlpool of narrowing attention, since that's the way worship invariably goes, until his work was ruined and his career destroyed—all unbeknownst.

No . . . understanding—even obtaining—the property of "purity" for one's revenge was not a problem. What surprised me was the discovery that Penner had painstakingly pored over Dr. Goebbels' *Diaries,* which had been published with some scandal and fanfare. The lesson that he drew from them became central, if not essential, to the achievement of Transcendental Retribution. Goebbels was a professional liar. His ministry was a ministry of deception. The delicious irony was that Goebbels himself became both deceiver and deceivee. He fell for his own line—hook and sinker. This was a kind of "eureka" for young Penner. Of course Joseph Smith ("Joseph Smith!" Penner's journal exclaims) didn't receive the Book of Mormon as he claimed, "on gold! plates! and in Palmyra, New York! for Pete's sake!" Nor had Mohammad, nor Moses, nor any other glory guy, taken Allah's dictation, or found the Tablets of the Law by climbing to a mountaintop and seeing them leaning against a rock. But the liar who lies long enough, the liar who wants his lie to be the truth, the liar who sees belief in other people's faces, for whom his lie is honey to their ears, is eventually a believer too, sincere as sunshine, clean as stream, faithful, too, as old clubfoot was, to his hope-filled falsehoods, and to Adolf Hitler.

I suspected, then, that Luther Penner had absented himself from his home and town and little circle, from Harriet's expressionless ardor and self-serving attentions, hence from me and from his recent past, in order to remake his nature; for if Luther Penner wanted to revenge himself upon the world, how better to do it than to corrupt that world's consciousness and mislead its mind with a fresh religion, straight from the shop, perhaps with a bit of tradition for reassurance, a touch of the exotic for excitement, a whiff of novelty to suggest to all those sheepish feet that at last there was before them a new path.

Luther Penner, I thought, is somewhere sewing robes, and getting guruized. Then his social awkwardness, bad teeth, and poor complexion, his stoop, his shuffle, his oddly forceful, overly candid glance, would be an advantage. If the beautiful are believed to be stupid, the handsome are thought to be anything but saintly. Lucky for Socrates he had thyroid eyes. What, I wondered, would Luther be preparing? from where would his inspiration come? how would he save mankind? what must we do to deserve the gift of his word, his wisdom?

Every pitchman, huckster, con artist, liar, joker, pol, great

Satan and his hench-imps, needs someone to pitch to, to imp with, those gullible ears and empty heads and greedy hearts eager for the grifter's whisper . . . eager for the love of Lucifer . . . to lick their private fears, bestir their lusts.

So: secret revenges are secret when not felt to be requitals by their victim, who lives with a limp he learns to take for granted; and they become transcendental when even the inflictor is in ignorance of the nature of his deed. Such as the passing on of stupid ideas. Such as the sincere creation of illusions, no longer lies, but falsehoods served on porcelain and eaten with sterling.

Yet . . . what had the cardinal done to the cowbird? how come the cuckoo was offended? What was the cause, in Luther's case, of so general a grudge? A little schoolboy bullying could not account for it. His family seemed in no way to blame. What could explain Penner's profound sense of being wronged, wronged by Nature? Might it be the recognition, in himself, of a disparity between ambition and ability so great as to seem a natal punishment; the perception of a distance between wish and satisfaction so common and so painful and so vast that Luther Penner could accept it for Everyman, represent it, be the modest plain one on their behalf, holy and lowly, one more time: appear to give comfort to the meek, who will not—in truth—inherit the earth, only breathe its dust and eat its dirt, die and go into its ground. Unless . . .

Then an unsigned letter arrived in the mail for me, postmarked Gahanna, Ohio. Penner must have received some information about my inquiries. The note accused me of being nosy to no good purpose, and a few other things best left unreported. Months of silence followed.

When I heard of Luther Penner again, he had changed his name to Romulus. Simply Romulus. He was preaching a new paganism based upon the idea of multiplying sacred objects through certain rigorously formal acts of devotion, and in this way conquering the secular world. Eight hundred objects: scarfs, pans, potted plants, three chairs, several windowpanes, a staircase, ferris wheel, wooden canoe, similar items, had so far been rescued, and had had holiness conferred upon them. I gathered from a few scattered news reports, mostly snide and condescending in tone, that there were degrees of purity in this ancient, now revived, theology, as well as levels of worldly removal, and that even a used soup can had been elevated already a dozen steps toward rare.

His followers said they felt like magicians and gods because they had become capable of creating objects of spiritual devotion out of the most ordinary things: a puddle, for instance, which had to be replenished, a spoon and a shoe, a dill pickle but not yet its jar. One woman, who was otherwise average to an extraordinary degree, had been given, through Romulus' ministrations, a sacred ankle. He was, the reporter smirked, working to ennoble other parts. And one day, in the distant future, the world would resemble a museum full of priceless and useless and adorable things—icons of the ordinary: sand and snails and lipsticks—each equal in the sight of one another, even corncobs and slop pails, divinities like the divan upon which Romulus nightly reclined.

The world had really been holy once, with deities, in effect, who dwelt in ditches and shrouded peaks. There were divinities identified with the winds in the trees, the water in rivers, the smell of hay in the hayloft on a warm fall day, for both mayflies in clouds and crowds of flowers, so why not for a bent or broken nail? for a toy, or vase, or windowpane—each and all looked at in a special way, a way that (though there was a recipe for this sort of gazing only regulars of the religion might receive) rendered them priceless, yes, beyond price and pricing, made them rich in their benign individuality, rich in their resonance, rich in the richness of their multitudinous properties, full to the brim with Being—in short, infinite, and infinitely *soi.*

Salvation, I learned in a letter from a friend living in Columbus, Ohio, where the cult had holed up, was to be achieved when, like Boy Scouts accumulating merit badges, you had sanctified a sufficient portion of your local world. Everything was to be—and would be—saved. Romulus had seen Juno, he said, in her nightdress, lonely as a broken broom straw, waiting for her Godman to return from the office, night drawing on like a finger through mist: mist, finger, act of drawing, night—divinities in their own small right. No less than the whitebud in bud like a fountain when its shower has begun to shower.

You, whoever "you" were, would be saved, it appeared, only when someone saved you by paying a saving attention. Under a lamp. Some sort of light? The light of a devoted eye? Here sexual problems rose—they always do—because the breast with its tempting suckle center was not to be eyed and prized as a source of solace or stimulation, but for its curvature, its design, its iconographic history, and this was a dish more easily ordered than eaten. Nudity was practiced (rumor said) so as to produce a matter-of-fact state regarding the body which could then become contemplative, detached, and redemptive.

I had to be seriously puzzled. I possessed the briefest, most scattered bits of news, fragments of this philosophy drifted to me like ash; and I could only make guesses based upon a past I increasingly feared was deceptive. Did Penner now pretend to believe that the world was a work of art? since simply being seen would alter nothing in sight's subject—that was one virtue of vision, unlike tasting gazing didn't take a bite—it could only alter the attitude of the perceiver to what was being perceived. Though of course Bishop Berkeley, whom we must all hold in the highest esteem, believed quite otherwise: *esse est percipi,* he said—well—wrote. The principle is too silly to be said.

It occurred to me that to deprive objects of their instrumentality was to destroy their essence. It meant Penner was turning the world upside down: taking revenge by rendering the useful useless and the useless valuable.

Nor could I resolve the rather regular recurrence of urination as a revenge. Was this new cult going to make chamber music, as Joyce's poems did, one level of meaning getting even with another?

Suppose Penner had been adopted? Would that explain his predilection for role reversals, for multiple guises, for passing himself off, or his periodic regressions? Never being what he seemed. Or was he just pretending to be pretending?

Again, I heard nothing from or about him for a long time. My own researches were hit-and-miss and mostly intermittent. I interviewed Aunt Spatz again with ambiguous results. I wasn't in the neighborhood when Luther was born, she said. He's got to be someone's natural child, didn't I think? she guessed. Luther bore no likeness to his parents, but that often happened, didn't it, she offered. Had he, as a child, often wet his bed? Not that she knew, though it wouldn't have surprised her, Aunt Spatz answered, admitting that much.

Claude Hoch, whom I returned to as well, admitted that after his humiliation, he had done some angry research on the expression "piss on you." And while he was telling me the obvious, and calling Luther Penner a coward for substituting for Claude's limb Claude's innocent and hapless desk—and did I catch the symbolism of the drawer?—my thoughts wandered a bit until they encountered, vividly reenacted, Penner's gesture: the slowly lifted leg.

Principal McDill, no longer in that capacity, had little to add.

Luther Penner was the sort of sniveling little squit who brought out the worse in people. Penner was, he thought, a born provocateur.

I obtained, from Harriet Hamlin Garland, of all people, further, and later, notebooks. These I received through the mail after a few preliminary inquiries and not a little haggling over their price. Some entries did not deal entirely kindly with me. As I had feared. Penner had sensed some skepticism. For me, he wrote, the cock had crowed half a dozen times. Then he ungenerously added: "until its throat grew raw with roosterizing." Had he heard about and remembered one of my public jokes?

Many entries puzzled me. Penner had made a list of local churches, with jots, but why? The Saint Peter's African Methodist Episcopal Church, for instance, and the note, Holy Ghost Headquarters. Or the Apostolic Pentecostal home Bible study center, then the exclamation: a book, a sacred! book! Or the Prince of Peace Baptist, then in parentheses, with a question mark, the words (Serene Queen?). The Vedanta Society. The Church of God International (sounds like a business, he wrote). The Saint Bartholomew, the John Knox, the Saint Mark's, Saint Monica, the Saint Marcus United Church of Christ. Then underlined, Lighthouse Free Methodist. The Exciting First Baptist, fully graded choirs and orchestra. The Ethical Society, humanist of the year award (there's a thought!). First Assembly of God. The Korean Presbyterian (really?). The Fellowship Church, its purpose—to know God, its mission—to make Him known (motto?). And the Emerson Chapel, "laughter holding both his sides." Church of God Sabbatarian, the Concord Baptist, sun worship. And the Church of the Open Door (should be).

Finally, from Columbus, the tragic news came. The Society of Salvators (as it was now called) had been attacked by a gang of thugs, and Luther Penner had been killed by a blow which had toppled him over a railing. His Society had apparently managed to accumulate funds sufficient to buy a small abandoned Catholic church in one of Columbus' central slums. Members then began (using a mumbo jumbo I can only guess at) unnecessarily desanctifying the building (a priest had unfrocked it already, it was the custom) in order—when sufficiently secular—that it could be revivified, but now for pagan and polytheistic purposes. This program had been under way for some days, and news of the procedure and its aims had leaked out. Salvators of Serene Peace (as they called themselves) had gathered in the ex-choir of the ex-church to undefile a modest art-glass window depicting the previously blessed Virgin, in her customary blue robe, standing on a cream-colored cloud and gazing adoringly upward at still more sky, when a gang of Irish-type toughs (so early reports indicated) broke in swinging lumber, and in the melée Luther had been struck or pushed over a railing onto the chancel floor. Early indications were that his injury was a broken neck, not a bat in the back as might have been supposed.

I do not find Luther Penner's legacy to lie in the Serene Queen Salvation Society, which, as Romulus, he founded and, indeed, gave his life for, although it continues to grow in the slow small way of lichens over rock, empowered by the myth of a real Romulus and an unreal Remus, and gaining its little ground despite the enmity which attached itself to the group after the accident like the stink a skunk may spray on a dog (when one might have expected some sympathy, some understanding); nor, I think, can it be identified with Harriet Hamlin Garland's organization, now ensconced in Missouri, Colorado, and lower Wyoming, though more or less in constant movement (since her doctrines tend to have their greatest impact on first hearing, when their repulsive character is most strongly felt, most abundantly cheered). Instead, I believe Luther Penner presented us with a mordant yet magnificent metaphysics: life perceived not simply as if it were lived amid a maelstrom of conflicting and competing myths, but as if it were dressed up in illusions deliberately designed by those who have been previously misguided, and who are now getting even as only secret enemies secretly can. How many in one's own home or neighborhood—to examine a small sample—have been betrayed by isms and ologies of one sort or other, have given money to nutcase causes, and squandered much of the precious time of their lives in vain spiritual pursuits?

I have no doubt that had Romulus lived, he would have sanctified the secular in a new way, produced an appropriate text, and, whether his vision was accurate or not, I believe his example, his doctrines, would have given many lost people something to follow, as well as the feeling of being found. The meek, like the sacristan who serves his church, elevated by sharing Penner's vision of the beauty and possible purity of all things, will understand their value and find their vindication. I am reminded of the venerable philosopher Immanuel Kant, so high-minded a man he didn't dare put on a hat, and his worship of the *Ding an sich.* I expect my Columbus researches will reveal to me the nature of those rites whereby even a stained soul might be bleached back to virtue and accorded its whiteness again. A convert told the press that, following the attack, she knelt where Luther lay so soft and pale he looked like lather.

Romulus, that is.

I envision at least one self-help book emerging from these recipes and operations. To reclaim for people now the pagan worship of the world—what a concept! dust a divinity! grease a God! the least leaf valued like a Lord! not the way a beloved body—a faint scar's mystery, the eye's lashes, the ear's lobes—is kissed by its lover's scrutiny, but with an artist's marveling yet detached attention. To administer to all of creation a purifying catharsis! like writing's gray ghost on the washed wall.

Though at first I thought Juno a strange choice for the Society's titular spirit (the sister of Jupiter as well as wife!), and the flashlight an even odder symbol (hung in functioning miniature around each faithful neck), Romulus' world, unlike Luther Penner's, was . . . rather is, let us hope . . . intended to be a radiant one, full of tender scrutinies and loving realizations.

This is revenge? Ah . . . yes. So secret. So severe. So complete. So pure. So benign. So transcendent. Now one may, any night, awake in a frightened sweat to say, even to the sleeping world: "I am a creature in a myth. I am unreal." Even as the priest preaches, and the preacher prays, either may be under a Salvator's light, losing, in the very instant in which the holy words are said, their allegedly sacred but actually worldly, profit-making use; yet these are the same symbols that will be admired anew once they've been well scrubbed (like golf balls going round and round in their little round washers)—and when at last clean of their claims to the Truth—thus redeemed—they can be safely admired for their wisdom, their rhetoric, the history they represent; because in a polytheistic world, such as Romulus proposed (I hope, proposes), dogmas are disarmed at the door, and welcomed like visiting friends, like other makes of car. Freshly struck coins will never feel spent, but will become immediately ancient as Roman ones, and like valued antiquities from the moment of their minting. Bills will be admired for their engraving, for Benjamin Franklin's artfully rendered face, for the denseness of the money's clothy weave, for the subtlety of shading among its many grayed greens; later, it can be loved for the pathos to be found in its folds, stains, and other signs of passage, if it's undergone the disgrace of exchange. One of Luther Penner's spoons, with which he used to put a spin on his coffee and orchestrate his ideas, I forethoughtly pocketed after an evening at the Cow's Lick Café. It is preserved, now, in a clear glass cup—a kind of reliquary—and leans there, in a peaceful tilt.

However . . . who knows, when a fire has been lit, where its wildness will take it? Who knows? It was a man named Romulus whose neck was broken; meanwhile Luther Penner may have a few astonishing trump cards still concealed among the ruffles of his buried sleeve; because, before his demise, he'd become not only the master of secret revenges, but an artful contriver of reversals, fine guises, and logical regressions as well.

A charge of manslaughter has been lodged against the goons who knocked Luther over the rail. Rumor has it, however, that these young toughs were incited by the Salvators, and it may be that Luther (Romulus, that is) miscalculated the consequences again; that he meant only to have a few of the faithful buffeted about, and a gratifying persecution, always so necessary in matters of faith and truth, profitably begun. Perhaps he did not count on more than a small fall, and hadn't asked for martyrdom. Especially since the supportive and therefore holy text had been scarcely begun.

Luther Penner's remains, following the obligatory autopsy, were returned to the home of his parents, who arranged a quiet cremation for them, and an even quieter scattering of ashes; most contrary to Luther's wishes I am sorry to say, for I know he was hoping for a tomb which would invite and facilitate visits.

I shall always regret not having been asked to attend the ceremony, which I heard was small, sober, and simple, plain almost to a fault.

A NOTE ON THE TYPE

This book was set in Fairfield, the first typeface from the hand of the distinguished American artist and engraver Rudolph Ruzicka (1883–1978). In its structure Fairfield displays the sober and sane qualities of the master craftsman whose talent has long been dedicated to clarity. It is the trait that accounts for the trim grace and virility, the spirited design and sensitive balance, of this original typeface.

Rudolph Ruzicka was born in Bohemia and came to America in 1894. He set up his own shop, devoted to wood engraving and printing, in New York in 1913 after a varied career working as a wood engraver, in photoengraving and bank-note printing plants, and as an art director and freelance artist. He designed and illustrated many books, and was the creator of a considerable list of individual prints—wood engravings, line engravings on copper, and aquatints.

Composed by Stratford Publishing Services,
Brattleboro, Vermont
Designed by Peter A. Andersen